ALL THE TOMMYS IN THE WORLD

A ZOMBIE THRILLER

JAVIER GOMBINSKY

PIGFARM
PRESS

PRAISE FOR JAVIER GOMBINSKY

" . . . A terrific writer . . . "

— RICHARD MAREK, EDITOR OF *THE SILENCE OF THE LAMBS* AND BESTSELLING AUTHOR

"A sharp, entertaining zombie epic that gleefully defies expectations."

— *KIRKUS REVIEWS*

"...akin to an undead ouroboros in mid-molt — just when you think you've got a grip on it, this serpentine narrative sheds its skin and becomes something altogether more frightening and unforgettable."

— CLAY MCLEOD CHAPMAN, AUTHOR OF *WHISPER DOWN THE LANE*

"Fast-paced and never a dull moment...a meaty slice of a unique zombie thriller..."

— SARA TANTLINGER, BRAM STOKER AWARD-WINNING AUTHOR OF *THE DEVIL'S DREAMLAND*

"Addictive...gives you the kind of adrenaline rush that only good fiction can stir up, making you believe those characters are real and immersing you in an atmosphere so frightening that the only thing left to do is run—run fast, so the zombies won't catch you."

— Agustina Bazterrica, Premio Clarín Award-winning author of *Tender is the Flesh*

"A unique and intriguing entry into the zombie genre, *All the Tommys in the World* is an addictive horror epic with Gothic undertones. I greatly enjoyed this book."

— Sonora Taylor, author of *Seeing Things* and *Little Paranoias: Stories*

"...this genre-bending mystery keeps its audience and characters guessing, keeping the suspense alive throughout..."

— *BookLife Reviews*

"An Excellent apocalyptic novel where all the elements of the zombie genre converge and meet at a cemetery... the cemetery of Chacarita, an icon of Buenos Aires..."

— Hernán Santiago Vizzari, Investigator and historian. Distinguished Person of Culture of the City of Buenos Aires.

To Mom.

To Mili, this book's first, second, and third reader.

And to the friends and family I neglected while writing this book.

As the car spins out of control and seconds before it veers off the road, as tires screech and high beams slice the black night, he comes at me from the driver's seat. I grab his head with both hands, his face green by the faint light of the dashboard, his milky eyes glowing inches away from mine, his mouth and teeth reaching for my neck, and I manage to raise my knee between the two of us and force him back into the driver's seat. I jump him and push him to the floor, trying to grab hold of the wheel as inertia pulls my body away from it. His arms break off under mine, puffing a cloud of dust. I look into his eyes and ask him to stop, to please stop. But his teeth sink in. And I feel the burn, and I see his mouth pull away with my skin and flesh and blood, and I see black. And it doesn't feel bad at all. Or good. It just is. And I see it. Or, I understand. Or, I remember: The world, overrun with us, the dead; the rise and the fall of the zombie Slayers; the ancient cities turned to forests and jungles and deserts, burning under a red sun, so swollen and so close to the earth; the giant, cool underground cities, unhuman ant colonies, bursting with the movement of dead bodies. I taste the pungent tang of embalming fluid; I see corpses turning on corpses, in rage and in pity; and I see the last three human shapes, standing alone on a graveyard planet. I see more things. I see kaleidoscope eyes. A walk among the dead. And the untimely death on three-hundred twelve. And just before we hit the oak tree, Tommy. I see Tommy. And all the Tommys in the world.

ALL THE TOMMYS IN THE WORLD

PART I

1

BLOODY CREDITS ROLL UP THE TV SCREEN, AND LILITH GETS UP from the couch. She opens the blackout curtains, blinding Nate with sunlight.

"Well, that was a swift apocalypse," she says, looking outside.

"How does it look?" Nate asks. "Everything back to normal?"

"Mostly. They're almost done cleaning up the—well, cleaning up."

From his seat on the couch, Nate can only see blue skies. He can hear the faint sound of police sirens.

"Should I take a look?"

She turns to him. "No, Nate. It'll all blow over soon."

"You think we should've gone out?"

"What, with this crappy old thing?" she asks, patting her chest. "They got it covered."

Nathan wonders for a moment which of the two is least convinced of this.

"Watch another movie?" she asks, changing the subject. Now he knows for sure.

"Sure," he says, standing up. He walks to the camera next to the TV and talks to it. "Bye, um, boils and ghouls! I hope you liked our reaction video. Remember to Like, Share, and Subscribe!

New video tomorrow, so make sure to tune in! *We have such sights to show you!"*

He stops recording. "Your turn to edit this one."

"Yeah," she says, "I'll start tonight. All our fans are busy with the apocalypse, anyway. Have you checked the comments? The ungrateful fucks are pissed we're not out there."

"Fucking Slayers. They're eating this up. It's time we face it. A lot of horror fans were just violent psychos waiting for a chance to kill without any consequences."

"Yeah," she says. "Fuck 'em."

She pauses for a moment, her gorgeous green eyes gazing into his like she's looking for something.

"What?" Nate asks.

She bursts out in laughter.

"You were actually scared!" she says, wide-eyed.

"What?"

She smirks. "You've barely said a word the whole week!"

"You weren't so chirpy either," he says, "until you were sure it was over."

Her eyes widen and sparkle the way they do whenever she teases him. "You've been even paler than usual," she says.

"You've been even bitchier than usual," he says, and they laugh. "So, what's next on the playlist?"

"If you're up to it, we could go with a zombie movie."

"Ha. I thought even you were done with those. 'That whole genre is stale' and all that?"

"Fuck you. Yes, I was, but after this crap happening outside, I need *something* to get the bad taste out of my mouth. Let's watch a good one. Maybe go back to the roots. O'Bann—"

"No."

"I could warn you before the cemetery parts."

"Still no. And it's *all* cemetery parts."

"You know, the fans have pledged to up their donations if you do. Maybe we can fake it? I'll tell you what to say—"

"*Alien?*" he interrupts.

"Nah," she says, "no body horror today. Too realistic."

A faint sound distracts him. It's almost unnoticeable, but it seems to be coming from inside the apartment.

"What do you mean, too realistic?"

The sound is gone. It was probably nothing.

"Well yeah, Nate, you're a guy. For you, it's just a movie. But that shit could happen to me at any moment. It happens to people, Nate. For some, it's even some sort of sick compulsion. That's the real fucking horror if you ask me. So, no, Veto."

"Giving birth, you mean?" he asks. "The miracle of life?"

"The whole thing. Some creature growing inside of you? Feeding off your body? That comes out of your entrails? Spare me. No body horror. Too much fucking blood on the streets already. What about a clean, wholesome ghost story? *The Others? Lake Mungo?* Some good old secular horror to forget about the real whackos outside?"

"Sure, I could watch *Lake Mungo* again. Anyway, I thought it was supposed to be *natural*."

She grabs the remote on the couch. "Being mauled by a bear is natural. Wanna try that shit?"

A voice. Nate is sure he can hear a voice. Faint. It flashes like a radio being tuned in and out, but he definitely hears it. He signals Lilith to be quiet.

"What?"

"Did you hear that?" he whispers.

She looks around. She checks outside the window. "Hear what?"

He stands up and steps toward the window. He notices her eyes swelling.

"Nate, no," she stops him, raising her arms, serious. Scared.

The voice comes back, but somehow it feels like it's coming from nowhere. It's just *there*.

"Are you trying to scare me?" he asks Lilith.

She scoffs.

"No," he answers himself before she can say anything. "This isn't you. This is ... something else."

She looks at him weird. "Nate, are you alright? I don't hear a thing."

"Is there someone out in the hall? Are you *expecting* anyone? Anything?"

She scoffs again. "In a lockdown? They're not even delivering—"

And there it is again. Faint, but certainly there. Definitely a voice.

He gathers the courage to walk to the window.

"Wait, Nate—"

He paces forward and gazes down at the streets of New Southport. Between the towering buildings and around the tall white obelisk, the streets are brimming with cheering crowds, red with *Make America Great Again* hats, with guns shooting in the air. In the distance, streets leading to the waterfront seem more deserted, with people chasing shambling ghouls, and further away, in front of the river and Liberty Island, vacant streets are haunted by the odd rogue ghoul, walking undetected. Over here, the storm has passed. Some blood is being hosed down. Two pairs of feet on a stretcher are shoved into a truck. The vague echo of a dog barking. But nothing outside explains what Nate just heard.

Lilith stares at him like he's a bomb about to go off. "You're OK?"

"Yeah. Fine."

"Real blood doesn't—?"

"Nah," he says. "I'm OK with *blood*."

The voice is back. Yes, he's sure now. It's a girl. A little girl.

"Lil. Lil. Do you hear it?"

She shakes her head, confused.

He turns toward the hall leading to the bedroom. Away from the window, the sunlight fades out. The poster of Freddy and Pinhead with the words HORROR IS MY HAPPY PLACE is already shrouded in darkness.

Nathan grabs an empty beer bottle and walks slowly toward the bedroom. He walks across the dark hall and past the tall coffin-shaped bookcase, various creepy dolls staring at him from its shelves. The bedroom door is ajar, and the lights are on.

Behind him, Lilith says, "Maybe it's one of our fans asking us to join them for a zombie run."

Nate signals her to be quiet, but she doesn't see him in the dark. He tries hardening his face into a scary grimace, his hands clawing the air at her to try to warn her that something's wrong. No reaction. She can't see him.

"Or maybe it's a ghoul," she teases, "luring you into a trap. Or worse, maybe it's my parents, the model god-fearing couple, breaking the lockdown to brave the undead, and just popping in. That would be just my luck. Zombies are bad, but *that* would be apocalyptic."

He hears it plainly now. *"Nate? Can you hear me?"*

It's coming from the bedroom. And Lilith must have finally picked up on it, because her face turns to stone.

The whisper—and now he's sure it's Lilith's voice—says, *"Nate, I think someone's in the house."*

He runs to the room and swings the door open.

Lilith's whisper pleads, *"Nate! Nate, help me!"*

The room is empty. But a faint glare comes off from the TV. It's black, displaying a white title: VIDEO TO SCARE NATE — CASTING FROM LILITH'S PHONE.

Behind him, Lilith bursts out in laughter, and he jumps up and shrieks.

Lilith leans on him, snorting. "I can't, I can't. Oh shit, I ruined it, I can't believe it. I wanted to scream but I just—" and she bursts into laughter again. She's holding a camera pointing straight at his face.

Nate snaps out of it. Relieved, he tries to laugh, but he's still short of breath. "You motherfucker!"

"Oh my god, Nate, you should've seen your face!"

"You motherfucker! Oh, you have no idea what's coming to you!"

"No, Nate," she chuckles, her eyes red with tears. "You do know I have a heart condition, right?"

Nate hugs her, still laughing and panting. "Oh, I'll get you! I'll get you back! Wait, was the ghost movie proposal part of the shtick? How did you know I'd say yes?"

She laughs, finally catching some air. "You're *that* predictable."

Another, stronger lightning bolt runs through Nathan's spine, and he breaks the hug. He can see the surprise and fear in Lilith's face, too, because this time he knows he didn't imagine it: a loud, clear, repeated knock is coming from the apartment door.

"Lilith? Nate? Are you there?" says a familiar motherly voice.

"Open up!" says another familiar voice. "We don't have much time!"

2

LOOKING THROUGH THE PEEPHOLE, LILITH WOULD RECOGNIZE the woman's stark black long-sleeved gown anywhere. The man behind the big driving glasses is her father.

"Lilith," her mother blurts out. "Open up, please."

She unlocks the door, and it springs open as they hurry inside. Her mother slams the door shut and locks it, trembling. As she stands next to the coffin-shaped bookcase, Lilith hates how much her mother's gown matches her apartment's style.

"Lilybug," the old man says, walking up to her. He grabs her by the shoulders. "We found gas."

"What do you need gas for?" she asks, seeing her own reflection in his mirrored glasses. "Just stay home a few more days. The lockdown is almost—"

"We're leaving town," he says, gravely.

"The four of us," her mother adds, looking for Nate and smiling at him when she sees him behind Lilith. She raises her arm, the light fabric of her black sleeves floating up in the air, and looks at her watch. "The man with the gas is meeting us in three hours."

Lilith chuckles. "You're kidding, right? The apocalypse is over."

9

"Over how?" Her mother asks. "People are dying! The dead walk!"

Lilith sighs. "Yeah. Barely."

Her mother looks at her in horror. "*Barely?*"

"Pack your bags," her father says. "Now."

Lilith walks back to the couch and slumps down.

"Look, Pa, the Slayers got it. Even cleanup is almost done. They're working on a big bonfire for the bodies, for god's sake! It's over!"

"Still," her mother says, finally allowing herself to take a step away from the door. "We think we should wait it out somewhere quiet. You know, just in case."

"Come," Lilith says. "Sit down. Relax. Want some coffee?"

Her parents stare at her in silence. They clearly didn't expect her to put up a fight. Her father takes a deep breath and starts a slow walk across the living room.

"So odd," he says, looking out the window, "You two, of all people, playing scaredy cats, hiding in here with your make-believe horror movies while a real-life horror movie plays out right outside your window. Letting the Slayers—your fans, prob-ably—save the day. After everything you've *seen*—"

"Renwick," Ophelia interrupts, shooting him a cold look.

Lilith gives her father's mirrored sunglasses a death stare, and he quickly buckles under its heat, turning his face to study a bookcase across the room. "Too bad we can't just *book* those zombies to death, right?"

Ophelia seems shocked. "Stop it. Let's all just go and—"

"You used to be curious," he continues. "Impulsive. Gotta wonder what happened."

"You know what happened," her mother mutters, losing her patience.

"Yes," he says. "Your heart condition."

"Look," Lilith says, trying to control her breathing. "I get it. You're scared. This is clearly overwhelming for you. So go. We'll see each other in a week, tops. And we can talk on the phone—"

"A week?" Ophelia asks.

"Tops. And we can talk on the phone if it makes you feel any better."

Ophelia's tone changes. "Stop it. Stop it! This is not about *us*!"

Lilith looks at Nate. She needs the calm of his brown eyes, or she'll explode. "Then who?" she asks carefully.

Her mother looks down at the floor. "I know, you've been better—"

"Much better," her father adds.

"Yes, much better," Ophelia repeats. "But this? Why risk it, staying in the city?"

"What your mother is trying to say," her father interjects, "is that you're two aging gray-haired *youtubers*, barely scraping by, who never had a real job—"

"Renwick," Ophelia says with her eyes wide open.

"How much longer do you think you can keep this up?" Renwick continues. "Especially now that all your *fans* know that you're too pussy to go out in an actual zombie apocalypse."

"Renwick," Ophelia repeats, horrified. "What's gotten into you?"

"This is your day!" he continues. "Today of all days, you could be out there, leading this, using your useless movie trivia knowledge, making something of yourself, and here you are, hiding. And these Slayers are the ones who have it under control?"

Lilith clenches her jaw. "I'm not hiding."

He tilts his head. "You've *been* hiding. You've *been* sabotaging yourself."

"Renwick Kane!" Ophelia shouts.

"Ophelia Kane!" He snaps back without taking his eyes off Lilith's. "You're sleepwalking through life. When's the last time you two took a chance? Did something actually dangerous? Socialized? Overcame a fear, tried something new? You cannot keep escaping from real life in your books."

"They're not a threat," Lilith says, trying to stay calm. "Like, at all. Just don't walk too slow and you'll be fine. Bash their heads in, cut off their head, you'll be fine."

"Cut off their hea—??" her mother asks, shocked.

He laughs. "Ha! And you even got *that* wrong!"

"What?"

"They do run."

"No, they don't."

"I saw one running, with my own eyes," he says.

"You saw *what*?" Ophelia asks.

"Yes, just this morning. I dropped my glasses, went back a few steps, picked them up, saw one running. I didn't want to worry you, and he wasn't coming our way, so I said nothing."

"What?" Lilith asks with a spark of interest.

"Yeah. This zombie was crawling after some guy, and when the guy gained some distance from it, the zombie sped up the pace and, well, let's just say it caught up. It's like it was *luring* him there, like a trap or something."

Lilith's stomach sinks.

"No, no," she says in a daze, standing up. She walks up to the window and points outside.

"Look, Ma, you see? They *actually* shamble. They *actually* groan. They get shot in the head, and they drop. We've seen this a million times. This is every shit movie in the last fifty years."

She notices Nate looking away.

"It's trope after trope out there," she says. "It's almost ..." And she stops.

"Suspicious." Nate finishes the sentence for her.

Lilith turns to him. "It *is* a bit too much like the movies, isn't it?"

Still sitting on the couch, Nate's languid figure seems out of this world. His black T-shirt hardly moves as he breathes, and the white waves on the imprint move so slowly it's almost hypnotic. She can't tell if he's cool about this or if he's about to have a nervous breakdown.

"And you *saw* a zombie running?" she asks her father. "It

wasn't just some psycho pretending to be one, or kids playing some stupid game?"

"Looked pretty convincing," her father says. "Half his torso was chewed off."

"You even used the word *lure*. Believe me," she says, "that's creepy for many reasons."

She turns to Nate. "What do you make of that? In your, erm, *experience?*"

Nate seems catatonic. She's never seen him this scared. "They're dead," he exhales. "They're not stupid."

Lilith's mind starts to race.

"Too bad," Renwick says behind her. "About your heart condition."

Ophelia hits him in the shoulder. "Are you *trying* to get them killed?"

"She's not going to go," he says, as Lilith looks outside. "Deep down, she's reasonable. And she's terrified. She will come to her senses and come with us."

"It's not just my heart, you know," she grumbles. "Nate really shouldn't be outside these days."

"Oh!" her father bellows, "this whole thing, you hiding here, it's only to keep *him* inside? How magnanimous of you."

Ophelia can't believe what she hears. "Renwick, what's up with you today?"

"Really, Pa," Lilith says, turning around. "What the fuck?"

"Well, careful with Glass Boy!" Renwick says. "She's the one with the weak heart!"

A low hum outside swells into a police siren. It approaches, fills the room, passes by, and fades out. Lilith's heartbeat pounds in her chest.

"Go," she snarls.

Her parents share a look again.

"Lilith," her mother says, trembling, "we're not asking. We're your parents—"

Lilith's father steps toward Lilith. "And we're telling you, we're going. The four of us. Now."

"Actually," she snarls, "We can't. We're going out. We're gonna go get chased by a zombie. Like those tourists." She turns to Nate. "Right?"

"Ha," Nate manages to mumble.

Ophelia looks horrified. "What? Why?"

Clenching her teeth, Lilith tries to sound casual. She tries to smile. "The heart wants what the heart wants."

Ophelia looks at her, red-faced. "Wipe that silly grin off your face!" she snarls. "You think you know everything, don't you? You have all the answers. Well, this is real! We're in danger! And, running? You've been better, yes, Dr. Patel said you can try some more strain. But this? Why risk it with *this*?"

"The heart wants what the heart wants," Lilith repeats. "We'll go running with the zombies. It'll be fun! We'll *socialize*, make friends with other runners, and make a day out of it," she says, grabbing Nate's hand.

Renwick pierces her with his gaze.

"If you change your mind," he says, "meet us on the corner of Fifth and Market at five."

"Don't wait up."

"Be there," he says, placing his hand on Ophelia's shoulder.

"Have a nice trip," Lilith says. "See you in a week."

"Come, honey," he says, turning Ophelia to the door and reaching for the handle. "She'll come around."

"See you in a week, Ma."

Ophelia nods, turning to Lilith with glassy eyes. She's saying goodbye.

3

High above the corner of Seventh and Mill Road, a freshly severed head hangs from the electric wires. It looks peaceful in the morning sky. Clean. Shaved. Hair neatly combed, except for the messy patch where the hook bites into the scalp. His lips are flat and dry. His milky eyes are open wide, dreaming, gazing at the blinding sun.

A gust of cool morning wind caresses his cheeks and howls inside his ears, swaying him, turning him around. As the blinding light moves away, he desperately scans the new landscape: every empty car, every piece of burning garbage. At the far end of the street, a wall of smoke shrouds the rest of the city in darkness.

And behold, something moves. Out of the wall of smoke, two tiny figures emerge, running as fast as they can, coughing, squinting, looking over their shoulders. A woman whose broad smile is noticeable even from afar, and whose faint laughter echoes off the buildings. Her black hair sticks to her sweaty face, and her big green eyes burn with joy. She holds hands with a tall pale man running silently next to her, his chest heaving under his black T-shirt with white waves.

"I. Thought you were. Joking," the man huffs. "About. The running."

Her smile widens. She looks tired and sweaty, and her face is red. But she smiles.

"Just. Another. Block."

"Having—fun?" he asks, gasping.

"Old man. Got me. Curious," she says, almost out of breath. "It's our. Last chance. Aren't you. Glad. We didn't. Miss this?"

He looks behind him at the advancing wall of smoke and picks up his pace. He doesn't reply.

To their left, a hardware store door chimes, and the woman turns to it just as a small boy in a light-blue hospital gown comes out, shuffling in his hospital slippers, holding a white box against his chest.

She pulls the man's arm and rushes to the boy.

"Come on!" she yells, and her voice travels and bounces up the street. "The ghouls are coming."

The boy tries to look back as he's pulled by the couple. His box almost slips as he tries to hold it with his other hand, and his slippers shuffle with clumsy, tired, uneven steps as they zigzag through the debris.

"Are they after us?" the boy asks, trying to look over his shoulder.

"Come on!" she says, cheerful. "Enjoy it! We're being chased by ghouls!"

The man looks back at the wall of smoke. He doesn't look amused.

"Lil," he says, panting. "They're. Actually. Not. Far back."

"Quit worrying!" says the woman. "This is the first time we've had fun in this godforsaken city and its fake shiny smiling people! Are you getting this? Start recording!"

She pulls the boy's hand toward a narrow corridor in the debris. The pale man follows them, slowing down to fumble in his pocket, and looks behind his back. His arm freezes. He pulls out his hand, empty, and swings his arms to run faster.

"Lil," the man says, catching up to her. "Maybe. You should. Be more. Scared. This time."

She turns to him. "What? I've been preparing my whole life for this. Enjoy it! Get rid of your fear once and for all and enjoy it!"

"Lil—"

"Come *on*!" She yells, waving her arms and hair dramatically, the hollow echo traveling down the empty street. She grabs the boy's hand and laughs. "Don't you see? They're cominggg!"

The boy steps on a can and slips, losing his balance. The woman pulls him up.

"Thanks," he says looking up at her, smiling. But she keeps running, eyes front, face red and sweaty, eyes popping out of her head.

Behind them, five more figures emerge from the wall of smoke.

The woman runs into a charred smoking car and stops. She looks around, grabbing her knees, trying to catch her breath as the boy stands next to her.

"Shit!" she says. "We should have gone with the Slayers."

"They're psychos, Funnyface," the pale man says.

"Yeah. But they're *our* psychos."

"No," he says, looking around. "Just. Psychos. Come."

The pale man speeds off around the car. They follow him.

They get closer to the intersection. The head can see them more clearly. The paper-white man breathes heavily as he runs. He looks down at the boy and stretches his hand down to him.

"Seriously—kid," he says in between breaths, "Gimme. Your. Hand."

The boy struggles to keep his pace. He presses the box against his chest, tightens his lips, and shakes his head.

"Kid," the pale man repeats between breaths. "Let. Go. The fucking. Box."

The boy looks over his shoulder. He tries to see past the debris.

"Are they still after us?"

She jumps over a pile of luggage. The pale man waits for the boy to jump over.

"Are they still after us?" the boy repeats.

The man grabs him and pushes him over the bags. The boy stumbles as he lands and looks up at him in fear.

"Catch up," the man says, jumping over.

The woman grabs his hand, and with a grimace, the boy picks up the pace. He sprints, he strides, he paces, and goes back to shuffling his feet.

"I'm sorry," the boy says. "I can't."

The woman is not smiling anymore. As they approach the corner, the bags under her eyes become more and more noticeable.

"What's—what's your name again?"

The boy looks up at her. She still faces forward, squinting, eyes almost closed.

"Fran—Frankie," says the kid in between breaths.

She looks down and meets his gaze. His eyes look big, even from above, as does his open mouth.

"Frankie, I'm sorry," she whimpers, and her voice breaks. "I'm really sorry. Please don't come back for me."

The boy doesn't blink. His mouth stays open. He stammers, trying to speak, and she does it.

She lets go of his hand.

The boy hits the asphalt flat on his face, and the white box rolls down the street. As he tries to get up, as he reaches for the box, he looks up at the wall of smoke closing in on him.

The man turns to her. He smiles a tired, worrisome smile. "You. Did. Good. Honey. You. Had No—"

She looks straight ahead and wipes the tears from her eyes. "I know."

Her mouth moves with each of her steps. "One, two, three, four ..."

A piercing shriek fills the street, something made out of the boy's voice and of something else entirely.

She turns around. The cloud of dust has swallowed the boy and is growing arms and legs and heads, all reaching out for them.

"Four," she says to the pale man, pacing, tired, eyes front. "This was a big fucking mistake. You're right. We *are* getting too close."

He keeps running, eyes front. "No, Lil," he says. *"They* are getting close."

She looks straight ahead as if she hasn't heard him. She turns to him, then back ahead.

"How did this happen?" she asks. "We let ourselves get outsmarted by *fucking ghouls*."

"We were sloppy," says the man, looking over his shoulder. His chest heaves. The white waves on his T-shirt move up and down. "We got too comfortable."

The wind blows again around the hanging head, and the city spins like a toy globe. Now he sees an empty street, with vacant buildings, and another wall of smoke. A big white staircase leading to a big white building, and a scorched ambulance cooling off in front of it.

"You think ..." the man's voice says somewhere down below, "you think this is it?"

"What do you mean?"

"You know what I mean."

Silence. Nothing but tired steps trudging on the asphalt.

"Door three-twelve," he says, panting.

Her steps come to a stop. "Shut up!" she yells.

"No," she says. "No, this is *not* it."

"OK," he says, panting. "OK. Come on, we gotta—"

She sniffles. "Besides," she says, "only *you* die on three-twelve, remember?"

"Right. You're. Right."

A busy rumble gets closer.

They turn around and sprint, their feet pounding heavy on the pavement. The head can hear their heavy breaths coming in shorter and shorter bursts.

"What now?" Their voices dance as if they are looking around in all directions. "Where are we?"

"I don't know," the woman says.

"Maybe ..." says the man. "Maybe this *is* it. If we split, maybe they'll only follow one of us."

The woman begins to wail. "This is not," she takes a sobbing breath. "H-how I. Pictured it. Shitstain."

"Me. Neither. Barfbag."

The rumble grows.

"They're getting closer," the man says. "We talked about this."

"OK!" she sniffles. "OK. But this isn't it!" Her voice is growing stronger. "We look for each other later! I'm not done scaring you! This isn't it!"

The view of the white building starts to shake. The rumble is closer and closer.

"I'm. Not. Done. Scaring you. Either!" he yells over the din.

Her faint, sharp-pitched chuckle echoes among the growing rumble.

"Find the Slayers!" she yells.

The sound of steps hitting the pavement moves away, carrying the woman's wail farther and farther.

The pale man appears again, running in the middle of the street toward the charred ambulance. He sprints around it and climbs the white staircase, craning his head to look inside the open entrance doors. As he disappears inside, a horde of reanimated corpses swarms the street.

*　*　*

IN A SMALL DARK TOOL SHED, a freshly dead hand closes into a fist. Two deep lines are carved on its back. It hangs by a string from a wooden panel, between the open hands of a small child and an old woman, among dozens of open hands of different shapes, colors, and sizes, all carved with patterns of lines and crosses.

A German shepherd barks madly at it.

"Shhhh," says a soothing voice. The dog calms down as its master approaches.

He examines the fist and turns to a sheet of paper with a list. For number two, in crude letters, it says "Hospital."

4

____

Turning the corner, Lilith examines the empty street. Her heart hammers against her chest, and all she can think of is *Nate, Nate, how did it come to this?* She slows down, trying to catch her breath, trying to stop her cheeks from burning, and wipes her teary eyes. The city seems blurry. The looted shop windows. The signs. The ads. The coffee place. The sports store. The electronics emporium. And it hits her.

She knows this street.

She knows many streets. So what is it about this one? Her heart races again. It feels like the buildings are about to fall on her. It's not just the worry about Nate, but something else, somehow, something urgent about it. She can't tell what it is exactly, but something about this place ...

A trash can hits the ground, echoing in the empty street, and her blood curdles.

She clears a lock of hair stuck to her sweaty face. "What's the matter, Lil?" she says to herself as she wipes tears from her eyes. "Suddenly you're not so fearless?"

She looks at the trash can on the sidewalk, rolling down from a narrow alley into shards of broken glass, and quickly glances around. Next to her, the broken window of a hardware store, already looted clean. She looks up at the alley again, her breath scorching hot. She can feel her blood pumping through her body with every fierce heartbeat.

Three figures trudge out of the alley, wandering, their heads resting idly on their shoulders as if they were asleep. Maybe this is how broken necks look.

They turn in her direction. Lilith gasps. She hasn't been this close to them before. They smell like whatever the city has been smelling like, only stronger, and the itching feeling in her nose is almost unbearable.

She gasps again. Her eyes swell, and her pupils seem to retract as if they wanted to escape, to walk backward, to hide inside her head.

They're looking up at her. Their gaze is empty. Their open jaws hang idly, and Lilith can't help but stare at the dry lips around them. Somehow it looks like they're *trying* not to smile.

She turns around. Behind her, across the street, something buzzes. She sees the first line of the group, and as they approach, more of them. Dozens of them. All coming at her. She remembers Nate's words. Maybe this *is* it. She looks back at the corner where she left him, murky with smoke and fog. Will he still be there? Why hasn't he come back already? Where *is* he?

To her front, the three broken-neck ghouls are getting close. Behind her, the larger group paces steadily, taking up the whole width of the street. She scans her surroundings. She can't go back. The fog is too risky. Dodging the three sleeping beauties and entering the alley is suicide. Weapons? There is nothing around she can use.

The faint sound of an engine approaches. A car. Alone. Speeding across the city.

And she remembers.

"No," she says. "No ... No, no, no."

She checks her watch. "That's impossible."

Her heart hammers against her chest again, and the world

curls over her. Up ahead, in the corner of the street, a beam of light paints the pavement from the left, coming in fast.

She looks up at the evening sky. It's darker than she thought.

She turns around. She can see the decomposed faces of the ghouls, all locking eyes with her like it's personal, grinding their teeth with anticipation. They look nothing like she expected. They look like rotten meat. The holes and missing parts in their faces make their heads hollow. It's impossible. They shouldn't be standing. They shouldn't be moving. They shouldn't be so close. They shouldn't have taken Nate away. The roar of the engine gets closer.

She runs to grab the trash can, getting dangerously close to the sleeping beauties, and lifts it.

She throws it at them, and it works. Two of them drop flat on their asses.

"That's for Nate!" She yells, her mouth trembling.

She hurries to grab the trash can again, getting only feet away from the standing ghoul. It's an old man. He looks like a sweet man, but mad, enraged. Her arms are numb. They tremble.

A glass bottle rolls out of the trash can, clinking against the pavement. Lilith grips it firmly and, getting close to the ghoul, she strikes. Her eyes clench shut, and as the world goes dark, she yells again. "You took Nate!" Her voice is trembling. She almost doesn't recognize it.

When she opens her eyes, the ghoul is lying on the street on his stomach, trying to get up.

The deafening roar turns to a screech, and out the corner comes a cloud of gray smoke that skids and smells like burnt rubber, entering the street just before the wall of ghouls takes over it. A chrome bumper stops two feet away from her blood-soaked knees.

She looks up. Behind the windshield, a man is grabbing the wheel and moving his mouth angrily at her. His window cracks open and the sound finally breaks out. "Get the fuck in!"

She explores his face like it's a puzzle. "Dad?"

She looks at the passenger seat. Her mother is looking straight at her.

Lilith cannot speak. She only mouths, "Wait."

She turns her head up, searching for the street sign, and the beating of her chest becomes heavier. The letters on the sign seem to beat along with her heart, mocking her, laughing at her, fucking with her.

Fifth and Market.

Fifth and fucking Market.

"That's impossible," she mouths.

"C'mon, get in!" her mother yells.

Lilith's head is spinning. Behind the car, ghouls are filling the street, and getting closer.

"Get in!" Renwick repeats.

Behind her, the trash can rattles again. In the dark alley, the ghouls are getting up. She lifts the trash can over her head, but her arms are weak, tired. They tremble. They give in, and she drops it onto her face. She can taste her own blood.

"Lilith!" her mother yells.

Lilith looks around, defeated, and walks over to the car. She pulls the door handle.

The door is locked.

"What the hell?"

Ophelia opens her eyes wide and turns to Renwick. Lilith turns back and sees the angry ghouls only a few feet away.

With a bolt, the door unlocks.

The putrid smell of the corpses is so close it stings her nose. She pulls the door open, jumps inside, slams the door shut, and fumbles for the lock until she hears the bolt again.

Her father is chuckling. "What?" he says. "There's no danger, remember?"

"Good one," she says, catching her breath. Ophelia stares at Renwick with her mouth open, speechless.

Thump. A fist punches the window right next to Lilith, and an old, angry face cranes down and stares at her. The head is split open like a peeled banana, and the halves, inches apart, dangle as he hits the glass. Between the ghoul's eyes, she can see the city stretched out behind him. Above his grinning teeth, she looks at the ominous, impossible street sign: *Fifth and Market*.

Renwick floods the gas.

5

Lilith sinks into the familiar, burgundy-upholstered back seat, letting the suede cushion of the headrest, the shape of her head still imprinted in it, cradle her spinning mind. The old worn fabric feels like home. The sound of the engine becomes a relaxing hum. A sweet old voice singing *Que Sera, Sera* drowns out the noises of the street; the rumble of trucks, the sirens, the yelling and the gunshots. The smells of smoke and rotten meat fade away, overpowered by the aromas of the ever-present chrysanthemum car freshener and her mother's perfume. The fragrance of her childhood. The smell of home. And of course, if this isn't the most familiar view: her father's hands on the wheel like it's a calm Sunday drive. Her mother, sitting up straight, head on the headrest, like nothing ever happened. Lilith could fall asleep right now. She gazes at the empty city speeding away, and her eyes start to feel heavy.

What have you done? Did you just split? Forever? Are you really never gonna see him again? Nate? Your Nate? And now, you're just gonna ... Sleep?

"Take ... this ... old ... people ... shit ... off ...," she mumbles.

"She came!" Ophelia yells. "She came!"

Lilith's eyes spring open. Her mother, turning to her, kneels on her seat and throws her arms at her. Her eyes are wet and tired. She's been crying.

"Of course she did," her father says, dodging the charred carcass of a car in the middle of the street.

Her mother's eyes linger on Lilith, waiting for the hug. Lilith stays still. Ophelia's smile fades away, and she retreats back to her seat. "I almost didn't think you'd come," she says, wiping the tears from her eyes.

"Of course she would," her father says, completely calm, his hands resting comfortably on the wheel. His driving is hypnotic. "Jesus, Lil, reek much?"

Lilith frowns. "That's just it," she says. "I wasn't."

Her mother's glassy green eyes look at her through the sun visor mirror. Her father's sunglasses look up at her from the rearview mirror. Lilith is in a daze. "I didn't," she adds. "You said Fifth and Market, so we went the other way. A different part of town. Shit, how much did we run?" She takes her hand to her chest and checks her heart. She's OK. "I ... Really, can you take this shit off?"

He just smiles. "Deep down you must have changed your mind."

"Meant to be," her mother says, delighted. "Meant to be."

Lilith can't wrap her mind around it. Her mother turns back and smiles at her. She stretches her arms to hug her again.

Lilith's reflexes get the best of her, and her hand stops her mother cold by the neck.

"I'm sorry," she says, shocked. "It's just ..."

Her mother freezes. Her terrified eyes are red with so much crying.

"Nate and I split up," Lilith says.

"Oh," says Ophelia, pulling back to her seat and turning to Lilith's father. "We ... didn't want to ask."

"It's OK," says Lilith. "It's the right thing. You guys should do the same."

"We've talked about this—"

"Yes, we have," says Lilith. "And you *really* want to be the one to have to chop *his* head off, don't you? Or would you rather have *him* kill *you*?"

"Lil, don't start—"

"No, *yes* start. Because there's no other choice! Face it. Shit *is* coming our way, and it better find us all alone. Speaking of which, drop me off—"

"You worry too much," her mother says.

"What?"

Her mother makes a pause, trying to defuse the situation. "Que sera, sera."

Lilith looks at her father. "What's she talking about?"

"All this sudden concern for the future. Just—you know. Let it be."

"*Let it Be?* What is it with the musical references?"

"Yeah. Go with Nate if that's what you want. You think you're a rebel, but you're such a stuck-up."

Lilith can't believe what she's hearing. "I'd just rather be alone when—"

Lilith's father looks at the road, almost enjoying this. "But you *did* come."

He looks up at her in the mirror. He's wearing his big old driving sunglasses, the ones he's had ever since Lilith was a little girl.

Lilith is confused. "Yeah. Fucking Fifth and Market," she says. "It's impossible."

Dad grins. "Well," he says, "you're not as unpredictable as you think."

"You know Lil," says her mother, popping a mint in her mouth, "strange things have been happening to me, too. Just this morning—" She adjusts her visor mirror and looks at Lilith through it. "Just this morning, I had a terrible deja vu. I saw—"

Lilith looks out the window. "Wait. Where are you going?"

"I told you," her father says. "The city is doomed. We're going to Leatelranch."

Lilith looks confused. "Leatelranch?"

"Remember Leatelranch?" he asks. "You know what they say about Leatelranch. Everybody's *dying* to visit."

"Stop the car, right now."

Ophelia turns slightly to Lilith. "What?"

"Stop the car!"

Renwick is caressing the wheel. He's enjoying this. In the mirror, under his mirrored driving sunglasses, he has an irritating smirk on his face.

"First of all," Lilith says, "the city is almost clean. We're winning."

"Really?" asks Renwick. "Is that why you just split with your boyfriend?"

" … And second of all, Leatelranch is literally a fucking cemetery."

Lilith looks to her mother for approval, but she's looking straight at the road. It's getting dark. The trees, the signs, and the road are becoming different shades of night.

"Right? Ma?"

Her mother just looks straight ahead. She rolls down the window, and a cold draft hits Lilith in the face.

"I thought it was a swell idea," Ophelia says.

"Everybody knows it's full of freaks," Lilith says.

"Lilith!" Ophelia cries.

"Leatelranch is a joke," Lilith says. "A punchline. You know how people look at me when I say I'm from there? How they laugh at those backward rituals and stuff?"

"Sounds like it's right up your alley," Renwick says.

"All myths," Ophelia says. "Nothing but urban myths."

"It's a town," her father says. "It's your *hometown*. And it's a small town. Fewer people means fewer *walkers*, or whatever you call them."

"It's a town," Lilith says, "built around a ginormous cemetery."

"Built around a ginormous cemetery," he repeats, and chuckles. "Yes, genius, where they're all bundled up and inside stone crypts

and marble niches. Who's more prepared to deal with the dead than Leatelranch? It's what it was founded for! They were probably the first ones to kill them or lock them inside. Remember those big tall walls around the cemetery? What's better than big, tall—"

Ophelia grabs his arm. She looks at Lilith over her mirror.

"Oh. Right," he says. "You remember."

"Fine," says Lilith. "You go. But drop me off first."

With a screech of the tires, her father stops the car. Lilith's head whips forward with a sharp pain to the neck.

Renwick's mirrored lenses glance at her in the mirror. "Is right here good?"

Lilith looks out the window. It's dark. On the side of the street, ghouls turn to the car and trudge their way toward them. Lilith's fingers freeze around the door handle.

He steps on the gas again, laughing. Her fingers caress the handle and go back to her lap.

"You know what I meant," she says, looking outside. A continuous progression of ghouls roams the streets, and her confrontational tone goes down a notch. "As soon—as soon as it's safe."

A smile draws on the side of his face. "And guess where that will be." The smile fades to a grimace. "Really, Lil, that smell."

"Maybe someone we hit," her mother says.

"No," he says, "that smell is coming from inside."

Lilith sniffs her clothes. She can't tell any more.

The hum of the engine dominates the cabin for a few blocks. Around them, the world burns.

"Where are they?" Lilith whispers to herself. *"Where are the Slayers?"*

"Exactly," says her father, butting into her personal conversation. "Those *Slayers,* supposedly in control ... Where are they? Nowhere."

Lilith stares out the window as they drive. Ghouls seem to roam freely along both sides of the street.

"It's not like you're gonna go back to find Nate anyway," Renwick adds, shrugging.

Lilith looks for him in the mirror but finds him staring out at the road, cowering behind his big sunglasses. She exhales and gazes out the window again.

"Those fuckers ..." she says, giving into the fact that this is now a dialogue. "They must be up to something."

Her father cranes his neck and looks at her in the mirror.

"What do you mean?"

"Well, look at them," she says, motioning toward the ghouls trudging aimlessly on the street. "They're shambling idiots, and yet, the way they closed in on us ... the way they seem to be *everywhere*, even though we keep killing them. And that one with the split head. Why do some of them die with a blow to the head, but clearly that one didn't? It even seemed to smile as we left. It's as if they're *playing* dead."

"Lilybug," her mother says. Her voice is thin and weak.

"What?"

Her mother takes a deep breath. "Listen, Lil," she says. "I've been thinking. You and Nate have known each other since your teens. It was meant to be. And because of that, you're going to be together your whole lives. You feel that, don't you?"

Lil's chest starts to race. She looks back and feels her throat closing.

"Ever since you met him, he's been your whole life. Like your father is to me. And of course, I don't want anything to happen to your father. But when it does, I want to be there." She extends her hand to the side and places it on his shoulder. He turns to her. Under his driving glasses, he's smiling.

"Because in the end, you cannot choose when it ends, but you can choose where to be when that happens. And that's what will matter then."

Lil looks at them, so happy and careless, oblivious to the hell around them. She notices her mother's hands are slippery. Sweaty.

"So maybe," Ophelia says, "what I mean is—" Her voice breaks. "Maybe you *should* stay and look for Nate."

"She'll die!" her father bellows.

"She's a grown woman," her mother says without another crack in her voice.

Lilith looks back. It's getting darker, but the chaos suddenly doesn't seem so threatening after all.

"Leave me here," she says.

"What?" asks Renwick.

"Let me out here. I'm going back for him."

Ophelia sobs and lowers her head.

"No, no," Renwick says. "None of that. You're coming with us. Look, the highway ramp's coming up."

Lilith sees the traffic bottling up in the ramp and realizes this is her last chance. She clenches her teeth and silently fingers the handle. She pulls, pushing her whole body against the door. It doesn't open.

"Child lock," her father says with a grin.

Lilith looks back. "Nate ..."

Renwick turns the wheel and takes the ramp. As they climb toward the highway, making their way among the other cars, Lilith notices the stars shining in the dark sky. Night has fallen. Her eyes start to readjust. The cabin takes on a ghoulish green tinge from the eerie glow of the dashboard lights.

"You can take your glasses off now," Lilith tells her father.

"Oh," her mother says, "he never takes them off when we're on the road."

Lilith looks to the sides and then behind her. "So many cars," she says. "Now it makes sense that the city's empty."

The car slows to a crawl as they join the thick traffic on the highway.

"Why's everyone's driving so slow?" Lilith asks, looking around.

"Well," her father says, patiently. "Hospitals are out, so

nobody can afford to get hurt. Besides, it's not like zombies can drive and outrun us."

Her mother looks up at her mirror and pretends to check something on her face. Lilith can't look away from her greenish face. Her mother's eyes gaze into hers, and she makes a strange sort of gesture. Her eyes look nervous. They're alarmed. They signal toward Lilith's father.

Lilith doesn't understand. "Wha—?"

"So!" says Ophelia. "Leatelranch! It's going to be weird after all this time, right?"

Lilith can tell she's nervous. "I want out," she says.

"Lilybug ..."

"OUT! I WANT OUT!"

She kicks her door, but it doesn't budge. Her father laughs. "Lils ..."

"Maybe we should let her out," says Ophelia. "She's a grown woman."

"She'll come around," he says.

Ophelia inhales, gathering up her courage. "Renwick Kane! You let her out right now!"

"Now?" asks Renwick. "In the middle of the highway?"

Ophelia takes a second. She's petrified. Her voice breaks as she tries to sound natural. "Y—Yes. Now."

Renwick turns to her and smiles. "Sure," he says. "Sure."

The car slows down to a stop.

Ophelia's eyes lock into Lilith's through the mirror. "I'll open your door, sweetie," she says, getting out.

Lilith can hear the noisy fumbling of her mother's fingers as they search for the door handle. And she frowns. Because that's *all* she hears. No engines. No horns. No chaos.

She turns around and looks outside. Behind the rear window, out there, it's pitch black. The traffic around them has stopped dead. They are surrounded by cars, but all the headlights have gone off. She can see the outlines of human figures inside the cars nearby. They're all ... waiting for them.

Ophelia unlatches the door. Lilith feels the fresh air and hears the night crickets from the open road. "No, Ma, wait!" she yells.

Her mother stays outside, holding the door open for her. Lilith gets out of the car and looks for her mother in the dark.

"Ma! We have to—"

Her body spasms with fear when she feels her mother's hands on her shoulders, and her alarmed voice in her ear.

"There's something wrong with your father!"

6

Nathan enters the hospital and finds himself in a pitch-dark hallway, his chest heaving. He leaves the hospital door ajar, slowly and silently, as he tries to steady his breathing. As the last sliver of light enters through the door, he checks the street. The crowd hasn't followed him.

It looks safe. Maybe I can go back. Maybe they stopped following us. Maybe they ran past us. They're dumb enough. It's possible. They're clumsy enough.

He scans the street. A low rumble grows, like a stampede.

Shit.

He closes the door and it latches with a clean and silent *click*, leaving him alone in the buzzing, hungry darkness.

He steps softly on the linoleum. Each step is slow and careful, ready to step back upon the first sign of obstruction, whatever he might not be seeing, just like he did all his life. *No use in being scared*, his father would always say. *You can't depend on flashlights. You run out of batteries on the other end, how are you gonna get back home?*

His breathing calms down. His eyes adjust. White walls. White linoleum floor. White trays and stretchers along the walls. A portrait of a friendly nurse smiling at him. Even though he hates the dark, this place feels *cozy*.

A short *zap* comes from the end of the hallway, followed by a low hum. Nate stops his foot in mid-air. It seems to come out from behind a door on the far side of the hallway. A blueish glow breathes under it.

Nate sets his foot down slowly. He paces carefully, silently, toward it. As he's about to walk past a door, his gaze shoots up. There's a number on it: 107.

"Shit," he says under his breath. "Numbered doors, check. Staircase ..." He looks around. Right down the hall, just before the door with the light creeping out from underneath, there's a staircase. "Shit. Shit."

Whatever you do, he thinks to himself, *you do not take the stairs*.

He walks past the first door, and his eyes search the hall for the next one. As he creeps toward it, the silvery embossed curves of the numbers shine in the dark like the blades of a knife: 108.

"Do not go to the airport unless you've booked a ticket already," comes a faint, ghostly voice from the far end of the hall. His heart skips a beat. "Tickets are sold out."

Just ahead, on the floor, he notices a white tray surrounded by syringes. He treads carefully between them, slowly, and as his foot is about to step on the floor again, he freezes. That noise. Children. Laughter. Shouting.

"There, there!" the voices say. They seem to come from behind the glowing door. Nathan lets his foot down on the floor and continues his walk toward it.

"Don't move!" a little kid's voice says.

Nathan freezes.

"There, there," says another kid's voice.

"Stop jiggling it!" a third voice says.

A female voice shouts, like an explosion, and Nate's blood freezes. She immediately lowers her voice. It's a TV news channel. The sound reverberates all along the hall like a megaphone.

"The zombie threat appears to be ending, thanks to a movement calling themselves the Slayers."

Nate walks past rooms 109 and 110. The walls are covered

with drawings. A crayon Frankenstein monster, smiling. A kind of cemetery with friendly round tombstones.

"... In a coordinated effort they're calling The Bonfire ..."

A blue crayon blotch that is probably Superman. A huge banner made with handmade cutout letters: HAPPY HALLOWEEN.

Cute, he thinks. *This isn't brooding. This isn't gritty. See, Lil? No clichés here.*

"Humanity is, and I'll say it again: *Humanity is winning.* No thanks to the military, which has been disbanded until further notice after entire sections were decimated by their own troops."

Nate reaches the door with the buzzing light. It's ajar.

"Same goes for most police and National Guard squads ..."

His foot lands on a can of soda, which tumbles across the floor with a metallic clank that echoes through the hall. He strides toward it and crushes it with the whole weight of his body.

"Guys," a voice whispers behind the door, "did you hear that?"

7

NATHAN STANDS IN THE DARK, VERY STILL, THE WEIGHT OF HIS body on the crushed can of soda. Another whisper comes from behind the door with the blue glow.

"Hear what?" it asks.

He cranes his neck to peek through the crack in the door. Inside, the blue glimmer of a TV reveals children moving around, and something crawling on the floor near him. Something small. Nathan tries to adjust his eyes. It's a boy, curled up on the floor. He's wearing something bright, or colorful. Red and blue.

Superman?

"See anything outside?" Another boy asks.

The tiny Superman turns to Nate, the blueish glimmer bathing his face. He's grinning. And he's looking straight at Nathan.

Nathan's heart races. Why? Why is that creepy kid looking at him like that? Why is he suddenly scared of a boy? He must be around seven or eight years old, but that grin looks nothing like any child grin Nate has ever seen.

Superman's grin disappears, and he turns to the other kids.

"Suckers," he says, and bursts out in laughter. "You should see your faces."

43

"You idiot!" another kid says, "I almost shit myself. Close that door!"

The boy in the Superman costume locks eyes with Nathan again, and the door swings closed, muffling the protests from the other kids.

Nathan has to take a moment to react. His body is shaking.

Slowly, he pushes the door open again. Through the crack, he sees a dark room. Bathed in the blueish light he saw under the door, he sees the Superman boy again, hunching against the corner of the room, fumbling with some cables, almost hiding behind a hospital bed. A sign that reads HAPPY HALLOWEEN covers a window. A boy wearing a black and red Star Trek costume stands in the middle of the room, staring at the black-and-white buzzing of a TV on the wall above him.

"Stop yanking it!" he yells.

To his left there's another bed with two boys sitting on it, also young, probably around ten. One of them is bald, and has needles all over his head, and he's dressed in a black leather suit. Not a bad Pinhead costume, Nathan recognizes. The other is dressed like Austin Powers. He wonders again why he's still afraid of a bunch of kids. Why not announce himself? Or just leave? Or at least relax about the crushed can of soda under his foot?

"I just don't get why you're so *excited* about this," says the boy in the Austin Powers suit. "Zombies are dumb and violent. Ghosts are clean. Vampires, they're clean. Sophisticated. What's so cool about zombies?"

"Oh, I'm tidy, I'm immortal," the Pinhead boy mocks him. He pulls Austin Powers' blue tuxedo jacket, and Nate can hear the fabric rip.

"It's just death, moron," he says. "Better get used to it."

Austin Powers' eyes swell, and he checks the hole in his costume. He looks up at the bald bully. He's panting.

He doesn't reply.

"Don't just sit there and take it, Les," the boy in the red Star

Trek shirt tells him, still fixated on the buzzing TV. "He's afraid, too, you know."

Pinhead stares at Austin Powers defiantly, waiting for him to make a move. But Lester, breathing heavily, just straightens out his jacket.

The TV zigzags and buzzes, a voice comes through again, and they all look up.

Cables in hand, Superman looks up as well. He looks paler and thinner than the others.

The TV comes alive. "That's right, Kendra," says news anchor Robert Macomber.

The boys cheer.

"That's him!" the boy in the Star Trek costume yells. "That's him!"

"Instead," the man continues, "we owe much of our success to this new group called the Slayers that apparently has found a way to keep from turning into them."

The boy in the Star Trek costume jumps up.

"See?" he yells, "I told you he was alive!"

Nathan sneaks his head past the door. The title bar reads ROBERT MACOMBER REPORTS: THREAT OVER?

"Shit, Kenny, your dad's old," says the bald Pinhead boy, sitting on the bed. He turns to Austin Powers. "Right?"

Austin turns to him and smiles reluctantly. "Ha," he adds.

The bald boy turns to Superman. "What do you think, *Superdork?*"

Superman glances at him and turns back to the TV. He looks too weak to respond. Holding the TV cable seems to be taking all of his energy.

"Shh," says the boy standing in the middle of the room, eyes locked on the TV, and taking a step closer to it. "Shut up."

The news anchor stares vacantly at them. "The Slayers," he says staring at the teleprompter with disdain, "are reporting that they've-quote-found the ghouls' Achilles heel, *blah blah,* planning a bonfire, *blah blah blah* ..."

He stops. He looks deeply into the camera, and his face turns into a grin. He seems to gaze straight at the boy in the *Star Trek* costume standing still in the middle of the room.

"Hi, Kenny."

Lit by the TV rays, the kids' jaws drop, and they all turn to Kenny.

A buzz stuns them and fills the room. The TV is dead. Superman looks for the dropped cable, fumbling his hands on the floor. The other boys are still stunned. Frozen.

The bald boy snaps out of it first. "Fix it!" he yells, "fix it!"

The boy in red just stares at the dead TV.

Superman grabs a chair and stands on it, fumbling with the cables as they go up to the TV, and Nate notices there are also cables going to his arm. White and transparent tubes sway with every one of his movements, stretching, pulling, connecting the boy's arm to a machine. Nate notices a dark shiny spot on the boy's arm. He's bleeding.

The TV comes back on. Robert Macomber is still grinning. "Well, I'm here to tell you: *not quite*." His face twitches. "Not quite. Not. Quite. Not quite. Haha. Nope."

The kids look at each other, confused.

"Not—not ... Quite."

The camera moves back to his co-anchor. She laughs nervously. "Robert, what's wrong with you?"

Her eyes dart between him and the camera. "Quit the theatrics, please!"

Superman turns to watch the TV, and his arm pulls a tube, and the tube turns a heartbeat monitor to face Nathan. The display is silently flatlining.

Robert Macomber grins at the woman, his eyes so wide, they threaten to pop out of their sockets.

"*Quit the theatrics!*" he explodes. He seems to find it funny. "Kendra, you don't know just how right you are!"

He turns back to the camera with wild eyes. There's an

uncomfortable silence in the studio as the camera zooms in on his face.

"OK," he says. "Here's the scoop." His face turns into a grin. "I'm coming to get you, Kenny."

Kenny turns to his friends. Nathan can see tears coming down from his eyes.

Still grinning, without blinking, the man lifts his arm and points to the camera. Blood comes down from the side of his chest. "I'm coming to get you."

Robert Macomber bolts up, and a scream fills the studio. The camera loses focus, moves, and suddenly he's not there anymore. His chair is spinning, and a terrified Kendra looks at the camera. Her panicked "What the fuck?!" are the last words viewers hear before all hell breaks loose in the studio.

The bald boy jumps off the bed. "C'mon," he says. "We gotta go."

He puts his hand on Kenny's shoulder and starts walking toward the door. Toward Nate.

"Wait," Austin Powers protests. "We gotta wait for Frankie."

"No time," the bald kid says. "Didn't you see that? We gotta go, now."

Austin tries to look defiant. "Yes, time," he says, and his voice cracks up. "Yes, time."

Kenny's cheeks are red and shiny with tears. "Guys, I want to go."

Austin jumps off the bed. "You think your father is coming here?" He walks up to Kenny and points at the TV. "That's—He's probably just—"

"We need to go!" says Kenny.

Austin takes a step back. "But what about Frankie? I'm not leaving him behind! If we can just wait a bit, just wait here—"

"Fuck Frankie," says the bald boy. "If he didn't come back already—!"

Austin looks at him gravely. "Shut up!"

Kenny sobs. He puts his hand on Austin's shoulder. "Please,

Les. He's coming."

Nathan shudders. He checks the dark hall behind him. He can't see anything, but he's sensing the same rush as he did moments ago when he was being chased by ghouls out in the street.

Austin looks at his friend in red, whose face is shiny with tears. "OK. OK, Ken." He turns to Superman. The boy looks exhausted. "Need any help?"

Superman comes down from the chair, taking the machine, and Nathan's heart skips a beat. The cables are definitely connected. The display is definitely flatlining.

The boy is dead.

Inches away from him, the bald boy grabs the door handle, about to open it. Nathan is petrified. He knows he should move, but he can't.

"He's back!" One of the boys says.

The bald boy turns to the TV again. Nate closes in again to watch, inches away from the boy's pins. The kids are standing still, their faces turned to the TV. Robert Macomber is back. His face fills the screen now. He stares straight at Kenny.

Kenny takes one step to the side, and his father follows him with his gaze. Kenny steps back. His father smiles and follows him with his gaze. His eyes are blood-shot.

"I can't wait to hug you," Robert Macomber says, savoring every word.

"Kenny," calls the bald boy, "come on. We're leaving."

As the door handle comes down, as Nate's heart starts to race, Superman drops the TV cable, jumps down from the chair, and grabs Kenny by the shoulders.

"I think you better wait till your father gets here," he says with a grin.

"What?" Austin asks.

"Oh, shit!" Pinhead yells, running for the door, springing it open in front of Nate, and bumping his head with dozens of thin acupuncture needles into Nathan's chest.

8

Out in the cold and dark road, Lilith's mother's eyes plead with her. Lilith looks around, trying to find a way out. The cars around them open their doors. Shadows are slowly coming out and sneaking toward them. To the side of the road, she can barely distinguish between the black trees surrounding the highway and the black sky above, faint stars blinking to the chirping sound of crickets, and the rustling of leaves coming from the woods. Next to them, on the side of the road, a sign proclaims, in gothic script letters dripping with rust, Leatel-ranch: Next Exit.

"Get in!" Renwick says from inside the car. "I think they're coming."

Lil looks again. What seemed like shadows moving silently in the night are now dark silhouettes.

"They're getting closer," Lilith says under her breath.

She looks back at the car and sees her mother zooming past her, running toward the shadows. Lil freezes as her mother raises her arms uncontrollably, fighting off the figures like a feral animal. She kicks and screams and punches like Lil's never seen her do. Her hands are lioness paws, clawing and pushing the figures aside.

Before she can react, her mother is running back toward her.

"Whoa, Ma, are you OK?"

"I'm fine," Ophelia says, panting, as she fixes her hair. "Lil, please, what do we do?"

Renwick turns on the lights. Lilith panics. The road around them is full of cars, all doors open, and between them, ghouls are closing in on them.

Ophelia enters the car, and Lil follows her. She sits down, and as she closes her door, she unlocks the child lock.

"Go, go—!"

Dad floods the gas.

"Ma!" says Lilith, staring wide-eyed at her mother's headrest in front of her. "What the hell was that? You looked ... feral!"

She sees her mother's shoulders going up and down, breathing heavily.

"Mother's instincts," Renwick says. "Never underestimate a mother bear protecting her cubs."

Ophelia says nothing. She keeps breathing heavily, looking straight at the road.

Renwick turns the wheel sharply. "Hang on!" he says, and the car skids off the highway, bumping and rattling in the grass, toward the woods.

Lil looks back. The ghouls calmly walk back to their cars, start their engines, and resume their solemn procession along the dark highway.

"Did they touch you?" Renwick asks Lilith, bumping to the sides as the car rattles. Up ahead, the car's high beams hit the first trees. He turns to his wife. "Are you OK?"

"Yes," says Lilith, trying to stay seated. "We're OK."

"They were dead!" Ophelia says as the green light from the dashboard flickers. "They were all dead!"

As they enter the woods, he slows down. The cabin steadies, and Lilith notices she's been clutching her hands to the sides of her mother's seat. The engine's roar becomes a faint purr. Thick trees pass by on both sides of the car as they roll on the soft ground.

Renwick turns off the lights. *Now* it's pitch black.

"We're alone now," he says. "Safe."

The woods start to thin. Moonlight falls intermittently on the car, bathing the cabin in flashes of white light. Lilith rests her head on the headrest, looks up to see the flickering full moon, and sets her gaze on her mother's headrest in front of her. As the vision blacks out and flashes intermittently, she notices a dark splotch among the white. There. She sees it again. What is it?

The car goes dark.

Up front, she sees a clearing. She readies herself and her terrible night vision to be as alert as possible.

White light shines again through the thick trees. As her fingers caress Ophelia's velvety headrest, she notices something wet and dark and strange in it, like an inkblot.

"Ma ..."

Moonlight flashes again, a perfect photograph of her parents sitting in front of her, and yes, right in front of her face, right in the middle of her mother's headrest, a big, dark smudge.

Lilith's body tightens.

" ... Yes?" Ophelia says, looking at her in the mirror.

The forest ends abruptly, sending white moonlight flooding over the seat in front of Lilith, and on the shining smudge. Below it, in the narrow space between the headrest and the seat, where her mother's neck should be, a meaty open wound bleeds, dripping drops of black.

9

WITH HIS CHEST BURNING FROM THE STING OF THE NEEDLES, Nathan pushes the spiky boy away. He paces toward Superman, who, pale as a ghost and lit by the gray static rain of the TV, holds Kenny in a lock.

"Stop!" he yells.

The pale boy in the Superman costume lifts his head slowly to meet his gaze. His grin sends a chill down Nate's spine. It's the uncanny expression you'd get if you forced a smile on a corpse. Something about the stillness of every muscle he's not purposely moving, a stillness Nathan remembers—

But the boy is still human, Nathan thinks. He's upright, he's moving, and this is just enough to let Nathan function. He grabs the boy's arm and breaks the hold on Kenny. The child's arm feels limp, lifeless. He doesn't fight back. His wrists are icy cold, and Nate tries to ignore it, to keep a hold on him, to fight the urge to run away.

"Now, kids—" he says.

But a tiny fistful of knuckles lands on his cheek. Nate struggles to hold onto Superman and turns around to find Pinhead about to throw a second punch.

"Stop!"

53

The Austin Powers boy charges toward him, about to throw a low, unfair kick. Nathan lifts his foot in defense, and the boy lets out a cry of pain.

"Stop!" Nathan yells, "I'm not one of them!"

A tiny foot kicks him in the ass, throwing him off balance and propelling him forward, and he takes Superman with him, falling on top of the boy, hands on his neck. The boy squirms, trying to escape, and Nathan struggles to keep him restrained.

He looks around the room.

"Where are your parents?" he asks, getting up, regaining his balance as he keeps his hold on Superman. Cold, dead, corpse Superman.

"He's dead!" the Pinhead boy yells, pointing at him. "Kill him!"

"I'm not dead!" Nathan yells, "I'm just pale! Your friend, on the other hand—"

A big red blotch comes at him, and Nate instinctively turns around. Kenny Macomber jumps him and wraps his arms around his neck, trying to strangle him, the red polyester of the Star Trek costume burning his mouth, and makes him almost lose his grip on the dead Superboy. He can't believe he's still doing it. He can't believe he's not running away, screaming his lungs out, looking for a place to wash his hands and shower and forget about this whole thing.

"Your—friend's—dead!" he mumbles.

Superman's squirming comes to a stop.

Nathan feels Kenny sliding down from his back, landing behind him, and stepping away. Pinhead and Austin are in front of him, frozen, looking at him.

"What?" Austin asks, confused.

"No, he's not," says Pinhead.

Nathan catches his breath. He shows them the blood. "Look!"

Kenny walks around him. He keeps a safe distance and examines Superman. He looks at his face, his neck, his arms.

"But ... he didn't try to kill us," he says.

"Touch him!" Nathan yells. "Feel his pulse!"

The boy in the Austin Powers suit walks up to Superman with a white cable. He touches Superman's cheek, and his face turns to stone. He puts a heart rate sensor clip on his index finger and looks him in the eye. Superman doesn't bat an eye. In the corner of the room, the heartbeat monitor display a flat line and emits a long, high-pitched *beep*.

"Shit."

The boys stare at Superman, and Pinhead takes a step closer.

"He's a zombie?" he asks. "Why isn't he ... doing anything?"

Superman's shoulders are limp. He's unresponsive. He's a corpse.

"There," Nathan says to the boys, pointing at the TV. "Bring me that cable."

Pinhead walks up to the TV, walking past a petrified Austin Powers.

Nathan grabs Superman by the shoulders and shakes him. The boy's face is hard as stone. Nathan does his best to keep his hold on the boy, even though all he can think of is running as far away as possible, and getting rid of this sinking feeling. A chill he hasn't felt in a long time.

"Why are you doing this?" he asks.

But the boy doesn't move.

"Are you guys ... giving up?" Nathan asks him. "Is that it?"

The boy's eyes come alive. They lock onto his.

"Is this a trap?" Nathan insists.

The boy stares at him, silent. His eyes are black and empty.

"I've just been outside with fifty of you," Nathan says.

The boy squints. It's like he's mocking him.

"I've *spent my life* among you," says Nathan, impressed by his own courage to speak to it.

The boy smiles.

"I've *hurt* many of you," he lies.

Superman giggles.

Nate shakes him again. "You don't know who I am, do you?" he shouts. "You don't know where I come from!"

The boy just smiles.

Nathan clenches his teeth. His face is burning.

The bald, spiky boy looks at Nathan. "You're not kidding anyone," he mocks him. "You look scared shitless."

"Yeah, man," Austin says. "Get a fucking grip."

Nathan turns to Superman again. The dead boy is grinning.

"Let me," the boy in black says, grabbing Superman by the shoulders. Nathan lets go, scared, and finally allows himself to shudder.

Austin leans in, getting dangerously close to Superman's face.

"What's going on?" he asks the corpse.

Behind him, the boy in the Star Trek outfit takes a step back, trembling. Nathan recognizes that look and realizes he probably looks about the same right now. He hasn't been this scared in years. He had forgotten how fear really feels.

Superman's eyebrows are frozen. His temple is relaxed and flat. He looks almost peaceful. His eyes are still. But his pupils. His pupils are boiling.

Nathan walks up to the window and looks outside. "How long have you been here alone?" He asks the boys.

"Two days."

"Have you eaten? Taken a shower?"

They don't respond.

"How about you? Austin?"

The boy in the Austin Powers suit sends him a cold, hateful stare. "Who's Austin?"

"Austin Powers," Nate says.

"What's an *Austin Powers*?"

The question stuns Nathan. "How *young* are you? You don't know Austin Powers?"

They all look confused.

"I'm Lestat," the boy in the shiny blue suit says, faking a weird accent. "A Victorian vampire."

Nate notices the plastic fangs in Austin's mouth and chuckles. "So that's why you've been talking funny, *Austin*?"

This gets a big laugh from Pinhead.

"What about you, Pinhead? Ever heard of Austin Powers?"

The Pinhead boy doesn't understand.

Pinhead stares blankly at him.

"Oh, come on. Who are you supposed to be then? Those pins?"

Pinhead bites his lip.

"Leave him alone," says the boy in the Star Trek costume. "His mom made it."

Nate sighs. "She's dark."

Pinhead narrows his eyes. "She's an acupuncturist."

"Wait," says the boy in the Star Trek uniform. "You come from outside. Have you seen Frankie? He was still wearing the hospital gown."

Nathan's blood curdles.

"No," he lies.

"He went to look for some medical—"

"No idea," Nathan interrupts him. "Sorry, kid."

Clank.

Nate freezes at the echo of a can falling to the ground somewhere out in the hall.

Austin and Pinhead turn toward the door. It's wide open, a hole containing all the darkness in the world. Nathan moves stealthily toward it, too, followed by Kenny.

"*Zombies?*" Kenny whispers with a trembling voice, scratching his red T-shirt nervously.

"Let's hope," says Pinhead.

Kenny and Austin turn to him. *"What? Yoshi, cut it out, you're not funny anymore."*

Pinhead points at Superman: weak, scrawny, tied to a chair. *"Look at him, you idiot,"* he whispers. *"Zombies are harmless."*

Another sound echoes through the hallway. It sounds closer.

"I'd worry," Superman warns, his eyes vacant.

Kenny paces slowly to the door and takes a peek outside. As

he scans the darkness out in the hall, with his mouth trembling and his face turning into a grimace, he whispers.

"D—Dad ...?"

His voice echoes through the dark hallway, then dies out.

Silence.

He turns to Superman, looking him dead in the eye.

"Can we outrun them?" he asks, trembling. "Do they shamble like idiots, or will they catch us?"

Superman just stares at him.

Pinhead scoffs and points at weak, scrawny Superman. "Does it look like they can run?"

"Answer me," Kenny repeats. "Can they run?"

Superman grins.

"They almost caught me," Nathan says. "But they weren't really running. We just ... got cornered. We had bad luck."

"Ah," says Pinhead. "They *almost* caught you. And if an old guy like you could outrun them, it should be a piece of cake for us."

An echo interrupts him, approaching from the hall.

Grumbling. Footsteps.

"Yes," the Superman boy says, slowly, savoring every word. "I remember this."

His voice sounds off. A tired, calm voice, like an old man telling stories by the fire. A voice like rustling dry leaves. He stares at the wall, lifeless, the TV cable wrapped around his chest hanging loosely.

"They should be climbing in from the windows now," he says, as though he's conjuring an old memory. "Approaching us through the halls. Filling them. Closing in. Killing you in front of me."

"Weapons," Nathan says. "Now."

He looks around the room for something he can use. The room is harmless. But next to Kenny, he notices a fire extinguisher that's the perfect size and weight.

Before he can say anything, Superman turns to Kenny and raises a lifeless finger toward it: "Your head gets crushed with that fire extinguisher."

"Ha," says Pinhead, amused. "Kenny, take that fire extinguisher, *please*."

Kenny's face goes red with anger and fear.

"No!" says Austin. "Kenny, don't!"

Pinhead smiles. "What? Aren't you curious?"

Clank, goes the hallway again.

"Fuck this," Pinhead says, opening the door. "Follow me."

Nathan catches Yoshi just before he makes it out the door and looks down the hallway. Shadows approach them in the dark. Sluggish. Ghostlike.

"We gotta hurry," Pinhead insists, escaping Nate's hold. He sprints back toward the door, his sneakers squealing in the dark.

"Come on, guys!" he yells, and now his voice travels throughout the entire floor, loudly, unmistakably.

Kenny and Austin hurry toward Nathan, who blocks the door and looks into the dark. He can make out shapes, human shapes, moving inhumanly toward Yoshi; legs and arms crawling with uncanny speed through the darkness like scurrying cockroaches.

Kenny panics. "Oh shit. Oh shit. Oh shit," he repeats, as Nathan scans the room again searching for something to use as a weapon. Austin and Pinhead are looking at him, frozen, scared.

But all at once, the noises in the hall stop.

Nathan looks in the dark again. The pack of ghouls, or whatever that mass of buzzing darkness is, is not approaching them anymore. It looks uneasy. A faint hissing fills the hall, like buzzing insects, like a storm of a thousand screams repressed into whispers. And in those whispers, something familiar. Almost like ...

But no. That's impossible.

Zombies don't speak.

And suddenly, just as fast as they were approaching, the ghouls move away. Their hissing moves away, far into the darkness, and disappears.

Kenny frowns. "They're going *back*?"

"They got spooked," Austin says. "Something spooked them."

Pinhead paces back into the room. "What scares off a zombie?"

Nathan turns to Superboy, ready to question him again, only to find the chair knocked over and the TV cable lying on the floor. Superboy scuttles to the door, squeezes between him and the kids, and runs into the dark hall to follow the other ghouls.

The kids look at each other wide-eyed.

Nathan takes a breath.

"OK," he says. "They can run. Let's just thank our luck and get out of here."

"No," says Austin. "We need to wait for Frankie!"

"He's probably dead and evil by now," says Pinhead. "Let's just go."

"He's probably safe," Nathan says, trying to sound casual.

"Safe where?" Austin asks.

"You mean, with the Slayers?" Redshirt and Pinhead ask at the same time.

And it dawns on Nathan. He had forgotten about the Slayers.

"Yes!" he says. "The Slayers! That's where she'll be! He, I mean. Your friend. We need to head—"

"What do you mean, *she*?"

Nate pauses. "My girlfriend might be there as well, and this is the perfect opportunity to get her. Come on. We have to go."

He exits the room and lets the boys out.

As they leave, Kenny turns to Pinhead and whispers in his ear, "Did you hear them talk, too?"

10

LILITH SINKS INTO HER SEAT AND LOOKS AT THE GHOULISH apparitions sitting in front of her. Their faces glow green by the dim light of the dashboard. Her cool-as-fuck father, driving, unaware of any danger, and her mother's stone face in the mirror in front of her. They both look straight ahead as the car bumps and rolls on the soft ground. Dark trees parade slowly around them. The shaky mirror shows her mother's thin flat mouth, bathed in sickish green. Needle-thin branches scratch the window next to Lilith's face.

"That was close," Renwick says.

Lilith searches for his gaze in the mirror. She lifts her eyebrows, trying to get his attention, but his driving sunglasses seem fixed on the road. Hell, it's so dark, it's hard to tell if he can even see anything behind those. Lilith looks around for a clearing, a gap in the trees that will shed another flash of moonlight and let him see her face. But trees, trees seem to be everywhere now.

"Look!" he says, raising his arm right in front of Ophelia's face, pointing to the side. "Over there. The old Citizen tracks! They will lead us straight into Leatelranch."

This is it. Lilith stares into the mirror, waiting for him to look.

"It's ironic, isn't it ...?" she says, but he keeps looking straight.

" ... We're following the tracks of the *dead train*," she continues slowly, aimlessly, "just to ... escape the dead."

"That's not ironic," he says, serious, still looking up front.

"Well, you know," she tries again. "You always said, Leatelranch was founded because there were too many corpses in New Southport, and now we're fleeing there for the same reason." As she talks, she opens her eyes wide, hoping to catch his attention, her gaze darting between the green face in his mirror and the one in her mother's.

"Yes," he says. "It made sense then, and it makes sense now. I don't see the irony."

She opens her eyes so wide they hurt. She cannot possibly open them any wider. He doesn't seem to be taking the hints.

"What's *ironic*," he blurts, "is that you always hated when I talked about history, and here you are ..."

"Hah," she goes, trying to get him to look at her.

He doesn't.

"Remember?" he asks idly, without a care in the world. "I used to take you to see *The Citizen*, at the museum. You seemed so bored ..."

"Well—"

"And then you became a total *groupie* of those horror movies about the dead coming back to life and trying to eat everyone."

"Brains," she says, and this is sure to get a reaction from him because he hates it when she corrects him. "They eat brains."

"Yes. So, in the end, Leatelranch got to you, didn't it?"

"What do you mean?"

"Well, speaking of *irony*, I'm sure you appreciate how you were practically *born* in a cemetery, hated everything about it—the history, the *facts*, hated *us* for teaching you about it—but you were perfectly happy living in those zombie movies."

Lilith waits. He *has* to look at her now.

He looks forward.

The scratching on the car softens, and Lilith sees that the forest outside dwindles. The moon casts a blanket of white light on the car, and Lilith's eyes are drawn to her mother's headrest once again. She catches her mother's gaze in the mirror, piercing her with her deep green eyes.

"I know you can see it," she says.

Lilith's heart skips a beat. "Wh—what?"

"I said," Ophelia repeats, "I know you can see it."

Lilith's body clenches. She wants to look at her father, ask for help, see if he's hearing this, but she can't break contact with those terrible green eyes. She wonders what her father is doing, how he's reacting, just outside her field of view.

"What do you mean?"

Ophelia's eyes look straight into Lilith's soul. The car hits a bump, and for a second, the mirror is filled with her ample, green smile.

"The hole in my head," the mouth says, "of course, dear."

Lilith freezes. She tries not to blink. She thinks. She tries to think. Without blinking. The image of the car trembles. So, it has come to this. She tries to hold her tears. *It's easy,* she says to herself. *You've bored people talking about this. You've imagined how to combat ghouls all your life. Why be numb now? The seat in between is nothing but fabric and stuffing. And she's even strapped to it, for fuck's sake. So, if it was so easy to fight the last one, how come it's suddenly so hard to move?*

"Pa ..."

She tries to find her father in her peripheral vision. Just a blur, but she can see he isn't moving. He keeps driving, unaware. She glances at the rearview mirror, looking for her father, then quickly looks away. Staring out at the darkness, she scans the image she saw, like a picture burnt into her retina.

A grin.

Her father was grinning.

He chuckles.

Ophelia turns to him and smiles.

"You look nervous!" he says. "What's the matter?"

They burst into laughter. Lilith's so tense her muscles hurt. She grips the door handle.

"Why the long face?" Her mother mocks her. "Aw, you didn't see this coming, did you?"

"OK, OK, this is our last chance," he says, turning to Lilith. "I want to know what you think about this now. While you're still ... you know."

Lilith doesn't move. She can't move.

"What was your favorite house?" he asks.

She scans her door, the other door, the thinning woods outside. *Which way? How? Now? Stall them?* The engine in the car is roaring, but it's nothing compared to what's going on in her head.

"What?" she asks.

"What's your favorite house? Your place in New Southport? Or our place in Leatelranch, where you were born? Do you even remember it?"

Lilith remembers. She spent her entire childhood there, and part of her teens. She had friends. She had adventures. She had losses. She met Nate there.

"It was your whole world for years," he says. "It gave you shelter. All your zombie movies, what do they have in common? They're about finding shelter, aren't they? And yet ..."

"Honey—enough already," says Ophelia. Only this is not her usual agreeable tone. This one's *hungry*. It can't wait.

"Two days ago," he says, "when I died ..."

Lilith is stunned. "What?!"

"*What?!*" Her mother shrieks like a parrot, stabbing Lilith with her gaze through the mirror, and Lilith's mouth closes shut.

"Two days ago," he says again, slowly, "when I died ..."

Lilith can't believe what she's hearing. "You—"

"*You died?!*" Ophelia shrieks, mocking Lilith with a hysterical grin.

Lilith turns to her. "I thought—"

"*I thought Ma was the dead one!*" her mother taunts, imitating the exact words Lilith was about to utter.

He looks out the side of the road. "All right, enough of that. We're coming up."

Ophelia turns to him and smiles. Her eyes are gleaming. Something meaty is dangling from the back of her head. The corpse places her right hand against the dashboard and grabs Renwick's hand with the other.

He floods the gas.

He turns toward Lilith and leans toward her until his face is inches from hers. Lilith's nose itches. That smell. That smell was coming from him. He takes off his glasses, and Lilith gasps. His eyes are dead. Big. Murky.

"You were right about one thing," he says. His breath smells like roadkill. Her muscles tense, and she fights to pull her head back. Her hand trembles on the handle.

"We *are* playing dead."

Lilith pulls the door handle with her whole body but hears the loud mechanical *thump* of her father locking it again with the push of a button.

"What's the matter?" he asks. "Planning to escape?"

A wave of rage washes over her. She stretches forward and pulls up her mother's headrest, seeing the two metal spikes coming up, and she thrusts forward with the weight of her whole body. Her father's face is still next to her, smiling, and her mother sobs. Looking front, Lilith sees her white-knuckled hands pushing the headrest onto the front passenger seat, stabbing her mother in the back. It drips blood on her feet.

"Why would you stab *me*?" her mother sobs, and then laughs. "Me!? Mommy!?"

Her father's face, inches from her face, laughs too.

Lilith pulls the plush headrest and stabs her father in the chest. Her hands tremble. Stunned again, she sees him moving back to his seat. Out front, the woods around the car get thicker. A wall of oak trees is coming up.

He clenches his teeth. "We're gonna tear you apart!"

Lilith strikes again, nearly tearing off his chest. Her parents are still interlocking fingers like this is nothing.

"Are you scared, Lilybug?" he asks with a smile, his face green by the faint light of the dashboard.

She stabs him again, hitting him in the cheek, and tearing it off. He gives a hollow chuckle, and Ophelia mocks her again. "Are you gonna cry?"

In an instant, his mouth and teeth reach for her neck. Lilith raises her knee and forces him back into the driver's seat. She jumps on top of him and pushes him to the floor, and the car starts to skid. Lilith opens the driver's door and sees the dark ground and patches of grass speeding down below. She catches her first breath of clear, fresh air.

"Wait," her father asks, curled into a ball under her. "How did you do that? This is where you—"

She looks up through the windshield. The car is heading straight into an oak tree.

"I know," she mumbles, and her eyes swell. "This is where I die."

As she jumps off, as she hits the cold hard ground, she hears her parent's voices moving away with the car. "How did she do that? This isn't—"

The car skids in the mud, loses control, and crashes into the tree.

11

THE GIRL IS HOLDING FLOWERS. IT'S A TWENTY-TWO-STEM bouquet with damask roses, white carnations, and three types of chrysanthemums. She looks up at the beeping box, a glass monitor with a green line jumping around. As her parents talk to the doctor in whispers that barely resemble English, she recognizes only short phrases: " ... *brain death* ... ," " ... *two minutes under* ... ," " ... *best not upset her* ..." She watches the friendly green dot bounce and squiggle, like a ball teasing her to catch it. *Beep. Beep.* She imagines she's about to catch it, then *beep*, it wriggles up again. It sounds funny and warm. And there, suddenly, in a reflection in the screen, she finds her grandmother's calm, sleeping face. She looks a bit thin, like a prune version of her Grann. Her lips are closed and slightly crooked to the side. Her eyes look tired, darker, like they're floating on black puddles. They are closed, but still, they are rumbling. They are restless, they are ... busy.

"She's waking up!" her father yells.

The doctor rushes past them, and the girl quickly grabs her father's hand again, pressing tightly. She doesn't like how her Grann looks right now.

The old lady in the hospital bed moves her lips. " ... Eeth ..."

The doctor moves to her side. Renwick grabs Grann's hand, and Ophelia holds the little girl by the shoulders, keeping her away from the bed.

The doctor listens carefully. The woman wets her lips and speaks again.

"Sheeiit."

"What?"

The old woman frowns. She's struggling. "Guddamit," she says.

The girl giggles.

The woman opens her eyes. Renwick's face lights up. He smiles.

Grann looks up at him and around the room. She doesn't smile. "Whaddafuck ...?"

Ophelia smiles at the girl. "She's in a mood, huh?"

"Hey, sleepyhead," says Renwick. "You're back!"

"What?" says her Grann, eyes still wandering.

"You were ..." Renwick begins, then starts again. "For almost two minutes, you were completely—"

The doctor looks at Renwick and shakes his head, signaling for him not to continue. Behind him, Ophelia's eyes are watery. Renwick stutters.

The doctor leans over Grann, making sure she can see him smile. "Do you know where you are, Miss Kane?"

Grann's eyes look around her. "I ... I ..."

"How are you feeling?" asks Renwick.

"What ... happened?"

"Come," says the doctor, putting his hand on Renwick's back and walking him outside. He looks at Ophelia, too. The three of them exit the room and close the door. The girl can see them through its tiny glass window.

She turns to the bed and just stands there.

The old woman turns her head and looks at her. From where she stands at the foot of the bed, the girl can only see her Grann's forehead and a small portion of her eyes. She seems angry.

"Lilith," she says.

The little girl jolts. She grips the flowers nervously with both hands, squeezing the stems.

"Is that you, Lilith?"

"Yes, Grann."

The old woman sits up with a sigh. She's sluggish and confused. Lilith sees the tubes and cables moving around, following her grandmother's movements like a puppet. She finally can see her lovely, wrinkly face. Her eyes are almost closed shut from the pain.

"Do you have a headache, Grann?" asks little Lilith.

Grann, still groggy, tries to put her thoughts together. She struggles to smile. "I dreamt about you."

"Really?" asks Lilith. "What about?"

Grann grabs her head and tries to open her eyes, but the white hospital light is obviously hurting her. Her head is falling to the side.

"You ... You were ... I was you ...? Wait ..."

She talks funny, like she just bit her tongue. She tells Lilith a lot of strange, silly things. Things that Lilith doesn't understand. Things that don't make sense. She would never like a boy! Ugh. Grann says a lot of scary things, too. Lilith looks out through the glass window on the door and sees her parents talking to the doctor. She grins. She's listening to adult stuff. Grann is finally treating her like an adult, telling her things that adults usually keep from children.

Now, Grann is talking about her new red coat, pointing at it with her frail trembling finger.

"You can't remember that, silly," says Lilith. "We bought it this morning before coming to see you!"

Grann looks confused.

"But I ... was there, wasn't I? Or was I? Why, if this was just moments before we—"

Grann's eyes dart around the room. When they finally settle on young Lilith, they seem not to recognize her.

"But wait, if you ... so young ..."

She stares at the wall behind Lilith, and her eyes finally open entirely. Her black pupils retract deeper and deeper, and her face turns into a painful grimace.

"OH NO!" she yells, "Please, help! You can't let me go back there! Don't let me die! I don't want to die!"

The door opens. The doctor barges in and moves Lilith to the side. Mom and Dad follow him into the room, and Mom holds Lilith against her. Lilith tries to free herself.

"But I want to hear about the car crash!" she says. "And Tommy!"

The doctor picks up a needle and holds it close to his face, reading from it. Grann sways her arms around. "Don let me die again! Please!" She hits a lunch tray and sends it crashing to the floor.

"Oh no, oh no," says Renwick, turning to Ophelia with tears in his eyes. "Take Lil outside."

Mom picks her up.

"No!" Lilith yells as they take her away from the room. "She dreamt about me! She dreamt about me!"

12

LILITH ROLLS AND TUMBLES ON THE GROUND, ON HARD ROCKS and sharp sticks, until her back hits a giant dead tree and the wind gets knocked out of her.

She struggles to get up. She has a metallic taste in her mouth. She wipes her hand across her face and sees blood. Her left leg throbs with pain. Coughing, hurting, she looks at the car wrapped against the tree like a steel-winged gargoyle. Plumes of smoke escape the hood. The smell of gas and oil fills the air.

The cold ground cracks under her feet. She notices the full moon behind the thick foliage, but its light doesn't reach the dense forest full of invisible trees and branches. She takes out her phone. It's dead.

"Gotta get back," she says, trying to get her body to stop shaking. "Gotta get back."

As her eyes adjust to the dark, she sees a spot that's lighter than the rest. She puts her hands in front of her to fend off the thin branches coming from everywhere and walks toward it. Her left leg is in pain. The light behind the foliage grows brighter. She's getting closer.

As she makes her way between two branches, bright moonlight hits her face. It's a clearing. A wide corridor, bathed in moonlight, in the middle of the dense forest.

"What the ...?"

Her foot stumbles onto something hard. She hears a deep, metallic noise, and she falls face first onto an old wooden plank.

She gets up and looks both ways. The gleam of two steel railings stretches on the ground as far as she can see. They're connected by old wooden planks that look almost luxurious, like antique furniture. The planks are bigger than any train track planks she's ever seen. The two steel railings are also wider apart than those of a regular train track. But this is for no ordinary train. It's monstrous. She's standing on the old *Citizen* tracks.

"Gotta get back," she says, shivering, like a mantra. "Gotta get back."

She looks to the left, trying to make out where it ends. Nothing but dark. She looks to the right. Far in the horizon, the tracks disappear into the night, and she sees something moving. She narrows her eyes and takes a step forward. She tries to focus. Small black dots, crawling in a formation, like ants. She shudders. It's the highway. Cars are slugging along with their lights off.

"Shit."

She turns around. She looks at the gleaming steel beams disappearing into the night, and she sighs. She starts following them.

The wood planks beneath her feet are rotten. They look ancient. As she's about to set her foot on the next one, she freezes. Something is moving in the dark patch of black soil between the wood planks, like worms, but bigger. Two clusters of bony fingers squirm and twitch. An open mouth coming out of the ground seems to gasp for air. Dead lips, black, like dry mushrooms. They open and close, with small teeth biting away at the night in a demented frenzy. Lilith enjoys hearing the bones crack under the sole of her boot. She smiles as she walks past it.

"Lilith."

A shiver runs through her spine.

The wind. Has to be. Either that or a mocking whisper.

"Lilybug ..."

She turns around.

"Dad?"

She looks around. Nothing but still, dead trees. She's alone.

She looks down at the ground. The black lips have stopped moving. They're curved, like dead caterpillars. Like smiling.

"'Tis the wind," she says to herself. "'Tis the wind and nothing more!"

She huffs, looking around. "Not the best reference right now, Lilybug."

Her teeth chatter. She steps on the cold planks and looks around. Nothing but darkness.

Lilith.

A jolt runs through her spine, and she bolts, her feet stepping on the tracks like hammers hitting nails. She looks down and focuses on the planks and carefully jumps them two by two to avoid falling, and she runs, runs, runs until her ribs hurt.

She paces herself. She controls herself. She takes two breaths in, two breaths out, and she evens her breathing until her heartbeat steadies. She uses the moonlit wooden planks to normalize her steps. She was always afraid of running. Now she's getting good at it, and her heart is fine. She looks at the planks passing by under her feet, and she notices that they are starting to get fuzzy. So are her feet. A light fog laps at her legs and knees, and suddenly she can't see her own ankles, as if she's a floating ghost. An image of the boy (*Frankie, was it?*) landing on the pavement fills her head. She slows down. Nothing is chasing her. *No need to risk stepping on broken planks you can't see.*

Shivering, trembling, she stops. She feels her way to the next plank with her feet, and looks up. In front of her, taller than the treetops and madly covered in creepers, rises an impossibly large concrete structure with a brutal arch opening its mouth to swallow the tracks. Above the concrete arch, two vacant black holes where the military checkpoint offices used to be, and above that, a carved sign. Creepers are twined around the embossed concrete letters, rendering it unreadable. But she doesn't need to read it. She knows what it says, and even remembers the somber, brutal, timeless lettering in which the name was carved. It's the same lettering that she saw in street signs, offices, stores, and buildings throughout her childhood.

Leatelranch.

What she remembers as a menacing gray skull is actually just a bureaucratic building. A military post back from the plague days.

She had forgotten all about this. As she walks into the open mouth, she wonders what else she's forgotten about Leatelranch.

13

Nathan looks out the door. There's a light at the end
of the long corridor. Sunlight.

Behind him, the boys talk in whispers, hissing, murmuring.
The boy in the Austin Powers suit bolts up on his bed.

"Are they really gone?"

"I think so," Nathan says. "It's too dark to tell."

Yoshi tries to squeeze his head between Nate and the doorframe, and his pins get caught. He lets out another *ouch!*, and it
echoes down the hallway.

"Take those off," Nathan says.

Yoshi looks up, dead serious. His head has broken pins and
blood on both temples.

"Don't tell me what to do, you coward," he says, strings of
blood falling down his face.

"Dude," Lester says, "you're bleeding."

Yoshi touches the gash in his head and looks at his bloody
finger.

"Ha," he says, and chuckles. "I am."

Nate scolds him with his eyes. "Take those off, you moron!"

"No!"

"His *Mommy* put them in," Kenny says.

Nate exhales. He steps out of the room and looks around. It's empty.

"They're ... gone?" he says, confused. He turns to the boys, and he places a hand on Yoshi's shoulder. "OK, boys," he says, "now, slowly, quietly ..."

"Don't touch me, you asshole!" Yoshi says, wriggling out of Nathan's grip and disappearing through the door.

Before Nathan can react, Lester and Kenny run off, following him. They run in the dark, surrounded by the hospital doors, the numbered doors. They look clumsy, their hands stretched forward, feeling their way, blind, reaching out for invisible obstacles.

Just ahead of them, on the floor, there's a spilled tray of syringes.

"Stop!" Nathan whispers. "Don't step on those."

"Shut up, loser!" An echo says in return as the boys head to the noisy syringes.

"Shit," Nathan curses under his breath.

He looks at the shiny numbers stalking the hall, mouse traps ready to spring, and wonders if there's any chance Lilith has gotten the number wrong all this time.

"Shit," he mouths again.

He sprints past the boys and jumps over the fallen tray, stepping between a scalpel and scissors, and turns to the boys, who grab clumsily at the air with dilated pupils, exploring the darkness. They're about to step on the syringes. They're about to slip and fall, be loud, call out for the monsters again.

Nathan grabs their hands, gets close to their incoming faces, and whispers, "*Stop!*"

They jolt. They gasp. They freeze.

He kicks around the syringes on the floor, and the boys look down.

"You didn't see that?" he whispers. "What are you, blind?"

"Oh, shit," says Yoshi, recognizing the voice, recovering from the fright of his life. "It's just you."

"See what?" asks Lester, looking around with eyes wide open. "It's pitch black."

Nate kicks the syringes again. They scatter with a loud noise.

"What's that?" Lester asks, confused, looking down at the floor with dilated pupils. "How did you ..."

"I had a strange childhood," says Nathan.

"Ooh," Yoshi mocks him, "so mysterious, such a troubled motherfucker, trying to outdark the cancer kids. What happened, daddy didn't buy you the ice cream you wanted?"

Nate exhales. "Listen. If we make any noise ..."

"Who cares?" asks Kenny, still looking around, trying to focus on anything. "They're gone."

"You don't know that," Nate says. "You can't even see."

"But they said—"

"Don't listen to him!" Yoshi yells. "Come on."

He bolts toward the street door, trying to get past Nate, and steps on a bedpan and slips. Nate catches the boy in mid-air. He grabs him with both arms, dodging the needles as the boy wriggles and squirms in his arms.

"And where are you going?" he asks the boy, who keeps looking at the open door.

"Come on!" Pinhead repeats. "We need to follow them, or we're dead."

Nathan doesn't get it. "Are you insane?"

Yoshi, sure that Nate can't see his bright, bald head in the dark, looks up at him with contempt.

"You didn't hear?" he says, scratching his head, pins waving up and down, "They were running away. Scared. From something called the Delegate. And we need to—"

Nate freezes.

"I heard that, too," Lester says, still trying to focus on anything in the darkness.

"Yeah," Kenny says.

For a moment, the room is filled with just the murmur of gunshots and faint music coming from the street.

"Wow," says Yoshi, staring at Nate.

"Mister, are you OK?" Kenny's voice trembles.

"I think I can see your face now," says Lester.

"You just became even paler," says Yoshi. "If that's even possible."

Nate places his hand on Pinhead's shoulder. He moves closer to him until he can feel his own breath bouncing off his face.

"Are you sure you heard the word *Delegate*?" He forms the word carefully, like it's made of glass.

Yoshi plays serious, mocking Nate's face. "Yes."

"Where? How?"

"From the zombies!" Kenny says.

"They're running away from it," says Yoshi. "Whatever it is, it should be close. We should stay close to that. We need to see what it is, if it can scare zombies like that."

"Fuck no," says Kenny. "That's actually why we should stay away from it."

"Shit," says Nate. He glances around. He's looking for a magical exit, a miracle cure. He stares down at the tiled floor and stomps on it. "Shit, shit, shit. Goddammit, shit fuck motherfucker."

The boys stare at him.

Nate takes a deep breath. "We need to get to Leatelranch."

"Nu-huh," says Lester. "We need to find Frankie."

Nathan's mind races.

"Trust me. This is more important."

"What about your girlfriend?" Yoshi asks in a mocking tone. "Is this more important than her, too?"

Nathan bites his lip. The world becomes a haze.

The children look confused. "Why? What's in Leatelranch?"

PART II

14

RENWICK KANE ENTERS THE HALL WITH A LAZY SUNDAY stride, wearing his favorite blue pajamas and holding a steaming cup of coffee. He has the sun on his face and drags his slippers on the floor. He grabs the door handle, but he stops to look at the drawings on the door. The morning sun highlights all the crayon colors, making them more beautiful than he remembered. He smiles, takes a sip of his coffee, and opens the door.

A gust of fresh air hits him. The Monkees's "Daydream Believer" is playing, and the room is flooded with morning light. Looking out the open window, the girl is on her tiptoes, her elbows leaning on the windowsill.

"Good morning, Lilybug."

As she turns around, her black hair glides with the wind and sways across her face. Her big green eyes burn with excitement. "Hi, Daddy!"

He walks up to her and checks the view. Outside, in the park, children are playing and running around. There is laughter. Dogs are barking. Couples sit on the benches. A string of colorful market stands surround the park, and people walk by slowly, browsing the goods on display.

"Seems like someone wants to go out to the park," he says. "Let's go. Get dressed—"

But Lilith is looking to the left. She's craning her neck, trying to see past the gray wall that borders the park.

"What *are* those things?" she asks.

He looks at the black smoke billowing out of the crematory.

"That's just a chimney. A tall, round brick—"

"No!" she says, playful. "Those things, hanging on the wall!"

"Oh, those? Those are just old oil lamps. Listen, Lils, why don't we—"

"But they're so *big*."

"Oh, those," he says. "They're just decorations. What do you say if—"

"Is that a *gargoyle*?"

"No, gargoyles are the winged guys, like from the pizza place, remember? I'll show you in a moment, when we go out."

"They play music sometimes," she says, fixated. "There. Inside."

"Well, it's because of some religions," says dad. "They believe it helps."

"And is it true?"

"Some of it," he says, trying to intrigue her, to make her turn around. "Look, let's just go out."

"We're going out?" She says, still looking at the wall.

He looks at her messy morning hair. "Yes," he says. "Don't you want to go out? To the park?"

"But when can we go *there*?" she asks, pointing at the wall.

"Ah, you don't want to go *there*," he says.

"Why? What's in there?"

"Nothing. Just nothing."

"But people go inside all the time. Lots of people. And cars. Those long, black ones, even. There, see?" She points at the big cemetery entrance, with the large portico, on the far side of the park. Tourists are queuing to enter.

"Well, baby," he says, "that's a place for grownups."

"Like that bar downstairs?"

"Yes."

She turns to him, skeptical.

"Well, no," he says. "Not really."

He bends down on one knee. "That's where people go when they go to heaven."

Now he's got her attention.

"It's the oldest in Leatelranch. In fact, Leatelranch was founded because of it."

He sits her down on the bed. She sits next to him, crossing her legs, leaning in to listen.

"Didn't they tell you about the Jesuits in school?"

"No." She sits up, ready for a story.

"Many years ago, this was just a small ranch."

She smiles. "That's why it's called Leatelranch!"

He laughs. "Yes, I guess it is."

He has her whole attention now.

"A group of Jesuits owned this land."

"Jesuits?"

"Yes. Like priests."

"Oh."

"And one time, New Southport—Remember New Southport, where we went last year?"

"Ah-ha."

"Well," he says, "there was a very nasty flu, and many, many people died. So many, that they didn't have any place to bury them all."

Her pupils are burning. She's eating this up.

"So, they bought this ranch from the Jesuits and decided to build a big cemetery. They built our train station, which was the biggest at the time, and even had a special train to travel between New Southport and Leatelranch many times a day, to bring in all those people."

"You mean the dead people."

"Yes. Can you guess what that train was called?"

"The Citizen?"

"Yes. Exactly. That locomotive we see in the museum, that you think is so *boring*," he tickles her tummy, "was very important back then. It was the fastest, and the strongestest train in the world."

"Strongestest?" she asks, chuckling.

"Yes, the strongestest. But then, of course, they needed people to tend to the cemetery and the brand new train station, so they built houses for people to move here. And those people needed stores, and parks, and restaurants. And that's how Leatelranch was born."

She stands up and looks outside again.

"And what's that, daddy?"

He stands up and looks outside the window, grabbing her soft cotton shoulders. He bites his lips.

"Those ... trees?" he asks.

"No," she says. "That. The big triangle."

He crouches down to her level and looks at the cemetery. She can already see a green patch of grass to the left, and the gray stone necropolis to the right.

"You're getting tall," he says, fixating on the inverted white pyramid that stands out among the crypts on the other side of the wall, held by four pillars in its corners.

"I'm growing up," she says, cheerful. "I can even see the little gray houses. It's like a miniature city over there! It even has little streets and pavement and everything!"

"Look, never mind that, Lilybug," he says. "Forget about that."

But she's still staring at the cemetery. "OK," she says, excited, savoring it with her gaze. "Let's go out. Let's go to ... the park!"

He sighs. He lunges to tickle her. "You trickster!" he says. "Why are you so obsessed, huh? It's *boring*! It's for *grownups*."

"I wanna go," she protests in chuckles.

"That's ... a messy subject, Lilybug."

"Why?" she asks, and pouts. "Why are grownups always so serious?"

He grabs her shoulders. "Because we care about you. And we want to protect you. We will always, always protect you."

She nods.

"Tell you what. When we go pick up Mommy, we'll swing by the used movies stand and choose another *Rainbow Team* movie."

"I told you, they're boring. I want to see gargoyles. And cemeteries."

"Ok," he says. "Maybe we can pick up another zombie movie. You liked those, didn't you?"

Her face lights up. "Really?"

"Really," he says. "But not another word about that place. All right?"

"Sure, Daddy," she says, unable to stop herself from immediately turning back to the view beyond the wall.

"Let's go," he says loudly enough to startle her, and this manages to make her turn to him.

Behind her, a purple cloud surfaces from above the inverted pyramid, twisting and turning around it like a giant dancing cloak, and wriggles back into the inverted pyramid's entrance.

15

THE OLD CHOPPER MOTORBIKE GROWLS AS IT CRUISES AMONG the tombstones. It's an old model, but it still glistens in the morning sun. Groundskeeper Marcus Warner guns the throttle and presses on toward a narrow path surrounded by crypts and mausoleums, his skin worn by the sun and the years, his gray beard fluttering in the wind. Behind him, a scared seven-year-old wraps his arms around his stomach, pushing his pale face against the man's back. Even though he can't see the boy, the man knows he's clenching his eyes shut.

"Some fresh air will do you good," Marcus says, slowing down as they enter the alley and looking both ways on every corner. He checks every crypt door, stained-glass window, and lock. "You're spending too much time at home. You're white as a ghost."

Marcus sees something in one of the alleys, and he slows the bike to a stop. He turns off the engine, and the rusting of trees and the chirping of birds takes over the air. It really is a beautiful day. He walks over to the crypt door and kneels in front of its rusty lock. It's broken.

He looks back at the boy still sitting on the bike and sees the fear in his eyes as he takes in his surroundings.

"Isn't this beautiful?" Marcus asks him, inhaling the fresh morning air. "All of this stone and marble, built to last forever?"

The boy just looks at him. His neck jolts to the side, as if he heard something.

"We're alone, son," Marcus says. "You don't have to worry."

The boy doesn't even respond. He looks like he's about to get jumped by someone. Or something.

"Look," says the groundskeeper, pointing to a statue of an old man with glasses, smiling broadly in his perfectly ironed suit. "Here, people pass from a fragile body to clean stone, for all eternity. This is a good place."

But the boy still looks worried. The man stands up, rusty lock in hand, and walks up to the bike where the boy sulks. He opens the saddlebag and searches for another lock.

"Have you seen her again?"

The boy doesn't respond. His gaze is lost on the horizon.

"The lady with kaleidoscope eyes. Has she come again?"

The boy shakes his head, looking around.

"No?" the man confirms. "Good. You see?"

The man replaces the lock and pulls it to check that it doesn't open. He checks on his son and finds him looking up at a stone angel that looks to be his same age. The boy mouths a "hello" just before noticing he's being watched.

Marcus smiles. "You probably just overheard some ceremony. Used to be, people put coins in people's eyes." He turns to the boy. "Some people still do."

He walks back to the bike. He gets on and starts it. The boy straps his arms around his chest so hard that he almost draws all air from his lungs.

"Whoa," the groundskeeper says, smiling. "Easy there."

They ride through rolling green hills, checking on the tombstones on the ground. One of them has dead flowers. He stops again and gets down to put them in the trash.

He walks back to the bike. "Scooch over."

The pale boy looks up at him, his eyes still half-closed to block out the sun, and his face lights up.

"That's right," Marcus says.

The boy smiles and moves to the front seat. Marcus gets on the bike again, sitting behind his son. He places the boy's hands on the handlebars. His short arms can barely reach.

"Don't worry, I'll help you."

The boy gets comfortable. He hangs from the handlebars and lets his back hang, trying to imitate his father's seating stance.

The man puts his hands over the boy's and starts the engine. He takes a deep breath. "Smell this beautiful air," he says. "It's good for the ghost."

The boy twitches, alarmed. "What ghost?"

Marcus chuckles. "What ghost." He pats and tickles the boy's chest. "The ghost in here. You."

The boy keeps silent, but Marcus can feel his chest finally relaxing.

"The cemetery is a puzzle, son," the groundskeeper says. "A puzzle waiting for the pieces to fall into place." He checks the mirror for a reaction. A smile. A nod. But the boy looks straight ahead, only reacting to the wind in his eyes. "It's the one place where nothing is ever lost, ever again."

They approach a long tall wall full of names, numbers, and photographs. Some of them have flowers. In the middle of the wall stretches a high Roman arch.

"No," the boy says. "Please. Not there."

"Don't worry, son," the man says, taking his eye patch from his pocket and strapping it on his left eye. "Everything's all right. It's a beautiful day."

They ride under the arch and roll down a long ramp into an underground gallery several stories tall. A cold shadow casts over them, and Marcus feels the boy's grip tighten against the handlebars. He switches the eye patch to his other eye. Suddenly, the dark, cool halls seem brighter to his left eye. Vaults with names parade on both sides of the motorbike, reaching all the way up to the ceiling.

"Oh," the boy says.

"See? Don't worry, I got you."

"But ..."

"There's no one here but us." His voice echoes along the clean white hall.

The boy looks around. He's trembling.

The rumble of the engine takes over and echoes through the halls. The endless walls are a mosaic of marbled names. Some have flowers. Some have string dolls hanging from them. Marcus checks every hallway, every plaque, every flower holder, every wastebasket. All clean.

"You see?" he says, looking around. "Nothing to fear."

They climb up a ramp. They take a wide road, and the sun shines on them again. Marcus switches the eye patch to his other eye, and this time the boy shields his eyes from the sun and dares to look around.

Marcus smiles.

The chopper approaches another area with crypts. The crypts here are not as flashy as the marble-and-stone ones. These are older. Gray. The boy doesn't think much of them.

Towering over them, however, coming up on the side of the road, the charred stone inverted pyramid held up by four pillars already throws its massive shadow over the road ahead.

The boy's head is clearly turning to it.

Marcus cups a hand gently over his son's eyes, clenching his fingers tightly together to make sure not even a sliver of light slips through.

"I'm sorry," he says, "some things, you're not supposed to see yet."

He turns to a small passage and, after some twists and turns, gets back on the main road. Only then does he take his hand off his son's eyes.

They ride past the last of the crypts, through a large green clearing, and around the empty green hills until they reach a house at the end of the cemetery.

The boy gets down from the bike and walks to the house. The caretaker smiles.

"See, Nate?" he says. "It wasn't so bad."

"I guess."

The boy stops to stare at a closed gate at the far end of the cemetery walls and exhales.

"There's nothing out there for you, Nate."

The boy looks back at him.

"Out there, there's nothing but suffering and decay."

The boy looks down at his feet. "I know."

"Want to go see Mom now?" Marcus asks.

"No."

He smiles. "Ok, son. I'll be right back. Take this inside, will you?"

He takes out his eye patch and gives it to the boy. Nathan runs into the house.

The caretaker guns the engine again and rides among the green hills until he reaches the familiar tombstone. He stops the bike and walks toward it slowly, a shy smile already spreading across his face. His cheeks burn. He lies on the ground. He caresses the tombstone, and his fingers travel through the carved letters. They read ELEANORE WARNER. Above it, there is a grainy black-and-white picture of a woman, mouth slightly open, two coins covering her eyes.

He smiles. "Hi, baby."

16

THE GIRL HUFFS. HER FATHER IS SLOWING DOWN AS HE WALKS near the swings. She can tell he's trying to look uninterested, waiting for her to say something, to run and play, but her little feet stride confidently toward the end of the park, where colorful tourists queue to enter the cemetery.

"Look," he says, extending his arm right in front of her face, "I think I see an empty one." He points to a single red swing dangling between two boys soaring back and forth.

Lilith can't resist a swing. She runs to it and jumps on. She propels herself upward with all her strength, trying to reach as high as she can, trying to look inside the walls. Almost there. She climbs in the air, and the huge gray wall starts to look a bit smaller, almost like it's crouching, like it wants to bend down and let her see inside. She can almost taste it. The tiny city she can see from her window is just behind that wall, so near. She gets higher and higher, and something black shows behind the wall. Something black and big, clearly taller than the wall, but not close to it. It's the strange triangular house she can see from her bedroom. Only now it looks huge, bigger and bigger, as she soars higher.

"Careful, Lilybug!" Renwick calls out from below.

Lilith propels herself backward and swings by him, and when she reaches the summit again, she leans back, ready to shoot forward. She swings by her father again at a hair-raising speed and prepares to see behind the wall. She climbs up, reaching the same height as the old oil lamps on the cemetery wall. She reaches the height of the not-gargoyles, the mysterious fixtures above them. She reaches up further, and for a moment, she's flying—she's floating in the air, the swing barely attached to her.

"Careful!" her father yells.

She holds on to the chains and lets herself down. As high as she can reach, the wall still won't let her see.

She jumps off the swing and lands on the ground.

"My god, Lil!" her father says. "I told you to be careful."

"I'm sorry, Daddy."

He kneels down and hugs her. He caresses her back. "I think after picking up Mommy we'll be going right back home."

"No!" Lilith protests. "Let's go a little more. Please?"

"Do you promise to do as you're told?"

Lilith knows he's bluffing. He wanted to go out just as much as her. She makes an effort to sound apologetic. "Yes, Daddy."

He nods with approval.

They continue their walk and reach the menacing monument in the center of the park. He stops with a noisy shuffle of her feet. "Good. We need to follow the doctor's orders. Exercise is good, but we have to know our limits. No strenuous activities. No big shocks. Have I ever told you the story of Salomone Francis?"

Lilith huffs, blowing air into her bangs, and doesn't stop walking. "Only like a million times."

Their path is now lined with market stalls. Lilith sees this market from her window every day. It's at the end of the park. The entrance to the cemetery must be close.

Her father stops at one of the stands and looks over the goods on a table covered in red cloth. Lilith pulls from his hand, but he's not moving.

"Look, Lil," he says. "Aren't these pretty?"

Lilith stands on her tiptoes and reluctantly skims the table. It is piled high with colorful dolls, or toys, or decorations, or something.

"Meh."

"Meh," her father repeats, raising his shoulders. "You know, this is kinda what you'd see inside the cemetery. I told you it was boring."

Lilith checks the table again. Tiny little stone houses. Long gray boxes. Colorful skeletons with flowers. They are kind of cool. She reaches for one that looks like a church.

Her father's hand crosses hers and grabs a tiny gray creature. "And—and this is what a gargoyle is. You know, like we were talking about before?"

She takes it in her hand to examine the stone animal. "Cool," she says. "Can we see the ones inside?"

"Yeah, cool. But really, there are more of them outside of the cemetery than inside. If you like, we can go see my favorite one right across the street—"

"But I want to see the ones *inside!*"

"Come," he says, and they keep walking. "We'll see. Mommy must be closing the shop already, and we need to pick her up. We thought you could help us today."

"Yay!" she yells. "But after, can we go in?"

"We'll see," he says. "If it's still open. We'll see. Come. It's time. Oh, look, speak of the devil."

Right after a couple of stalls, where the market ends, Ophelia Kane is closing one of the metal panels of the kiosk. It looks like a metal flower. She kisses a small black-and-white picture of Grann that hangs from one of the panels, then closes it. She turns around just in time to see them, and waves.

As Lilith waves back, she hears some tourists speaking a strange language. Close to them, beyond her mother's stall, a queue is gathering. Behind the crowd of people she spots the marble steps. From there, her eyes travel up the massive columns, up to the wide triangular portico that reads WESTERN CEMETERY.

"Mommy, Daddy, can we go inside?"

"Lilybug," Renwick says gently. "You're not old enough."

"Why?" she asks. "Old enough for what?"

She notices her parents looking at each other. "Some things," Ophelia says, "once you learn them, Mommy and Daddy can't kiss them better anymore. Come," she says, and she takes a pink rose from the kiosk. She wraps it in cellophane along with some baby's breath (*It's called* Gypsophila, her mother would often say, *but doesn't baby's breath sound so much better?*) and hands it to Lilith.

"Go," she says, pointing with her chin at a couple kissing on a bench. "Tell them it's a gift."

Lilith looks at them kissing. "Ugh," she says.

Her father chuckles. *"Ugh?"*

"Trust me, that'll be you in a couple of years," her mother says.

Lilith looks back at her. "Me? Ugh! Never!"

Her parents share a laugh. "You'll come around," her mother says. "Now go. You want to work with Mommy and Daddy, or not?"

She crosses her arms, rejecting the flower. "You give out flowers for free? Nice way to do business."

"What's with you today?" her mother asks.

Lilith can't believe she has to spell it out. "I wanna go inside the cemetery!"

Ophelia is visibly angry. "Lilith, you'll do as you're told."

"No."

Her father looks at her and sighs. He looks serious. "I guess it's her choice," he says. "Look at her. She's a big girl now."

"But—"

"Don't worry," he says, "I can finish up here while you take her inside."

It's her mother's turn now to look at Lilith wearing a face Lilith has never seen before. She looks ... sad. "Are you sure?"

"Honey," he says. "It's time."

"But her heart?"

They look at each other, and Lilith notices them having a conversation with their eyes. She knows how this usually ends.

So she bolts. She scurries among the tourists and runs up the marble steps. Her head spins around as she walks through the tall columns and toward the black iron gates. The entrance is wide, and what she thought was a queue is actually just a lot of people going in and out freely through the wide entrance.

She freezes when a guard smiles at her.

"Are you alone, little girl?"

Lilith looks behind him. Inside, people walk down little streets in the miniature city she's used to seeing from her window. On those little streets are little gray houses, and little churches, with scary towers and pointy windows. They look kind of like the ones around the city. But something's off. Something about their size, and how there's no room for anyone to really live in them. And the windows. Even in broad daylight, the windows are all dark.

"There you are!" Ophelia's voice is strangely soothing, despite the anger in her tone. "Lilith! Do not walk away from us!"

"We're closing in five minutes," the guard says.

"Oh," Lilith says, turning around, looking for the safety of the flower kiosk.

"You can still go in," the guard says, "just come out as soon as you hear the bell."

Lilith takes a step back.

"No problem," her mother says behind her, grabbing Lilith's hand. "We'll take the chance."

"Mom?"

"Your father's right," she says. "It's time." She doesn't sound too happy about it. She exhales, and adds, "Que sera, sera."

Lilith's feet are heavy, and her legs are so numb she has to force her body to keep up with her mother's pace.

It's not so bad. They enter a nice green miniature square and take a path covered in tall bushy trees. It's like a miniature street, tailor-made to her size, and all around her are miniature houses, each of them a different shape, a different color, a different stone, or metal, or whatever they're made of. Across the path are more miniature streets and pathways. And all around, there are strange statues of people with wings. Monsters. Angels. Houses that look like little churches, with glass pictures on their windows. She can tell they are supposed to be colorful, but the colors are faded. The glass is old and dusty.

"So, what do you think?" her mother asks, turning a corner.

Lilith looks back at the infinite maze of narrow zig-zagging streets, and she wonders how they will find their way back.

Ding-dong-dong-dong, tolls a distant bell.

Lilith grabs her mother's hand. "All right," she says. "Let's go."

"Nah," Ophelia says, holding her hand. "Don't worry. We still have a few minutes."

Next to her, Lilith sees a window that's low enough for her to peek inside. The glass is broken and sharp, and inside, it's all black. She approaches it carefully and looks through the opening. Inside, there's a rotten wooden box with its lid slightly askew.

She takes a step back.

"Easy, there," Mrs. Kane says, placing a hand on her shoulder. "Don't go so near."

The girl glances behind her and is relieved to once again see the entrance, where people are gathering and funneling out of the cemetery. "OK," she says, "I'm ready to go."

Her mother smiles. She seems relieved.

But Lilith feels her father's hand on her shoulder. "Nonsense!" he says, almost out of breath. "We're here already. And you wanted to see, right?"

"You're here?" Ophelia asks.

He smiles. "Wouldn't miss this moment for the world!"

In the distance, Lilith hears the rusty moan of a gate closing. She spasms, and her father's heavy hand holds her in place.

"Don't worry," he says with a smile. "I'm sure they'll let us out."

Ophelia seems to be struggling to stay silent.

He gets down on his knee, bringing his eyes to Lilith's level, and smiles. "Now we have the whole place for ourselves!"

"I'm cold ..." Lilith says, looking back the way they came. "The sun is going down."

"We'll go home in a moment," he says.

"Daddy," she protests, "please ..."

He smiles. "Well, didn't you want to come inside?"

An iron door opens again. This time, by the sound of it, it's a smaller door, and it's closer to them.

"But they're closing!" she protests. She's shaking.

In complete silence, like a ghostly vision, four people walk past them carrying a long wooden box. They carry it solemnly, stepping without a sound, heads down, toward a closet-like wall at the end of the street that Lilith didn't notice before.

Lilith looks up at her parents, and they look at each other, terrified, and turn to her with a fake calm.

"You see, Lilybug—" her mother begins. But Lilith slips out of her grip and runs away.

17

DING-DONG-DONG-DONG, SOUNDS A DISTANT BELL.

Standing in a narrow alley, Nathan looks at his father with pleading eyes. "Can we go home?"

The man chuckles. "Those bells are for them," he says. "We don't need to go anywhere."

The boy looks at the world outside the front gate. The buses running by. The bustle of people coming and going. The colossal train station where people go to faraway places.

Nathan grabs his father's hand. "Please," he says. "Let's go. Just today?"

Marcus looks into his son's brown eyes. "Nathan. We *are* home."

"But I don't like it when the people leave."

"Well," he says, squeezing the boy's hand. "Don't worry then. We still have a few minutes."

Nathan watches the people walking around them and marching out. "But—"

"Look!" says the caretaker. "Look at these columns! These angels. There are so many unsung artists whose work can only be appreciated here."

The boy peeks inside another broken stained-glass window.

The room is poorly lit, but he can see a large shelf on the wall, a black-and-white picture of a woman, and an old wooden box covered in a dirty, fancy blanket. "What's that?"

The caretaker looks inside. "That's called a *pall*. It's like a cloth. Like a blanket."

"It's all dusty," Nathan says.

"Well, it's been here a long time."

A couple of old ladies bump into them. They look friendly and happy.

"The cemetery's closing," one of them says.

"Yes," the caretaker says. "Thank you."

He turns to Nate. "See? There's still people around."

Nate watches as the ladies walk away from them. He looks around at the other alleys. They're all empty. The cemetery is falling silent. He can't hear any conversations anymore. Or food wrappers. Or camera clicks.

They turn toward the house at the end of the cemetery, and as they reach the corner, Nathan notices that the alley doesn't end in a dull crossroad with another alley, like the streets outside; here, around six similar alleys like the one they just traversed lead up to a small fountain. He turns around the fountain, looking out at the paths, and he sees the cemetery as an infinite maze. From here, all the alleys look the same. *Which way is home?*

A flock of birds circles the fountain. The fountain spray and the birds chirping are the only sounds Nathan can hear.

In the distance, the rusty moan of an iron gate signals that all the visitors have gone.

"Don't worry," Marcus says with a smile. "I'm still here with you."

Nathan clings to his father's hand as they enter another alley. The sun no longer shines on the stained-glass windows. The sky is darker, and it paints the crypts a darker shade of gray.

They hear something. People. Conversation. Nathan smiles. He tries to speed up, but his father stops him. He puts a finger to his lips, signaling Nathan to be quiet, and walks to the end of the alley. He cranes his neck and looks to the left.

Nathan sneaks between his father and the cold black marble of a crypt wall. He peeks out around the corner. One of the crypts, with a symbol of a broken egg with a triangle inside, has its iron gate wide open, and four people are lifting and storing a coffin inside.

Nathan tightens the grip on his father's hand. He tries to pull him away. "Father ..."

He looks Nathan in the eye. "Don't look away," he says, putting his hand on his son's shoulder.

Four people dressed in gray uniforms slide the coffin onto a shelf inside the crypt, but the coffin isn't made of wood like the other ones he's seen. If it were, it wouldn't be making the screeching sound making Nathan's pale skin feel ice cold. Once inside, the coffin fits precisely between the shelves, like a drawer but without a handle. Nathan moves his shoulders like he's shaking something off. "Brr," he says, "but now it won't be able to open."

Two of the men enter the crypt and hammer each side shut. They bring a bucket and paint the side of the coffin with a sticky gray putty.

"What's that?" he asks his father.

"Cement."

"But now he won't be able to breathe," Nathan says, and he tries to wiggle free of his father's heavy hand on his shoulder.

"Don't look away, boy. Don't look away."

They lift a massive block of marble and place it as a cover over the whole coffin.

With another rusty sound, they close two iron wings on both sides of the coffin, like gates, enclosing it. They are engraved with iron bows and angels.

"But now he won't be able to get out!"

"Don't look away," his father says, rubbing his shoulders. "These things, you have to learn them."

The men close a lock between the iron wings. Another man comes from outside wearing a face mask and carrying a rusty tool. As the others leave the crypt, a white light sparkles from inside, and sparks fly out. The masked man comes out, and like a ceremony, the first two men enter again and grab the iron wings. They try to pry them open. Nathan gasps. It almost looks like they're testing its strength.

And then it's the skewed marble crypts falling on him as he trips and runs, the shaky view of the cemetery as he gasps and breathes and runs away, the parade of tombstones filing past him on both sides, the clouds watching, idle, complicit, the trees and the silence sheltering him from his father and his horrors, the lock on his house, the handle, the shut door, the wooden floor, and tears, and tears, and tears.

18

THE CLOUD OF FOG AROUND LILITH MELTS INTO THIN AIR AND laps at her knees, shining ghoulishly white under the bright moonlight. Up ahead, tracks and fog are eaten by a huge dark mouth. The building looks like it's been abandoned for years. Its silvery shape glows in the night like a giant.

Such a huge train station for such a small town.

Lilith follows the wide tracks inside. She reaches a fork where they begin to merge with a system of narrower modern train tracks that lead to newer platforms with narrower arches. The railings look smaller, cheaper, and show recent use, and they seem to lead to the main hall of the beast. She follows them.

The bones of the massive gray behemoth stand cold and damp. The platforms, full of no one, wait just for her, and the building's coldness pierces through her skin as she follows the tracks inside. Her steps echo off the tall ceiling and along the vast hall. When she finally reaches the platform, she sees a glimmer of light reflecting off a dusty bronze sign: MAIN HALL.

She follows the scratched, uneven floor of the platform, eroded by centuries of mass transit, luggage cart wheels, and the dragging of trunks and suitcases from the days of the plague, and reaches the entrance to the main hall. It's vast and dark, except for a pale column of moonlight that shoots from the tall ceiling and casts its ghostly light on a marble bench. The bench seems to *grow* from the marble floor like a natural appendix. The full moon shines on it through the broken dome.

She walks toward the light, stepping softly on the marble floor. Her sneakers squeak and echo in the vast silence.

On the bench is a bouquet of dead flowers wrapped in cellophane. Next to it, a silvery metallic greeting card with a weeping angel.

She grabs the metallic card and climbs up onto the bench. A flash of pain travels through her wounded leg, almost throwing her off balance, but she steadies herself (*could be worse, Lil, you did just jump out of a car*) and uses it to reflect the valuable rays of moonlight around the station. The reflection dances in the vast darkness, finally coming to rest on a window. The old ticket booth, its curtains down. Her tired, trembling hand moves the beam farther to the left, where she makes out another bench. She tries again. A giant clock overlooking the station. Something gray floating in the dark.

A hat.

A gray hat. Floating in the dark.

Her blood freezes. The light starts to shake, and she fights to control it. Below the hat, the white dot of light reveals a face, staring at her, mouth open, eyes open, crying for help.

Her legs shake and seem like they want to run. She steadies the light and notices the face isn't moving. It's grainy. Even if it's hard to tell in the dark, she realizes she's only seeing black and white. It's a picture. She moves the light around. A man is looking at the camera and crying, holding in his arms what seems to be a body covered in a shroud.

Oh. Right.

The light travels left along the wall of the station, revealing more pictures from the days of the plague: A warehouse full of stretchers, the sick lying everywhere. Blurry-faced workers loading bodies onto the wagons of *The Citizen*, a mighty iron beast. (*An advanced machine, even by today's standards*, her father would say. *It has its own track-changing system*, whatever that meant.) A picture of this very hall, sparkling and new, filled to the brim with people crying and mourning and pushing over each other. Salomone Francis, the architect and founder, overseeing the construction of the front gates, and a few crypts behind them. Then, color pictures, modern pictures of the same landscape, and the same crypts. Only, behind them, more. Many, many more.

She remembers these pictures. She remembers this station. And she remembers the story. Pa used to recite it over and over. *Yellow fevered*, she used to say when she was little. New Southport, decimated by a plague. The need for a new, huge cemetery. The purchase of a Jesuit ranch outside the big city. The huge undertaking. The industry. The station. The *dead train*. The staff. Death as a spark of life. The town that grew out of a cemetery. The golden age of Leatelranch.

The beam of light hits on a rusty iron sign covered in dust. It shows the directions for the Leatelranch Museum, to the left; the exhibition of *The Citizen*, to the right. And the exit to Leatelranch town square and Leatelranch cemetery, straight ahead.

Her light beam follows the arrow and zooms toward huge doors, all boarded up.

She lights up her way toward the door, checking for obstacles, and jumps down from the bench. She walks in the dark until she can touch the boarded doors. She feels her way around the wooden planks and finally reaches the borders. She slips her fingers between the rough splintery chipboard, pries them open, and peeks outside. And it hits her.

"Ugh," she says. "Home."

19

LILITH SQUEEZES THROUGH THE ROUGH SHEETS OF PLYWOOD boarding up the station doors and, stepping clumsily with her bad leg, reaches the portico outside with a flash of blinding pain. Fresh air and crickets welcome her, and street lamps bathe her again in the ghoulish white light of her childhood. She takes a deep breath. In front of her, a long staircase rolls down to the street below, giving her a wide view of the street, the park in front of her, and the cemetery gates to her right.

What now, Lil?

Leatelranch is a ghost town. Cars are neatly parked along the empty street in front of her. Across the street, the park with its neatly cut grass is also empty, dimly lit by the white light of its street lamps. To the left, her favorite pizza place, a stone building with big bullet-shaped windows, has its lights turned off, but the fans inside are still spinning. The ashy gray gargoyle holding a pizza on top of the corner entrance has a lost gaze, like it's sleeping with his eyes open, almost about to drop the pizza on the empty sidewalk below. Next door, the locksmith shop, and her childhood favorite, the granite angel with keys on both hands, also seem to sleep. Above her head, with a *clack*, an old traffic light turns green.

Where is everybody?

To her right are the tall Roman columns with the huge trian-gular pediment resting on them, carved with its original name: WESTERN CEMETERY. Behind the columns, the black iron gates that close off the entrance to the cemetery seem to be closed. Nothing moves behind them. She can see the first couple of stone crypts, also untouched. The cemetery looks as dead as the city.

And that wall. That horrible wall.

But just before the wall starts, she spies the kiosk. Her parent's flower shop next to the gate. It looks closed. No flowers in sight. But it's still there. After all this time, someone's still selling flowers at her parents' old spot. The kiosk is much smaller than she remembered. Spots of rust open wounds in the now faded green and eggshell paint.

Between the flower stand and the wall, next to all the graffiti, is where the line of cars begins. The black stretch limousines. The hearses.

Though she'd rather keep looking at the entrance and the columns, the cars and the market stalls, the vision of the wall surrounding the cemetery is unavoidable. An impossibly high concrete wall that goes on forever, enclosing the cemetery and running along the side of the vast park, separating the two. The ancient lamps are still there, hanging from the wall, throwing their horrible dim light, placed so far from each other that large sections of the wall remain dark. And on the top part of the wall —between the lamps, where the light doesn't reach—those *things.*

She steps down the broad marble steps to the sidewalk, hearing the echo of her footsteps, and, without thinking, her path skews to the left, away from the cemetery.

She reaches the first car and looks inside, hoping, for some stupid reason, that she'll find the keys waiting for her in the igni-tion. Of course not. She checks the seats, waiting for a miracle. No keys.

She looks around again. She hits the window, and her arm

bounces back, full of pain. The alarm blares, echoing through the park, bouncing on the wall.

She crosses the street toward the pizza place and glances at the wall again. Across the park, even though the dark spots between the lights are pitch black, it's like they're looking at her, like the many eyes of a spider, somehow following her with their gaze. She hurries toward the sidewalk to her left, away from them.

She steps carefully, checking for loose tiles, trying not to draw any attention, and looks around for any signs of people, dead or alive. The tall gray houses facing the park, where her neighbors used to live, seem empty. Windows are all black. Some are square, some are oval, some are thin with a gothic arch, like wide-open eyes. All watching her, all blind.

She checks every angle and every crevice. The concrete architecture of Leatelranch is full of twists and turns that cast sharp shadows everywhere, and tonight, more than ever before, she can appreciate how scary her hometown really is. Leatelranch is a little more run-down than she remembered. Old. Broken. Shops and buildings are empty. She walks by dark doors, all standing below that typical Leatelranch embossed lettering that always depressed her so much. MVSEVM. ALIMENTVM. TABERNA. Hanging above her least favorite marble shop, a concrete sharp-angled angel with deep rhombus-carved eyes looks down on her, its prism fingers folded up in prayer. She looks at its stained-glass windows and remembers how on nights like this, when all the houses in the neighborhood had their lights on, its dimly lit colorful stained glass depressed her. But now, somehow, it looks different. In the back of her head, she can't help but think that there's something actually cool about this place.

Fucking whacko, she thinks. *Who styles a town after a cemetery? No wonder none of us grew up to be bubbly Instagrammers.*

She reaches the TOKENS shop, and the window looks just like she remembers it: Flowers, stones, crosses, stars of David, wooden stick dolls, knots of hair, color strings, dead beetles, strange talismans she never understood from strange religions.

She sees a bronze bell with a white cord, and a tasteful, old-time illustration of the cord going underground into a coffin, for the convenience of the discerning taphophobe.

She looks inside the HEADSTONES shop, labeled so with another concrete sign. This is the fun shop, the one she used to love. Lit by the streetlights, she sees a parade of grave markers made of marble, granite, concrete. Round, square, soft, sharp. She stops to read the sample inscriptions, as she used to do with Nate. JOHN DOE. JANE DOE. I TOLD YOU IT WAS SERIOUS. YOUR NAME HERE. Behind them, from deeper inside the shop where the streetlights can't reach, a pair of glimmering eyes looks out at her.

"Fuck!" she blurts out as the shadow hides further inside, and she sprints across the street and into the park, hiding, kneeling, enduring the pain in her leg. *So there* are *people here.* She steps on the soft grass and walks among the bushes to get away from the houses and closer to the wall. She looks at the bullet-shaped windows and their stained-glass textured eyes. In the dark, a shadow stares at her. She narrows her eyes. *Is that a face?* She scans the hundreds of windows overlooking the park. She knows she's being watched.

She looks over her shoulder and glances at the hideous wall. Her feet hesitate before turning around. She takes a nervous step toward it, and another, dragging her feet. The pain is gone. Fear is all she can feel. She sets foot on the path in the center of the park and, emboldened by fear, she squints, trying to see between the lamps into the dark parts, to those huge casket-shaped marble artifacts. And finally they appear, looking timeless as the wall, like diamond-shaped, laser-focused pupils, shining as they watch her.

A bolt of lightning shoots through her legs as she sprints away, feeling the wall chasing her. She looks over her shoulder, and this time she knows she can see them. Maybe it's her eyes having finally adjusting to the dark, but for the first time she can see the artifacts in full splendor, not imaginary eyes but real huge marble coffins on the wall, and marble tombstones protruding from the wall above them.

She runs down the cement path, keeping a safe distance from the wall to her right and the houses to her left, under cover of the plump treetops scattered around the park. She zips through the playground, where the swings make a rusty, squeaky sound. Short of breath, she runs until the wall on the other side of the park finally ends and turns a corner to haunt some other street (*not just any other street, Lil, but you know that*). She sees REQUIEM, the bar on Rodney Street, with its big red awning, a spot of color among so much gray, and she's glad some things never change. But this is no time to reminisce. *We need to find a way out of here.* She passes by the monument to the dead, a circular scene where open-mouthed skeletons surround the founder and architect of Leatelranch, Salomone Francis, in creepy sharp-edged cubist form, the man made entirely of edges and angles, with thick oblong boxes and prisms for fingers and lips. She remembers the familiar sight of the park and Salomone's back as she was growing up.

And behind the statue, she sees it.

Between two taller church-looking concrete buildings stands a small white brick house. It's older and simpler than those around it, with two black windows on its second floor that overlook the park. The lights on both her parents' bedroom and her own are off, just like the ones throughout the rest of the town. As she walks toward the house, she remembers herself looking out that window. She cranes her neck, trying to make out what her bedroom looks like now, but she can't see from here. *Maybe if I get closer.*

As she crosses the empty street from the park to the sidewalk in front of her childhood home, the lighting dims. Her block was never quite as well-lit as those surrounding the park.

She stands on the doorstep. It looks just like she remembers it. She touches the door and examines it, enjoys it, recognizes it, the shape, the texture of the wood.

She looks at the buzzer, lit by moonlight. Her name is still scratched on the bronze plaque. She looks at the angry, hollow indentations filled with moonlight, following each double-, triple-, quadruple-grooved letter, and remembers how hard she'd scratched with her key that afternoon.

Her memory is interrupted by a shadow whooshing across the doorway.

She turns around and looks up. A dark figure crawls and leaps from one sharp-angled roof to the next, parkouring along Leatel-ranch's uneven skyline.

"*Wolfram!*" she whispers to herself, smiling, and runs after him.

20

TAKING SHELTER IN A CORNER OF HER HOME, THE OLD WOMAN stands very still. Her husband's footsteps come from the area where their rosewood coffee table must be. They move through the darkness behind the Chesterfield, near the old ottoman sitting against the tall ogival window. The black silhouette of his arm lifts the glowing white curtains, and he peeks outside, the shape of his face cutting against the caramel-and-white checkered pattern of the stained glass.

Elvira fights the knot in her throat. "Are they still there?"

Ulfred closes the curtains and turns to her. His eyes are nowhere to be seen in that black shadow of a face, but a glimmer gives him away. He's crying. As she gazes into what she thinks are his eyes, into eyes that she hopes are gazing into hers, she feels like a teenager again, falling in love for the first time.

"OK," she says, and nods. "OK."

Elvira slithers to the window and catches the dangling curtain to get her own peek outside. Standing on her lawn, bathed in the white light of the Leatelranch street lamps, a line of pale faces smiles at her. The Guzmans. Mrs. Morton and her little boy. The Saint-Domingues. The Malinowskis with their twins. She lets out a whimper and jerks her head back. She looks through the narrow

115

crack between the curtains and the glass. To the sides, as far as she can see, a wall of dead neighbors has formed around the house.

She closes the curtain until it covers the window completely. The murky gray shadows drawn on it seem to move. To expand.

"I think they're coming," she says, covering her mouth, muffling her own voice. *"I think they're coming!"*

She paces toward the front door, stubs her foot with a chair, and, limping, she makes sure the lock is set. As her foot throbs, she slumps her whole body against the door and clenches her eyes and her face until her jaw hurts.

Knock, knock.

Elvira jolts and yelps.

In the dark, standing halfway up the stairs, Ulfred asks, "They *knock?*"

"Ulfie," she says. "Help me with the door."

"Stay put," he says. His feet shuffle up the linoleum steps.

Elvira leans against the door with her whole body. "Ulfie ..."

"Just—give me a moment," he says.

"Will it still work?" she asks. "The gun?"

The steps make a pause. She can hear him sighing. "It's old. My granpapa brought it from Haiti. We'll find out."

"Forget about it, please," she says. "Come help me with the door."

His steps resume their climbing upstairs.

Knock, knock.

She feels the vibration in her back, and it travels along her weak legs.

"Why do they *knock?*" she whimpers, pushing herself against the door. She turns her neck and tries to see through the peephole. Her body feels light as a feather against the hammering knocks.

Knock, knock.

The stairs make that shuffling noise again. Ulfred's steps. She watches for his approach and notices a bluish glimmer in the dark.

Knock, knock. The metallic lock rustles next to her ear.

"Ulfred, darling, my legs, I can't keep—"

"There's only one bullet," he says.

The tone of his voice says it all. She knew it. She just knew it. She tries to keep her voice from faltering. "Then we keep it. For him."

The steps get closer to her.

"Elvira," he says, his voice now warm and close, "he's not coming."

"Yes, he is."

"No. He's not."

She sniffs. "Please," she says. "Save it for him. In case he comes."

For a moment there is silence, and Elvira feels something hovering in the darkness in front of her. Ulfred's familiar arm draping around her neck. His face leaning into hers until their noses touch. The hard gun being pressed against her left shoulder.

"*Listen to me,*" he whispers. "I left the car blocks away from here."

She searches the dark for his eyes, puzzled. "What? Why?"

"Even if he comes for us, he'll think we're not home. And he'll go away. Wolfram is not coming."

Tears rain down her cheeks. His face is close to hers.

"He'll be safe," he says.

She closes her fists and hits him in the chest, pushing him away. "You bastard!" she yells. "He won't be safe! God, he won't!"

His arms wrap around her, pulling her away from the door. She tries to fight him, and he holds her tighter. She stops fighting. Her arm stretches up to his hands on her shoulder, and she grabs the cold steel of the gun.

"I don't want to be one of them, Ulfred." She gently moves the barrel of the gun downward until the muzzle rests just above her left breast. "Please, help me."

Their eyes remain locked. Ulfred's breath is warm. Heavy.

"I'm scared," she says. "I don't want it to hurt. The radio said it would hurt. They bite, and chew—"

Knock, knock.

Elvira shrieks and shakes her head to the sides. "Ulfie, Ulfie, I can't take this anymore, Ulfie!"

The spell broken, Ulfred lets go of his wife. He steps back into darkness.

"I won't even see it coming," she continues to beg him. "It will be painless. Sudden. It will spare me from god-knows-what horrors. God, I know, it's selfish, I know, I'm sorry. I'm sorry, Ulfie."

He takes another step back.

"There's no telling how much it will hurt when those things walk in and grab us and tear us apart or eat our brains or whatever it is they do. And what about afterward? What then? Maybe it hurts even worse. The pain, the pain, the pain, oh, Ulf—"

A flash of light. A deafening shot bounces and echoes around the living room. Elvira's ears ring.

"Ulfred?" she says, without hearing herself.

She stretches her arms. *"Ulfred?"*

She feels movement on the floor in front of her.

"Ulfred?" she asks, reaching for the darkness with the tip of her fingers, the ringing in her ears clouding everything. "Oh, god ..."

The ringing starts to fade away. She hears a faint, faraway voice. " ... will only hurt a bit."

She sighs, relieved. "Ulfred? You're all right?"

A warm mouth on the side of her neck jolts her, and before she can scream, teeth cut into her flesh. A jaw springs shut, taking muscle and vein and artery in a powerful pull that sends waves of pain through her body, knocking her to the ground. Wanting to scream, she inhales, but only blood fills her lungs. She gasps and tries to breathe in some air just to be flooded again with the same metallic taste. She's suffocating. She inhales again, and a heavy sludge streams deep inside her. *Calm down,* she thinks. *Best to calm down and stop breathing, just stop and avoid that sinking drowning feeling. Think. Focus.* Ulfred's shoes are next to her face. She's on the floor. She doesn't remember falling. She hears him spit out something, and a bloody piece of flesh lands next to her eyes.

She looks up at the monster that used to be her husband, his chest now a shiny puddle of dark crimson. He's calmly looking down at her, waiting for her to die.

As her world fades to black, she hears it one more time.

Knock.

Knock.

Elvira stands up and turns the door handle. As it opens, the gray ghoul on the porch turns around to join the others, already marching down the street.

The newlydeads follow the throng to their neighbor's house, which was built to resemble a quaint sixteenth-century gothic chapel. As the pale grayish bodies spread out across the lawn and along the sides of the house, Elvira and Ulfred approach the back door, and, politely, knock.

21

LILITH RUNS AS FAST AS SHE CAN, STRAINING HER ACHING LEG, eyes fixed on the shadow crawling across Leatelranch's sharp, uneven skyline. Her throat burns. Her mouth is dry. *Fuck reanimation. If there's anything truly fantastic in zombie movies, it's all the goddamn running everyone manages to do.* She wonders how much longer she can last. She feels naked, watched by the dark windows around her.

The silhouette hops between rooftops, silent as a cat. His cotton hoodie camouflages him against the dark skies, but as he jumps in the air, it slides just enough that Lilith can see his face shining under the moon. *Wolfram, it is you.*

Wolfram lands on a tilted roof, hops along it, and jumps again over the ledge. He lands swiftly on a hump-shaped roof and paces toward a tall knife-shaped chimney stabbing the night sky that's twice as tall as he is.

"Show-off," she mumbles, a smirk drawing on her face. She allows herself to slow down. She leans over a wall bearing a graffiti that reads OUR BODIES ARE MOLDED RIVERS and tries to catch a breath.

"Let's. See how. You get out. Of this one."

The shadow gets a foothold on the flat side of the knife-shaped chimney, grabs the ledge, thrusts himself up, stands on the curved edge, and jumps to the next building. He spins in the air and lands on the other side of the gap with a silent roll.

"OK," says Lilith under her breath, "so you got good at it."

The shadow stands on the skewed roof of a house that looks like a chapel but with a futuristic angled roof, a huge bullet-shaped front window, and smaller windows on the top. He climbs down to the middle of the roof and stops. His head turns to each side, checking for witnesses. Then he cranes his neck over the ledge and looks down on the silent dark house, planning his descent.

Lilith frowns. "That's not your house," she says, trying to steady her breath.

The shadow grabs the ledge and climbs down. His feet dangle in front of a window, and he lets go, landing with one foot on the window ledge, and he continues his fall, and his hands magically grab the window ledge. With his feet now dangling halfway to the porch floor, he swings his body and lets go, landing smoothly on the porch, where the streetlights finally shine their white light on a man in a gray tracksuit. He quickly turns around and faces the door, showing Lilith a gray, anonymous back.

Lilith crouches and runs stealthily toward the house, hiding behind a car, peeking over the hood.

The man turns his head. He looks around. Wolfram looks just like she remembers him, though maybe a bit more buff, more grown up. He has a beard now.

He knocks on the door.

A pair of eyes peeks out from a window on the porch and disappears. The door creaks open, and out of the gap comes the head of an old fragile man.

"Wolfram," he whispers. "Go home. Your parents must be worried sick."

Wolfram glances at the house across the street. Lilith recognizes the caramel and white checkered pattern of its stained glass windows. Nostalgia washes over her. *That's* Wolfram's house.

"Hi, Mr. Tooms," Wolfram says, looking nervous. "They aren't home yet. Can I wait for them here? Inside?"

"Sure," the stranger says. He looks around, vigilant. "Come on in."

Wolfram enters, and the door closes behind him. Lilith crosses the street in a crouch and heads up to the porch. She peeks through the window. The lights are off, but the street lamps reveal Wolfram's muscled silhouette being escorted through a living room by the old man.

Lilith crouches in front of the door and looks through the keyhole.

Mr. Tooms is looking at Wolfram. "Do you know what's going on?"

"I hear that in the cities we've almost beat them," says Wolfram, "but best stay on the safe side and not leave the house."

"Yes," says the old man, "I'm sure it's for the best."

Wolfram walks further inside, looking around, and he freezes.

Lilith gasps. Standing around him, populating the living room, sitting on the couch, sitting at the table, standing next to a tall lamp, Lilith makes out other figures, blending in with the darkness. Wolfram turns his head, looking at them.

"Uhm ..." he begins, "are ... are you also hiding out?"

A calm voice comes out of the dark. "Just friends."

Wolfram makes a sudden jerking motion with his hands around his head. Only then, Lilith hears the buzzing. Flies, lots of them, circle around in the dark.

"Coffee?" asks Mr. Tooms behind Wolfram. Lilith can't see his face, but it sounds like he's smiling.

"S—Sure," says Wolfram, still looking around.

Mr. Tooms goes to the kitchen. Lilith hears a cabinet door opening, a cutlery drawer being pulled.

"Your parents are probably fine," Mr. Tooms says from the kitchen.

"I'm sure," says Wolfram, looking around at the strangers.

Lilith's eyes finally adjust to the darkness enough to identify those faint glimmers in the dark. Teeth. They're smiling at him.

A gunshot echoes high in Leatelranch's sky, jolting Lilith. Wolfram turns around to the big window next to Lilith and looks across the street. "What was that?"

"Oh dear," comes Mr. Tooms's voice from the kitchen. "Best not ponder on these things, sonny. Everything will be all right."

With her ears buzzing, Lilith turns around. Ghouls are now walking down the street, unaware of her, looking at Wolfram's house.

She crawls along the porch and hurries around the side of the house. Through the kitchen window she spies the old man, mindlessly clanking an empty glass pot against a coffee mug.

"But it's good that you wait here," he adds.

She hears trees rustling behind her.

"Shit," she mutters, "what now?"

Staying low, she scurries behind a clutch of trash cans just seconds before an old couple comes through the trees, holding hands. *They might look familiar,* Lilith thinks, *if it weren't for the mangled bloody bits hanging from them.*

Suddenly a memory clicks into place. "*Ulfred?*" Lilith asks the night, her whispered voice dripping with pain and anger. "*Elvira?*"

They knock on the kitchen door. The door opens, and Mr. Tooms smiles calmly at them. In complete silence, they walk in. He turns around, showing a deep bloody dent in the back of his head, and closes the well-oiled door.

Lilith's mind races. *What's going on?*

She crawls back around the house and finds a bullet-shaped purple window. She raises her head slowly and carefully. The strangers lining the walls stare fixedly at the kitchen, smiling. They're all still. Only Wolfram, standing in the middle of the room, moves. His eyes dart in every direction, searching for an exit, and finally his head turns toward the window where Lilith is crouched.

When Wolfram's gaze meets Lilith's, his mouth springs open.

Lilith throws a menacing look at him, prompting him to right himself and play it cool. Behind him, three dark shapes emerge from the kitchen. Their arms hang stiffly beside their bodies, their legs march as if they are disjointed, feverish, and their feet plod like dead weight, connecting to the floor as if they have to remember where it is with each new step.

"Watch out," says Mr. Tooms with the friendliest of voices. "Coffee's hot."

22

———

LESTER CAN'T WAIT TO GO OUTSIDE. AS NATHAN CRACKS OPEN the hospital door, a burst of sunlight blinds him. Outside, helicopters thunder, sirens wail, and it sounds like there's a large crowd gathering nearby, maybe a few blocks away.

"What's that rumble?" Yoshi asks, excited, behind him.

"Psychos," Nate whispers. "People who think this is fun. My girlfriend is probably with them."

"And Frankie?" Lester asks.

"And your friend, probably, yes. I'll take you to the Slayers. I'll check if my girlfriend is there. And then I'll get to Leatelranch. They probably have cars."

"Psychos?" Kenny asks.

"They have guns," Nathan says. "They can help us. You'll be safe with them."

Lester's eyes adjust. Through the crack, the street looks deserted. The wind drags trash around.

Yoshi rushes and tries to slide through the opening, bumping into Nathan.

"Come on, then! Let's go!"

"Wait," Nate says, stopping him. "Slow. Don't make a sound."

127

He steps outside and holds the door open for the boys. Yoshi and Kenny walk out and look around at the empty street, squinting.

"Wait!" Lester yells, tying his surgical mask. He walks outside, shielding his eyes from the sun, and tries to focus. "Here," he says with a muffled voice. "I brought for everybody."

Yoshi turns his back on him. "Fuck off."

Lester frowns and shakes the masks at him in anger. "You need them for outside!"

Yoshi scoffs at him and jumps down a few steps toward the sidewalk, drawing a snarky look from Lester, who puts the masks back in the left pocket of his cheap Austin Powers suit.

"That's a real pocket?" Nathan asks, impressed.

"Of course they're real," Lester says.

Kenny looks around. His red shirt shines under the sun. "Where are all the zombies?" he asks.

A string of gunshots echoes around them. A crowd cheers.

"Mostly lying dead on a pile," Nathan, trying to find the direction of the noise. "That way."

Kenny looks up at him with puppy eyes. "Can we go with them?"

"Yes," says Nate. "We're going with them."

But Lester hears something else. He looks at the other end of the empty street. Yes, it's definitely coming from there. Some fuss, like shuffling on the pavement. He wanders toward it, motioning the others to keep it down, and as he reaches the corner, he looks at the street to his right.

He freezes, in shock. In the distance, maybe two blocks away, there's a small group of people. They're far, but there's no denying it.

Their bodies end at their shoulders.

The headless bodies circle around something and bend down, then get up again. They seem to carry something.

Yoshi and Kenny catch up to him and peek from over his shoulder, shielding their eyes from the sun.

"Wait," Kenny says. "Are those ...?"

"Yes," Yoshi says, excited. "Zombies."

"That's gonna be us someday," Lester says.

Kenny frowns, worried. "What are they doing?"

"Shut up!" Nathan scolds, louder than intended, then corrects himself in a whisper: "*Be quiet.*" He stands behind the boys, placing his hands on Kenny's shoulders, and tries to digest the scene unfolding before them. His hands are shaking.

"Impossible," he says, wide-eyed. "That's impossible. That's impossible."

Kenny looks the other way, trying to locate where the party noises are coming from. "I wanna go where the guns are," he says.

"Yeah," says Yoshi, turning to Nate. "You shouldn't let kids boss you around. Show some spine, man. You're the adult here."

"*Shut the fuck up,*" Nate whispers as he stares at the headless zombies. They seem busy. "And don't call me an adult," he says, dead serious, glancing at the boy with the pins in his head. "I'm not even forty." Yoshi smiles nervously and steps back.

Lester can't shake off the feeling that there's something off about one of the zombies. He looks for a place to hide that will let him get a closer look. Only a few empty cars dot the deserted street, so he crouches and hurries behind one of them.

"*Kid!*" Nathan whispers. "*Kid!*"

But Lester doesn't care. He needs to see what's happening.

"Call him *Austin,*" Yoshi jokes, his voice already distant, and Lester takes a deep breath to calm himself. He can hear the man preparing to call him again.

Nathan whispers at the top of his lungs, *Lestat!*

Better. But Lester keeps skirting between the empty cars, getting closer and closer to the pack of zombies, who have now somehow managed to organize themselves into a circle. All but one are the same height and headless. The last, the one that Lester can't stop wondering at, is smaller and still has his head.

Finally, Lester is close enough to hear the zombies growl and shuffle their feet on the pavement. He can almost make it out …

Out of nowhere, Nathan jumps him and carries him behind the car, pushing him against the passenger door.

"What were you thinking, kid?" he asks, inches from Lester's face.

The boy's eyes scan him. "I think I saw something."

"We all saw something," the pale man says, checking on Kenny and Yoshi and motioning them to stay there. It's useless. The boys are already running toward them. They crouch and hide behind the car, next to Lester.

"This is so cool," says Yoshi, excited. He peeks his head up from the hood. "They're ... *working together*," Yoshi says.

Lester takes another peek through the window. He counts five or six headless zombies, plus a smaller one, a boy, with his head still attached. Lester gasps. He recognizes the boy's face. And his turquoise hospital gown.

"Look closer," Lester says. "Do you recognize something?"

Kenny ignores him. He keeps looking around, as if he's being preyed upon by every shadow around him.

The man exhales and shakes his head. "Get down," he says under his breath, crouching. "Let's get out of here." The boys look at each other as he starts to crawl back toward the hospital. "Let's go."

Lester doesn't want to blink. He doesn't want to miss a thing. His mind races. That's his friend, right there. "Wait!" he insists. "Look!"

Yoshi and Kenny raise their heads over the hood.

"Wait," Yoshi says, squinting. "Isn't that a gown? From the hospital?"

"Frankie!" Kenny yells in horror. "They've got Frankie!"

The boy in the turquoise gown is now standing in the center of the wretched circle, facing away from the boys. A headless zombie with one arm walks up to Frankie and pokes him with his only hand, and Frankie straightens, as if in acknowledgment. Then, inexplicably, he opens his arms wide.

"Guys," Nathan says, "You don't need to see that."

"We have to save him!" Lester cries.

The one-armed zombie returns to his place in the circle around Frankie. The group takes hold of Frankie by the hands and feet.

"No," Lester says under his breath.

The zombies begin walking in every direction, stretching Frankie's arms as they go. They start to grunt. And suddenly the man's hand is covering Lester's eyes.

"Let go!" Lester says, trying to get away.

"You shouldn't have to see this," Nate whispers in his ear. He sounds terrified. His voice is muffled by the rising sound of the zombies' struggle. Of bones cracking.

"Let go!" Lester yells, pushing away the man's hand and focusing again on the scene. The zombies are pulling away, twisting Frankie's arms as they strain to move forward, wrenching them in grotesque, inhuman angles, but Frankie stays silent. Bones crack again.

Kenny throws up behind him.

"You shouldn't see this," Nathan repeats. "Not yet. Not yet." He throws his hands back over the eyes of Lester and Yoshi, but both boys shake him off once again.

"Who do you think we are, mister? You sure seem afraid. Maybe *you* should look away."

An arm comes off, and a gush of green shoots out. The zombies stumble. One of them drops the arm on the pavement and helps the others bring the boy down. They pile above him like a pack of rabid dogs, so strong that his body convulses with every pull over the pool of green goo forming under him. They dislodge the other arm with a *crack* and throw it away.

"Frankie!" Lester yells, and for a moment it seems like the boy under the savage pile of zombies looks up and turns to him with a smile.

Knees and elbows saw their way into his flesh, and the head rolls over the pool of green goo.

Nathan covers their mouths this time. Lester is crying.

"They're turning against each other," Yoshi says, his voice muffled by the man's hand.

"No," says Nate. "They're working together. I think your friend was already one of them."

The struggle is over. There is silence around them. It almost sounds like a beautiful day.

"What? Shut up!"

The zombies stand up and take a step back. They spread out like perfectly coordinated soldiers, leaving the headless, armless torso lying on the pavement. Two of them carry the arms toward a large duffel bag and throw them inside. Another one grabs the head by the hair and walks toward Nathan and the boys.

"OK," Nathan says. "Fun's over. He's coming over here. Let's—"

The headless ghoul holding Frankie's head begins climbing a ladder leaning against the streetlight. As it rises, the head, hanging from its hair, sways and turns in the afternoon sun, facing the boys.

"Frankie," Kenny says to the head, waving goodbye to his friend.

The ghoul on the ladder freezes. It leans its torso toward the boys, and a growling sound emanates from its chest. Instantly, all four headless soldiers on the ground abandon their duties to turn directly toward them.

"Fuck," says Nate, pushing them back toward the hospital. "Run. Run! Run!"

Lester looks over his shoulder and resists. "But, Frankie!"

Nate pushes him forward. "That's not Frankie anymore! Run!"

23

ALL THEY CAN SEE IS AN EMPTY STREET, YET THE CHEERING grows louder and louder. *Whatever that is*, Kenny thinks, *we're getting closer to it*. He runs as fast as his itchy suit allows. His red shirt catches the sun's rays and turns them into a scalding hot oven for his arms, and the black polyester pants imprison his knees and legs. But fear is a strong cold fuel, and stopping is not an option.

"We need to go back!" says Lester behind him, his voice muffled by his hospital mask. "Get ... Frankie!" He breathes with a difficulty Kenny knows all too well.

"Forget Frankie," says Yoshi. "He's one of them now!"

Kenny turns to Nate, who is silently staring straight ahead, focused on running. Nate could probably outrun all of the boys, but it seems to Kenny that he's slowing himself down to match their pace.

Tossing a glance over his shoulder, Nate's already pale face turns even whiter. "Just run!" he yells. "Follow the noise!"

Kenny picks up the pace, scraping his legs and arms even harder against his sweaty, rough suit, and musters the courage to look back. Lester and Yoshi are behind him, also running as fast as they can.

Behind them, four headless bodies maintain their pursuit relentlessly, with no signs of getting tired.

Kenny feels a knot in his throat, a vibration, as if too many screams are trying to escape at the same time. His legs try to run even faster, stretching the seams of his tight polyester pants, brushing against the fabric so hard that he thinks he'll catch fire.

"Wait up!" yells Lester with his muffled mask voice.

"Over here!" says Nate, turning the corner toward a massive electronics store. Kenny is startled by a large TV in the shop window showing a crowded street that looks to be the perfect illustration of the cheering sounds they've been following. *No, it can't be ...*

He's relieved when the group turns another corner only to hear the cheering grow louder than ever.

Yoshi's voice comes from behind him. "Are those ...?"

Kenny notices something at the end of the street. A yellow barricade. Actually, the whole corner seems barricaded.

"Yes!" says Nate. "We made it!"

Behind the barricade, two people walk around, aimlessly, carelessly. To Kenny, they look like the bored people he's seen in the waiting room of the hospital.

A sound like thunder rattles Kenny's body. He covers his head and slows down, then looks back to check on the zombies. Instead, he sees Nate yelling at him. "Keep going!!"

His feet are heavy. His knees won't bend.

And that's when he sees them. Those men at the barricade. They have long guns, and they are shooting them up into the air. Beyond them, turning the corner, is the noisy cheering crowd.

People are bursting out of the barricade, thousands of them, cheering, dancing.

Safe, Kenny thinks. *Safety. Shelter. Protection.* His body is still blazing hot, his legs still burn on contact with the coarse pants, but he starts to feel like he can handle it.

"Hey!" Nate shouts at the figures behind the barricades, waving his arms, a shadow of relief drawing over his face. "Hey!"

Kenny smiles. If Nate smiles, he can be optimistic as well.

One of the guards turns his head around to them and whistles. The other one turns as well.

"Yes!" Nate yells, triumphant, smiling and waving even harder.

Both men run up to the yellow barrier. But instead of jumping over it to aid the struggling group, they stop and kneel down on it. Lester hears the metallic sound of guns being cocked.

"Stop right there!"

Lester sees Nate slowing down and looks over his shoulder. He knows the headless zombies are still chasing them, but they haven't yet rounded the last corner. He looks again at the guards. Behind their guns, they're taking aim. One of them drops a can of beer to the ground and aims at Nate.

"Fuck," says Lester, his voice muffled by the hospital mask.

Kenny freezes. He looks back at Yoshi, who's already looking straight at him. He mouths, *Did he say fuck?*

"Don't shoot!" yells Nate.

But the guns keep pointing at them. Kenny squints to avoid the glare and tries to get a better look at the barrels.

Now they're both pointing at Lester.

"What's with the sick boy?"

"He's OK!" Nate calls back to them.

Kenny can hear the guards hissing and whispering. Their automatic guns remain firmly locked in their positions.

"He's just an idiot," yells Yoshi. "Would we be hanging with a sick kid about to turn?!"

Kenny and Lester share a look.

"We don't give a shit!" yells one of the guards in a thick Southern accent.

"That's how you stay alive around here," the other guard explains.

"Great, Ron," says the first one, "go ahead and tell the enemy our secrets."

"Go ahead and tell them my fucking *name*, you—"

"We don't care about your names!" yells Lester at the top of his lungs. "We're not the enemy! We're alive—!"

Ron points his gun at Lester. "So, why's that kid wearing a mask?"

"He's just weird," Nate says.

They cock their guns.

"He's not sick! He's not sick! He's just weird! He's not gonna die, c'mon. Would a zombie stop running when you ask him?"

They seem to concentrate on their aims.

"They're kids!" yells Nate. "You're gonna shoot at kids?!"

Ron turns to his buddy and ponders the question. "They could be midgets."

"We're not midgets!" Kenny shouts. "We're kids. And look at us. We're alive, right?"

The other guard addresses Ron. "They look alive to me."

"Well, we are," Kenny presses on. "We're kids, we're not midgets, and we're *not zombies*."

As Ron thinks about it, Kenny looks back. The headless zombies are rounding the corner. He raises his voice as loud as he can over the knot in his throat. "They're coming!" he yells. "They're coming for *me*!"

Yoshi explodes. "Fuck me dead!" he yells. "They're coming, you morons! Make up your minds!"

Ron looks behind them. "This could be a trap."

"*Walkers* don't set up *traps*, you moron," says his buddy.

"Fuck it," says Ron, and he lowers his gun. "Come on in. Hurry!"

His buddy stands down his weapon, and the group runs toward the yellow barrier. Kenny smiles as he pushes his suit-prison to its limit. When he sees the relief on the faces of Nate and Yoshi and Lester, the knot in his throat goes away so fast, he feels hiccups coming.

"Cabal of walkers," Ron yells suddenly, stopping on his way to open the gate. He kneels on the floor again and taking aim. "Twelve o' clock."

"Roger-Roger," yells his buddy.

Lester looks at Nate. "Did he say *cabal*?"

Nate looks back at him with a confused look.

"A cabal," says Ron in a military tone so exaggerated it could easily be mistaken as a joke, "is a group, band, or cell of enemies."

Yoshi opens his mouth to talk, but Lester beats him to it. "They're fucking nerds," he says under his breath.

Nate throws them a scalding look. He points his index finger to the armed men. "Shut up!"

A storm of gunshots rattles Kenny's brain, deafening him. Out on the street, the headless zombies fall to the ground, green blood splattering the pavement.

"Yeah!" Ron and his buddy yell at the top of their lungs. "Yeaaaah!"

They look at each other and smile, proud. "Did you see that?" asks Ron. "I got one in the nose! I got one in the fucking nose!"

"Nose?" asks Kenny under his breath. "They're headless."

They high five. "Fuck yeah!"

Ron pats his buddy in the chest. "Check this out, check this out."

He reaches into his vest pocket and takes out a grenade.

"Oh, Ron," says his buddy with a smile, "you're crazy, man. You're crazy."

Kenny looks around and panics. Nate is throwing them a warning look. He looks back at the zombies and covers his ears.

The little cylinder flies across the sky over their heads and falls near the zombies with a faint *clink*.

"Shiiiiiiiiiiii—!" yells Lester.

A deafening explosion interrupts him.

As the ringing in his ears starts to fade away, Kenny hears the cheering louder than before. A cloud of black smoke flies over them, and he starts to cough.

A hand comes through the fog. It's Lester's. It's handing him a mask. Kenny takes it, coughing, and puts it on. Suddenly the air coming out of his mouth is as hot as his arms and legs. The heat is unbearable.

The cloud of smoke dissipates. Nate and Yoshi are now wearing masks, too.

Finally, Ron opens the yellow barrier and slams it shut behind Nate, who has wasted no time thrusting the boys through in front of him.

The cheering is loud. The street is filled with people, cheering, dancing, shooting at the sky.

"Welcome to the Slayers' little party!" Ron yells, his voice barely audible over the cheering.

"Thanks," Nate replies, wary of the guns, trying to keep his eyes on the boys as the crowd threatens to envelop them.

"Don't mention it, buddy," says Ron, smiling.

Nate puts his hand on Ron's shoulder, causing a reaction from him: a shudder, a short but definite reach for his gun.

"Who can I ask about a car?" asks Nate.

"What?"

"A car," Nate repeats under his hospital mask.

"A car?" asks Ron. "I don't think so."

"Are you the one who'd know so?"

Ron throws him a cold look.

Kenny grabs him by the sleeve, pulling down, desperately. "Please," he says. "They're coming for us. They're coming for me."

"Coming for you?" asks Ron, amused. "I guess they are, aren't they? Come, follow me," he says, and he turns toward the crowd. "I'll take you to the one that'd *know so*."

Nate smiles. "Thank you. Looks like no door three-twelve for me today!"

"What's that?" asks Kenny.

"Death," Nathan says. "Never mind. It's an inside joke with my girlfriend. Her grandmother once ... Just, just never mind. Come on."

Kenny jolts as a hand lands on his shoulder. It's Lester. "Cheer up," he says, "we're with the Slayers now. Your father can't come here. We're gonna be fine."

Kenny tries to smile. He turns again toward Ron's gun, and, without a word, he shuffles his feet toward the cheering crowd.

24

LILITH LIFTS A TRASH CAN AND THROWS IT AT THE PURPLE window, making it explode with a loud *crash*. Shattered glass flies inside the dark living room, where a dozen heads turn to her in surprise. Their eyes, glimmering in the faint glow of the street-lights, lock on to her.

"Wolfram!" she yells. "C'mon!"

The leftmost pair of eyes comes closer, and just as Lilith identifies them as Wolfram's, something blocks the window. A blood-stained shirt. Someone's back. Wolfram's father, Ulfred, is waiting to greet his son.

Lilith grabs the other trash can and throws it at Ulfred, sending him flying to the floor. She enters awkwardly through the window, steps on his back, kicks him in the back of the neck, and kicks, and kicks again with the heel of her foot until the head comes off and rolls over with a surprised look on his face. Wolfram's father looks much older than she remembered.

Wolfram is petrified, looking at the dark silhouettes surrounding him.

"Wolfram," yells Lilith, "watch out!"

He turns around just in time to see a shadow, his mother, pouncing at him, teeth first.

"M—Mom?" yells Wolfram, clumsy and shocked as he tries to duck her attack. He points one fist up in a defensive stance, which she dodges as she lands.

"Punch with your other hand!" yells Lilith.

Clenching his eyes, Wolfram throws a wild punch with his right hand. It sinks into his mother's right tit before stopping at her hard chest, throwing her fragile body backward.

"I'm sorry," he whines as the ghoul hits the floor.

"Catch!" yells Lilith, and she grabs a loose purple shard from the window and throws it on the floor next to him, the glimmering glass shining in the dark. Wolfram kneels to pick it up. His hands tremble.

"Come on!" yells Lilith. She can see the other ghouls closing in on Wolfram.

He stretches over the fallen ghoul, and, with a whimper, stabs Elvira's neck again and again. He jumps up and kicks the head until he can see it rolling over. Lilith can hear him sobbing.

"You had no choice," she calls out to him. "And you don't have time to deal with it now."

His voice trembles. "Lil? Is that you? What are you doing here? What the fuck is going on?"

"Not now, Wolfram!"

Two of the other ghouls step in, their teeth going for Wolfram's neck. He pulls his arm, preparing to punch again. The ghouls look straight at him and jerk their heads to the sides in a dodging motion.

"Kick!" says Lilith. "Jump kick or something!"

He jumps and spins in the air, kicking both zombies. He lands gracefully as they hit the ground.

"How are you doing this?" he asks.

"No idea, I'm just making it up as I go."

The ghouls get back up. Wolfram tries to take a defensive stance as they move around him, but he stumbles, falling to the floor and dropping the shard of purple glass.

As the ghouls close in on Wolfram, Lilith jumps in. She head-butts the largest zombie right in the teeth, then pushes the others down on top of it. The ghouls sprawl in a jumble on the floor, their heads right next to a heavy-looking antique chair. She lifts it and drops it on their skulls, which sound like cracked eggshells as they burst open.

Wolfram stands up, dazed by the darkness around him.

"Shit," he says, "it's like they can see in the dark."

"It's worse," says Lilith. "I think they can see, like, the future."

"What? How ...? What?"

"I'll explain later."

Heavy footsteps come at them.

"Oh shit," says Wolfram. "Left or right? Left or right?"

"Surprise yourself!"

"Middle, then!" Wolfram kicks and hits the ghoul between the legs. There's a heavy thump. He feels around and finds a heavy glass lamp. He grabs it and finishes the ghoul off with a blow to the head that sounds like a thousand windows shattering.

"Fuck this," says Lilith. She walks toward the door and feels around the wall. She flicks on the light. It blinds her.

The room is nothing like she had imagined. It's smaller. Old. Walls are painted with a faded olive green and are filled with old racks and shelves full of black and white pictures, old plates, and porcelain figurines. The room is full of antique furniture, the solid and sturdy kind made of polished wood. And among the furniture, a group of rotting corpses, standing very still, unusually tall, hunching over them, grinning, with milky white eyes that seem to dream.

She turns to Wolfram. He's in shock, staring at his beheaded parents on the floor.

The standing ghouls shamble toward them, arms up, steps heavy, legs stiff.

"Wolfram. Look alive."

He stares at her and opens his trembling mouth, speechless.

"Right," she says. "Sorry."

He doesn't look amused. "What's this?" he asks. "They can *act* alive?"

"Worse."

Wolfram rips out the shattered shade from the lamp, keeping the heavy brass base, still slippery with his mother's blood. "Take the cord," he says, holding to the lamp. "What do you mean worse?"

Lilith yanks it. "I think they're just *posing* as ghouls."

She coils the cord in both hands and tightens it, eyes fixed on the ghouls and their gray hands, almost close enough to touch her. The one in the front walks toward her with empty eye sockets, a strange goo pouring from where his eyes used to be.

Wolfram turns to Lilith, overwhelmed. "What?"

More zombies begin to stream in through the broken window.

"Shit," says Wolfram. "The lights! We attracted them!"

Lilith pushes one of the ghouls away and turns toward the door. She yanks it open and takes Wolfram's hand. "C'mon!"

25

LILITH EXITS THE HOUSE AND CHARGES DOWN THE DESERTED street as fast as she can move. The pain from the crash still radiates along her leg. Crickets chirp around her, as if the world hasn't caught up yet to the infested house behind her, so teaming with ghouls now that they're climbing out every window.

"What now?" she asks, panting.

Wolfram runs past her without breaking a sweat and heads to a dumpster on the side of a house.

"Follow me."

"Oh, no," she says, "I've seen you and your parkour shit. Do I look like I can parkour?"

He turns to her and smiles his broad smile. "You seemed pretty limber back there, showing me the moves."

"I guess I did!" she says, trying to catch her breath. "You picked up a lot, by the way. When did you become such a zombie fan?"

"I'm not," he says, walking toward the dumpster. "I hate those dumb movies. I just did as you said. How did you know how to do that?"

"I didn't really believe it until I saw you doing it," she says, following him.

He fakes an old teacher voice. "You have potential, but you need to apply yourself more."

Lilith laughs. "Mrs. Ravenscroft?"

"Remember her?" he says, sizing up the dumpster for a place to hold. "Anyway, c'mon, we'll take the easy route."

"Remember, I have this heart thing ..."

Wolfram turns to her, confused. "Oh, right." He checks the street around them, looking for another way.

Lilith can hear the ghouls approaching. "I need your help. I need to get out of here, I need to get back to New Southport and find Nate."

He climbs the dumpster and turns to her. "We'll help you out. Right now, you need to follow me."

She looks around. Every darkened doorway to every darkened house is opening, as far as she can see. Out of each one, shadowy figures are emerging and walking directly toward them.

"Shit," she exhales, "We? Follow you where? Where are we going?"

Wolfram crouches like a gargoyle and reaches down for her, and she extends her hand.

"Police station," he says. "I just left Wednesday and everyone there. It's safe."

Her hand freezes in midair. "Oh. No, no."

"We need to go!"

"Is Mr. Girardot still there?" she asks.

"He's the chief. Look at me. Look at me." Wolfram stops talking until Lilith complies with his request. "I know what you're thinking. But now's not the time to be shy. Just push through it. Like tearing off a Band-Aid."

"Ugh." Lilith looks around for another way out. The street-lights show the parade of dark figures growing close.

Wolfram stretches down, bringing his hand closer to her. "Come on."

"And Wednesday," she says. "Wednesday is also there. Oh, no. I can't. I hope you guys are safe. I'm glad you're still together and all. But I really need to go to New Southport and find Nate."

Wolfram bites his lip. "Lil, Jesus."

"Don't you get it? I need to go!"

"Lil," he repeats, slowly, like he's addressing a wounded animal. "*It's OK.*"

Lilith exhales. "Shit! Shit! Shit!" She takes his hand. "But promise me, *promise me* you'll help me get to New Southport."

He pulls her onto the dumpster effortlessly, and she struggles to her feet. Behind them, more figures are stepping out of their houses.

"I'm sorry," says Wolfram. "Is Weirdo Cemetery Boy OK?"

"His name's Nate," she says.

Wolfram examines the ledge above the wall closest to the trash bin. "Yes," he says. "Him."

"I'm sure he's OK ... We just had to split up. I need to contact him."

He turns to her. "How do you know he's not—?"

"He's not," she finishes abruptly.

She doesn't like the worried glance he throws at her.

"Well," he says, "then maybe you should lay low for a while, you know? Stay with us—"

"I can't," she says. "Really. I just need to find him. Scare the shit out of him before this is over."

"*Scare him?*"

"Yeah," Lilith says. "It's something we do."

"That's the priority right now?"

"The heart wants what the heart wants," she says, trying to smile.

Wolfram jumps as high as he can, trying to reach the ledge, but it's just out of reach. So he sticks his hands to the wall. Lilith can't see what he's holding on to, but he starts climbing up the flat surface like a goddamn spider. He taps twice on a brick, making sure Lilith sees it, and steps on it.

"Anyway," he says, holding on to a rusty pipe, "I'm glad to hear about him. I knew you guys would still be together. I'm sure you can contact him from the police station."

She turns around. The front lines of the ghoul parade are about to enter the alley.

"So, what brings Lucky back here?" he asks.

"My dead father. Literally."

Wolfram reaches the roof and jumps onto it effortlessly. "Nothing to it."

"Fuck you," Lilith says under her breath.

His head pops back into view, and he extends his hands down to her. "What? Grab my hands and climb on the wall."

She grabs his hand. She puts one foot on the wall, flexes, and a flash of pain shoots up her leg. She slips.

"Fuck," she says. Regaining her footing, she continues. "He— he brought me."

"Why?"

"Fuck if I know. But it probably means we should get as far away from here as humanly possible."

She finds another foothold on the wall, pulls on Wolfram's hands, and secures her other foot against it.

"You know what they say about Leatelranch," he says, and she wishes he'd shut up and not finish the goddamn tired old joke. "Everybody's dying to visit."

As Wolfram pulls her up, Lilith scratches her elbows on a brick, and her chest scrapes the rough ledge. Suddenly she's on a rooftop, surrounded by the gargoyles large and small that slumber on the ledges of Leatelranch. She stops to catch her breath. The night air is fresh and sweet. The roof where they stand overlooks the cemetery. She can see the miniature city of crypts and alleys, quiet and clean, and behind it, the vast green hills with scattered clusters of gray tombstones.

"This place is a lot cooler than I remembered," she says.

He looks around. "Hasn't changed much. Maybe it's the new perspective," he jokes. "You guys left, what, ten years ago?"

"I think more like fifteen, or twenty," she says.

"God, I haven't seen you since—"

"I know."

"You disappeared ..."

"My parents took me away. I wanted to stay."

"But you never called ... or anything ... " he says quietly.

"It was hard, OK?" she says. "Not as hard as this climbing-roofs thing, but hard."

An awkward pause falls over the old friends as they creep quietly toward the far side of the roof. Lilith's leg is throbbing.

Wolfram breaks the silence. "So, how's life in the big city?" he asks. "Got kids?"

She scoffs. "Can you imagine?"

"Not ready yet, huh? Yeah, we were just now thinking about it ourselves," he says.

"God," she groans, "you, too, Wolfie? *You've* turned into one of those? I swear, everyone you think is cool, eventually they just ... *turn*. What happens to you people?"

"We grow up!" he says, laughing, looking forward. "You will, too, you'll see. Never say never."

Lilith doesn't need to say it—her glare makes those words perfectly clear.

"Listen," Wolfram continues. "Back there. You said they could see the future. Is this about what your Grann told you in the hospital?"

"I told you about that?"

He chuckles. "You're kidding, right? Don't you remember why we called you Lucky? You could see the future. One doesn't just forget about that."

The world spins around her. Leatelranch spins around her. Her childhood spins around her.

"I *told* you about that? When?"

"Of course you did! Way back when. Before you traded our gang for that boyfriend of yours." Lilith slaps him on the arm. "I'm kidding, I'm kidding. So what else do you remember?"

"A lot of images. Things that ended up happening. But after

the car crash, it was all gibberish."

"Damn. Bet some of it woulda come in handy right now. What do they want? How do we stop them?"

"I don't know. Let's just get to the station."

"Good idea," he says, gauging the size of the gap between where they are standing and the roof of the next house. Lilith imagines Cthulhu could probably walk through it without disturbing a single slumbering gargoyle. "Let's regroup. I'm sure a good ol' blanket and cup of coffee will help."

Wolfram jumps across Cthulhu Alley and lands gracefully. "Come on!"

Despite a throbbing leg and serious misgivings, Lilith jumps across the chasm and lands on a concrete rooftop. The alley is now crawling with people. She follows Wolfram along the roof, and he jumps a small gap to the next ledge. She reaches the ledge and prepares to jump, but she stubs her foot on a gargoyle's tail. She loses her balance, her leg going numb as she falls on her back, and manages to grab the ledge as she slips and falls. Before she knows it, her feet are dangling in the air.

"Help!" she cries.

Wolfram turns back. "Shit," he says. "I can't make the jump. You're on the ledge. If I jump over there, I may step on you."

"Help," she repeats pitifully, watching as the ghouls close in on them in the alley below.

"You can do this."

"I can't."

"Yes, you can!" Wolfram pleads from the other ledge.

"I can't," she cries, still looking down. Her fingers are slipping. "I can't do shit. I'm done. I'll never see Nate again. I wanted to scare him one more time—"

"Come on! You're Lucky!"

"I'm—slipping," she winces.

"You can wing it!" he says to her. "You just taught me how to kick those zombies' asses. You can do it. Just don't think about it—"

"N-Nah," she says, trying to lift herself up, and failing. "I just told you to wing it, and you did. YOU can. I've never winged shit. I had my visions to help me my whole life, and now they're gone. That car crash was the last thing. I'm fucking useless now."

"You are *not* your visions," Wolfram says. "Forget about those. Do your own thing."

"I can't," she says, trying again to pull herself up.

"You're afraid. It's not gonna be easy. Just try, for once."

"I—already tried," she says. "It never goes well."

"Aw, come on. Never? Never worked *once*?"

She thinks about it. "Yes," she says, staring over at the horizon. "Once."

"When? When was that?"

A smile sneaks up to her and clears her frown. "The night I met Nate."

Trying to push herself up, she kicks from the hip like a fish out of water and hits a pipe next to her. She steps on it and uses it to push herself up. Suddenly her elbows are on the roof. She makes a final push and finds herself lying on the roof, heaving.

"Yes!" Wolfram yells.

He jumps the gap and lands next to her. "Are you OK?"

"Yes," she says, dusting herself off, trying to catch her breath. Her arm muscles burn. "But ... look."

She points down at the street. It's densely packed from end to end with dark figures, and still more are coming, as far as they can see in all directions, marching along, getting closer and closer.

"The house lights must have attracted them."

"They knew," Wolfram says. "They were waiting for you."

"Maybe we're the last ones," she says.

"Maybe the last ones they know about. Let's keep going. The others are waiting for us there."

From the corner of her eye, a yellow light suddenly shines in the dark skyline. She turns around. A bullet-shaped window lights up. A pale figure, sitting still, stares at her. Another window shows what looks like half a girl, as if she's standing inside a half-open closet, looking straight at Lilith through her long black hair. But it's just clothes. It has to be only clothes. More windows light up. Spreading like fire, yellow lights, white lights, and colorful stained-glass windows lit up like kaleidoscopes. Shadows, human shapes, stand behind them. A chill runs through Lilith's spine.

Leatelranch is awake.

Wolfram looks back over his shoulder. "My god. We're surrounded. The whole town is dead."

Lilith can't believe what she's seeing. "I think we're really the last ones, Wolfie."

He turns to her and winks. "Aren't we lucky? But don't worry. As long as we're up here, we're OK." He jumps to the next ledge, and Lilith follows. "Let's just get to the police station."

Another silence falls over them, and this time it's Lilith who breaks in. "So, how are things with Wednesday?" she asks.

"Good."

"That's great. What about the rest of the gang?"

Wolfram turns around. He gives her a strange look. "You mean Doyle?"

"Yes," she says. "Doyle."

"Well, that's a name I haven't heard in a while," he says. "I thought you'd ..."

"Forgotten?"

"Forgotten, yeah. And here I was gonna say *repressed*."

Lilith looks down at the roof tiles below her feet.

"He left," he says, breaking the silence. "Right after you did."

"Oh."

"It was probably harder on him, too—"

"I had no idea," Lilith interrupts.

"Of course not," he says. "Why would you? You left."

They climb the roof tiles and reach the peak. Many roofs away, across a broad avenue, stands a tall gray building with spires, like a fairy-tale palace gone wrong. The word *Vigiles* is engraved in its concrete facade.

26

MRS. RAVENSCROFT LEADS THE CLASS IN SINGLE FILE INTO THE museum hall. The squeaking of dozens of children's sneakers fill the air. Lilith skips carelessly, jumping, laughing, reaching up high to keep her hands on Wolfram's shoulders, and holding fast to her Raggedy Ann doll with her pinky finger. She laughs at the boring old-timey shovels and helmets in the exhibitions around her, and the boring old black-and-white photographs covering the walls. The tall ceilings trying to make all this seem *so important* are definitely *not* cool, and she makes that clear by ripping more squeaks from the old museum floor, skipping and jumping higher.

"Cut it out!" Wednesday whispers behind her, laughing so loud that Doyle and the others behind her start to crack up as well. "What's up with you today?"

"Whoa," Wolfram says with his eyes fixed on the center of the room, "we gotta get in there."

Lilith follows his gaze and notices *The Citizen*, the famous iron locomotive in all the pictures. It really is a beast, taking up most of the huge hall, not to mention ugly and boring, but it's surrounded by red velvet rope and the ever-tempting DO NOT TOUCH sign.

Behind Wednesday, Doyle, shorter than the rest, sticks his head out of the line. "Guys, this is a museum. They'll kill us!"

"Yeah, cut it out," the boy behind him says, flashing impossibly blue eyes.

But Lilith is already exploring the locomotive with her gaze.

"Look," she says, noticing a big hatch behind the red velvet rope. "There's the entrance!"

"All right," Mrs. Ravenscroft says, waiting for the kids' chatter to die down. "Make a circle, now."

The class rearranges itself with more squeaking, and Lilith skips around a few times before stopping.

"First of all, let's all welcome Lilith back," Mrs. Ravenscroft says. The old woman is tall and pale, and her black gown is somewhat like the ones her mom uses, but older looking, with lace shoulders and a ridiculous high ruffled neck.

"As you know, Lilith had to take a few days off, and we want to be supportive. We love Lilith very much, don't we?"

Lilith doesn't enjoy the murmuring that rises up around her.

"This place is boring," she complains, loud enough to shock all the voices into silence and to earn a scolding look from Mrs. Ravenscroft.

Everybody laughs.

Mrs. Ravenscroft bends down to Lilith's eye level. Her smile is wide, and her thin lips are almost invisible in her pale skin. Her eyes are murky and old.

"What's your doll's name again?"

"Baby," Lilith replies, holding her worn doll tighter, caressing her red hair.

"Hi, Baby," Mrs. Ravenscroft says. Her teeth are all old and rotten.

"You know, Lilith," Mrs. Ravenscroft starts. "There once was a king who was sad, and he asked the wisest poet in the kingdom to write him a phrase that would cheer him up in dark times, but that would also help him stay humble in times of happiness.

Everyone thought it couldn't be done. Such a phrase would be nothing short of magic! But you know what happened?"

Lilith loosens her grip on the doll, invested in the story.

"After a few days, the wise poet returned, and he told the king: *This, too, shall pass.*"

Lilith's eyes widen. She squeezes her doll.

"So," the old woman says, wearing her ugly old-woman smile, "whenever you're sad, just remember: This, too, shall pass. Even our sadness."

Lilith represses a sigh of wonder. She looks around at her friends and clears her throat.

"Still bored," she says.

The class cracks up.

"I mean, thank you, Mrs. Ravenscroft!" she says, turning to her friends and smirking. She can feel the old woman's gaze linger on her for a while, and is relieved at last when she hears the teacher's footsteps walking away.

Mrs. Ravenscroft turns to a museum wall and starts talking about the black-and-white pictures.

"Now!" says Wolfram. "Let's go!"

He bolts, and Lilith follows him, giggling, excited, trying to outrun him. Wednesday and the boys follow close behind her.

A voice echoes in the hall. "Hey! Kids!"

A grumpy-looking guard walks up to them, signaling with his hands to stop.

"No running!" he yells.

Mrs. Ravenscroft turns to them, startled. "Boys! Girls! Come back here."

They giggle as they get back in line.

"Stop embarrassing me," the old woman says. "This is no place for running. Pay attention!" she says, before turning back to the wall and continuing with her boring presentation.

"Happy now?" Doyle says.

"Let's go again," Lilith says.

"No!" says the boy with the impossibly blue eyes. "You'll get us in trouble!"

Something about that iron behemoth calls to Lilith. Yes, it's boring, but there's something oddly familiar about it, a secret calling out to her from its hollow cabin. She tries not to think about it, but what she's trying to forget is a nightmare, and *this* beast is real, a physical object right in front of her. They can't both be the same thing. Fighting her fears, she reaches into the nightmare and, like pulling thick cobwebs from her eyes, pulls out a small nugget. Just one memory. Just this once.

"Hey, Ricardo!" she yells.

Her friends try to contain their laughter, but the guard turns around, and it's clear by the look on his face that she got the name right. He searches for Lilith's voice as it echoes around the massive chamber, then follows it down a corridor behind the gathered children.

"Now!" says Wolfram.

They bolt again, sneaking past Mrs. Ravenscroft and under the red velvet rope. They climb a small iron ladder and scuttle inside *The Citizen*.

The cockpit is wide and dusty. They sit on the floor against the dark iron panels on both sides of the compartment, red-faced, panting and laughing.

"How did you do that?" Wednesday asks her, her voice metallic with the echo in the cabin. "Do you know him?"

Lilith hugs her doll. "I can't believe it worked," she says to it with a big smile, hugging it as hard as she can. "I can't believe it worked."

"Yeah," Doyle says. "How did you know his name?"

"How do you think?" Lilith says. "I got lucky."

"That's *too* lucky," Doyle says. "Did you overhear his name? Have you been to the museum before?"

She smirks, looking around at the cockpit like it's a dream come true, and points to a small unmarked lever sticking out from the left side of the locomotive's front panel.

"You wanna see lucky? Try that lever. It opens a secret hatch."

Doyle, next to it, turns to it suspiciously. "It's all dusty."

"Pull it, you wuss," says Wolfram.

Doyle pulls it reluctantly, and next to Wednesday, a small hatch disguised as a smooth black panel gapes open like a mouth. Wednesday jumps up and stifles a scream.

Lilith breathes heavily, euphoric. She loves this. It's like she has superpowers. It's like a dream. *No, it's better than a dream. Because it's real.*

They all look at her with a bit of fear.

"Have you snuck in here already?" Wolfram asks, suspicious.

She snorts. "Um, *no?*"

Wednesday is confused. "Did we read about this in school?"

"You mean in How to Drive a Weird Old-Timey Locomotive class?" Lilith snarls. "Yeah, it's right before math."

She can hear herself, and it's like somebody else is putting words in her mouth. She sounds defiant. She's so happy, but she sounds so angry. *Well, so what.*

"What's going on, *Lucky?*" Doyle says, somber. "Really."

She scoffs. "Grann told me about it."

"Grann?"

"My Grann."

The squeaking noises from the museum hall fill the iron cabin.

The boy with the impossibly blue eyes puts his hand on Lilith's shoulder. "Are you OK?" he asks, almost whispering.

"So you *have* snuck in here before?" Wolfram says. "And she gave you lessons?"

"No, it wasn't *lessons*," Lilith says, trying to avoid her friend's gaze. "Wow, it's like I remember being here. But I remember being here now."

"You can see the future!" says Wolfram, looking at the lever with a big smile. "That's the coolest toy ever! You really *are* lucky."

"I guess I am," she says, and her cheeks burn. She looks at her doll and smiles at it.

"This is no toy," says the boy with the impossibly blue eyes.

"This is huge! We gotta *use* this! What else did your Grann tell you?"

Wednesday looks inside the hatch and takes out a humanlike figure, slick with oil and charred, like a doll made of grease and coal.

"Ew! What's this?"

The moment Lilith's eyes fall on the figure, everything goes dark. All the air is sucked out of the cabin, and a cold chill runs through her body. The images hit her like so many shovels. Hazy shapes that turn into nightmarish images from a horrible ... future? Whose future? On the outside, she appears to stare blankly at the figure, her eyes far away, unfocused. But she's looking inside herself, backwards, to the past, to a murky memory. She doesn't notice her doll slipping from her limp hands. If the guard's name was real, and if the hatch was real, then maybe these images that taste like vinegar in her mouth are ...

"What's wrong, Lil?" the boy with the impossibly blue eyes asks. "You look like you've seen a ghost."

Lilith tries to speak, to ask for help, to say that she's not lucky at all, but her mouth doesn't move: *Grann really is gone. And what she said really is happening. And if they heard it, they'd freak out. Dead people ... everywhere? Only three people left in the world? A car crash? Whose car crash? Grann never told me she was in a car crash. Was she talking about me? Should I stay away from cars now, my whole life? But who gets into a car with a dead man driving it? It doesn't make sense. It has to be a dream. But that figure ...*

Just stay away, she says to herself. *Stay away from cars, from everything, and maybe these nightmares will stay where they belong: in my head.*

"Do it again!" Wolfram squeals.

Lilith starts to come to. "N—Nah."

"What? Come on!" Doyle insists.

She raises her arm (so heavy, suddenly) and points idly at a side panel. "That knob will turn on the lights," she lies.

Doyle tries it with a big grin on his face, but nothing happens.

They all turn to her.

"Oops," she says, grabbing a handle next to the exit hatch. "Must be wearing off. Let's go." And with that, she starts to climb out of the cabin.

"Wait!" Wolfram whispers. "There's Mrs. Ravenscroft, looking for us. You gotta tell us when it's safe again!"

"Yeah, you just missed once," says Wednesday. "We believe in you!"

"Come on," says Lilith, walking away. "Who cares."

"Lu-cky! Lu-cky!" they whisper-chant behind her.

With a lost gaze, almost catatonic, Lilith goes out.

"Come back!" Wednesday whispers. "Lil! You left your doll here!"

"Leave it," she says as she walks away, dragging her gaze along the cold marble floor.

Mrs. Ravenscroft's shriek pierces her ears. "There you are!"

Two pairs of footsteps power their way to her, and her teacher and the guard each grab one of her arms.

Mrs. Ravenscroft is fuming. Lilith can notice the anger, the nervous trembling of her teacher's voice, but she's not afraid. Not of this.

"Where were you?"

But Lilith doesn't care enough to answer. Her teacher's grip on her arm tightens.

"What where you thinking?" Mrs Ravenscroft insists. "Answer me, Lilith, or your parents are going to hear about this!"

But Lilith just stares at the floor, unable to concentrate or even look up.

"Whatever."

27

IT'S BLAZING HOT UNDER THE BLANKET. THE BOY TRIES TO hold his breath, puffing his cheeks like a blowfish, until he has to let go and exhale, making his cozy lair even warmer. He tries to inhale, and the air burns his lungs.

He pokes his mouth out of the blanket, just enough to catch some fresh air, and he clenches his eyes shut until they hurt. Ah, sweet fresh air. He relaxes his body and tries to fall asleep, even if his hands are on his face and his knuckles weigh on his eyes. Small price to pay to keep the blankets tight. He could stay like this forever, even if sleep won't come.

He tries to think of tomorrow. Another day of learning the ropes. *You get to work like a grownup*, he thinks, *and here you are, whining like a boy*. He changes position. He relaxes, and finally, he starts to doze off.

Something hits the floor.

His eyes spring open to see the shadow of a tree creep over his bedside lamp. His hands have shifted in his sleep, stripping the safety of the blanket from over his head. Like lightning, he brings the covers back up, plunging his face back into the cozy, oven-like darkness. But it's already too late. He can't unsee what he saw.

Before the blankets went up, in that microsecond, he saw that shadow crawl up the lampshade.

The night plays tricks on everybody. It's the fear. And the panic. And the shivering. They can fool anyone.

Tock. Tock.

A finger, a finger is thumping on his window glass.

Tock. Tock.

He clenches his arms and brings the covers right next to his face. He closes his eyes and slowly turns into a ball, careful not to let anyone see any sudden movements.

It was the wind …

Tock. Tock.

Father probably heard it. Father will come. Father, the master of this cemetery, who travels it daily and knows not to be afraid, will have an explanation for this. *Ghosts can't hurt you*, he's said many times with a smile. And it was an honest smile. Who knows better than the cemetery caretaker? *Ghosts can't hurt you.*

But that doesn't mean ghosts aren't *real*. It doesn't mean a cemetery is a place for the living to sleep. *If ghosts do exist*, the boy realizes, *they'll be here.*

Father's not coming. Nathan makes a careful opening in the covers to peek straight at his door, wary of not looking anywhere else.

The door is closed. No footsteps-on-the-floor noises. No one but him, alone, in this night.

Tock. Tock.

And if that's Father outside? Wouldn't that be funny? No ghosts! And his father, safety himself, right there with him, right next to his bed! Why would ghosts knock on his window, anyway? It's him, coming back from some night job.

The boy moves his head slowly, peeking out from under the blanket. He sees his desk next to the door, his lamp next to his desk, the curtains next to his lamp, and the window frame next to his curtains. He takes a deep hot breath. Slowly. Very slowly. *Don't let it hear you.*

The window is empty. Just the tree with its bony arm and fingers, in the frontline of the thick forest before the cemetery. The thin branch touches the window glass. *Tock. Tock.*

He sighs, relieved. He smiles, wishing his father could see him now, bravely peeking his head out of the blanket, breathing the fresh air, checking on that noise like a grown man.

Creak.

He yanks the blanket back over his head. The squeaky sound came from inside his room. Someone is stepping on *his* wooden floor.

Creak.

Slow. Silent. The sound is muffled by the blanket, but it's unmistakably close. It sounds, even, as if it's coming from under his bed.

Ghosts can't hurt you.

He slides the blanket down slowly, silently, until his face is bathed again in the fresh air of the dark room.

He opens his eyes.

Horrible face. Big bright yellow eyes, like golden sunglasses. Open mouth full of rotten teeth.

He dives back under the covers, curling into a ball as fast as he can, clenching his whole body and pressing his hands to his face and his arms around his head, pulling the covers with them, his feet feeling the chill of the open air. He tries to kick and fix the covers without looking, but he's kicking the cold fresh air, and now the covers are loose and floating in the air over his head.

Creak.

Exposed. Seen by the ghost. *This is it. This is the brave juice Father talks about. No hiding anymore.*

He forces himself to open his eyes.

GHOSTS CANNOT HURT YOU.

"How did you get in here?" he asks, getting shivers from hearing his own voice in the darkness of his room.

The face just stares at him.

With his body shaking and jittering, Nathan forces himself to let go, to relax his muscles and let himself move, to move his heavy stiff arm closer and closer to the figure standing next to his bed. His jittery index finger won't go near it, but Nate pushes on, pushes until the force field is broken, until his finger, no longer part of his body but just a finger lingering in the air, dares to touch the cold skin.

There's a hiss, like a cat, or a whisper, and a sharp pain in his finger. With a thump, his window springs open, and the shadow crawls out and disappears into the thick forest.

Nathan jumps up, bolting for the door. He grabs the heavy handle and pulls it down with all his strength.

Then he freezes, turns to his open window, and lets the handle back up slowly.

He won't believe me. Father won't believe me.

He walks toward the window. The trees and the grass look friendly and peaceful. The lights are on as far as he can see, illuminating his perfect park.

Ghosts can't hurt me, he repeats to himself as he places both hands on the window frame, the graze in his finger still stinging. He lifts one leg over it, then the other. *Ghosts can't hurt me.*

28

____

NATHAN FEELS WEIRD WALKING IN HIS PAJAMAS OUT IN THE
open. The grass feels cool under his bare feet. But lit by the
silvery moon, and by the lampposts shining their yellow light
everywhere, he feels invincible. *Ghosts can't hurt you. This is your
chance to shake off your fear, once and for all.*

He enters the woods. Tall thick trees surround him, but a
clear path filled with lamps welcomes him, so bright that he can
read the names on the plaques below each tree. Gomez. Lemarc-
hand. Bukeela. He could swear the trees are moving. *Something* is
moving. He squints, trying to focus. One of the lamps casts its
yellow light on a shadow just as it moves out of sight. He follows
the shadow out of the forest, past the ARBORETVM sign, past a
solitary lamp out in the open field, and down the path toward the
next one.

The shadow escapes through the tomb-filled hills rising in
front of him. Crooked mossy tombstones with crosses and snakes
around their inscriptions rise above him, threatening to crash
over him like waves. He steps on the fresh grass and climbs the
small hill. The shadow is still there, in the distance, maybe closer
now. As he walks downhill, he steps on something hard. He looks

165

down. Next to his foot, a name is carved in marble, and a picture of an old man smiles at him. He's reached the graveyard.

When he looks up, the ghost is gone.

You can see in the dark, like a pirate. The boy wishes he had his father's eye patch. He covers one eye before entering the dark. He walks along the yellow-lit grass, details fading as he moves further away from the lighted path. Soon it all turns to black. He takes a couple of extra steps and switches eyes. The closed one, accustomed to the dark, can see the grass. It's now a ghoulish dark blue.

Nate spots the dark figure crawling past some bushes. He sees the ghost's hunched back, its arms swinging back and forth, casting long shadows as it walks away from the yellow hue of the lamp, until it finally fades into the dark. Nate looks ahead and gasps: The ghost is walking toward the crypts.

He looks over his shoulder, craning his neck to see above the hill, but he can't see his house anymore. His breathing intensifies. *It's cold*, he thinks. *Maybe I should go back.* He looks again at the crypts.

The ghost has disappeared.

He remembers what his father told him. *When you want to find something, ignore it.* He looks to the side of where the ghost should be, and his peripheral vision finds it. It works! After a few seconds, the ghost fades out. He again looks at the other side of the ghost, and the shadow appears again. It walks into thin air and disappears. The boy blinks, blinks with all his might, and, like a series of moving pictures, the figure becomes clear again, clearer than ever, reaching forward with both arms now, walking on the grass.

The boy fights his trembling legs and follows it. He walks past the last lamp and gets closer to the crypts section, the miniature city, the blind windows that always stare at him. His hands shoot up to cover his eyes like a reflex, but he forces himself to keep them down. He clenches his fists and walks with his arms stuck to his sides. The light goes dim, and as he starts seeing the first alleys and monuments, the lights go dimmer and dimmer, and the ghost disappears again.

You can see in the dark, like a ninja. He looks at the ground ahead of him, memorizing it. He closes his eyes and squeezes them shut tightly. He paces, hands forward, ready to fall, and he notices he's in the same position as the ghost was. When he feels he's reached the darkness, he opens them again. His eyes still take time to adjust, but he can see the crypts now. An iron skeleton in a hood towers over him, leaning on a shovel.

Glass shatters, and a cold shiver runs through his spine. He runs inside, seeing the shiny pieces reflecting the moon on the floor ahead of him, and he runs through the narrow corridor. He follows her into a narrow alley, and an iron door creaks nearby.

The crypts seem empty, but he can't tell. The paths and alleys are pitch black. He squints with both eyes and walks softly along the tile floor. *You can see in the dark, like a ninja.* Next to him, glass windows stand out from the dark with their dim reflections, and the tiled floor becomes distinguishable from the black marble. He steps carefully, checking for loose or broken tiles.

An iron hinge twists, and out of the darkness, a hand reaches out for him. He runs off like hell, but not before something cold and hard hits him clumsily in the head.

He runs, and runs, and runs in the dark, unafraid of anything that may come ahead. Nothing can be as terrible as what's behind him.

There's a light at the end of the alley. Maybe past it. His legs outrun each other, each step becoming a long stride, and though his chest beats like a drum, he's never felt so light, so free of his own body, so free that he could fly. This is what he was born to do. He's not a ninja. He's a runner.

He runs past the last crypts and exits the alley, stepping on the grass again, and he keeps running toward the lamp, which he now can see is hanging from a gray wall. He reaches it, and touches it, and stops. He leans on the wall and looks around. He's never been this far away from his house. He's on the opposite side of the cemetery.

He looks back. The only way back home is through the crypts.

As he recovers his breath and his ears stop ringing, he hears something.

Music.

He turns around, scanning the grassy patch between the wall and the crypts. Empty.

His eyes search the crypts. The paths, the empty windows. Still. Silent. Terrifying.

The music is coming from outside.

And the music is happy. Angry, but happy. It doesn't make him afraid.

He walks along the wall toward the next lamp. There. A green door. It's half-covered in moss, with a rusty chain along its handlebar, secured with a combination padlock. He tries to peer through the cracks on each side. A street. Passing cars. The music is coming from a house with a red awning. There are people going inside.

His nervous fingers try a number in the padlock.

It springs open.

29

THE PLACE IS NOTHING LIKE SHE IMAGINED. *THIS* IS WHAT WAS so intimidating? *This* is the ultimate *adult* place in town? The red awning outside does REQUIEM no favors. Inside, the bar is cozy, warm, and friendly. The Ramones blast from the speakers, loud and distorted. Lilith's fingertips burn from her cigarette, and she puts it out. She smiles and takes another sip of her soda. *If there is an opposite of Grann's prophecy*, she thinks, *this must be it*.

The bartender looks at them, suspicious. He raises his voice over the music. "I haven't seen you guys before, have I?"

"First time," she says. Wolfram and Wednesday smile and nod, nervous.

"Are you sure you're OK?" he asks. "Folks know you're here?"

"Again, yes," Lilith says. "Thank you."

She takes another sip of her soda. Yes. This. This is the opposite. The opposite of what she's been doing every night, the opposite of staying home and meeting whatever fate she's supposed to meet tonight.

The song comes to a stop, and the bar sinks into silence. The jingling bells over the door announce a new customer's arrival.

"No way," the bartender says, staring at the door. "It's him!"

As the kick-drum starts the next song, Lilith looks around. "Who?"

"The freak," the barman says. "Hey, Hemlock, Arcana, remember that one I told you about?"

The couple in the next booth turns to look at the door, and Lilith follows their gaze. They all stare at the pale boy entering the bar, looking around like he's lost. He's wearing raggedy gray pajamas. Out in the street. In the cold. "Now, that's an entrance," Lilith says. "Who's that?"

"Some weirdo," says Hemlock.

Lilith smiles.

"I can't believe it," the barman says. "I told you he existed!"

Wolfram looks at the door and seems amused. He bolts up from his chair and walks over to him as Lilith and Wednesday share an awkward stare. Then he comes back, hugging the strange boy.

"Girls," he says, "this is Nate."

Nathan lifts his hand to wave an awkward hello. Lilith frowns with suspicion.

"Wednesday," says Wolfram, pointing at Wednesday. "Lucky," he adds, pointing at Lilith.

Nathan looks surprised. "Is that your name? Lucky?"

Lilith stares at him. This isn't supposed to happen. She left home. She tried to avoid it. Did she get it wrong?

"No," she says. "It's Lil."

"Oh," he says. "Why does he call you that?"

"It's a long story—"

"She can see the future," Wolfram says. His eyes brim with excitement. "And she got spooked by you."

"Well, speaking of the future," Lilith says, her gaze burning Nate's cheeks, "I'm not interested."

Wolfram can barely contain himself. "Whoa! So it's true?"

Nathan looks confused. "Not interested in what?"

"You," she says. "This."

Nathan stutters. "I ... I ... I just ..."

"Uh-oh," says Wolfram to Nate. "Looks like she saw you in one of her dreams." He turns to Lilith. "Why? Who is he? What did he do?"

Lilith looks down. "I don't know," she says. "I don't know him."

"Yes, you do," Wolfram teases her. "Come on. What? Some prophecy involving pajamas?"

Lilith turns to him, serious, and Wolfram explodes with laughter. "Oh my god! Really?"

The deafening beat of a drum stuns them. A new song starts.

"Come," Wednesday says, pulling Wolfram's hand. "I like this song. Let's dance."

They bounce toward the center of the small bar, twisting their hips as they go. The few people sitting in the booths nearby stand up and join them.

Nathan looks around, amused. "What is this music?"

She looks at him like he's an alien. "Did you just ask, '*What is this music?*'"

"Yes."

"It's one of the coolest bands in the world," she says. "The Ramones."

"Ramones," he says to himself, smiling. He turns to the small improvised dance floor. "Well, sorry to bother you," he calls over his shoulder as he joins the dancing crowd.

The drums boom in Lilith's chest, as if her own heartbeat is coming from the room. "Fuck it," she says, standing up and jumping into the growing swarm of moving people. She bumps into Wolfram and Wednesday, and the three dance together.

Wolfram turns around and begins scanning the small crowd.

"Stop it," Lilith shouts at him over the music.

"Stop what?" he asks without even turning to her. Lilith knows he's looking for the boy, and it won't take him long to spot him. His pajamas make him stand out in the crowd. Not to mention the pale face.

Wolfram jumps over next to Nathan, slamming up against him, hard. Nathan smiles at him awkwardly and keeps hopping.

"Leave him alone," Lilith says.

"So what's the deal?" Wolfram asks. "Why so pale, man? Don't get out much?"

"I don't know," Nate says, smiling an innocent smile. "I'm just pale."

Wednesday moves closer to him. "Where are you from?"

"Yeah," Wolfram adds. "Where are you from?"

The questions sound friendly, but Lilith knows Wolfram's mocking the poor guy. She elbows him in the ribs. "Stop it," she whispers.

"Around," Nate says.

"Oh, yeah? You live near the cemetery?"

Nate frowns. His jumping peters off. "Do I ... Do I *know* you?"

"Haven't seen you at school," Wolfram continues.

Wednesday slaps him in the back of his head. "Just ask him, you idiot."

"Leave him alone!" Lilith yells. "God. So much pressure to be the cool guy."

"OK, OK," says Wolfram, laughing, inhaling, ready to talk again.

Nathan stops jumping. His face becomes plain and serious, and he makes eye contact with Wolfram. "Did you lose somebody?"

Wolfram and Wednesday freeze on the spot. Wednesday is speechless. Wolfram looks at him wide-eyed. "Is he for real?" he asks.

"I mean it!" Lilith yells just as the song screeches to a stop, and she elbows him again.

Wolfram lets out a resounding *Ugh!* that alerts the barman to trouble brewing.

"All right, you kids," he says. "Fun is over. Out."

"No!" they plead. "Please!"

"Out. I won't say it again."

"No way!" Nathan yells, bouncing around once again as though the music never stopped. "Never! This is great!"

Lilith follows Wolfram and Wednesday toward the exit. As they walk outside, she grabs the door handle and takes a last look inside. The pale boy is still jumping up and down in complete silence, alone, as everyone stares at him.

As the barman walks up to him, Nate turns to Lilith and meets her gaze. And smiles.

The door chimes as it closes behind Lilith, and bursts open again a moment later.

"What a great place," the boy in the pajamas says, practically falling out the door.

Lilith is surprised to agree. It sure wasn't boring. "Yeah ... It is, isn't it?"

"Do you ... Do you live nearby?" he asks, rubbing his hands in the cold.

She looks at him funny. "Kinda. What about you?"

He seems tight-lipped. "Kinda."

There's an awkward silence as they both look straight ahead at the park.

"Well, bye," he says. He rubs his arms, looking deathly cold, and walks away.

"Weirdo's afraid of his own shadow," Wolfram says, watching after him. "Well, let's call it a night. Everything's closed, anyway."

"Wolfie," Lilith says. "I can't go home. Hang out with me a little longer."

"Why?" Wednesday asks. "Why can't you go home? What happens there?"

Lilith exhales. "I don't know. But I don't want to find out."

"So what's the problem?" Wednesday asks. "Home, Pajama Boy, what?"

"Not sure," Lilith says. "I don't remember exactly."

"Well, you gotta go home eventually," Wolfram says. "Just go. You'll tell us what happens tomorrow at school."

"Cowards," Lilith says, trying to decide which direction to

walk in to find someplace open this late at night, and deep down knowing the answer already. "Go. I'll manage."

Wolfram and Wednesday laugh. "Go home, weirdo," Wolfram calls out over his shoulder as they walk away.

Lilith stands on the cold sidewalk, then mindlessly crosses the street to the open park.

In the center, away from the prying park lights, a patch of darkness hides the ever-dependable swings. She only has to step one foot on soft grass of the park before the familiar screeching sounds of the swings' long metal chains reach her ears, and a few steps later the apparatus reveals itself to her against the dark night. The ground is mushy, and the smell of fresh grass is exhilarating. The music from the bar grows distant, and crickets take the night. The cold wind rocks the swings, or so she assumes—until she sees it. A figure, sitting still on her favorite swing. Her legs turn to stone.

As her eyes adjust to the dark, she notices the raggedy gray pajamas.

She looks back. The way home is clear. Her warm cozy bed waits for her. But what else is there? What else? Her mind swims with words she can't connect to one another. Haunted words, like *fingers, three-twelve,* and fucking *kaleidoscope eyes.* Who knows what they even mean? Who knows if they're even that bad?

And who knows what *good* things Grann left out?

Fuck it.

She approaches him.

Cheering fills the street. Music blares from military speakers wired to the streetlights. Gunshots echo around the tall buildings and up into the sky. People dance in the crowd, bumping against each other. Kenny has never seen a party like this. He follows Ron as he makes his way around the sea of people. The tall bodies give him shade, but the scorching air inside the mass of people, the heat coming from the collective human blob that they're forming, only makes the suffocation worse. His suit is warm and wet, and it sticks to him as he walks. The sole of his boot sticks to a newspaper that reads "The Dead Walk."

Hovering over him, Kenny sees glimpses of faces—tired, joyful, drunk, pissed, relieved. Some revelers hold flares, waving them around over their heads, their pink and red smoke making the path even murkier. Kenny coughs. People kick him and push him around. The street is littered with empty cans and food. People hold painted steel pipes. Bats with nails on them. Water guns filled with strange dark fluids. A girl is wearing a DO NOT RESUSCITATE T-shirt. Another one reads WELCOME TO THE RAPTURE.

Yoshi's voice comes from somewhere inside the crowd.

"They've had time to make T-shirts and everything? Where were we?"

The girl hears him and turns around. "I had it before zombies were cool," she yells with a smug tone.

"This is it?" asks Yoshi, disappointed, from somewhere inside the crowd. "This is what we've been missing out on?" he asks. "These morons?"

"We got six more *walkers*," Ron's voice comes from above. He leans into the word *walkers*, savoring it.

"Whoo," another voice comes back as a response. "Six more *walkers*!"

The word carries through the crowd. "Six *walkers*? Cool!" Voices underline the word as if it's some kind of code. As it passes around, others call them *zombies*. *Zeds*. *Pus Bags*. *Deadites*. *Biters*. *Stenchers*. *Munchers*. *Shamblers*. It's a competition. They look at each other, gauging their reactions, trying to come up with the cleverest name for them.

Up ahead, Kenny sees an opening in the crowd. A bright spot of fresh air. An area where the sun still shines on the pavement, clear of people. He opens his mouth to let the air in. The air is hot, and he tries to slip between the warm limbs blocking his way. Yes. There is a patch of sunny, fresh, empty street, leading to a massive pile of dead bodies up ahead. He swims toward it, squeezing his arms and legs as the crowd pushes on with its scorching current. He crawls past his friends, getting glimpses of them in between arms and legs, and pushes on.

He stretches his leg forward and feels it hovering in the air, untouched by any people. He puts his foot down on the asphalt and, pushing out of the crowd, he slowly emerges from the sea of people, constrained only by the polyester sticking to his body. The cloud of pink dissipates. He savors the fresh air as the beads of sweat falling down his face start to feel cooler. He's standing on a small patch of empty pavement, the intersection of two streets. Next to him, he sees Nate, who is followed by Ron and the boys.

Ron looks up and whistles. "It's bigger than this morning!"

Kenny turns to the towering pile of dead bodies in front of them. It stretches across the entire street and reaches the third-story windows of the buildings around them.

"Whoa," Nate says. "What's that?"

"A bonfire!" says Ron. "*The* bonfire. Where have you been? Once we done roundin' them up, we'll light it up and enjoy the barbecue!"

Also standing in this clearing are a group of six or seven Slayers, who shoot at the dead with endless amusement, aiming for the heads and faces, not keeping count of the bullets. They *whoop* and they *yeehaw* and they *yesssuh* with each bloody explosion.

The gunshots echo through Kenny's wiry frame. Jittery, he looks around for a pathway through the crowd, but his eyes keep returning to that pile. That evil, disgusting pile.

A beer can flies by and hits a guy in the head, who jerks and turns, ready to fight. But when he sees the can, he laughs. He fires two shots toward the sky. "Woohoo! Yeah!"

"Watch out," says someone, "Ghoul coming through!"

Kenny steps aside just as three men walk past him carrying a dead body. They walk toward the pile and throw it toward the ever-growing heap.

"So," Nate asks Ron, also looking at the pile. "Who can I ask about a car?"

"A car?" a woman's voice asks. She's in her fifties, chubby, and looks like she hasn't skipped smoking and drinking a day in her life. Her chubby arms are filled with prison tattoos of eagles and flags, the greenish ink fading into a sickish hue. The people who surround her are drunk, like everybody else, but make an effort to listen carefully to whatever she says.

"*Today* of all days, you need a car?" she asks.

Ron laughs. People around them start laughing.

"He wants to go find his *girlfriend*," Yoshi says.

Nate moves him aside. "I know how to stop all this. And I need a car."

The woman takes a step forward and looks him in the eye.

Kenny notices the gun hanging from her belt swaying back and forth. He sees Nate's eyes drop to it as well, but without any hesitation, Nate raises his gaze back to looking her square in the eyes. She spits on the floor and sizes him up.

A halo of silence envelops them. People stop laughing and form a circle around the pair. Lester is very still. Even Yoshi has stopped smirking. Neither Nate nor the woman change their stances. Kenny starts to feel the sun burning his shoulders.

The woman is the first to break the silence. "If you're talking about the virus ..."

"This isn't a virus," Nathan says.

"Oh, isn't it?" she says, amused. "Then how come my *Mr. University* guy tells me—"

"I don't have time for this," says Nate, unimpressed. "I need to get to Leatelranch."

The people around step forward, ready to jump in and defend her. Nathan doesn't flinch. There's a cold disgust in his upper lip. Without taking his eyes off her, he says, "I'd suggest you all back away."

She seems amused. She raises her hand to stop them. She tilts her head and smiles. There's a tattoo of a Confederate flag on the back of her neck.

"Sure, Mr. Savior," she says, breaking the stare down and striding away. "I'll get you a car. Come with me."

Kenny looks at Yoshi, who looks at Lester. They all raise their eyebrows in surprise.

"What?" Nate asks them as they scurry behind her.

"You looked tough," Kenny says. "Like, not afraid at all."

"It was starting to look like you had no balls at all," Yoshi says.

Nathan hasn't looked this serious all day. "I'm not afraid of *people*," he says.

The boys share another look. "Badass," Lester says.

As the woman walks past a subway station entrance, two people come running up onto the street from below and run toward her. Kenny spasms at the unexpected invasion. "Mrs. Momma! Mrs. Big Momma!" they yell.

Nathan looks at Ron. "*She's* in charge of all this?"

Ron looks him in the eye apologetically. "I know, a woman, right? But don't worry, she's cool."

"That's not what I meant—" Nathan starts to say, and his face turns to a scowl.

Kenny doesn't like the look on his face. "What?"

Nathan turns his head slowly, looking around, and his face transforms. Kenny tries to follow his gaze.

"Gun nuts," Nate says under his breath, describing the scene around him. "Idiots. KKK. MAGA morons. Frustrated losers. Pre-teen gamers. Doomsday preppers. Religious nuts. Rapture enthusiasts. People who *couldn't wait* for the world to end." He exhales. "*These* are the zombie fans."

Ron turns around. "What? You say something?"

"No," says Nate, still calm.

A red Make America Great Again hat drops on Yoshi's head. He takes it off, looks at it, and throws it away. "*They* did this?" he asks. "*They* killed the zombies?"

"Something's off here," Nate says.

"Relax, man," Ron says. "We won!"

Ron and the subway men follow the woman as she walks toward another yellow barricade that separates the crowd from another empty street. Nathan and the boys follow them, and Kenny tries to keep up. But his itchy suit has grown so sweaty and constrictive, he can barely walk anymore. He looks at Lester in his bright blue polyester suit, and Yoshi, worse, in his leathery body suit. "Aren't you guys hot?"

They seem to think about it. "I'm OK," says Lester.

Yoshi looks at him in disgust. "What, little girl can't handle being outside?"

Lester smiles sympathetically. "Don't worry, Kenny. We're safe here."

A group of armed pimpled teens leans on the yellow barricade, having a heated argument. They're red-faced, each holding a can of beer in one hand and a gun in the other.

"*Call of Duty: Zombies* was the best," says the one with a swastika tattoo on his arm.

"Shut up!" says a girl dressed like an elf, "It doesn't hold a candle to *The Last of Us*."

Big Momma points beyond the barricade. The street outside is littered with burnt cars, trash, broken suitcases. In the distance, there's a faint sound of dogs barking.

"That way," she says. "Pick any car you like. I think you should be clear all the way up to Leatelranch. Keep us posted on your arrival. And let us know how the roads are." She lets out a horrible doglike laugh.

Nathan seems confused. He looks around, and Kenny follows his gaze. Something moves in the distance, but it looks like it's more of those ghouls, wandering around.

"But, do you have keys or something?" Nathan asks.

"Keys!" she laughs. "Listen, sonny ..." and she interrupts herself in an explosion of laughter. "Keys! Har, har har."

Kenny is afraid to ask. "What's the matter, Mr. Nate?"

"The KKK just took my baby away," he says under his breath.

"I thought you were supposed to find your girlfriend here," Kenny says. "What's so urgent now about going to that Leatel-ranch place?"

"Wherever she is," Nate says, looking around, "she's safer if I get there and stop this madness. And she's probably better off not coming with me."

"Is that true?" Kenny whispers to him. "Can you really stop all this?"

Nathan's mind seems to wander. He starts to nod slowly, but his face turns worried. Sour. Suddenly, he looks like a scared little boy.

Kenny takes this as a *yes*. Nothing that scary would be an option if it wouldn't save the world. He puts on his serious face, trying to appear grown up. "Then we'll get to that place, Leatel-ranch, one way or another," he says.

Nathan smiles and pats him on the shoulder. "Thanks, kid." His hand feels scalding hot on Kenny's already sweaty shoulder.

"Look," Big Momma says, "one of our teams is away with the bus. I guess after today, our work is done here. So, you can probably take it."

"Really?" asks Nate.

She smirks. "I reckon buses are about to become dirt cheap. And the city's almost clean, anyway."

"Thank you," says Nate, on the verge of tears.

"More *walkers*!" Someone yells.

"Good," the pimple-faced teen says. "More shooting practice. Hey, is that a mime?"

In the middle of the street, a group of ghouls slowly shambles its way toward them. They are spearheaded by a scrawny man in heavy white makeup, his jaw hanging loose. There is a large bite missing from his neck, and his cheeks and upper lip, still attached to his face, are unusually red.

"Nah, he's just a dead man," says the girl in an elf costume. "That's mortuary makeup, probably."

"Bah," says the boy. "Boring."

Big Momma raises her hand and points at the group.

"Yeah, yeah," the boy says, aiming his gun. "We never get any mimes."

"Well," another teenager says, getting ready to aim, "look behind him. The she-hulk. That woman's completely green. What's up with that?"

"Yeah," the girl says, "and hey, isn't that the guy from the news?"

An icy, familiar shiver runs through Kenny's spine.

31

KENNY STARES, PETRIFIED, AS THE SHAMBLING GHOULS GET closer. They're less than half a block away, and he can already see their faces. On the right—*Yes, definitely him*—his father alternates between walking like a zombie, arms forward, gaze lost, and looking straight at Kenny with a hint of a grin. Kenny looks at the teenagers next to him, pointing their guns at his dad, and feels a horrible relief.

"Wait!" Ron says, turning to the kids. Something in his hands shines with the sun, and the reflection slices across Kenny's eyes. Ron smiles. "You kids ever shoot a gun?"

"Just go on and shoot," Nathan barks at Ron, taking a step toward Kenny. "This isn't a game, and we're not psychos—"

"I wanna try!" Yoshi interrupts him.

Kenny can't believe what's happening. "What?"

"Don't do it," Lester says to Yoshi.

"It's real easy," Ron says, taking a step past Nate. He hands Yoshi the gun. "Just aim for the head, and go to town on the bastards!"

Kenny's heart is about to burst. "Guys!"

As the ghouls get closer, Yoshi takes the gun and examines it.

Ron holds him by the shoulders and positions him behind the barricade. "Just point and shoot."

Lester takes a step toward Yoshi. "Yoshi," he says, "don't."

Kenny screams. His father, and the rest of the ghouls, are getting closer. "Yes, Yoshi, do it, please, just do it!"

Yoshi squeezes the trigger. Kenny covers his ears too late, deafened by the shot, and hears the bullet ricocheting off one of the burned-out cars several feet away from the still-advancing ghouls. The sun must be playing tricks on Kenny's eyes, because his father seems to wink at him.

Two of the pimple-faced boys get ready to make a move. Ron quietly signals them to stand down and turns to Yoshi again. "Go on, son."

Yoshi shoots again. Next to the green-skinned woman, closer this time, the windshield of a car shatters to pieces.

The Slayers laugh. "We're lucky those fuckers are slow!" Big Momma jokes.

Yoshi tries again. This time, the dead woman jolts back, and a burst of green blood gushes out of her shirt. Her green flesh, torn to pieces by the bullets, flies in the air.

"Yes!" Yoshi yells, and the pimple-faced teens hoist their cans in the air.

But the green woman keeps coming. Behind her, the others keep following her.

The Slayers laugh. "The head, idiot! Shoot the head!"

Kenny notices Nate alternately glancing at him with pity and at the Slayers with contempt. They grin proudly, oblivious to Nate's glare or simply not giving a shit.

"Don't pay attention to these psychopaths," Nathan says to Yoshi, putting his hand on his shoulder. "They're cowards. They wanted to kill people before, they just didn't have the guts. They had to wait for an apocalypse. They're fucking pussies, Yoshi. Don't you be a fucking pussy."

A burst of gunshots burns the air, and the green woman is cut in half, both parts of her falling heavily to the pavement. Behind her, the standing ghouls get showered with bullets. A head explodes. Mr. Macomber's shoulder gets ripped to shreds, and a single, final bullet hits him right in the middle of the forehead.

He slumps to the ground.

Kenny holds his breath. A puffy cloud of smoke shrouds the group of zombies. Nothing seems to move inside, but the smoke is so thick, Kenny wonders if he'd be able to notice any movement.

One of the teenagers burps. Still holding his assault weapon, he turns to Yoshi and raises his eyebrows, pointing his chin to the clearing smoke. The green woman's torso crawls along the pavement, trying, weakly, to stand up with her hands.

"I fixed it for ya, kid," the teenager says. "She ain't movin' anymore. Just finish her off in the head."

Kenny looks at the torso trying to get up. Behind him, inside the dissipating cloud of smoke, his father's body lies on the ground, lifeless. Still. He exhales, relieved. "Dad."

Yoshi gives the teenager a snarky look. "I wasn't aiming for the walking ghouls," he says. "It's just—This thing is heavier than I thought."

He raises the gun, pointing high above, and he shoots again. Something, a round thing hanging from the power cables over the street, spins around.

Big Momma steps forward and leans over the yellow barricade. "I'll be damned," she says. "You got it! You got ... What is that?"

A girl steps forward, squinting her eyes. "Looks like a white balloon."

The balloon stops spinning and starts a slow swinging motion. It's hanging from a thread tied to the cable.

"It's a head!" Ron says.

Kenny squints. Yes, it's definitely a head. And he sees its face. It's a pale, dead face, with a hole where one of the eyes used to be. Gun-smoke is coming out of the hole.

Ron turns to Big Momma, ecstatic. He pats her back. "Motherfucker!" He says. "A friggin' head! Did you do that? Did you hang that up there?"

Big Momma looks puzzled. "No," she says.

"Looks pretty fresh, too," Ron adds. "That thing ain't been dead for more than a day or two."

"Well, don't look at me," she says. "Wait. We've been here since yesterday. You mean to tell me that's been here the whole time?"

"Hey," the pimpled girl says, "that TV guy's still standing!"

Kenny's heart skips a beat. He kneels below the yellow barrier to get a closer look. The green woman's torso keeps crawling her way to them. Behind her, as the smoke clears, a few bodies still stand and walk. Among them, sure enough, is his father. He's bloody, but less rotten than the others. He looks almost clean. Almost alive. He's smiling. His eyes are wide open. He picks up the pace and looks down, locking eyes with Kenny. "Hello, son!"

Kenny's body freezes.

Big Momma doesn't look so smug anymore. "Hey, guys?!" she shouts back at the crowd. "We need some backup here!"

Behind them, the block party hasn't noticed a thing. The music is loud, and under the current circumstances, the sound of the groups' recent spate of gunshots wouldn't have sounded out of the ordinary.

"Bus is coming," someone yells cheerfully in the crowd.

Yoshi shoots again. Mr. Macomber still trudges heavily, grinning, closer and closer, as the ghouls next to him get pumped with bullets.

"C'mon!" Lester yells. "You're doing that on purpose!"

"I'm not!" Yoshi says. "My hand's trembling!"

"Guys ..." Kenny pleads.

Mr. Macomber is getting closer. Out of the cloud of smoke now, in plain daylight, they can see his bloody clothes and his crazy determined eyes unflinchingly fixed on Kenny. His thick black glasses hang crooked from his face.

"Kenny," Nathan yells, "run back!"

Kenny can't move. He just watches as the ghoul's shadow towers over him, blocking the sun.

Lester swoops past him, takes Yoshi's gun from his hands, and slides past the yellow barrier. He jumps Mr. Macomber from the back, clings to his neck, and hits him in the head with the gun. Mr. Macomber raises his arms to grab him, but a second jab from Lester cracks his skull, and the gun plunges deep inside his head, splattering green blood and brains all over Lester's hand.

Mr. Macomber's body falls to the ground. Lester rides him all the way down, stabbing and hitting him in a violent frenzy.

"Ouch!" he yells when his knees hit the pavement, but he keeps swinging his arms up and down, digging inside the hollow bowl that is now Mr. Macomber's head, yelling in rage. Then he gets up. He kicks Kenny's father in the head, and then the ribs, and then his ass. Kenny watches in silence as Lester finally steps back, trembling, and sits down next to him. They both stare at Mr. Macomber's body as a pool of green blood crawls slowly toward them.

"Austin!" Yoshi yells, walking toward Lester and patting him on the back. "You did it! Are you OK?"

Lester shudders. He looks at a tear in his blue Victorian suit and tries to put it back together. He looks back at Mr. Macomber. "Ugh," he says. "They're ... naked. You can see the death all inside them. They're ... we're ... so fragile."

Kenny sniffles. His eyes are watery.

Yoshi crawls toward the body, and he silently picks up Mr. Macomber's thick black glasses. He walks up to Lester.

"Don't," Nate says.

Yoshi puts the glasses on Lester's face, who just stares at him, motionless, still breathing heavily, clenching his teeth.

"One of these days you'll get a beating," Nate says, as Lester stares into Yoshi's eyes, looking exactly like Austin Powers.

A group of Slayers picks up Mr. Macomber. Sniffing, crying, half-scared and half-relieved, Kenny watches as they drag him away and throw him on the pile.

"Should we burn them?" Ron asks. "I think we should start burnin' em."

"Not yet," Big Momma says.

"Why not? What are we waiting for?"

Big Momma turns around to face him. "Are you questioning my orders?"

Ron steps back. "I just want to know," he says.

"First we pile 'em, then we burn 'em," she says. "Once this starts smoking, it's gonna be harder to move around."

"That's why you're the boss," Ron says.

Lester puts his hand on Kenny's shoulder. "He can't hurt you anymore, Ken."

Kenny hugs him. His face burns, and he starts to cry.

32

Wolfram knocks on the iron door with his ring and turns to Lilith. "See? You *can* parkour after all."

Panting, sweating, leaning on her knees, Lilith looks up. "Fuck you."

He knocks again. *Knock. Knock knock knock—Knock. Knock.* Nothing.

"What is that?" asks Lilith. "Morse code?"

Wolfram doesn't respond. He tries again. *Knock. Knock knock knock—Knock. Knock.*

Nothing.

He turns to Lilith, wide-eyed.

She says it first. "Maybe they're—?"

A hollow mechanism turns inside the door. It reminds Lilith of submarine movies. The door unlocks. As it opens, a voice comes from inside. "Wolfram!"

The door opens, and Wednesday jumps up from inside, hugging Wolfram. She looks at Lilith.

"Who's ...?" Her eyes open wide. "Lilith?" She turns to Wolfram. "What's she doing here?"

"Hi, Wednesday," says Lilith, forcing a smile.

Wolfram looks around at the city's flickering lights, and the dark shadows looking back at them. "Let's go inside."

They enter an old concrete stairwell. Wednesday closes the huge door behind them and turns the cogs and levers. It *clanks* shut like a bank vault.

Their steps echo in the concrete tube as they take turn after turn down gray steps lit by dim yellow gas lamps. Finally, they reach a bullet-shaped arch that welcomes them to the main hall.

"So this is how it looks from the inside," Lilith says.

The police station reminds her of an old church. She hasn't seen this kind of architecture in years. It just doesn't exist in New Southport. The place looks old and dusty, but it's only because of the concrete. Modern lighting and only a few pieces of furniture make it actually clean, Zen-like. The front door is closed shut with the same iron mechanism as the one in the rooftop. In the back, there's an office where a dozen officers hunch over a table and work hastily on something. There is an old-style elevator, the kind that looks like a black iron cage, in the middle of the hall. And there is a front desk facing the entrance. A young-looking officer sits behind it.

And there's something off about him.

The guy is sitting still. Too still. Still as a bug. His fake lively eyes open a bit too much and don't blink.

He notices her.

Lilith gasps. He tips his hat and smiles at her. His eyelids slide down unnaturally, slowly, like slugs on a sticky surface, and stay closed for just a bit longer than usual. It's like he's remembering how to blink.

She freezes before her foot lands on the next step, spreading out her arms to stop Wolfram and Wednesday.

A tall imposing man enters the hall followed by two officers. It's Wednesday's father, Mr. Girardot. The chief of police. He notices Lilith, Wolfram, and Wednesday up on the stairs. There's not a hint of a smile on his chubby face. His lips are a flat line underlining his thick gray mustache.

"I take it your folks didn't make it," he says to Wolfram, and his mustache moves along with every word. "I'm sorry."

He looks at Lilith. "Lilith Kane," he says, and he approaches her with arms wide open.

Lilith looks like a deer caught in headlights. She peers at the impostor officer at the front desk. He's giving her a cold look. She wants to say something, but she can't move her mouth. She's paralyzed.

"Chief," the man at the front desk shouts, standing up, "She's one of 'em!" He raises his arm, his hand holding a gun, but his head is blown away by a loud bang. The body slumps on the old wooden chair, making a squeaking sound.

With his gun still pointing at the ghoul, Mr. Girardot turns to Lilith, puzzled. "You can spot them." It's a declaration, not a question.

The two officers behind him run to the corpse, grab him by the arms, and drag him to the front door. His shirt collar slides, revealing a small, clean incision in the back of his neck.

"You saw that, too?" Lilith asks him as Wednesday runs down the stairs.

Mr. Girardot holsters his gun. "I'm chief of police," he says, just before Wednesday jumps to hug him. He hugs her back and grabs her face. "You OK?"

She nods.

The officers each take a handle on each side of the door, turn them heavily to unlock them, and toss the body outside. They close the door and turn the handles again and walk swiftly to the back office. They bring three gas masks. They give one to Mr. Girardot and put on the other ones.

"All right, listen up," Mr. Girardot yells, holding his mask. His voice echoes around the hall, and everyone stops what they're doing. "Something's coming," he says, and somehow the silence becomes heavier. "Since the beginning of this ordeal, all police and military stations have arranged a heartbeat signal every five minutes. As you might know, many dropped on the first day and second day. But some remained stable. We holed up. But for the past couple of hours, each of the remaining stations from New Southport to here has been dropping, one by one."

People look around at each other. Some of them stare at the gas mask in the chief's hands.

"Shit," Lilith sighs. "Nate."

"This elevator," Mr. Girardot says, pointing to the metal cage, "will take you to our safe room, where you'll find gas masks, like this one. You will use them, effective now. There's enough food and supplies to last us months. It's gonna be crowded, but we *will* manage to have an orderly, quiet wait until this blows over. Any questions?"

The hall is a tomb.

"The rest of us will join you downstairs in a moment," he adds. "Go."

The people closest to the elevator fill it to capacity, and with a noisy electric surge, they disappear into the ground.

As Lilith climbs down the stairs, Mr. Girardot walks up to her. He hands her his gas mask.

"You, follow me," he says, walking toward the back office.

She looks at the people waiting for the elevator. Wolfram's already queuing, looking around for Wednesday.

"How're the folks?" Mr. Girardot asks Lilith, and she starts walking to catch up to him.

She examines the gas mask. "Dead."

He stops for a second and keeps going. "I'm sorry," he says. "Any kids? Family?"

"Me. I'm their only—"

He turns to her, serious.

"Oh, you mean me," she says. She blows a raspberry. "God, no."

He looks surprised.

"I mean, no, Mr. Girardot."

He puts on his mask. "Around here, please call me Chief."

He takes two other masks and hands them to the guys hunched over a large poster of some kind spread across the desk. When Lilith gets closer, she sees it's an old hand-drawn blueprint with gothic markings and legends. CREMATORIVM. ARBORETVM. MAVSOLEVM. NECROPOLIS. COMPLETORIVM. Scattered across its face are miniature police cars, tanks, tiny metal soldiers.

Wednesday enters, brushing past Lilith. "Papa, what's going on?"

"Later," Mr. Girardot says, joining the huddle over the blueprints. "For now, please, just put on your mask and join the others."

"And what about Lilith?" Wednesday asks.

The chief looks at Lilith. "She spotted one of 'em. Maybe she can help us with the siege."

"But, Dad ..."

He turns around and grabs her by the shoulders, looking deep into her eyes. "Peanut. We'll be safe here. Doors are sealed, they sure built things to last back in the plague days. But just in case, you need to go downstairs. Now."

Wednesday looks into his eyes through the mask, worried, but if her concern stirs any reaction in him, he doesn't reveal an ounce of it. She turns to Lilith, then looks at the table, which only makes her more confused. "If she's staying, I'm staying."

"Yeah," says Wolfram, making his way into the office.

The chief takes a deep breath, allowing it.

Lilith still looks down at the mask in her hand, puzzled. "My boyfriend's still out there."

"Speak of the devil," he replies, looking back at the map with the layout of the cemetery.

"I need to get to him," she adds.

He hunches back over the table. "First things first."

"Look," she asks, still examining the mask, "whatever's coming, why do you think it's in the *air*?"

He exhales deeply and looks her in the eye. In that second,

the image she'd always held of him as the ultimate tough adult in control vanishes, replaced by that of a scared and fragile man.

"This afternoon," he says with a defeated tone in his voice, "just before the signals started to drop ... the fucking morons burnt a whole heap of them."

33

A shriek of feedback pierces through the air, and Kenny has to cover his ears. A voice comes through the speakers. Sober. Serious.

"Ladies and gentlemen, this is a broadcast from HQ: I have an announcement to make."

Silence. A throat clears. Nate and Ron look at each other.

"Oh, hell, I'll just say it: WE WON!"

People explode in celebration, and Ron throws his arms in the air like Rocky.

Nate frowns. This is all too easy.

The speakers continue, and the cheers slowly die out.

"War is over. OVER! Ghouls are easy to kill with a blow or shot to the head, and our contacts worldwide are all telling us that the cleanup phase has almost begun. The worldwide undead uprising will be over in a matter of hours. So, for fuck's sake, celebrate! Go mankind!"

"Not quite the Independence Day speech, but it'll do," says Nate to the guy next to him. He raises his arms in celebration. The other guy gives him a thumbs-up and takes a sip of beer.

"I am giving the green light to start the bonfires. Let's light these sumbitches up!"

"Yes!" yells Ron. He walks down the metro station steps to

help two other Slayers lug a military-green suitcase and a gas can up to the street. Others follow with more gas cans.

Nate looks at them, pop-eyed. "Is that gas? We've been standing on a stash of gas cans?"

"Relax," Ron says as they lug them to the base of the pyre, "It's not like they're smart enough to light it."

He heaves the large can of gas and starts spraying the corpses. The others spread and do the same. Each one empties their can and makes way for the next one until the bodies at the bottom are drenched, their hair and clothes saturated, and a puddle of gas starts to spread around the pile, making everyone take a few steps back.

Ron opens the military suitcase and takes out some flares.

"Ok!" he yells, "This one's for America!"

Lester presses his hospital mask tightly against his mouth and nose. He looks at Nate and the boys, his eyes pleading for them to do the same.

"OK," Nate says. "OK."

Lester reaches into his pocket and gives Nathan a mask. Then he offers masks to Yoshi and Kenny, and they all put them on. Finally, he offers one to Ron, who takes it without looking, still checking around to make sure everyone's stepping back. He puts it on without a second thought.

Ron starts a flare and throws it to the left of the pile. He starts another one and throws it to the right. Another one, center. Another one, left. Another one, center.

Kenny looks at the fire. It starts to spread. He searches for his father's corpse among the others. His cracked head sticks out. He looks like he's sleeping, mouth slightly open. The flames start to lick his face. They spread. They cover him, eat his face. He's engulfed in the fire now. And for a second, just for a second, his eye springs open and stares right at Kenny. All that is happening and all that has happened can be summed up for Kenny in that white fiery eye. It strains like a fist and, just as suddenly as it opened, it closes again.

Kenny points at it and turns to his friends. "Did you see—?"

His mouth lingers on the words. He looks around and suddenly feels alone in the middle of a dancing crowd. People cheer. Guns are raised to the sky in victory. Smoke from red and pink flares curls its way up into the air, hiding the crowd in a fog that grows thicker and thicker. He can't find his friends.

He turns back to where his father lays sleeping, being eaten by the flames.

Lester appears through the mist. He hugs Kenny, and they watch the fire burn together. "Death is not the end," he says, trying to comfort his friend.

"Oh, shut up," Kenny says. He's heard it a thousand times. He stares at his father's body as it burns. "Do you think they could be *playing dead?*" he asks. "Letting us think we won?"

"Pff," Lester scoffs. "Why'd they do that?"

"I don't know."

"Well," Yoshi says, "If they *were* playing dead, it *would* be impossible for us to know."

Behind them, people are dancing. A drunk ginger-haired teenager gets pushed out of the group next to them. He raises his arm, shoots Mr. Macomber in the forehead, and jumps back into the party. Kenny opens his eyes wide and looks at his father's corpse. It doesn't move. The face starts to burn and melts under the fire.

Pillars of black smoke rise as far as the eye can see.

34

SITTING ON HIS SWING, TEENAGE NATHAN CAN'T HELP BUT stare at Lilith. She propels herself upward into the night sky, her hair flowing behind her, and as she swings back, she's smiling like a little child. He looks up and imagines himself flying, like her.

"Aren't you cold in those?" she asks as she swings by, looking at his pajamas.

He looks down. He forgot he was wearing them. "I don't care, I guess."

She swings by again. She seems impressed. "Too cool to care, huh? Swing! Come on!"

His feet are anchored to the beaten patch of dirt under his swing. Squeezing the iron chains, he tries falling back, carefully, and lifts his feet off the ground. The short sway forward catches him off guard, and he clenches his hands until they hurt. She, and her hair, swing by.

"What's your favorite zombie movie?" she asks, looking up at the sky.

He seems confused. "Oh," he says. "movies. I know what you mean. I haven't seen them yet."

As she swings by, she glances at him like he's an alien. "What do you mean?" she says, shooting back up toward the night sky. "Zombies! The dead coming back to life? Braains?!"

She reaches the summit again, and she seems to be looking to the side, trying to see past the tall wall.

He tries to propel himself forward. It doesn't work. "Oh," he says.

"Yeah. What do you like? Campy, gore, terror, thriller..?"

"I guess ... I guess I don't know any. My father doesn't want me to get myself distracted by things like that."

She buries her feet on the ground, stopping almost immediately as the ground crunches. "You live in Leatelranch, and you don't know any zombie movies? It's the living dead, dude!"

"Well—"

"Do you, by the way?" she asks, launching herself upward again. "Do you live here? I've never seen you at school."

He nods toward the wall. If it weren't there, he could see the first crypts already looking back at him. "There," he says. "I live there."

"Yeah, right," she says, chuckling. "That means we're neighbors!"

"Huh," he says, trying to look away from the wall. He can hear the chains of her swing squeaking behind him, coming and going, like a pendulum. The squeaking slows down.

When he turns to her, she's staring right back at him, mouth open. Her eyes dash left and right, looking for a way out of here.

"Wait," she asks. "Are you ... dead?"

He chuckles. "I'm not one of them, you idiot!" he says and laughs. "I really do *live* in there. My father's the caretaker."

Her face transforms from fear into mad, burning interest. "No!"

"Yes."

She's not blinking. "No!"

"Yes," he says.

"That's so cool."

"Clearly you've never been inside."

"No," she says. "Never."

He thinks about it. "It's true," he says. "I don't think I've ever seen you in there, either. How come?"

Her mouth tenses as she stares at him.

"You've never lost anybody yet?" he asks.

She looks away. When she turns back to him, he can tell she hates him for asking.

"My Grann. I was young." She blurts it out like the words were burning her insides. "Here we were, talking nicely about zombies, and you have to come and bring up death."

"Sorry," he says.

"It's OK," she says. "Actually, it's very OK. She foretold something for tonight, but it looks like it's not happening. So it's good. It's all good."

"Really?" he asks.

She laughs nervously and snorts. "Never mind. I know you don't believe me."

"No, really. What did she say?"

"Can't help you there. It was mostly gibberish."

"So how do you know if it happened or not?"

"Well," she says, "I have, like, *keywords*. Believe me, I'd notice if I saw it."

"Cool."

"You don't believe me," she says. "I don't care."

"It's a confusing life," he says. He exhales. "I've seen things, too. And you should hear the things my father has to say."

"Anyway," she says. "I'd *kill* to live in there. Be the first line of defense against the zombie horde, you know?" She swings both arms and mimics hitting something in front of her.

"Wow," he says, looking at the stars to let himself process it. "You ... You laugh at them."

"It's an escape," she says. "If you don't laugh at them, you let them get to you, right?"

"I wish I could do that," he says. "But they scare me too much."

"Nah," she says. "Movies today have become shit. Zombies are not scary anymore."

"I told you. I haven't seen any movies. I mean *them*."

She frowns. She seems confused.

"And the way they smell," he continues. "I still have the stench in my mouth."

Her face hardens. "What."

He looks down at the ground. "Earlier tonight. One of those, how did you call them ...?"

She's stopped blinking again. "No," she says. Her mouth stays an open O.

"Yes," he exhales.

"*You* saw a zombie."

"Yes," he says. "Maybe. I don't know. I don't know *what* it was."

She grabs his hand. Her mouth is still open. "Well," she says, "I wouldn't worry. Sure, it would be cool. But it was probably just someone sneaking in or some boring shit like that."

He chuckles. "Sneaking in? Have you seen how tall those walls are?"

She explores the wall as far as she can see. "I bet I could sneak in through one of the doors, if I wanted to."

"No, you couldn't."

"Yes, I could."

"Anyway, forget about it—"

She raises her voice. "Forget about it?! You're kidding, right?" she asks, already starting to look excited.

He turns around and looks at the cemetery gate. "Anyway, I should go back," he says. "Father might notice I'm missing."

She follows his gaze to the wall. "Nah. Stay here," she says. "Look at these beautiful stars."

"I can see them from inside, too, you know," he says.

"Or I could join you," she says, still gazing at the walls. "Just so you're not scared. I'll kill those zombies for you." She laughs.

His heart skips a beat. "Really? You wanna come?"

She giggles nervously. "What?"

"You could come," he says, "just for a minute. I'd feel safer if you come and show me this isn't so serious. You seem immune to it."

Her laughter stops. She looks deep into his eyes. "You really are scared of it, aren't you?"

"Yes."

She laughs again. "Why? You know, in most movies, you can kill them with just a blow to the head. And they can't even catch you, they're so slow. At least in most movies. The good ones."

He looks at her as if she's magic. "I still can't believe you laugh at them."

She laughs out harder. "And you don't mind telling this to a girl?"

His cheeks suddenly burn. "What do you mean? Anybody can be scared."

Her eyes twinkle as she looks into his eyes. "You're just so cool. Everyone around here is always *trying* to be cool. And here you are, in your pajamas, not giving a shit, telling me how scared you are. There's not a bullshit bone in your body, isn't there? Now *that's* cool."

Nathan is so excited he's almost afraid he's wagging the back of his swing like a dog's tail. "So," he asks, standing up, fueled by this sudden surge of courage, "does this mean you want to come inside?"

Her laughter stops all of a sudden. "I'd love to," she says. "But I can't."

"Why?"

She looks away. "I gotta stay outside. The heart wants what the heart wants," she jokes.

"You're scared, too, huh?"

She stops dancing in her swing. "Well, I can't just up and *go* into the cemetery in the middle of the night, right?" She snorts with laughter.

"Sure you can," he says. "I'll let you in."

She looks annoyed. "Look," she says, "I'm not following a complete stranger into a fucking cemetery, OK, wacko?"

"You know where I live. You just said it. We're neighbors."

She looks down at the ground. She seems ready to get up. "You're insane, dude."

"I'm sorry," he says. "I'm sorry. And anyway, I shouldn't try to put anybody else through it."

"I'm sorry," she says, and she slowly starts to swing again. "I shouldn't have called you that."

"No," he says. He lets out a deep sigh as she gains momentum again. "You're right. Nobody else seems to see her, anyway. Maybe it's up to me to find out what's behind the kaleidoscope eyes lady."

Lilith's hands slip from her swing's chains, and she goes flying forward, falling face first on the ground.

He grabs the chains of his swing, trying to get up. "Are you OK?"

Still on her hands and knees on the ground, she turns around. "What did you say?"

"It's just ... What I call her," he says. He keeps talking, trying to ward away the vacant stare Lilith is throwing at him. "The lady. The zombie or whatever. I don't know *what* it—What? Why are you looking at me like that?!"

She takes her time to get up, never breaking eye contact with him. "Do you believe in fate?"

"Yes," he says, "I see it every day. It's not nice."

"Ha," she says. "No. Really."

"Yes, really."

She pauses. "My grandmother mentioned that," she says.

"Yeah, my dad says it comes from a famous song—"

"No," she says. "I think she mentioned the lady in the cemetery."

Nate looks at her in disbelief. "Stop. Just stop."

She stares at the ground in shock. "No," she says. "No. No, no no no. This is impossible. This is all too—" She looks up at the wall as she dusts off the dirt from her hands. "Well," she says, her voice trembling. "I guess it's time, after all. I guess I'm going in."

35

Nathan sneaks his arm through the rusty doors and fumbles with something. He pulls a heavy chain toward the opening, trying to get a glimpse of it in the dim lighting of the park, but the chain doesn't budge.

"So I'm finally gonna do it," she says, more to herself than to her new companion. "I'm going inside the cemetery."

He leans over the wall and stretches his arm further inside, concentrating. Lilith hears the turning of tiny metallic wheels.

"You really never came in here?" he asks. He's trembling. "Why? I thought I'd seen everyone in town, but not you. Everyone comes in here at some point. Even just for fun."

"What are you doing?" she asks.

Still concentrating on whatever's behind the door, he doesn't reply. The lock behind the door goes *click* and unlatches.

"Wow," she says. "Impressive."

He pulls the chains and opens the door. Inside, a narrow path stretches before them, lined with shrubs and trees.

Lilith steps forward, but he cuts in and enters first.

"Whoa," she says, "suddenly you're *eager* to go in?"

Nathan looks extra pale under the moon. "I'm scared stiff," he says as he walks in. "I just don't want you to go first."

She's startled. "Oh. Thanks, I guess," she says, stepping in after him.

Nate secures the door behind them and the two begin down the pathway, away from the lights from the park. Lilith stumbles on the broken tiled floor, and Nate grabs her hand tightly, helping her keep her balance.

"Thanks," she says.

His hand is shaking. But as her hand presses into the warmth of his body, she can feel him relaxing, too.

The path quickly grows pitch dark. She searches the sky for the lights of the park, but it seems the high walls lock them out as effectively as they have Lilith herself. Only at the end of the path does the darkness begin to lift, and she knows they will soon reach the crypts she can see from her bedroom window. Old gray stone crypts. And yet, here, among the green, a new fresh air fills her lungs. It smells sweet.

She follows Nate farther down the path. Her feet shuffle on the floor, ready to stumble again. As they walk past the plants, she inhales all kinds of new scents. Delicious smells. Celery. Chocolate. Strawberry. Onion. Horrible and dark smells. New smells, like no flower her parents' flower shop has ever sold. It's beautiful. And up ahead, she can already imagine the life-sized versions of the crypts she can see from her window. A miniature city made of crypts of all shapes and sizes. She remembers, vaguely, walking the streets of that city once. But she ran out before she could see much. It's funny. All that time, she's been afraid of *this*?

"Are those Cypresses?" she asks.

"I don't know. I don't know the names. The cone-shaped ones are there to raise the souls up to heaven, I think."

"Wow."

"Yeah," he says. "And at night, the smell of the plants really rises up. So, you've really never been in the cemetery before?"

The path finally ends, and in the dark, she can sense they're entering the narrow alleys of the miniature crypt city. "Sort of," she says.

"Oh," he says. "I'm sorry."

"No, it's not that. Well, actually, I didn't make it that far inside ..."

"We don't have to talk about it if you don't want to."

"How *old* are you? You sound very mature for a guy out in his pajamas."

She lets his hand guide her and tries to make something out of the many shines and glares from the glass windows reflecting the pale moonlight. Still, there's nothing to see but tiny lights floating around her amid a sea of black. His hand pulls hers as he turns a corner, and she shuffles her feet to avoid any obstacles as she turns and steps into what she thought was a black wall.

"How can you see anything here?" she asks.

"I have my tricks."

They march forward in the dark. The sound of crickets surrounds them. The night is calling for them.

His hand starts trembling again.

"Are you OK?" she asks. She gasps. Her voice turns to a whisper. "Did you see something? Did you see her?"

"No," he says. "I thought I did. But it's nothing."

Lilith laughs. "You're pretty cowardly for someone who lives in a cemetery."

He paces in silence. Her sight is adjusting to the dark, and she can see the angles now, surrounding her. The borders. The broken windows. The rotten doors.

"So," he says, his voice trembling. "Is this like in your zombie movies?"

"Only thing missing is the fog," she says.

"Oh, there's fog all right," he says, "only not here. Up north, where the caskets are buried. It's all grassy plains there, and some mornings—"

The tone of his voice sends a shiver down Lilith's spine. "I was kidding," she says.

"Well, I'm not," he says. "I've seen it plenty."

"Wait," she says. "There can't be fog. I live right outside, and I've never seen fog."

"I'm serious!" he says. "I wouldn't lie to you."

She surveys the cemetery around them. The dark crypts seem more menacing now.

He pulls her hand. "I'll show you."

Angels and gargoyles shine under the moonlight around her, watching over them as they run in the night. Up ahead, at the end of the corridor, she sees a clearing, a lighter patch of dark, under the bright full moon. Her lungs fill with the briskness in the air, the sheer purity of air that's not being breathed by anyone else, multiplied by the trees, somehow purer than the park itself. It's got the dampness of the stone crypts maybe, or the earthiness of recently dug graves, but whatever it is, it's the freshest air she's ever breathed.

"Wow," she says. "I never knew the cemetery had such an open field after the crypts."

"Oh, yeah," he says, "the crypts are just the beginning."

She turns around and searches behind the tall wall for her home. All she can see is the open night sky. They are far away from anything she's ever seen from her window.

"God," she says, running after him, stepping on the mushy grass. "This place is huge!"

"Follow me!" he says, running up a small hill.

As she climbs toward him, she can tell he's staring at something. When she catches up to him, her jaw drops. Further ahead, among the vast greens and hills, the night sky is interrupted by a ghostly arch above the cemetery hills. A black-and-white rainbow. Like a ring made of mist, or a ghostly fog.

"What the hell is that?" she asks, marveled.

"It's called a fogbow," he says.

"Ha ha," she mock-laughs. "You're shitting me."

"No, really. Actually, this one's a *lunar fogbow*. See how the moon shines on it?"

"Wow."

"We also have rainbows, the colorful kind, sometimes. But I think these are way cooler."

She tries to catch her breath. "I'll say."

He points at the horizon, at a dark woodsy patch.

"And over there, that's my house."

"You live here? You see *this* from your bedroom?"

"No. I see trees."

"Oh. That's not so bad."

"Well, they're people."

"What?"

"It's the environmentalists or something. They bury people in these pods and make them grow into trees."

"That's nice, I guess."

"No, it's not. Not when it gets windy, it isn't. Come on."

He walks her along the border of the crypts and into a roundabout. In the center is a statue of a giant black egg with webbed wings spread wide, like it's a bat about to fly away. A circular park bench surrounds it.

They sit, still holding hands, and look at the gray lunar fogbow. Lilith looks carefully at him, at how he sits, to sit down at the exact same moment, so that they don't have to let go.

He turns to her, and she looks away. She stares up at the sky.

The fogbow starts to disappear. The sun is rising.

"I don't think she's coming out anymore today," he says, looking around. "I'm sorry."

She turns to him. "You're *sorry*?"

"Well, yeah, you wanted to see her ..."

"I don't mind," she says.

His hand is shivering.

"Sorry," he says, looking down on his hand. "I can't help it. I know I'm not like your cool friends—"

"I like that you're not like them," she interrupts. "I like that you can be scared."

"Yes," he exhales. "I'm sure it's what every girl looks for in a boy."

"No, I mean, I like that you're not afraid to show it. You're un-ironic. Everyone seems afraid to be themselves, actually, except for you."

"I think I know what you mean," he says. "I see them at the wakes. Pretenders."

"Yeah!" she says. "Pretenders. You know what? Everyone I know out there, all of my life. *They're* the zombies."

Crickets fill the night.

"Boo!" she goes, breaking the silence, stunning him, and he smiles.

She raises her voice, letting the words travel in the open night. "What the fuck's wrong with being afraid, anyway?"

He sighs. "Well ..."

She looks at him. "I think you might be the ballsiest guy I've ever met," she says, and she leans in to kiss him.

36

THE OFFICE SMELLS MUSTY. IT HASN'T SEEN USE IN YEARS, AND yet the wear and tear evident on the dusty chairs shows this was once a busy area. Lilith watches as the officers gathered around the large table mutter to one another and point at different markers on the map of the cemetery. The paper is so yellowed and worn, and the lettering so old—even for Leatelranch standards—that it's hard to believe it could still be useful. Filling the shelves, wall to wall, are water bottles, canned food, first aid kits, neatly folded blankets. There's an empty coffee machine next to Wednesday and Wolfram.

"Jeez," she says to Mr. Girardot. "Think it's enough?"

"There's plenty of supplies," he says. "We won't be running out anytime soon."

Somehow, even as he says it, he doesn't look confident.

"Surely you don't plan to stay here for long," Lilith says, forcing a chuckle, pretending she's not waiting desperately for his answer.

He hunches down on the table and places his elbows on the map. He sighs.

"That's great," she says. "Just remember, I need to go *now*. I don't care if they burned them, if you lost contact, I know Nate is

OK. Of course he is. I just know it. I still have some scares left on me. And you said—"

"I know what I said," he says, focused on the map. "We will help you. But we sure can use your help, too. So if you want to survive, then stay a while, answer some questions, help us get to the bottom of this, and you have my word, I'll send some officers to get you there."

Everyone around the table shoots her an icy look.

"I know how this plays out," she says. "You adults always say that, and in the end, you'll find a way for me to stay."

He turns to her, confused. *You adults?* he repeats. "Look. You're free to go. Right now, if you want. But I can't send any of my men out with you right now. Not until we figure this out. Help us with the plan—just speak out if anything sounds wrong or stupid—and I promise, we'll help you. We could be missing something. Tell me how you spotted that ... zombie, for starters. We need to find out what drives them. How they think."

"How they think?" someone asks.

The chief turns to them, serious. "Yes."

"OK," Lilith says. "I trust you. It's just that, lately, no matter what I do, things have a way of going another way."

"Well, not this time," he says. He turns to an officer sitting in the corner of the room, her hair black as night. "Morelia," he says, "try the radio again, see if you can catch some signals. Prioritize New Southport."

Morelia's face turns to stone. "But Chief," she says. "Washington. London."

"Prioritize New Southport for now."

Morelia nods and turns back to the radio, handling the dials.

Lilith sighs, relieved. "Thank you, Mr. G."

"She can do it," Wolfram says. "She's an expert in this zombie stuff."

The men and women around the table throw her a raw look. "Those are movies," Lilith admits, blushing as she tries to ignore everyone's gaze. "This is real life. I know that."

Wednesday is visibly upset. Lilith can feel her glare burning a hole in the back of her head.

"Well," Mr. Girardot says, "real life is looking a lot like the movies right now. What happens in the movies?"

Silence. Lilith feels everyone's eyes bearing down on her. She stutters. "Ehm ... Erm ..."

The soldiers look at each other. "We're supposed to risk our necks for her?" someone says.

"Give her a moment," Mr. Girardot says.

"OK," she says. "OK. What do we know so far: I haven't seen them run, but I'd bet they *do* run. It would make sense that they don't get tired, either."

"We know that much," Morelia says.

Mr. Girardot turns to her with a scolding look. Morelia turns back to the radio.

"First things first," Lilith says. "Let's discuss the rules. Every genre has them."

"This isn't a genre," someone says. "It's real life."

"Every genre has them," Lilith repeats, trying to focus. "And this is how you get to kill them."

The mumbling in the room fades out. They seem to be listening to her.

"They are *revenant* zombies. Meaning, they are still who they were. At least kind of. They remember. They talk. They think. They ... act human," Lilith says. "They pretend. But they make mistakes."

Words pour out of her. Her heart pumps faster. This is exhilarating. It's exactly like the movies. People around the table are hanging on her every word.

"Like Sergeant Wilkes back there," someone says. "What kind of mistakes?"

"Well, if I had to put it into words, I'd say that they forgot how to act human. And they're just bad at it. They're the same, they keep their memories, but they also seem to have a sort of collective memory of the future, and maybe that's too much to handle—"

The room starts to whisper and mutter. "Future?" someone asks. "What? Chief, is this a joke? How do you know all this?"

"I think they've watched these movies," she continues, "the same ones we watched, and they're *playing* the zombies we know from TV ... They're counting on us to expect movie tropes. But in reality, they seem different. They know the future. And they seem to be able to communicate with each other— no, not communicate, but it's as if they have a common plan they've agreed to beforehand."

"But—"

Lilith's mind races. "Actually," she says, "maybe they never hatched a plan. Maybe they just all want the same thing. Maybe they all ... agree."

Someone scoffs. "Yeah. They're all Ph.D.'s, and they *concur*."

"Oh, they're *smart*," Lilith says. "They tease us. They play us. They don't just want to kill us. They trap us into specific situations. My parents could have killed me in the city, but they brought me here."

"My neighbor waited for my parents to try to kill me," Wolfram adds.

Chief Girardot locks eyes with Lilith. His mustache dances as he says, "Why?"

"Isn't that the question?" Lilith says. "But if this is some sort of plan, or strategy, and they're counting on it happening, then the right move for us would be to go against it, whatever it is. Be unpredictable. They want us to go left, we go right. If we want to survive this, we need to mess with their plan. Prevent the future, whatever it is."

"Bullshit," a deep voice says. The officers around the table make room, and a tall man leans on the map and looks at Lilith. "I've seen them shamble," he says. "They didn't seem smart to me."

"Yeah," someone else chimes in, "how come some of 'em are smart, and some of 'em are dumb?"

"Maybe there's a timeline from infection to nonverbal killing machine," someone else replies.

"They're faking it," Lilith says. "All of it. They know something. They *understand* something. They seem to know how things will end."

"They're laughing at us," says Wolfram.

Someone scoffs. "Gimme a break."

"Lil," Wolfram says. "Tell them."

Mr. Girardot turns to him. "Tell them what?"

"About why we used to call you Lucky."

Wednesday stares at Lilith and gnashes her teeth, red-faced, about to cry. "*Yes, Lilith*," she says in a mocking tone, "*tell us*. How do you *know*?" She looks ready to explode.

"My grandmother," Lilith replies. "She died, she saw something, and told me."

This seems to keep Wednesday from exploding.

"That's why we called her *Lucky*," Wolfram says. "She can see the future, too. Thanks to your Grann, right?"

"She pointed some of them out," Lilith says, "so I kinda learned how to notice these ... coincidences. These weird moments. I always had them in my life, but lately, they're getting crazier. I think it's related to them somehow."

Mr. Girardot seems very interested. "Related how?"

"I don't know." Lilith racks her brain. "I don't know."

"What about the rules of infection?" A short, stalky woman asks. "How does this spread?"

"That's easy," the chief says. "Death. No virus or anything. Dying will turn you into one of those."

One of the officers smirks. "So, what kills them? Silver bullets? Stakes? Exorcism?"

"That's werewolves," Lilith says. "And vampires. And fascist bullshit."

"What if they're demons?" the officer asks.

"Wow," Lilith says to the chief. "You really *do* need me here. *Demons?*"

"Simmons," the chief says to him. "Please shut up."

"Blows to the head don't work," Lilith says. "Some of them pretend to be struck down, but I've seen one with a cracked skull, still going."

"Fire," Morelia says. "Fire kills everything."

Lilith snorts. "Tell that to Russo. In *Return of the Living Dead*, they try to burn them, and it only creates a cloud of smoke that turns you into a zombie when you inhale it. Chief, how did you know they shouldn't be burnt?"

"Common sense, dear."

"Let's hope this isn't like *those* movies," Lilith says looking at the cemetery map. "I better get to Nate fast."

Mr. Girardot puts a hand on her shoulder. "You've become quite the intellectual."

She blushes. "Thank you, Mr. G— I mean, Chief Girardot."

"What do you do?" he asks.

Lilith is confused. "What do you mean?"

"For a job. What did you study? What's your line of work?"

"Film critic," she says, "sort of."

Chief Girardot chuckles. "Of course! Good old Lilith. Your parents got you hooked on those horror movies, didn't they? They told me all about it. You had your whole life planned out. It drove your hippy parents crazy! How you'd meet a mysteriously dark boy, become a big, successful horror filmmaker ... I'd be surprised if you ever *did* go off script."

"So, this means you'll help me?" she asks.

"I told you I would. I will."

"I really need to go find Nate."

"I know."

"I don't doubt you, it's just— You promise you won't change your mind?"

The radio fizzes, and a high-pitched noise interrupts her.

"No," Mr. Girardot says. "I promised."

Lilith smiles. She looks at the cemetery map. "Isn't Leatelranch full of dead people?" she asks. "Why storm the cemetery first?"

He lifts his eyes from the map and looks up at her. He sighs. "According to the last census," he says, "the total population of Leatelranch is 32,211 souls," he recites. "The cemetery holds over 300,000 bodies." He points at the gates in the map with a firm, steady index finger. "Those," he says, "those are their barracks."

The radio goes *whizzwhawhisss* again, and all the heads in the room turn to it.

"Is this really the first time you've come back to Leatelranch?" the way the man's mustache moves when he talks is hypnotic.

"Yes."

"In all these years?"

"I've been busy," Lilith says.

"It's so close," he says. "Your hometown!"

"Well," she says. "You know. Life."

"Is it because of ...?"

Lilith avoids Wednesday's gaze. "Well," she says. "It's hard."

"I know. I don't blame you."

Her eyes go watery.

"I don't blame you," he repeats. "It's OK. It wasn't your fault."

"Wednesday sure does," she says.

Mr. Girardot looks down. "Yes, she does."

The radio crackles with static. Mr. Girardot's eyebrows shoot up, and the whole room turns silently to it.

A voice comes through. "It ... trap ... all a trap ... *fizz* ... Slayers ... —ead ... —yone ... dead ..."

They all look at each other, frozen.

"Av—oid ... big cities ... *fizz* ... Washington ... —outhport ... lost ... *fizz*!"

The air gets sucked out of the room. Lilith turns to stone. The room becomes a small light at the end of a pinhole, and silence fills her head.

"No," she says, taking a step back. "He can't be dead."

The chief puts his hand on her shoulder.

"This can't be it," she says with a blank stare as tears run down her cheeks.

"But you saw more things, right?" Wolfram asks. "What did you see, you know, after? This can't be it."

She exhales, staring into space. "Door three-hundred and twelve."

"What? What did you see?"

She sniffles. "Everything I can remember already happened. I've spent my life avoiding moments, rebelling against prophecies, but now, these are the last ones. After the car crash, after door three-twelve ... there's nothing."

She turns to the cemetery map on the table and wipes the tears from her eyes.

"Wait a minute," she says, her eyes darting from one corner of the map to the next, looking at the miniature soldiers and tanks and military cars as she remembers. "A walk among the dead."

She bursts into tears again, and the chief hugs her.

The radio goes silent. The room goes silent.

"Try other frequencies," Mr. Girardot orders Morelia.

She turns the dials idly but gets nothing. She shakes her head.

"All gone, Chief."

Mr. Girardot looks behind at the cans and water. "We have defenses. We have air filters. We have supplies to last us years."

Lilith is frozen as he speaks.

Wednesday sobs. "Years?"

"Whatever it takes," Mr. Girardot says. "I'm not risking anyone outside right now."

Wednesday hugs her father, and Wolfram joins them. Mr. Girardot opens his arm and waits for Lilith.

She wipes the tears from her eyes and joins them.

37

FLAMES SPREAD FAST AMONG THE PYRE, SETTING ABLAZE hundreds of bodies. Threads of smoke escape from every opening, turning darker and darker and reaching for the sky. Pale hands and limbs turn golden. White cotton shirts turn brown. Shy flames grow bolder, stretching like tongues and tentacles out of every pore, and wriggle and squirm and touch and destroy. As the air grows hotter, as the huge black cloud of smoke starts to flail like a fat snake in the wind, Lester steps back and presses his surgical mask against his face. He checks on his friends and lets out a muffled sigh of relief when they do the same. Behind them, everyone starts to cough and cover their itchy eyes.

"Dude," someone says, coughing, "this smoke is *thick*."

All around them, the coughing grows worse. People try to breathe through their shirts. Some of them kneel on the ground, their chests swelling and contracting as they struggle for air. They lie on the floor in fetal positions, whining.

The boys turn to Lester, alarmed.

"See?" Lester says under his mask.

Beer cans fall to the ground. People on the ground begin to convulse.

Lester's eyes grow huge, and his heart pumps faster. "Oh, shit!"

The kicking and screaming of the fallen Slayers becomes more violent by the second.

"We need to move," says Yoshi. "Fast."

Lester looks for a way out. What was a crowded maze a minute ago is now a large open street carpeted with people. There are bodies as far as he can see. "Which way?" he asks. "We're surrounded!"

Nate accidentally steps on someone's belly, and he sinks, softly, down into it. The body doesn't complain. "*Any* way!" he says, holding his mask to his face. He and jumps ahead, landing on someone's back. Again, not a peep from the body on the ground. "Follow me!"

A hand reaches up and grabs his ankle. "Help," it mutters.

Nathan shakes his leg, jittering, and jumps back to the small island of pavement where the kids still stand.

"Welcome back," says Yoshi.

A wall of ghouls comes walking down the empty street. They walk straight, without any affliction or difficulty. They climb over the yellow barriers.

"Quick," says Nate to Lester and Yoshi, "grab a weapon."

They look around at the last mighty warriors and *Call of Duty*-ers weakly falling to their knees, trying to breathe through their clothes, but their limp fingers can't hold on to anything anymore.

Yoshi moves toward the girl with the DO NOT RESUSCITATE T-shirt. He tries to take the crowbar from her closed hand, struggles with it, and pulls out the entire arm, getting splashed with green blood. He wields the arm as a weapon and whips it to the sides, practicing his moves. The bones crack as the severed arm twists unnaturally in the air.

"Goddammit Yoshi!" yells Lester. "Have some respect! That's a person!"

Yoshi hears his friend but ignores him. Lester can see a half-cocked smile on the side of his face. He practices a swing as he looks around for trouble. "You need to get it, Les! Nothing but dead meat! That's what we are!"

Lester is getting angry. "I swear to god, Yoshi—"

"Lester! Focus!" Nate's voice comes clear as day. Lester just doesn't know from where. He scans the field of fallen unconscious people and finally finds a bat with nails on it lying loose, away from any claimers. As he reaches down to grab it, he hears a wail building up behind him. It's Kenny's terrified voice.

"No, no, no ..."

Lester lifts the bat and turns around. "What is it, Ken?"

Kenny's face glows orange as he stares into the bonfire. He shakes his head to the sides and whines. "Daddy ... No."

Lester turns to the big pyre. From his bed of flames, Mr. Macomber is getting up.

"What?" Lester mouths.

Among the fiery, convulsing bodies, he climbs out, leaning on bones and limbs. His face is still recognizable, but his body is a thinly fleshed skeleton, lit like a torch. It walks down from the pile, flames coming out of his eyes and ribcage, stepping on heads and fingers that awake and wiggle and prepare to rise. It walks straight toward Kenny. Kenny steps back, holding his mask. He looks around him. He scans the ground. A fat ginger man dressed in *Lord of the Rings* armor struggles to breathe and lifts his arm toward Kenny, holding a steel pipe in his hand. *Help*, he mumbles. Kenny pries the pipe out of his hand and turns back to his father.

Close to him, scorching the air around his face, the fiery rotten head opens its jaw with an expression of surprise. He's mocking him. The charred lips grin, revealing blackened teeth inside its smoldering mouth.

Blam! A shot hits Mr. Macomber in the forehead.

Ron steps toward the burning ghoul. He's wielding a gun in one hand and holding a hospital mask to his face with the other. "Die, motherfucker! Die!"

Mr. Macomber turns to him. The gunshot is but a smudge on his otherwise destroyed head.

He grins.

"But—but that's impossible," says Ron, coughing.

A female voice comes from behind him, from within the smoke, coughing. It's Big Momma. "Shoot him in the head, moron! In the head!"

Ron turns around. "Oh! In the head? *Really?* Don't you think I did that?!"

He shoots again. Mr. Macomber's head whips back, then slowly comes forward, sporting a brand-new gunshot. He trudges on, getting closer and closer to Kenny.

Ron looks down at the gun in his hand in disbelief.

Kenny moves his head to the side, escaping the heat emanating from his dead father's body, and swings the heavy steel pipe as hard as he can, getting pulled forward by its sheer weight. Mr. Macomber dodges it as if they had choreographed the perfectly timed move in advance. Kenny's arms twist to the side, and he feels an unbearable heat on the side of his face and on his entire body. The ghoul opens his arms and wraps them around the boy, and the polyester Star Trek costume fizzles and booms ablaze. Kenny struggles, but the bony hands strap to his back, and the burning torso presses against his face. As he catches fire, he tries to escape his body in a loud scream.

Lester covers his mouth, unable to close his eyes. The burning corpse's bony arms trap Kenny in a hug, its fingers of death brushing softly against his back, setting his red costume alight. Father and son fall to their knees in a sunshine hug.

"No!" yells Lester, running toward him. Nate grabs him tight, holding him as he struggles to break free.

"Motherfuckers," Yoshi screams.

"We'll kill you!" Lester yells. "We'll kill you, you hear!?"

He starts running toward Mr. Macomber, but Nate gets a hold of him. Lester tries to fight him off.

"They're getting up!" says Yoshi.

Kenny and Mr. Macomber, two human torches with glad smiles, are walking toward them.

"Someone get me one of them masks!" Big Momma yells. Lester whips another one out of his pocket and gives it to her.

Around them, the fallen *Slayers* are losing the struggle. Coughs die out, and slowly, silence takes over. Bodies stop convulsing. They all just lie there.

"Quick," says Nate. "If we hurry, we can go through this sea of people—"

The smoke rises and covers everything, blocking the sun. The mirrored buildings are now truncated above the third or fourth window, and the cloud covers everything like a ceiling above them.

Carpeting the street, bodies lie in all sorts of strange positions. Lester scans the crowd. The faces. The colors. And he finds her. The red DO NOT RESUSCITATE T-shirt, and the beautiful girl wearing it, her head tilted to the side, her hair covering another person's face. One arm and both of her legs bent at grotesque angles.

Who sleeps like that? he thinks, and he pays attention to her chest. She's not moving. She's not breathing. As the last, feeble chest in the crowd slows to a stop, Lester is stricken by the image. He expects her eyes to open again. Her chest to swell again. Her mouth to smile again. Her arms, hands, legs, to wake up, to stand up, to dance again, for her to stand up and say that she's kidding, that she's OK, that this was all a big joke.

"Come on!" yells Nate. "Go! Go!"

And yet, when it happens, it's even more of a sight. To see a dead person getting up. Muscles waking, limbs straightening like a baby learning to walk. A chest that doesn't swell but moves nevertheless, like a puppet controlled by strings. People waking, standing, joining her, all moving, all lifeless.

Behind them, someone growls.

"What do we do?" Yoshi asks, waking Lester from his daze.

Lester looks around. An army of ghouls is coming down the street to the side of the bonfire. The newly reunited Macomber family is up front. And a horde of freshly slayed Slayers is gathering behind them.

Nowhere to go.

A pimple-faced teenaged ghoul grins an adult grin and raises his hands to Nate. He's wearing a pretend military uniform that clearly doesn't fit, and he's wielding a bloody kitchen knife. He throws it to the ground and lunges at Nate with his mouth open. Nate prepares to thrust his crowbar into the ghoul's head.

But the ghoul stops. He and every corpse around him simply stop what they're doing and run away from Nate and the boys like a choreographed flock of birds.

"Cowards," says Yoshi, his mouth smiling but his face pale with fear.

Nate frowns. "They run away. Again?"

As the army of ghouls clear the street, and their voices and grunts die down, a rumble grows louder. Through the black smoke and ash rising from burning human flesh on the move, an engine roars closer and closer. Lester strains to see between the fleeing bodies and the ash, but only catches a glimmer of something metallic and yellow. As the sea of ex-Slayers cracks open, as the cloud begins to dissipate moved by the sheer speed of the metallic beast, he finally gets a good look at what's coming.

A yellow freaking school bus.

NATE PUSHES THE BOYS AND JUMPS AWAY JUST IN TIME TO AVOID the speeding bus, which hits the lower side of the bonfire, blowing away the burning bodies and opening a path to the empty street on the other side. It crashes against an electronics shop on the side of the street, screeching and scraping its side against the wall, then crushes and bends over itself with a shriek of twisted metal, its center folding in like an accordion.

"Go! Go!" Nathan yells, pushing the boys toward the opening in the bonfire.

"That was close," says Ron, holding his hospital mask to his face and scrambling to catch up with Nathan.

"Too close," says Big Momma, trying to act cool, holding her breath, and finally coughing inside her mask.

"Follow us!" Nate calls to her, running alongside the kids. The pavement is burnt black and hot under their feet. To their sides, flaming bodies are trying to free themselves from the puzzle. The air inside Nate's mask is scorching hot, and it burns his throat when breathing in, his face when breathing out. They run next to the blazing bonfire and into the empty street on the other side.

"Wait!" a voice calls out. "Help us!"

Nate and Ron freeze in place and turn toward the sound.

Pressed against the windshield, the crushed faces of the bus driver and passengers are yelling for help. They're trapped inside the cabin, and the bus lies so close to the bonfire that its heat is rapidly turning it into a metal oven.

Behind the bus, a sea of ghouls is already rushing toward them. They are limber now. They fill the street like a marathon.

"Don't!" says Yoshi.

Nate takes a few steps toward the bus. People are piled up against the glass, crushed like sardines. They yell and cry out in pain.

"Help!" the driver pleads, his round face squashed against the glass, twisted. "Open the door! Please!"

"Oh, no," says Ron. "No way." Big Momma just smirks and looks at Nate, gauging his reaction. She seems too tough to care about the hell unraveling around them.

Nate scrambles to the bus door. He quickly checks the status of the ghouls closest to him. They're still struggling to climb over the pile, or to stand up from the pile. He drives the crowbar between the door and the frame and starts to pull. It makes a metallic wail that contrasts with the deep growl of the flames nearby. And faintly, behind the cacophony, he can just barely make out a faint wheeze coming from inside the bus.

It sounds like ... giggling?

He leans back away from the crowbar to try to peer into the cabin through a small gap in the twisted metal. All he can see is smoke-filled darkness.

"It's not working!" yells the driver, red-faced and alarmed.

"Pass it inside!" a voice calls out from somewhere behind the faces, twisted and crushed and monstrous, squashed against the door.

"Yes, pass the crowbar inside," says the driver.

Ron puts his hand on Nate's shoulder. "Don't."

"Let's just go," yells Yoshi.

Nate shakes Ron's hand away and pulls again, harder. He will not walk away. He pulls again. And again. But the door won't give.

Finally, one of the side windows slides open. A hand emerges through the gap, wildly gesturing for Nate to send the tool inside.

The crowbar disappears into the cabin before Nate hears the laughter. He takes a few steps backward, taking a good look at the bus driver as he does. *Why does he look like he's hiding something?*

Nate studies the ghoulish vision on the windshield. Scores of human faces and parts are crammed into a horrifying painting. He can make out the driver's face trying to smile, but he can't see any neck, or shoulders, or arms, or chest, that could possibly belong to it.

It's only a head. Maybe not even a head. A face.

He strides back farther.

Another giggle. The bus starts to rattle and rock from side to side.

Nate hears the sound of twisted metal ring out once again. As he steps further back, he sees his crowbar sticking out of the top of the bus. It's dancing to the shrieking sound of twisting metal, tilting back and forth like a shark fin.

Nate's blood freezes. *They're cutting their way out.*

The top of the bus tears open like a tin can, and a giant limb made of people punches through it. The sheets of metal fly off into the sky and crash down with two loud *booms* atop the marathon of running ghouls approaching Nate and the boys.

Once again, Nate spots the face that asked for help, but it's not connected to a driver. It's stuck like a smiling bandage to a godawful mass of human bodies squished together like putty. It seems to float toward the bus door, pushed by the squashed bodies around it, and all the faces Nate saw on the windshield follow him like a string of Pac-man ghosts.

As a synchronized unit, the mass of mangled body parts swings back to the other side of the bus, away from the door, slowly, then shoots forward like a giant arm throwing a knockout punch, blowing the door clear out of its frame.

The driver's face is now bloody red and missing half its jaw, but its eyes are fixed on Nate. Its half-mouth smiles a crooked, broken smile. Propelled by a giant limb that stretches its way out of the bus, it floats over the open street toward Nate, laughing at him.

Suddenly, the limb bends, and the driver's face gets squashed into the pavement, just a heel in a giant spider's leg. Another limb breaks free and stretches itself out of the bus window. It falls on the pavement, on the open street, sounding like a thousand bones cracking, then bends its giant knee-of-human-odds-and-ends to support itself.

Nate watches as a familiar form takes shape.

"Shit."

The monster stretches itself upright to the sound of human cries. The group watches in horror as the figure stands up, shaped like a human, made of humans, and towers over them like a giant, its upper torso soaring above the blanket of black smoke.

"Now run, maybe?" asks Yoshi.

Nate shoots him with a snarky look. "Since when do you ask for permission, Rebel Boy?"

They dart across the street under the shadow of the monster. The ground shakes as the creature chases after them, making waves in the black smoke. It flattens cars and cracks the pavement with every footfall.

A giant arm swings over them, missing them but sending a car hurtling into the glass panes of a mirrored office building.

"We can't outrun it!" says Lester.

Nate looks forward with a face of stone. "Just run!"

The creature swings its arms at buildings indiscriminately, destroying windows and walls. Glass and bricks and drywall and furniture explode everywhere, showering them with debris. Black smoke permeates buildings through broken windows, and people begin jumping to the ground from their once-safe high-rise apartments. If they don't simply splatter into a paste on the pavement, they convulse, get back up, and join in the hunt, making the streets more dangerous by the second.

Yoshi's face perks up as he motions ahead. "Do you hear that?" he asks.

"Hear what?" asks Nate.

"I hear it," says Lester.

Nate starts hearing a faint sound. A low, distant rumble.

"What is that?" he says.

The sound grows louder. Larger. Closer. And soon becomes clear. It's an impossibly large pack of dogs, barking madly.

Nate stops under the large awning of a building to look over his shoulder. The creature is catching up to them. Behind it, an army of ghouls races to get whatever scraps the beast will leave them. One of the giant legs stops in mid-air, ready to stomp whatever's unfortunate enough to be under its shadow. He can see the bus driver's bloody face grinning as it comes down.

He looks around him. Yoshi, Ron, and Big Momma are close behind him.

"Lester!" he says, "Lester's gone."

"Leave him!" Ron says as he runs past him.

Nate turns to him. "I'm *not* gonna leave him!" he grunts, and keeps searching among the chaos.

He freezes in fear. Just two blocks behind them, about to be crushed by the towering monster's giant leg, is Lester's tiny body, standing unflinching in the colossal shadow.

"What's he doing?!" Yoshi asks.

Lester turns to them and waves. "Don't you get it?!" he yells. "If we die, they won't come after us anymore! And we'll stay young! Forever! Why run from that?!"

"Are you crazy?!" Nate yells.

"It's OK, guys!" he says, smiling as darkness falls on him. "We're gonna die anyway! Might as well do it now!"

"Fucking whacko," says Yoshi.

"Leave him!" says Ron, slowing down but not stopping.

Nate turns to him and pierces a hole in his eyes. "We're *not* leaving him."

Nate sprints the two blocks back. The monster's leg is dangerously close. The many faces seem to suffer and smile as they fall down like a hammer. Nathan throws the boy over his shoulder and runs back. The column of meat lands behind him, shaking the ground and propelling him forward with its force.

"You should have left him there," says Big Momma when he catches up to the group. "Maybe he would've bought us some time."

Nate gives her a cold look.

The rumble grows louder and louder. It becomes a clear symphony of dogs barking. Too many to count. A crowd of dogs comes running down the street, a giant pack, covering the street as far as they can see, all running straight toward them. Dogs of all sizes and colors, but all mean, all fast, all obsessed, and all in rage. Their teeth are yellow and long and sharp.

"Goddammit!" Nate says. "Prescient zombies, MAGA mobs, human giants, and now killer dogs?! Leave something for the sequel!"

"There!" says Big Momma, pointing at a subway entrance.

Yoshi makes a run for it.

"No," says Nate, almost out of breath, "they're ... all ... locked."

"No," says Big Momma, also panting, "That's ... one of ours."

The head of the pack of dogs is less than a block away when they reach the station and leap down the stairs. The lights are on, and the entrance is open. Two figures stand guard at the iron gate.

"It's me!" yells Big Momma. "Quick! Close the doors after us!"

Sunlight disappears. Above them, the huge monster bends down to pluck them out of their hole with a single screaming finger, but the deafening pack of mad dogs jumps atop it like an ocean of muscles and rage. They cling to the creature's foot and cover it, and it carries them across the air in a huge kick. It shakes its wretched arm, sending more dogs flying, and begins crushing them under its feet, squashing them like balloons filled with blood. Still, more dogs keep coming, crawling up the massive tower of meat to bite and tear the dead flesh apart.

Ron and Big Momma join the guards at the foot of the stairs. "C'mon!" Ron yells.

But Nate is in awe. Holding on to Lester, who kicks and screams over his shoulder trying to break free, Nate looks up, looks everywhere, trying to take everything in. Behind the giant, Nate sees the bustling movement of people. The Slayers, all dead, have caught up. Dogs clash against them, and it seems there is no end to the sea of beasts. They are pure, raw instinct, enraged. Nate is astonished by the way they pull their necks after each bite, the way their teeth tremble with anger.

The giant, now riddled with the little beasts, falls to its knees on the street. It's being torn apart. Entire limbs, unidentifiable pieces of bloody pulp, entrails all drop to the street like scarlet rain. A hand hits Nate in the face, and he jitters and spits, struggling to keep his attention on the carnage.

A high piercing whistle makes the pack turn their heads. Their teeth and snouts are soaked with blood. They speed off toward the sound.

Nate looks at Yoshi and frowns. Yoshi is just as confused.

The giant, now in shambles, keels over, collapsing across the subway entrance.

Nate grabs Yoshi and runs the rest of the way down the staircase. They run through the gate, and, just before the stairway gets flooded with a sea of muscle, human, and dog, dead and alive, the guards push the heavy doors shut.

Slam!

39

THE GUARDS LOOK AT EACH OTHER POP-EYED AS THEY PRESS their backs against the beating, pounding metro station doors. Their sweaty faces shine under the white neon lights.

"What's going on?" one of them asks Big Momma. "What the hell was that?"

The ground shakes. Dust comes off the metro station's ceiling and walls. The columns tremble, but they hold.

"No!" Lester yells, squirming and breaking free from Nate's hold. He runs toward the door, and, between the two guards, he bumps his fists against the door. "No!"

One of the guards points his gun at him and cocks it.

"Stop!" Nathan yells, running to Lester and grabbing hold of him again. "Don't!"

Behind the door, there's growling. Dogs.

"They're still alive, you guys!" says Lester. "It'll be quick! We can live forever, all of us! We'll never get old! Just imagine—"

Big Momma steps toward Lester. Without saying a word, she brings her face closer and closer to his until he stops squirming. "Quiet," she says finally.

Lester's eyes twitch as she gazes into them.

Big Momma turns to the guards. "Well," she says, "since we

did make this unscheduled stop, why not take advantage of it?" She signals them with her hand, and they immediately point their guns at Nate and the boys.

"C'mon," she adds. "Take us to it."

Nathan looks at the boys. They seem as confused as he is. "Take us to *what*?" he asks, trying to look away from the barrels of the guns pointing at him.

But there's no answer. Big Momma strides toward the turnstiles. As she walks past Ron, she gives him a strange look, one that worries Nate. His concern only grows when Ron seems to acknowledge it. Nate throws Ron a mute but clear *What the fuck?* look, but Ron just looks away, his face sinking into darkness as he follows Big Momma through the turnstiles and down the dead escalators.

"Wait," Nate says as the guards push him and the boys forward. He starts to awkwardly climb the turnstiles. "Where are we going?"

Her metallic steps echo in the cool tunnel. "We're paying a visit to room three-twelve," she says.

Nate's heart stops. "What did you just say?"

She reaches the platform and goes directly to the tracks. She climbs down.

"Ron," Nathan says, "help me out. What's going on?"

"You'll see, soon enough," Ron says, and he climbs down from the platform. The guards reach Nathan and place the cold steel barrel on the back of his neck. "Down," they say.

He climbs down. Big Momma and Ron are following the dark tracks into the pitch-black tunnel, their steps grating on the gravel. He hears the boys landing on the gravel behind him.

"Hold on," Yoshi says with a smart-ass mocking tone. "There are no *rooms* down here. Are you gonna kill us?"

Lester jolts, excited. "Oh!" he says. "Yes! That would work, too!"

Ron turns to him. "Shut up."

The guards come down to the tracks and lead them to the

tunnel. Small emergency lights lead the way, lighting the tunnel just enough to make Nathan and the boys an easy target if they try to escape. Nathan's mind races. What kind of room is reached underground?

To their right is a series of small metal doors, each one lit by a small fluorescent bulb.

"Service rooms," Yoshi says. "That makes sense." He throws a look at Nathan that burns the back of his head. "Anything you want to say here? Now, for example?"

Nate looks at the numbers. Metallic and cold, they shine as he walks by them. 150. 152. His mouth won't scream, won't even move, as much as he wants to.

"Ventilation," says Ron, to pointing a door with his index finger. He turns to Big Momma. "Right?"

She doesn't respond.

As they walk, the narrow metal doors with their numbers parade next to him. Laughing at him. 304, 306, 308. He clenches his fists. 310. The next door looks just like the other ones. Just an average-looking door. With a room number sign in classic, unassuming letters. Three-hundred and twelve.

Nathan's feet bury into the gravel.

Big Momma turns around. "What?"

Nathan measures his words. "There's—There's gonna be a *walker* in there."

Big Momma smiles, licking her lips, scanning him with her eyes. She seems to be savoring this. She seems proud. "A couple of 'em, actually."

Nate doesn't understand. He's fixated on her tobacco-yellow teeth. Her crooked smile.

"But—"

"Go inside," she says.

The guards knock twice, pause, then knock again. The door opens with a rusty sound.

A man in a white coat welcomes them with a crazed, caffeinated smile. The bags under his eyes show many sleepless nights. His hair is messy, unkept. Even from outside the room, he smells awful.

"Big Momma!" he says warmly. "I've been meaning to call for you! I think I may have found something fascinating—"

Big Momma enters the room, ignoring him. "We found them out on the street," she says.

Nate looks at the empty tunnels. Maybe if he and the boys could get a head start, darkness would cover them. Without making a sound, the guards push him inside with their assault rifles.

Behind the man in the coat, four corpses sit in chairs, hands tied behind their backs. Dead-eyed. Lifeless. Grinning at him. No, not *at* him. They're looking *through* him.

"Hey! Don't push!" the boys yell as they enter the room. They spot the ghouls and freeze in place.

"Hello, boys," the four ghouls say in unison.

The boys' faces go pale.

Ron seems confused. "These fuckers talk?"

The man in the lab coat seems fascinated. His eyes sparkle. His mind is racing. "They've never talked before," he says, his mouth speeding to catch up to his train of thought.

Nate hears the shuffling of feet on the floor. The boys are pushing against the guards standing in the doorway, trying to leave the room.

"No! No!" Yoshi yells. "Let us out!" For the first time, he sounds terrified.

Nate looks at the ghouls. Their faces are beyond recognition, but something about them seemed to strike a nerve with the boys. "Are these ... your parents?" he asks them.

The boys seem confused. They explore the ghoul's faces.

"I—don't know," Lester says, making the ghouls grin.

Yoshi can't take his eyes off them. "M—Mom?"

Without waiting for the ghouls to react, Nathan jumps in with a warning. "They could be anyone, and they play tricks," he reminds them. "Don't let them fuck with your head."

"Yeah," Yoshi adds, fixated on the still corpses. "They're liars."

The ghouls just stare and grin. "Yes," they agree. "Who knows?"

Big Momma raises her chin, signaling something to the guards.

"Wait a minute," Nathan says.

The guards force Nathan and the boys down into chairs that form a circle with the ghouls. As his ass hits his seat, Nate looks up and finds himself almost face-to-face with one of them.

"But ... we helped you!" Nathan says.

"Well," says Big Momma, sharing a look with Ron and the guards, "the masks *were* nice. The station ... we'll call it a happy coincidence. But ultimately, you're nothing but trouble. That sick kid will get us all killed. And we need a suicidal boy in our ranks like we need a bite to the neck."

Nate turns to Ron. "You don't want to kill us," he pleads.

"Of course I don't, man!" he replies. "We're buddies!"

Nathan sighs, relieved.

Ron looks down. "But you *are* a liability."

"But—they're kids!" Nathan protests. He looks at Lester and Yoshi as they stare at their parents.

"They're a problem," says Big Momma, pointing at the boys. "We solve problems."

Nate turns to her. "You won't kill us. We'd turn into them and get you."

Ron opens a drawer and grabs a roll of cable and some zip ties.

"That's right," says Big Momma. "I can't kill ya. I won't kill ya. But ya won't be botherin' me no more."

Ron grabs Nathan's hands and pulls them behind the back of the chair. He binds them with a zip tie.

"You think zombies are the threat," Big Momma says. "But zombies are not as dangerous as people. If there's one thing TV shows have taught us ..."

"I don't watch TV," Nate says, furious.

"Ah, you're one of those. Well, excuse me, your highness."

Nate struggles to break free and notices Yoshi doing the same, but Lester is sitting still, calmly waiting for the zombie to break free and welcome him to eternal life. The ghouls don't move. It's like they're lifeless wax figures, sitting stiffly in their chairs, with loose, pointless ties around their wrists and disturbingly warm, kind smiles on what's left of their faces.

"All done," Ron announces, straightening himself up. Yoshi and Nate struggle with their bindings.

"Not so fast, Ron," Big Momma says, and Ron looks up at her, freezing when he sees the gun pointing at him.

Big Momma pouts. "You brought them in," she says.

"What?" is all Ron manages to say.

The guards walk behind him, grab him, and force him to a chair.

"What?" Ron repeats as they sit him down. "Are you kidding me?"

The guards tie him up, and the man in the lab coat puts black hoods over the ghoul's heads. The muffled sound of barking wafts down from the floor above, breaking into the silence that has settled over the room.

"What is it with those dogs?" Big Momma asks, looking at the ceiling.

Committed to their task, the guards take off Ron's hospital mask and put a zip tie around his mouth, gagging him. Then they walk toward Nathan as the man in the white coat places a black hood over Ron's head.

"Wait!" Nathan says. "I can stop this! I know about the Deleg—!"

The guards take off Nate's mask and wrap a thick zip tie around his mouth, pulling so tight that it prevents him from closing his jaw.

Nate tries to yell through the gag as the guards put zip ties around the boys' mouths and put hoods over their heads. Then, a smelly hood is placed over him, and the world becomes a hot black bag.

Nate hears three sets of footsteps shuffling away. A flick of a light switch, and the peaceful release of neon tubes being turned off. A squeaky hinge. A heavy metal door being slammed shut. A metallic lock turning with a heavy *clack*.

And silence.

"Well," one of the ghouls says through his gag, clearly unable to articulate. He lets out a wheezy laugh. "It theems id's thust uth now."

"Fugg you, thombie!" Yoshi yells, and the ghouls turn to him. "We'd nod afthaid of you! We'll deththroy you onth we ged oud oth here! Fidst Thrankie! Now Henny! I thwear do god ..."

"Guyf," Nate says. He can feel his hot breath on his face, and his own voice as if it's being whispered into his ears. "Led's just fogus on getting out of here. Gevenge if not the anfer. Kenny'f gone. Your other friend if gone."

"Never," says Yoshi, struggling with his gag. "We'll find the ghouls who did it and deftroy them. We'll pull out their armth and beat them with them."

"So," Ron asks. He sounds defeated. "Now what?"

Nate clenches his teeth on the thick plastic. "Fugg you," he munches, "dat's hut."

The dark draws strange doodles in front of Nate's eyes. Colorful shapes dance around in the night as his mind races for an answer. *Now what?*

"Now," a motherly voice says, "we wait for the spores to find their way inside."

"This room is closed shut," says Ron, whose plastic tie is clearly looser. "No spores are gonna come in."

"We'll see," says the woman's gentle voice.

Nate tries to bite the plastic, but it feels like his teeth are about to break. He decides to wait.

"Thad's why they're not efcaping," Nate says, his hot breath covering his face inside the hood. "They don't want to ruin their teeth. Their bodies. They'd rather wait."

"We have time," the motherly voice says.

"Well, we don't," Ron says. "I'm chewing my way outta here."

Nate hears the wet nibbling on the hard plastic.

"Of course," the motherly voice says. "You'll understand. Soon enough."

"So, what?" Yoshi asks. "We're gonna wait until thif plaftic *difintegrates?*"

The room is so peaceful. The silence is almost relaxing. Nathan waits for the next idea, the next voice, but all he can hear, barely, is breathing. He surrenders to the dancing figures in the dark and the rhythmic, steady breathing of his own body.

NATHAN SHAKES HIMSELF AWAKE. He can hear dogs barking far away, above them, up on the surface. The black cloth over his face is drenched with sweat and the heat of his own breath. *How long have I been out?*

Other than the sounds of the dogs, the room is silent.

"This is boring," Ron says. Nobody answers.

NATE WAKES UP. A chair is rattling and struggling.

"Whudd's going on?" he asks.

"Thust—Thdying—Do break free," says Yoshi, gagged. His chair rattles violently. "Aaargh!"

NATE JOLTS, awakened by his own voice yelling, "Ilith!"

NATE WAKES UP. He can see some light through his hood. The fabric is decomposing, and the room seems to be lit by some kind of faint greenish emergency light. He can make out Lester, Yoshi, Ron, and the ghouls sitting quietly, their hoods looking thinner also, their faces almost showing through the fabric. Nathan tries biting the zip tie. Still sturdy. *Fucking plastic.*

NATE WAKES up to a deep rumbling sound. The ground shakes. Dust and debris come through a hole in his hood, into his lungs. He coughs. Through the hole, he can see that one of the walls has crumbled and fallen, revealing the room next to them, where the ceiling has collapsed and lies in a pile of rubble. Above that, he can see the station hall, and a crack of sunlight gleaming from above. The barking from outside is louder than he remembers.

"Thit!" Yoshi yells. "The thpores! They'll get in!"

"Kid," Ron says, "They're probably gone by now." He sounds tired.

"HOW LONG HAS IT BEEN?" Nate asks, waking in a confused daze. His gag feels looser.

"Long," Ron says.

Nathan's mind races. "And are you thirsty? Hungry? Tired?"

Yoshi and Lester look at each other through their half-disintegrated hoods. They frown, confused. "No."

The ghoul facing Nathan continues to grin, and he wonders if its face ever changed under the hood. Behind the zombie's head, a crack in the wall lets in a sliver of sunshine.

"What's happening to us?" Ron asks.

NATHAN SLIPS in and out of consciousness. The crack in the wall is wider now. He wakes up. A green sprout has writhed its way inside. He wakes up again. A large plant grows behind the ghoul's head. He wakes up. The plant is dead. He wakes up. A small sprout has grown from within the dead plant's core.

Nathan checks the plastic of the zip tie with his teeth. Still sturdy.

He rests his eyes. A bright green vine has climbed across the wall, slithering through the ghoul's head and behind the its grin.

He dozes off. He shakes his head, trying to stay awake. The room is green and mossy. He wakes up. The room is brown and dry. He wakes up. Plants have broken in through the crack in the wall and widened it, pushing cold bricks away with tender stems. He wakes up. The room teems with foliage, vines and leaves and branches filling the entire cavern, brushing up against his bare arms. He wakes up. Everything in the room is rotten. He wakes up. The room, itself, is rotten.

"What's ... going on?" Lester asks. His voice is deeper, and there's stubble on his face.

PART III

40

THEY LOOK JUST LIKE PEOPLE.

Skin is tight. Faded. The half-cocked grins look permanent. Their teeth look solid. Their sunken eyes stare. Their frowns boil with something that looks like anger. And their chests. Those cold stone chests. Nate keeps waiting for them to swell. He listens, waiting to hear the sound of breathing. But the corpses sit as still as the ruins around them.

The boys are asleep. Ron is asleep. The black hoods are now thin, worn-out rags hanging from their necks. The mossy, cracked walls are covered in vines. Large plants have crept in and blossomed. Gusts of wind come through the collapsed roof in the room next door, whistle and howl over the sunshine-lit pile of rubble, and shake big leaves around the room, all around Nate, the boys, Ron, and the four tied-up ghouls. Outside, in the distance, Nathan hears the dogs barking. They are faint now. Distant.

He turns back to the ghoul in front of him. His eyes glimmer. His jaw moves slightly, and the plastic tie holding him to the chair slides to the back of his mouth.

"They don't know about the other boy," he says. His uncanny

voice sounds like air passing through a mechanical pipe trying to sound human.

Nate struggles with his own plastic gag. "What other boy?"

The eyes of all four ghouls pierce through Nate. One of them leans into him as much as the plastic gag lets him. "You left him to die," the ghoul's raspy voice says under his breath.

Nate's eyes swell. A whimper rises from the bottom of his chest and escapes, quiet but disruptive enough to rouse the sleeping teens and Ron.

They open their eyes and stretch their gagged mouths around their zip ties. They instinctively try to move their hands, to lift up their backs, to sit up straight, and the reality of the plastic ties binding them to their chairs slowly comes to them.

The ghoul sits up again, stares at Nate, and grins.

"Listen," says Nate to the boys. "Am I crazy, or is the barking dying off?"

The boys listen carefully. "I think so," says Yoshi, still waking up.

Ron lets out a sigh of relief. "Last week it was maddening."

"Thank god," says Lester.

"Oh!" says Yoshi. "He talks!"

Nate hasn't heard Lester's voice in weeks, maybe months. He hasn't even seen him move. Lester seemed to be happy this fate had befallen the group, to be waiting patiently for death to save him. In this moment, though, it looks like he cares about something again.

"What *are* those dogs doing, anyway?" asks Yoshi.

A nearby bark rattles them. Even the ghouls, still looking straight at Nate, seem to jolt in their chairs.

"Ask Mom and Dad," Nate says, looking at the ghouls. "Dogs seem to be making them nervous."

"Quit it, Whitey," says Yoshi. "They're not our moms and dads."

Lester looks at them, examines them, obviously afraid. The ghouls grin. But their eyebrows jitter nervously.

"You see?" asks Nate, and this time it's he who leans into the ghouls, stretching his plastic tie, letting it hurt him, and pull from the sides of his mouth and teeth as he smiles. "They *are* scared."

Ron tries again to chew on his plastic tie. Nate can see teeth marks, but the ties don't seem harmed by his chewing. They are still strong.

"You play tough," the ghouls say, "but you won't risk your teeth for this."

"It's true!" says Yoshi, raising his voice. "They *are* nervous!"

They grin. "We can wait."

Nate tries again to bite down on the thick plastic tie in his mouth. It hurts. The plastic doesn't budge.

"They're bluffing," says Yoshi. "They're bluffing!"

Lester looks at him with pity. "Don't do it, Yoshi."

"What do you mean they're *bluffing*?" Ron asks.

Yoshi starts munching on the plastic. His teeth slip on the smooth, hard strip, but he keeps trying.

"They're willing to wait until the plastic dissolves," Nate says. "Yoshi's right. We shouldn't wait. We can still heal. We can get out of here!"

Yoshi's face turns into a grimace as the biting hurts his mouth. He *ouches* and he *fucks*, he checks his teeth and gums with a look of pain, but he keeps going.

He looks up at Lester. "Lester. Munch."

Lester takes a look at the lifeless ghouls.

"No, thanks," he says. "I'm keeping my teeth. I'm gonna be one of them soon."

Nate stops chewing. "Lester!"

"You can do it, too!" says Lester, pleading to them. "If we died right now, we'd live forever, in these bodies. We'd never age another day!"

"Quit it, moron!" says Yoshi.

"Your teeth will be fine," says Nate. "You're alive, for now, like it or not. Chew."

Yoshi spits out a tooth.

"Well, not fine, but, you know."

Lester doesn't move.

Something snaps. Yoshi shakes his head to the sides, and his plastic tie comes flying off.

"Yes!" Ron yells.

The ghouls look at them patiently.

With his head now free, Yoshi leans forward and pulls, breaking open the plastic tie binding him to the chair.

"Yes!" mumbles Nate as he chews. He can feel the plastic giving, stretching.

He looks at the ghouls. Gone are their menacing grins. Now they seem submissive. Weak.

Yoshi stands up and breaks away the tie holding Lester's hands. "This is gonna hurt," he says, pulling the one around his mouth, snapping it.

"Ouch!" yells Lester, and he checks his jaw with his suddenly free hands. He stands up as Yoshi unties Nate.

Ron's tie snaps as well. He yells a battle cry as he pulls his arms forward and breaks free.

For a moment, Ron, Nate, Yoshi, and Lester face off. All four of them clench their firsts, ready to fight.

Ron, eager to turn the attention away from himself, turns to the ghouls. "What do we do with the walkers?"

They relax their fists.

"I say we kill 'em," says Ron, stepping toward the ghouls.

"Stop," says Nate. "It's safer to keep them like this. Let's just leave them here. Don't get near them."

He hears a cry of pain from Yoshi behind him. The teen is rubbing his shoulder. "I really got hurt taking off those ropes," he says.

Nathan freezes.

"What?" Yoshi asks.

A cold shiver runs through Nate's spine. "What's that on your arm?"

Yoshi looks confused. "I don't know. My shoulder feels sticky —" he says, still probing the area with his hand.

When he brings his hand in front of him and looks at it, Nathan, still frozen in cold horror, watches Yoshi's eyes swell up.

His fingers are covered in green blood.

Nathan quickly runs a frantic check on his body for bruises or injuries. His hands run over his arms, torso, and legs, checking for anything unusual. But it all feels normal.

"Shit!" Ron yells next to him. He's staring down at his chest. Green blood pours from a small cut. "I'm one of them, too!" he yells. "I'm one of them!"

"No, you're not," Nate says, looking at his fingers, also green and gooey. "Stop panicking. We're fine—I think. We're just ..."

Lester takes a step back and looks at them in fear. He checks himself frantically and is relieved that what's left of his old suit shows no new signs of violence beyond that brought about by his own body's growth.

Finally, Lester steps back and voices the question on everyone's mind:

"What the hell is going on?"

41

RON STEPS ON A LOOSE PIECE OF RUBBLE AND CLIMBS GINGERLY upward toward Nate, who stands on the floor above, reaching for him. They lock arms. Nate's face turns into a grimace as he tries to hoist Ron up. The piece of rubble gives, and Ron slips. Below him, where the ghouls are still tied to their chairs with zip ties, the boys stare up in shock as Ron's foot gropes around wildly, searching for a solid piece of concrete. At last, he finds a foothold, pulls on Nate's arm, thrusts himself up, and reaches the landing.

Nate helps Lester up next. The teenager, still wearing the ragged remnants of his blue Victorian suit, holds a fresh mask up over fuzzy teenage stubble and makes an awful face as he inhales. He looks around with disgust. Behind him, Nate helps Yoshi stand. His awkward teenage body struggles to move in his stretched out black leather costume, or what's left of it. It's torn to shreds. Like Lester, he's clearly outgrown it. He holds his mask even tighter and shivers at the smell.

"I know," says Ron. "Smells like my mom's kitchen after steak night."

Yoshi turns around. "You still lived with your mother? Aren't you like forty?"

"I'm forty-five," Ron mumbles. "The economy."

"Right," Yoshi says. "The economy."

"At least I *was* forty-five," Ron corrects himself, looking at the teens. "Who knows how long it's been."

"The economy," Yoshi mocks him, clearly ashamed, trying to change the subject.

The air is filled with floating dust. The walls are dotted with patches of some kind of fatty substance. The splotches swell and beat like a sick heart.

Yoshi frowns. He looks around, moving to the sides as he walks, trying to dodge the spores in the air.

"You know what this is?" Lester asks, holding his mask. He sounds invigorated. "I read about this. It's human skin. We shed it, like, all the time."

"But why so much?" says Ron.

"Isn't it obvious?" asks Yoshi with a feisty tone.

"Get over it, kid," says Ron, "it wasn't me who tied you up, all right?"

Nate freezes. He signals them to be quiet.

Ron looks around, on the alert. "What?"

Nate takes a step toward the far end of the station, where the lights are long dead and no sunbeams reach.

Ron chuckles. "Oh, no fucking way I'm going—"

"*Shhh!*"

The boys are listening closely. Ron tries to hear what they're hearing.

Then he notices a hiss. A faint hiss. A whisper, calling to them.

Nate walks into the darkness weirdly blinking his eyes. Ron watches in amazement as Nate seems to dodge invisible obstacles, his hands reaching into the air and making soft sounds as they touch solid objects.

"He can see in the dark, the freak," says Yoshi.

Lester steps forward and puts his hand on Nate's shoulder, mimicking his every move. Yoshi follows, his hand on Lester's shoulder.

"Oh, come on," says Ron. "Are we really doing this?"

He strides toward them and puts his hand on Yoshi's shoulder. If he'd have waited a second longer, he'd have lost them all in the darkness.

It's advancing slowly. It moves up, and Ron steps carefully on his left foot. It stops, and he stops. He's blind. Nothing in the world but the kid's shoulder, and the faint hissing filling the air.

Yoshi stops.

He seems to be turning to the right. Ron turns and feels his hand moving away from him. He follows.

As his eyes get used to the dark, Ron starts to see a dark grayish-blue rectangular shadow ahead, lighter than the rest of the darkness. It's an open door. Yoshi's shoulder moves toward it, and Ron hangs on to it.

"The hissing," Ron says. "It's getting louder."

"*Shh.*"

Ron has a bad feeling about this. He squeezes Yoshi's shoulder, and he feels it stressing, probably signaling the same to the guys in the front. But they don't stop. They are approaching the open door. And between the steps, the hissing is getting louder.

Something soft and leathery brushes against his shoulder. As he walks past it, the fabric hisses right next to his ear, "Ronnn."

His body jolts, and he jumps, bumping into Yoshi's back.

"*You OK, man?*" the teen whispers.

Ron turns back. He looks around. All dark.

Suddenly, something touches him. A dark splotch of black reaches for him. It hovers in the air, moving up and down like a massive insect struggling against its own weight.

"Gah!" Ron shrieks and hits it with both hands, panicking.

"What?" mumbles Yoshi. Nate and Lester whisper something nearby.

Ron points at the dark, where the hovering ghost just was. "Did you—Did you see that?"

"Quiet," says Nate. "I saw it. Just keep going."

"You *saw* it?" Ron asks. "What was it?"

"Shh. Don't worry about it. Move along."

"Are there ..?"

"No. That wasn't a ghoul."

"Then what ..?"

"*Quiet.*"

Ron looks around. His entire body shakes with fear as the others guide him toward the open door. There is a dim light on the other side.

As they walk past it, as Ron's eyes adjust to the light, the outline of the space they've entered becomes sharper. It's the station's main hall. Empty shops surround them, also covered in the black grease. And at the end of the hall, beyond all the dust floating in the air, there it is. Sunlight. The metro station's main entrance.

"OK," Ron says, letting go of Yoshi's shoulder. "Coast is clear. Tell me what the hell that was."

He can see Nate turning around. He looks scared, but also in control.

"A coat," he says.

"What do you mean *a coat*?"

"It was hanging from outside that ticket booth," says Nate. "And it just ... reached for you."

"Ha," Ron chuckles. "You're fucking with me."

"The freak can see in the dark," says Yoshi. "I believe him."

"It's a brave new world," Lester announces. The kid sounds almost cheerful.

Nate stops dead in his tracks and turns to Lester. "Is this funny to you?"

Lester meets his gaze. "Yes."

"Jesus," says Ron. "Leave the kid alone."

Nate steps up to him next. "And you. You still think you're in charge, don't you?"

"What's up your ass?" Ron asks.

"Fuck!" Nate explodes, his voice echoing through the empty hall. "I really don't give a fuck anymore!" Nate yells. "Go, live, die, do whatever the fuck you want," he says. "I'm trying to help. The world's over, my girlfriend is dead, and here you are, just thinking this is a *fucking game!*"

"We'll find her," says Lester. He's tired, but his face is relaxed, almost smiling. "We'll find her, just like we'll find Frankie."

Nate looks at him with a resolve that Ron hasn't seen in him in years.

"She's DEAD!" Nate shouts. "And your friend, too. DEAD! All dead!"

"On the contrary, mister!" says Lester. "Don't you see? There's no death anymore."

Nate breathes heavily. He looks at Lester like he wants to kill him. The boy doesn't seem scared at all.

"OK, OK," says Ron. "I'll go find us a way out. Settle down."

And that's when Ron notices it. Behind Nathan. Among the specks of dust floating in the air. Somewhere in the dimly lit hall. Hovering. Floating.

A bolt of lightning runs through his spine. His body jitters and readies to run, but his legs are frozen in place.

He looks again. There's no one behind Nathan.

Lester steps past Nate, looking more curious than scared. The kid saw it, too.

"What *is* that?" he asks, his eyes moving in every direction.

Ron never lost sight of the station entrance, never loses sight of it, so there can't be anything hanging there in the darkness. Yet, the sunlight seems to flicker, as if it keeps getting blocked, slightly, by something. As if a rag, or a ghost, was hovering in the air, moving up and down, to the sides, erratically.

Nate looks at Ron curiously, then follows his gaze to see what's caught his attention. "What the—"

"You see it, too?" Ron asks.

Nate answers with one word.

"Run."

42

RON KNOWS HE CAN OUTRUN THE BUNCH OF THEM, EVEN though he's the oldest of the group and has spent the same number of years tied to a chair. But he paces himself to let Nate lead the way to the escalators.

"Wait!" says Yoshi, breathless, in the back. "I can't run in this suit."

"Well of course, dumbass!" Ron says. "Look at you! You've outgrown them!"

The boys examine each other. They share an awkward look.

"I bet your underwear still has room to spare!" Yoshi says to Lester, but the boy in the shredded blue suit shrugs it off with a strange confidence. He's the only one in the group who doesn't look totally defeated. In fact, he looks spirited.

Nate reaches the metallic steps and begins climbing them two at a time. Ron follows and feels his boot slip on a slick patch on the heavy metal steps. He looks down and sees dark spots on the shiny surface of several stairs. The liquid is thick, like blood.

"What are you doing?" Yoshi asks. "Keep going!"

Ron resumes his climb and finally reaches the last steps. The vast hall is dim, but there's sunlight coming through dirty glass windows at the far end. There's a wide central aisle leading to a revolving door, behind which he can see the street. And at both sides of the aisle, around the large dark hall, human figures wait for them.

He reaches for Nathan. "Wait! Stop!"

But Nathan has already reached the landing and is running toward them.

Ron whispers as loudly as he can without shouting. "Nathan!"

Nathan stops, already surrounded by the dark figures, and turns around. "What?"

Ron's eyes start to adjust to the dark. The figures surrounding Nate are mannequins. This is a department store.

"N—Nothing," he says.

Nathan walks down the central aisle toward the door, and Ron follows him through the abandoned shop. His body is stiff with fear. In the dim light, mannequins seem to turn their heads as he walks by.

"So," Ron says. "Flying coats? Ghosts in the hallways? What's going on? What was that?"

"I don't know."

"It's those things," says Lester, waving his finger in the air. "Skin flakes. That human grease. It's all alive."

"And it's everywhere," says Yoshi, looking around.

The floor creaks as he steps onto the worn-out green carpet. A thin layer of dust covers the floor and lifts into the air with every step. Walls are greasy. Yoshi presses his mask tight against his nose and mouth.

"It's all because of our immortality," Lester says, whatever that means.

Ron turns to him so fast that his neck cracks. "Enough already, kid."

"Yeah," Yoshi says, fed up.

As they walk down the aisle, Ron notices more dark spots on the carpet. It's a trail of blood. And they're following it. "Looks like someone already took this exit," he says.

"I wonder if it will hurt," says Lester, excited. "But then, after that, we'll have our bodies forever!"

"Shut up," says Yoshi, "It's not funny." His voice is changing, faltering.

"We just need something painless. Quick. Something that won't leave a mark. This is so great!"

Ron takes a deep breath. "I swear to god—"

Ron steps on something soft. There's a pile of clothes on the floor. Broken pieces of mannequins and hangers lie around. And more blood. Everywhere.

"There was a fight here."

"So?" Yoshi scoffs at him from behind.

Yoshi picks up one of the hangers. He hands it to Lester. "Here," he says.

Lester examines it. "Here what?"

"Use it," Yoshi says. "Kill yourself. You say you wanna die, so do it."

Lester smiles. He's calm as a monk. "Not like that, you idiot," he replies. "It can't be violent. We have to stay beautiful corpses."

The other boy is getting visibly annoyed. "I think you're too late for that."

"Hey, beautiful," Ron says. "Go ahead and change, will ya? Put something on, chrissakes."

"We're not changing," they say in unison. "Especially not in here."

"You've been squirming in those clothes since we made it out of that room. Change."

The boys look at each other again and turn to the racks. They start browsing, avoiding the greasy patches.

"Why don't you believe me?" Lester asks. "It makes sense, doesn't it? We're gonna end up dead anyway, sooner or later—"

Something brushes against Ron's forearm. He jumps up, electrified.

"What now?" Nate whispers.

Ron finds a mannequin touching his arm and chuckles. "Oh," he says, relieved. "Sorry, I just— I thought ... never mind."

The boys emerge from the clothes racks admiring their new suits. "What happened?"

Ron can't believe his eyes. "Are you guys shitting me?"

They're wearing the same costumes as before, only now their cheap halloween costumes somehow look real. Lester dusts off his blue suit covering a puffy shirt that still makes him look like Austin Powers, and Yoshi tightens the straps of his new leather suit, now a shiny, seriously intimidating version of his kiddy costume.

"We found some grownup clothes, and adapted them," Yoshi says. "They were buried beneath other clothes, so none of that sticky grease, either."

"Underwear's different, too," Lester adds, making himself comfortable.

"Will you take those pins off, at least?"

Yoshi scoffs. "Um, no?"

Next to Ron, the mannequin's plastic lips part, and its mouth opens, revealing its hollow insides full of black grease, and as its hand stretches toward him, it exhales with the voice of wind blowing through dead pipes:

"Rooonnn."

Ron turns to the others. His eyes are wide open. The others look at him with the same expression of shock.

They bolt down the aisle toward the door, screaming like madmen, but Nate stops them before they burst out the exit. He and Ron do their best to survey the scene outside. The windows are so dusty that they barely let the sun in, making the outside look like an old photograph, or a still sandstorm.

"Do you hear that?" says Lester, turning around.

"What?"

The sunlight reveals the store to be even messier than it looked in the dark. Mannequins and clothes are thrown around on the floor. Blood is everywhere.

"Those mannequins are alive, kid," Ron says. "I'm not going back there."

"Shh," Lester says. "This is something else."

A slight hiss. A low whisper, like the rustling of dry leaves taken over by the wind. But there is no wind in the store. There is no movement at all.

Lester examines a rack of coats and takes a step toward it. His footsteps are muffled by the carpet. That sound, it's coming from somewhere close. Ron can hear it now, too.

The sound becomes clearer as they approach the rack of coats. It's weeping.

When they finally reach the display, Nathan looks down at the floor behind it, and he freezes.

"What is it?" Ron asks.

Nathan doesn't move. He doesn't say a word. They crowd around him to get their own looks.

It's just a head.

It lies face down on the carpet, moving its mouth like a fish out of water, its nose lifting it ever so slightly. It's weeping in silence, fighting to breathe. It's asking for help.

Ron speaks first. "A live head. But that's impossible."

Nate looks closer. "It looks like—It's Big Momma."

"But that's impossible," Ron repeats, his eyes widening almost to the point of escaping their sockets. "It's just a head. They're killed by a shot to the head, or cutting it off—"

Nate turns around. There's fire in his eyes. "Snap out of it! They're dead. They didn't die the first time, so what makes you think they'll die at all?" His breathing is frantic. He's heaving, red-faced. "Get it through your thick skull: They. Don't. Die."

"You mean *we* don't die," says Yoshi. His tone is low and devoid of hope. He chuckles. "Never. Ever. You get it now, Les?"

Lester is looking down at the head, in shock. He looks terrified.

The head looks up at him, eyes big and round, no eyelids to

blink. The skinless jaw seems to be smiling. It opens and closes, and a tongue tries to escape its mouth. "H-e-l-p ..."

Ron paces forward, his heavy steps muffled by the thick carpet, and steps on it. He kicks it, kicks it again, and crushes it under his heavy boot. He lifts his foot. The head, now a mush, still heaves and mouths its desperate, pathetic plea. The tongue dances like a slug that's been covered with salt, and they all stare at it in silence.

"You get it now?" says Yoshi, his voice trembling with fear. "Now that we *have* to live forever, we need to be *more* careful than before. Not less."

Lester can't look away from the heaving mush. His chest rises and falls in silence, as restless as the tongue on the floor. "Frankie!" he yells, all of a sudden, and he turns to Yoshi. "We have to help him!"

Yoshi looks at the squashed head. "How?"

"We have to protect him. Maybe we can put him back together!"

Ron tries to look outside through the dusty glass window. "Good luck finding him, first," he says.

Yoshi thinks about it. "And what good is that gonna do him?"

"We have to try, don't we?" Lester asks.

"Come on," yells Ron, holding the revolving door to the outside. "Let's get out of this crazy place."

THE IRON DOOR RUMBLES. BEHIND THE VIGILES INSCRIPTION, A heavy mechanism turns and slides. The giant wheel gyrates and something inside unlatches. The door makes a twisted metal sound and opens.

A formation of soldiers in military armors and helmets empties out onto the station rooftop. Lilith, Wolfram, and Wednesday climb the staircase behind them. Lilith has a hard time walking in the heavy armor, but she stomps eagerly on each step, ready to get her first glimpse of the sky in years. She trudges out into the sunlight and looks up. The helmet glass makes everything blurry and twisted and turns her breath into a near-blinding fog. All she sees is a tint of blue and the yellow stabs of the sun's flare.

As her breath dissipates, she notices one of the soldiers checking a device on her wrist and giving Chief Girardot a thumbs-up. A muffled, blurry vision of the chief takes off his helmet.

"Yes," Lilith says under her breath, and before the glass can be covered in her breath again, she takes it off. "Finally!"

She gasps for air. It's a clear day, and the air is fresh and new.

The soldiers take out their helmets and armors. Out here,

under the sun, they look different than under the white fluorescent lights of the bunker. She can tell they've all changed over the years. All that heavy training she saw them doing. All those pills and supplements and vitamins. They may be pale, and have bags under their eyes, but the small army assembling on the station's rooftop looks like they could take on the world. She must look like that as well. What else was there to do but join the training? She looks at her arms and torso. *Fucking hell*, she thinks. *They're as flabby as ever.*

The chief looks up at the sky, takes a deep breath, and smiles. "We've done it, boys."

His optimism is catchy. Lilith thinks of Nate, and how he should be here with her, alive, to be part of the revenge. He could have helped them clear the cemetery. It's his home, after all. *This one's for you, Nate.*

"Ready for Operation Full Sweep?" the chief asks.

"Yes, Sir!" the formation replies.

"Ready to clean up our town?"

"Yes, Sir!" they reply. They look eager for action.

"Ready to clean up the world?"

"Yes, Sir!" they reply, cheerful.

"Finally, after all these years of planning," the chief yells, "It's go time!"

They all cheer. Their voices go up to the sky and echo around Leatelranch. Chief Girardot steps onto the roof's ledge and surveys the street below.

"It's a brave new world," he says, shaking his head. "Look at that. Careful, now."

Lilith joins the others on the ledge. From their vantage point on the rooftop, Leatelranch looks like a ghost town. Green, mossy. The park and the streets surrounding it are swarming with ghouls, all standing still in silence, like a photograph.

"It's like the whole town is just frozen in time," Wednesday says.

"Surely not a problem for the tanks," Lilith says.

"But why aren't they coming up?" asks Wolfram. "After all these years, even the cemetery is still quiet. Why haven't they come for us?"

"All those guards we took," says Wednesday, sounding annoyed. "We lost sleep for nothing."

"They're up to something," says Lilith.

"Well, we're up to something, too," says the chief.

Lilith narrows her eyes and tries to draw more conclusions. "Even after all these years," she says, "they seem to rot, but they still keep all their functions. They can still walk, and see, and ... *think*."

"How do you know?" Wolfram says. "They aren't moving."

"They aren't moving right now, no. What worries me is the loose parts."

"What loose parts?"

"Look," Lilith says, pointing. "There. And there, on the grass. Limbs. Torsos. It's like there was a struggle."

"They *fought* each other?"

"And look," says Lilith. "That's new. There."

She points at a streetlight. A head is hanging from it, tied up by its own long red hair.

"What *is* that?" asks Wolfram.

"Laureant?" asks the chief.

"Yes, sir?"

"Shoot that down."

Laureant gets down on one knee and, with a bang, the head explodes.

"Should we change our plans?" asks Wolfram.

Lilith thinks about it.

"We go on with the plan," says the chief. "If anything, this only means they're less organized than we thought."

Lilith bites her lip. "I'm not sure."

"Well, I'm sure for you," says the chief. "It's one thing to be unpredictable. But a battalion doesn't change plans at the last minute."

"But Papa," Wednesday says with a trembling voice. "They're everywhere. What about the others? On the radio? Can't we get any more people to help?"

"We talked about this, Pumpkin," he says. "They can't be trusted."

"But ... the people on the TV—"

"Did you see how they looked?" Wolfram asks her. "Who were they trying to fool?"

"Even the untrustworthy signals kept dropping," adds the chief. "There haven't been any for over six months." He looks at her gravely. "We must assume we're the last ones."

"Aren't we lucky?" Wolfram says, glancing at Lilith.

"We will clean up Leatelranch ourselves," the chief says. "Then, the world. And it all starts there," he says, pointing down. "In the cemetery."

He turns to Wednesday. "Are you ready, Pumpkin?"

She and Wolfram share a look of enthusiasm. "Yes," they say in unison.

"Tanks are over there," he adds, pointing at a storehouse across the park. The front gate is made of iron, big enough to fit a plane, and surrounded by ghouls. "We need to open that. No way to open it manually. We need to start the generator—there." He points at another building.

"No problem," says Wolfram, and he pats Wednesday's shoulder. "We'll be right back."

"Be careful," says the chief. "You haven't done this in a while."

Wolfram looks around and starts walking toward a ledge facing a taller building. Wednesday smiles. "Don't worry, Papa."

"Remember," says Lilith, "don't be predictable. Don't get caught."

Wednesday smiles. "We won't," she says, and they bolt, sprinting and jumping to the next building.

Lilith turns to Chief Girardot. "What about the rest of us? How are we gonna get across that park riddled with ghouls?"

"We'll catch up," he says. "I know a shortcut. As for

you ... You wanted out, right? You wanted our help to get to New Southport? A promise is a promise."

She takes another look at the park. The dead swarm it like an anthill. This time, she finds herself checking their faces, trying to recognize them, looking for one face in particular.

"Nate's dead," she says. "There's nothing I can do about that. And I know full well, if we don't clean the cemetery, we don't survive. Not to go to New Southport, not to rebuild Leatelranch, not to do anything. I'm coming with you."

The chief smiles, proud. "Good," he says. "I'm sure he wouldn't blame you. Let's go."

IN DARKNESS, LILITH EXTENDS HER ARMS TO HER SIDES AND feels the soft earthy walls through her reinforced gloves. She struggles to walk in the heavy armor as her feet sink into the muddy ground. Her heavy helmet keeps leaning to the left.

"I hate this thing," she says, adjusting it.

She can barely see soldier in front of her who barks, "Do *not* take it off."

Chief Girardot calls for the small company to halt, and the soldiers comply. He points his flashlight toward the upper part of the tunnel wall. A small spark of fire, a match, shines its orange light on the chief's helmet. It floats toward the wall, trembling in the darkness. Lilith jumps as, with a *poof!*, it ignites a brighter flame that races toward her along a small gutter rigged to the cave's wall, shedding flickering firelight on the hunched soldiers in their black body armor.

"Well," says Chief Girardot, the echo carrying his voice along the tunnel. "Oil's still here."

The hunched figures rise and march forward. Lilith follows them.

"So, where are we going exactly?" she asks.

In the front of the line, Chief Girardot chuckles. "You'll see."

Lilith doesn't like the sound of it. She follows the line through the tunnel, looking at the earthy walls lit by the flickering light. It feels strangely cozy, even under the weight of the police armor.

The line stops. Up ahead, two tunnels appear like dark gaping mouths. Chief Girardot lights the oil gutter in the left tunnel, and the march resumes. As she walks by the fork, she sees a sign. It must be a hundred years old, at least. The rusty red handwriting reads PRESIDENTIAL ESTATE with an arrow to the left, and TRAIN STATION with an arrow to the right.

"Presidential Estate?" says Lilith.

A heavy hand lands on her shoulder.

"Don't stray," Chief Girardot says. "We discover new tunnels every day, and some of them lead to nowhere. I don't want to lose you down here."

She picks up the pace, catching up to the others, and the chief stays close behind. "I can't believe these tunnels actually exist," she says. "In school, they taught us about the Jesuit tunnels as an urban myth, something from before the foundation ..."

"Well, they sure exist," says the chief, speaking through his helmet.

"It's pretty cool," she says, looking around.

"Yep," he says. "It is pretty cool."

Lilith feels weird that they agree on something.

"This particular tunnel was renewed when they built the presidential estate," he continues. "Back when Leatelranch was the newest settlement, with good transportation and being the perfect distance from the city, the president decided to build his summer estate here."

"I must have been sick the day they taught that," she says.

"Yes. Sick. I'm sure you guys weren't cutting school."

The line stops again. The soldiers light another entrance.

"Yeah," says Lilith. "So, these tunnels will lead us to the cemetery?"

"Ah. You must have been sick that day, too."

"What do you mean?"

Chief Girardot looks at her and smiles. "It's funny you should ask."

She looks at him, puzzled.

"It's *very* funny you should ask," he repeats.

The soldiers resume their march, and the chief signals her to keep going. Lilith notices that the walls, lit by the flickering flames, seem to be closing in. Up ahead, the tunnel forks into two smaller openings. The soldiers have lit up the one to the right. Between the entrances, there is a plank of dusty old wood. It looks hundreds of years old. The letters carved on it are rudimentary. The handwriting, though, seems almost familiar. The left side says TEMPLVM. The right one says CVSTODIS.

"Well," says Chief Girardot behind her, "these tunnels precede the new cemetery. The closest exit is the old caretaker's house."

"Nate's house."

Chief Girardot is silent. Lilith notices the ground is beginning to slant upward. The tunnel is rising to the surface. She looks over her shoulder and sees the chief grinning behind his helmet.

"Nope," he says. "That's the *new* caretaker's house."

Lilith doesn't understand.

"Your dad never told you?" He shakes his head. "The current cemetery is new. It was created when the plague—"

"Yes, I know about the plague."

"Well, then you should also know, there was already a cemetery before that one."

Lilith's voice bubbles up her throat. "The park?"

"When the plague hit, they realized they'd need a much bigger one, so they moved the bodies to the current Necropolis, and transformed the old one into, yes—"

"The park?" asks Lilith again, baffled. "The park where we played as kids?"

He chuckles inside his helmet. "Creepy, huh."

Lilith stares at the tunnel wall. Her pupils dilate, and all she can see is a blur.

"And there's a house, maybe you noticed it, a little white brick house overlooking the park, that looks older than the other ones."

Lilith's mind races. Her condensed breath creeps up the helmet glass.

"That's because it was the first one on the block," Chief Girardot says. "Actually, it was there before there *was* a block. It's been there since the original cemetery days. The *first* caretaker's house."

As the slow march of soldiers comes to a stop, her mouth trembles. Someone calls for Chief Girardot from the front of the line. An old brick wall blocks the end of the tunnel. Chief Girardot signals with his hands, then grabs Lilith's armored shoulders to pull her back, away from the wall. The soldiers place something against the bricks, step back, and the wall blasts into pieces.

Up ahead, behind the settling dust, it looks exactly how she remembers it: Lilith's childhood living room.

45

RON TURNS THE RUSTY REVOLVING DOOR, AND A PIERCING shriek fills the abandoned store. He pushes with one hand and holds his mask with the other, and the boys see him making his way out to the street, almost disappearing behind the dusty, brownish glass.

He walks a couple of steps to the right, disappearing from the boys' sight, and reappears behind the window, which frames the scene outside like a cinema-sized projection screen. The dusty window makes it look like he's in the middle of a sandstorm, or a sepia-toned silent film. The yellow morning sun shines on his face, and he looks up at it, narrowing his eyes. He takes off his mask, and the boys can see that he's smiling. He takes a deep breath, smiles, and looks back inside, searching for them through the dirty pane.

"All clear!" he yells.

Inside, crouching behind a couch, Nate holds Lester and Yoshi by the shoulders. They keep a distance, so the fabric can't touch them. The cushions, like the walls around them, swell with greasy spots that beat like charred hearts.

Ron hits the window glass. "Oh, come on now!" he yells, inviting them, "the smell's a bit nasty, but otherwise ..."

He hears a noise in the street and turns around to the other end of the screen. He freezes.

"No," says Lester.

Two figures walk into the frame from the left. They look like charred bacon, and their bodies release black dust with each step, their legs charcoal logs scraping each other. One of them is shorter than the other. Smaller.

"Is that ...?" asks Yoshi.

The figures walk toward Ron, who looks at them in panic, his hands reaching for something, feeling their way along his pockets and sides, all empty. They close in. He makes a grimace that tells Lester that the charred figures smell *really* bad. One of the figures, the shorter one, turns and looks inside the store, looking straight at them. They can see the holes in his eyes.

"Yes," says Nate. "It's them."

Kenny Macomber grins, and his charcoal features rub against each other, sending splinters to the ground. He focuses again on Ron. Father and son take a step toward him.

Ron steps back. Even behind the brown glass, his face looks sheet white. But as they get closer to him, Lester notices that Ron's gaze is not stuck on the charred ghouls but is alternating between them and something else behind them.

That's when he hears the barking.

As the ghouls get closer to Ron, he glances over his shoulder, and his face goes from worried to desperate. The ghouls stop dead in their tracks and also seem interested in whatever's happening behind Ron.

The barking grows louder. Lester hears the muffled rustling of nails on the pavement, and judging by the way Ron is rotating back and forth, the sound seems to be coming from every direction.

It all happens in one split second: Mr. Macomber, the taller charred ghoul, opens his jaw and reaches for Ron, with more of a taunt than an actual attack. Ron lifts his arm to defend himself, and Kenny pounds on him in the right moment, as if he were waiting for that exact move. In the air, in mid-jump, it almost looks like Kenny turns to Lester, looks him in the eye, and taunts him.

"Shit," Lester says under his breath, and he hears Yoshi saying it at the same time.

From each side of the window, packs of dogs enter the frame and pounce on the ghouls like breaking waves of raw muscle and teeth. They knock them down to the ground and pile atop them, closing their jaws on every limb and tearing them apart. Ron witnesses the spectacle with trembling legs, covering his face with both arms, shaking with fear. The deep sound of growling fills the air, even inside the department store. Ron steps backward, trying to reach the revolving door again, when a loud, piercing whistle echoes in the street.

And the growling stops.

Mr. Macomber and Kenny get up, half destroyed. They look down at the dogs around them and lift their heads to look at something approaching from further away. They turn to each other. They hold each other's charred mangled hands.

Ron turns to the window again. His face trembles, shiny with sweat.

"What's going on?" asks Yoshi, craning his neck to get a better view.

Nate signals him to be quiet.

A pack of headless ghouls marches into view from the left. They walk among the dogs, cornering Ron against the window. Their headless bodies fill the window and, from the looks of it, the street. Ron desperately searches for a way out. His chest is beating so hard it looks like it's about to explode.

"Wha—? How ...?" he asks, his muffled voice coming from behind the glass.

The headless mob opens out to reveal a short man, his head still attached and looking alive, but with a face as expressionless as those of the ghouls around him. His black sunglasses hide his eyes, and a full-body black biker suit covers his body. A huge scar runs along his cheek, the only remarkable feature on the otherwise nondescript man. He walks confidently toward Mr. Macomber and Kenny, through the area filled with dogs, who make way for him as he walks. The charred ghouls are standing like broken statues, staring at each other with unbeating chests. Their hands remain locked.

"Why are they so still?" Yoshi asks. "Why don't they run away?"

"Don't look," says Nate, and the boys pay closer attention.

The stranger whistles. The headless mob closes in on father and son, their hands exploring their shoulders and faces, fingers slithering like worms inside their open mouths. As the Macombers tighten their grips on each other's hand, as they say goodbye, the ghouls pull their mouths open, jerking their jaws back until they crack. The pieces drop to the ground. Sleeping. Silent.

Ron exhales. He looks up at the stranger and smiles. "Oh, man, thank god—"

The stranger snaps his fingers, and the growling resumes. The dogs circle around Ron.

"What—wait—"

The stranger whistles again, and the circle closes over him like fire ants.

"No!" Ron manages to yell.

With a cracking sound, two arms shoot up above the pile, pulling off Ron's head in a thick spray of blood.

Lester is about to shout, and Nathan's hand covers his mouth.

The anthill spreads out. It sounds like Ron is crying. Before his body can slump down, as Ron's head wails down on the pavement, four headless ghouls grab him by the sides and pull, ripping his arms off. Ron's body stands, idle.

The stranger kicks the head toward the rest of the headless ghouls, who pick it up and place it in a bag. He approaches Ron's standing body and pokes it in the neck with two fingers.

"Shh," he says, and the scar on his cheek stretches like a pink worm.

Inside the bag, Ron shouts as loud as he can.

The stranger takes three fingers and jabs him in the ribs. "Tch."

The shouting stops.

As the dogs pounce again on Kenny and Mr. Macomber, tearing them apart, breaking them to shreds and spreading their ash along the street, Ron's headless body joins the formation of headless ghouls.

"Shit," Lester whispers to Yoshi, pointing at one of the headless ghouls. "Look at that."

It's shorter than the others. It's wearing a teal hospital gown.

"It's him," he says in a low voice. "Frankie's one of them."

The stranger disappears into the headless crowd again. The formation marches away, and the headless body in the teal hospital gown follows them.

46

Wolfram takes off his helmet and armor, puts on his hood, and joins Wednesday, crouching on the ledge of the roof. On the street, a thousand ghouls plague the pavement. The next building is an old one-screen cinema. After that, an empty lot, and then, finally, their destination—a small warehouse.

"There's the generator," he says.

"Shit," Wednesday says, "we still need to get across that alley. What is up with that smell?"

"Yeah. They're all rotten. They don't seem like much of a threat anymore."

"I don't know," she says. "Up here they can't hurt us. Down there ... there's too many. You think they can run?"

"I *know* they can run."

"You think they're faster than us?"

"No way," he says. "Come on. I'll run you for it."

He jumps down onto a window ledge and launches himself to the marquee of the cinema next door, hanging over the huge block letters. Within seconds, Wednesday is next to him, holding on to the giant sign with a smug smile. He crawls along the marquee to the side of the building, feeling the cold glass on his chest, then jumps to an emergency exit staircase and climbs down. He's about to drop to the ground in an empty alley when he feels the staircase shake. He looks up.

"You're too slow," Wednesday says with a grin, beginning her descent down the stairs.

Clank!

Wednesday freezes. There is a sudden, awful silence. Across the street, the ghouls in the park have stopped doing whatever they were doing to look in their direction.

"What happened?" Wolfram mouths to her.

They both slowly turn their heads to look at the marquee. It reads THRILL R.

"Oh shit," he says. And Wednesday doesn't need to ask, she doesn't need to turn around, because she can hear the shuffling of feet on the pavement behind her.

"RUN!" he yells.

They run back up the staircase all the way to the roof. Their urgent steps are heavy and move the metal structure, rocking it, making more clanking noises. Below, the gathering ghouls look up at them.

They reach the roof. As they sprint across it, Wolfram looks down. The ghouls on the street follow them like iron filings to a magnet.

"Ok," he says. "Once more, with feeling."

Wolfram looks down at the generator. The lot between the cinema and the warehouse is still empty.

"We'll never make it," she says.

"I have an idea," he says. "Look."

He points to the alley just before the generator. "C'mon," he says, "They'll never catch us."

"But they're so many—"

He climbs down to a window ledge. He looks down and calculates the fall.

"What's the matter?" she asks. "Stuck?"

He lets go and lands on the pavement with a roll. He looks up at her and smiles. "It's a high fall, but even you can make it."

"Fuck you," she says, and lets go. She lands on her hands and feet next to him, making a small splash. The air escapes her lungs as her hands sink into the puddled water and find the hard asphalt.

"You OK?" he says.

"Of course," she says.

Hearing a rumble, Wolfram looks over his shoulder at the crowded street. The army of ghouls stampede like a drove of bulls.

Wolfram and Wednesday look up at the window. It's too high to reach.

"Shit," he says.

"Fuck," she says.

"Fucking shit," he says.

"Shitting fuck," she says.

Wolfram searches the area for an opening, an escape, something. But the only way out is through the sea of ghouls. He points to the end of the flooded alley. "*Go!*"

He speeds off. She quickly catches up, then passes him, splashing splotches of dirt water at him. The first to reach the end of the alley, she jumps up onto a trash can, landing with her feet on both sides of its circumference, balancing herself. She looks back at Wolfram and smiles.

"Why so slow?"

She grabs hold of a thick line of exposed cables, pulls up, steps on it, and boosts herself onto a window ledge. Wolfram follows. She makes it to the roof.

Standing on the cables, Wolfram looks up to see Wednesday smiling at him, red-faced, sweaty, and beautiful. She extends a hand down to him.

"Need any help?"

He jumps, avoiding her open hand, and grabs the ledge. She moves back so he can climb to the roof.

She breathes heavily. "So ... they ... can ... run," she says.

"They can ... fucking run," he manages to say.

The ghouls take the alley with a storm of stomping feet and loud splotches, making waves, moving debris and black trash bags.

"What the fuck?" asks Wednesday. "Did it rain?"

"The park was dry," he says, "I think the sewer drains are clogged."

The alley is now busting with corpses looking at them, reaching for them.

"Well," he says, "they may run, but they sure can't climb." He turns to her. She's gone.

"Wednesday? Wednesday?"

He hears glass breaking down below and checks the building wall. Wednesday is climbing back down. She's holding to the window ledge, and one of her hands is bloody red.

"Wednesday?" he asks. "What the fuck?"

She reaches down to the thick blue bundle of cables and starts sawing away at it with the piece of glass.

"Shit," says Wolfram. "Be careful."

She keeps cutting, rocking her whole body from side to side until the cables finally split open and fall to the ground, barely missing one of the ghouls' heads. They throw pale blue sparks as they touch the water.

With a whipping blast, the entire alley is electrified. The ghouls convulse and rave as the volts pass through their bodies.

"They can dance!" she says, quickly working her way back up toward the roof and away from the electric blue waves down below. Her wet hands climb fast, and Wolfram can see the tips of her fingers slipping off the wet border of the ledge.

"Wednesday!" he yells, "Be careful!"

It's too late.

As she falls, her body skims the wall and the cables stuck to it, managing to get a somewhat graceful foothold on one of the ghouls' shoulders. Wolfram sees sparks. Her body jolts.

"Wednesday!" he yells.

She quickly springs back up and gets a hold of the wires still attached to the wall. She climbs up toward the ledge of the roof.

Wolfram reaches down to her. "Are you OK?"

She stretches up, trying to grab his hand. "Help."

"My God," he says, stretching his arm further. "Wednesday, are you OK?"

She catches her breath. "Yes, yes, I'm OK," she says, reaching for him. "Stretch down a little more."

Wolfram looks deep into her eyes. She's panting, blushed, and returns the gaze with a look of excitement. Of hunger. A blue spark rises inside her right eye.

He gasps.

"Wanna dance?" she says with a smile, revealing more blue sparks traveling around the insides of her mouth.

Wolfram gets up and runs. He jumps to the next roof, striding, and jumps again to the next one. He steps on black tile and cement and concrete, he runs through chimneys and towers and fences, sure that he's never run this fast in his life. When he lands on another roof and doesn't hear her behind him, he pauses to take a breath.

He should have known better. With an incredible show of strength, Wednesday manages to jump her way to the roof, and now she's only feet away, looking deep into his eyes.

"They can parkour, too," she says snidely.

He runs to the nearest ledge and looks down. The next house has a church-like pointed roof, too low and too steep to land on. There are no other options. He feels her hand on his shoulder. She slowly pulls back his hood with the other hand, then nuzzles her nose against his ear.

"*I gave you a head start*," she whispers, "*and you still lost.*"

He tries to give her a push, but she grabs his hands in mid-air, making him drop the key to the generator. She opens her jaw and closes it on the back of his neck, pulling away a mouthful of flesh and nerves. She grabs the keys in mid-air.

"We're gonna need those," she says, spitting out a piece of flesh.

"Yes, we will," he agrees.

He puts his hood back on and smiles. A glob of blood drips from between his teeth.

They make their way back toward the generator. They have tanks to set free.

NATE HOLDS HIS MASK WITH ONE HAND AND PUSHES THE handle on the heavy revolving door with the other, leaning on it with his shoulder. The boys help him push, and it finally lets them out.

The wind whooshes softly around them as if it were the only inhabitant of the dusty barren city. The street is empty as far as they can see. Plants have overtaken cars and buildings. Dark patches of grease pulse idly under the sun. In front of them, random pieces of clothes and bones on the street recall the shape of the fallen giant that chased after them a few years back.

"It really was the end of the world," says Yoshi.

Lester raises his hand to his face to remove his mask.

"Stop!" Yoshi yells at his friend. "What are you doing?"

"It's OK," says Lester. "Ron said it was OK."

"You mean Ron, the idiot who took his mask off and maybe turned into one of them immediately? That means shit. We keep them on."

"The air looks clean, actually," says Nate, looking around.

Yoshi doesn't buy it. "Yeah, but where did all the spores go?"

"Mhm," says Nate, thinking, looking around. "I don't know.

Maybe they've been absorbed by the ground? Or trapped in buildings and sewers, or gone to the sea? Who knows? But the air looks clean."

"I don't like this shit," says Yoshi.

"Relax," says Lester, his hand still on his mask. He pulls it down and breathes in, flexing his stubble-covered face and mouth.

Yoshi frowns and stares deeply at Lester, preparing to run.

Nate also has his eyes fixed on Lester. Waiting.

"It's clean!" says Lester after a long moment, and he inhales again. "It's clean! So, are we the only ones left?"

Yoshi looks at him with suspicion. He finally takes off his mask and breathes in. He looks mildly relieved.

"Other than that zombie-whisperer fuck, you mean?" he asks.

"No, I mean, where are the zombies?" asks Lester.

Nathan sees the buildings, taken by mold and time. He looks at the street, the aftermath of a combat zone, where garbage, disintegrated clothes, and human remains are scattered, forming bumps on the pavement in a shape that resembles a giant human, or the ground-corpse beast that almost killed them.

"It's ... like ... a cemetery," he says, his gaze still wandering around the surreal landscape. "The whole city."

"Look!" says Yoshi, pointing up. "The head that I hit. It's still there."

Above the street, an old, rotten, one-eyed zombie head hangs from a cable. It's facing them, and its jaw seems to be shaking and trembling.

"You thought it was going to just walk away?" asks Lester, examining the head.

"Shh," says Nate. "Is it ... trying to speak?"

The head chatters in the air at the same rate as him.

Nathan stares at it, baffled. "No," he says, looking at the moving jaw, feeling he can control it with every move of his own face. "He's *imitating* us."

He darts his head to the left. A familiar sound echoes through the empty street, coming from a couple of blocks away. It sounds like a machine, but deeper, hollower, and more desperate.

It's a pack of dogs.

"Come," says Lester, walking toward it. "We're going to get Frankie."

48

———————

CLOUDS BREW ACROSS THE BLOOD-ORANGE SKY. THE SUN sizzles and melts as it begins to set over the horizon. At the far end of the park, behind the horde of headless ghouls, behind the iron statue of Salomone Francis looking up in the air, behind the line of hedges and trees, behind the black iron fence and its open gate, and across the street, the doors on the white brick house open. A battalion of soldiers marches out, forming parallel lines on the sidewalk. An arm sticks up from the center of the formation and signals them forward. Silently, they cross the empty stretch of pavement to the infested park. As they march, they spread out, revealing the arm's owner, a man with a bushy mustache dressed in civilian clothes, who marches with a younger woman next to him. She has black ruffled up hair and green eyes brighter than the misty grass around her.

The formation marches in through the iron gate, still far enough from the ghouls to draw any attention. The ghouls, headless, run around, chasing, catching, and releasing each other, unaware of the soldiers.

The man with the bushy mustache looks to the far right of the park. Across the street, on top of the roof of a warehouse, two tiny figures give him a thumbs-up. The man gives another command with his raised hand, and the formation splits. Half of them make a beeline to the warehouse, moving swiftly across the dry yellow grass diving into a patch of hedges. As they make their way through the hissing bushes, they pass close by a group of headless corpses, drawing the attention of one of them, who turns its torso to them. By then, the first of the soldiers has already exited the hedges, and as the full line crosses the street to the large warehouse, the hissing dies down. The headless body turns back and joins the others.

The line stops at a small door in the warehouse. The door opens, and they disappear inside.

A low rumble moves the earth. The ghouls in the park all turn their chests toward the warehouse. Its large iron gate is opening. They turn to each other, curious. They grab their vibrating chests and pace in the direction of the movement.

Behind them, the remaining group of soldiers walks in the opposite direction, to the left corner of the park, hiding behind another patch of hedges surrounding the iron image of Salomone Francis.

Thunder rumbles in the sky.

The ghouls take the street and move closer to the warehouse. They walk inside the warehouse gate, the black void of an open mouth.

The vibrations are louder now. The entire park starts to rumble. Vision gets jittery. The electric wire trembles, and the head hanging from it, the head witnessing the scene, rattles.

Two large tanks exit the warehouse gate, speeding, powering through the mob, and enter the park. Behind them, two water-pressure trucks shoot streams of water into the sea of headless corpses, tossing them around, cutting them in half, leaving a wet mess of water and body parts behind them. More tanks follow them. Armored trucks. Reinforced army buses. They traverse the park, destroying every ghoul they encounter. They make a few rounds until the last body is squashed.

With that task completed, they find their places in the

preplanned formation around the playground, surrounding it with vehicles and guards.

Humans come out of the tanks and trucks and stand guard with their hands on the water cannons. One of them signals the mustache man with a whistle.

The small group of people in the corner comes out and walks to the playground. Among swings and slides, they discuss the plan as the two tiny figures resurface on the roof of the warehouse, climb down, and run to the park to join them.

The man with the bushy mustache puts his hands on his hips and looks around. He seems proud. "Not a hole in the ground," he says.

The girl at his side turns to him. "What do you mean?"

"You know," he says to her with a proud smile, "my grandfather was involved in the relocation of the cemetery. I expected to maybe see a hole or two, some remnants, but they sure did things right back then."

They look toward the big cemetery entrance.

"Buckle up, boys," he says. "We're going to war."

They take a deep breath, staring at the entrance, as solitary raindrops fall from the sky.

The couple that just climbed from the warehouse roof, two dark-skinned corpses posing as humans, stand next to the girl with the green eyes. She doesn't seem to notice they're dead. They look up and narrow their eyes, looking directly at the hanging head, sneering at it.

"Remember," the girl says, and the head's vision jiggles up and down as it moves its jaw, mouthing her words exactly. "We need to surprise them. Especially if you run into anyone you know. God, Nate, I hope you're not one of them out there—"

A raindrop falls on the girl's face, and she looks up. Her gaze wanders, looking for something. Finally, she notices the head. Her face turns into a grimace.

"Who'd do that?" she asks, and the group looks up, following her gaze.

"Who hangs a head from a wire?" she adds. "Why?"

"Probably a marking, or a signal," says the man in charge. "Guys."

One of the soldiers kneels on the ground and points a weapon at it. The head clenches its teeth in terror. She hears a whistle, an angry bee buzzing past it, and the snap of a cable being cut in two. Then it's the wind in her face, a thousand tree branches scratching her cheeks and ears and eyes, and rolling on the cool, moist ground until her temple is under a pool of mud.

49

THE FIERY SETTING SUN GLINTS ON THE TRUNK OF THE OLD blue Chevy. Hiding behind it, Nate, Lester, and Yoshi spy on the stranger with the dog army.

"That bastard has Frankie," Lester says.

"That bastard has *everyone*," says Nate, looking around at the bodies. His eyes are glassy and red, and they tremble as he explores the crowd. Lilith could be any one of them.

"We should we getting as far away as possible," says Yoshi.

"No," says Nate, clenching his teeth, vibrating with rage. "Let's get him. Who's with me?"

Lester nods at Nate, his face a reflection of Nate's determination and fury.

Yoshi is holding his arms, almost in fetal position, his eyes looking away at nothing.

"Yoshi?"

"What?"

"What? What do you mean what? We're getting the fucker who killed my Lilith," says Nate, "and your friend. That's what. You ready?"

Yoshi doesn't understand. He looks at the dogs and the army of headless corpses surrounding the leader.

"Get him *how*?"

"Cut the head, kill the snake," says Lester.

Yoshi looks at Lester's face as if it were the ugliest sight he's ever seen. "Wake up, you idiot. This is not *Dracula*. For all we know, even if that zombie-whisperer fuck dies, the zombie dogs will stay obedient to him anyway. He'll just be a *zombie* zombie whisperer. *Forever*."

Yoshi sees the spark of fear in Lester's eyes that he'd intended to light.

"Still wanna be one of them?"

"Ok, OK," says Nate. "Calm down. You may be right."

They hear an inhuman growl. Behind them, between the army of headless ghouls filling the street, Yoshi spots him. In front of him, one of the ghouls grabs a head by the hair and holds it in front of him. And it's talking. The jaw is moving up and down.

They can only see the man's back. He makes a strange clicking sound with his mouth, and one of the ghouls walks away. He comes back with a writing pad and a pencil. He walks to a bag and grabs a hand, and places the pad, the pencil and the hand on top of a car hood. He grabs the hand by the wrist.

"What's going on?" asks Lester.

"The hand ... It's *writing* something."

Nate's eyes are on fire. They're glassy. Watery. "We need to get closer," he says.

"Why?" asks Lester.

"There's a car over there," Nathan says. "It's closer to the corpses, but farther away from the dogs."

Nate's eyes tremble. His face is burning. "Go."

They run to the car and peek out. Still with his back to them, the zombie whisperer seems to talk to his own hand.

"He's holding something," says Nate.

"It's an ear," says Yoshi. "He's talking into a fucking ear."

The head talks to him. They cannot hear what it's saying. It sounds like dry leaves being swept in the street.

Nate tries to heighten his hearing. "Leatelranch," he says. "I'm sure he said Leatelranch."

The boys look at him. "What?"

"He ... I think he said ..." Nate stops. He struggles to make out the words. His eyes swell up like balloons.

"What?"

Nate closes his eyes and filters out every sound around him to put every ounce of focus he has on what the head is saying. He starts to whisper the words to himself as he hears them. *"Nate, I hope you're not one of them."*

His face lights up.

"She's alive!" he yells, loud enough to be heard.

The boys try to shush him.

"She's alive!" he says again, smiling, as Yoshi tries to cover his mouth. "She's in Leatelranch?! What's she doing in Leatelranch?"

The zombie whisperer is now hunched over the hood of the car, examining the pad, tilting his head. He raises his hand and talks to the ear. Nate hears the words "army" and "tanks." He glances up at the street, and the boys and Nate drop to the ground. A whistle cuts through the air, long and complex, like a bird call. The headless ghouls in the street spring into motion. They open bags and pull out arms, legs, and heads. Another group starts tearing their own limbs apart, grabbing and pulling at themselves until only one of them has an arm attached.

The zombie whisperer makes another elaborate whistle.

The headless army begins sorting through the limbs now covering the street and starts to assemble something. Something big. A structure. *It's like watching ants work*, Nate thinks, as fascinated as he is horrified.

Yoshi touches Lester's shoulder and points to a headless body wearing a teal hospital gown.

"Frankie!" says Lester.

The structure begins to sizzle. The limbs move by themselves, climbing each other, fingers creeping up torsos like spiders, legs wriggling and climbing the structure like worms. A recognizable form emerges: The scattered limbs have morphed into a scorpion the size of a bus. It has a tail, a giant ribcage, two arms made of other arms grabbing each other like tentacles, and three human heads on the front.

The stranger in the biker clothes strides up to the heads. He shows each of them the writing pad as he addresses them as a group.

"I heard it this time," says Yoshi. "*Leatelranch.*"

"We need to follow Frankie," says Lester.

The stranger turns to one of the headless ghouls and whistles, motioning to the scorpion figure with his head. The ghoul breaks formation and shambles toward it. The monster whips its tail and tears him apart.

"I'm not getting near that thing," says Yoshi.

"It kills zombies, you idiot, not us."

"You don't know that," says Yoshi.

A hundred legs and feet move below the buzzing beast, carrying it like a centipede, plodding with sick, heavy, drunk steps. It turns and advances toward them.

Lester stares at the monster as it gets closer. "Only one way to know for sure."

They hide behind the car and watch as it passes down the otherwise empty street.

Lester is the first to notice: The scorpion's giant ribcage is hollow.

"Jump in!" says Lester, grabbing Yoshi by the elbow. Yoshi jerks his arm away, scared, but then stands up and turns to Nate.

"You coming?"

Nathan chases after the boys, and while all of its heads are looking forward, they dive through the tangle of limbs and into the gaping ribcage.

50

THE RIBCAGE OF THE BEAST ROCKS AND SWAYS LIKE THE BACK OF an old truck. Lester, Yoshi, and Nathan sit tight against each other, holding their legs. The highway ahead is empty. They are alone in the middle of the cold crisp night. Dark clouds brew around the pale blue moon. Behind them, an army of headless ghouls fills the road, marching toward the conquest of Leatelranch.

"You're bleeding again," Nate says to Yoshi, noticing more green pus oozing out of the teenager's shoulder.

Yoshi brushes it with his hand to check himself, smearing bright green all along his arm. The cut keeps oozing.

"You must have reopened your wound jumping into this ... whatever it is," says Nate, motioning with his hand to indicate the bizarre chassis in which the three are riding.

"You're bleeding, too," Yoshi tells Nate.

Nate looks at his side. His black T-shirt is drenched. Pus keeps flowing out.

"Hey, morons," Lester says. "Newsflash: You never *stopped* bleeding."

Yoshi looks in horror at the pus on his hand. "So, are we dead? Or alive? What are we?"

"We're immortals," Lester says, looking very pleased.

Nate and Yoshi look at each other with a somber glance.

They look at the trees parading around the road. Nate rests his head back on the human-limb mesh and closes his eyes. The silence is magnificent.

Lester looks up at the starry night sky through the knit human limbs making up the vehicle, and something catches his attention. He kneels and crawls to the front. Among the grapevine of human arms and parts on top of the monster coach, sticking up like a periscope, are three human heads. One of them looks terribly familiar.

"Frankie?" he mumbles, waking up Yoshi.

"Frankie!" he repeats.

Yoshi crawls next to him. "Shh! What are you doing?"

"That's Frankie's head up there!"

"No, it's not," says Yoshi.

"Yes, it is! Frankie! Frankie!"

One of the heads notices him. It turns to the sides, looking for the source of the noise.

"Frankie!" he repeats.

"Dammit, Lester!" Yoshi says. "That's not Frankie!"

Lester's heart is beating fast. He crawls forward to the front of the mesh belly of the beast as it bounces with its thousand knees. He grabs a leg, steps on an arm, and climbs up the mesh. "Frankie!" he yells. "Frankie, it's me, Les!"

The face turns and looks at him. The pale moonlight shines on a deformed old woman's face.

"Oh no," says Nate. "No, no, no, no." He crawls to Lester through the mesh of arms and legs, balancing through the monster's swaying as its hundred feet march toward the ghouls, and sits next to Lester at the front of the cabin. He looks out through the mesh.

"Shit," says Yoshi. "It saw us."

The woman's dead eyes gaze at the horizon with a vacant look, missing them. The chain of limbs holding the head whips up again, pointing it forward.

Lester stops crawling. "It wasn't Frankie," he says, frozen. "It was someone else."

Yoshi crawls to the front with them. "Even if he was. He's one of the bad guys now, Les."

"We can make him good. We can bring him back."

Yoshi leans his head close to Lester. "There's. No. Bringing. Them. Back."

"Sure there is!" says Lester. "They're just dead. There's no reason they have to be even *angry* at us. Maybe they're just—"

"Or maybe there *is* a reason," Nathan interrupts.

"Yeah," says Yoshi. "Whatever shit they saw at the end of the tunnel, it seems to have made them really angry. Better leave it at that."

"You shouldn't be so afraid of them," says Lester. "The dead are not bad. Even death is not bad, anymore." He sits back.

"I'm not afraid of death!" says Yoshi.

Lester just looks at him. He turns his head, looking at the moving trees. "OK."

"What we *can* do is avenge them," says Yoshi, "that's for sure. Him and Kenny."

"Guys," says Nate, "can we just—"

"Shut up!" yells Lester. "You don't give a shit about us kids. All you care about is getting to your girlfriend—"

"That's not true!"

"Yes, it is," Lester protests. "Everybody loved Frankie. He was sicker than all of us, and still, he was always cheering us up. He joked with the nurses, played tricks on them, but he was still everyone's favorite."

"Yeah," Yoshi adds.

"And yeah, I miss him, OK?"

"*We* miss him," says Yoshi.

"Down there," Lester says, "in all the time we spent locked up, I've been dreaming more and more about him."

"That's good," says Nate. "It brings peace, doesn't it?"

"Yes."

"All the kids in our ward dreamt about the dead," says Yoshi. "Just before they died, too."

Nate nods silently.

"And all this death shit," Lester continues, "you know what's the worst part? When you die, it's like you never existed. Everything you did, everything you lived, everything you made ... Yoshi, do you remember when he faked a possession for that stupid priest?"

Yoshi chuckles. "Of course, man."

"And when we hid all the syringes? This was way back ..."

"The nurses went crazy!"

"Christ," Nathan says. "How long did you spend in that hospital?"

"Long," says Lester. "Longer than most terminal cases. And he was the first one there. What about when he convinced Louisa from the cafeteria that he had just had a sex change operation?"

Yoshi draws a blank. "When was that?"

"On her first day," he answers, and all three giggle at the old prank.

Lester sighs. "You see? Memory is fading already. Every day, everything is more distant. Until one of these days, nothing will be left. There'll be nothing left of Frankie." Lester breathes heavily. His chest heaves.

"You're right," Nathan says.

Yoshi turns around. "About what?"

"You should find your friend."

"Which part?" asks Yoshi. "Like it or not, he's gone."

"Not gone," says Lester. "No one's gone anymore. Not anymore. We find his head, we find him."

"Look at those," says Yoshi, pointing up. "Do they look alive to you?"

Lester looks at the heads. They are lifeless. They look forward, silent, eyes wide open.

He slumps back on the net of meat. "Maybe you're right."

"Well," Nate says, "Maybe if you can put him back together ..."

Lester feels an electric shock running through his body. "Yes!" he says. "He probably just wants his body back! If we could just find it for him ..."

"That's stupid," says Yoshi.

"We have to try. Just think what he's going through. Would you want to spend eternity like this? Like these loose body parts? He'd do the same for us!"

"Even if that would work," asks Yoshi, "how do you suppose we'll find all of his parts?"

"Actually," Nate says, looking around. "Didn't we see your friend just before the ghouls assembled this thing?"

Lester looks around at the hundreds of limbs forming the vehicle around them. There are hands and feet and elbows and legs of all colors, ages, and sizes.

"Look," says Nate, and he points to one of the arms holding the mesh together. "Isn't that like the one you had?"

Lester crawls to a small arm. "What do you mean?" he asks, examining it. He notices the thin small arm has a name tag on its wrist.

Francis Walton.

He pulls it from the mesh, and the hairy black arm holding it quickly stretches to grab the next one, closing the monster's wound. Frankie's arm wriggles in Lester's hands, almost springing free, but Lester catches it.

"So we got an arm," Yoshi says. "Big deal."

"It's something," Lester says, looking at it and fighting it.

Nathan looks up, browsing the mesh of limbs. "If they were cut at the same time," he says, "it would make sense that the other one is also around here ... There!" he points upward. "That one looks just like it!"

"Can it be?" Lester asks, crawling toward it. "Yes! Yes, it is!" He pulls it and holds it next to the other arm. They're identical.

A loud growl builds around them. The hundred legs plod on the ground, rocking them up and down, and though the beast has no engine and no breath, a stale tiredness permeates the air. Something has changed. The trio turn their attention away from Frankie's unruly arms to peer through the giant ribs out onto the street. Ghouls, the sentient, headed kind, walk around them, staring straight at them through the mesh of arms and legs.

"Oh shit, oh shit," Nate says under his breath.

Yoshi presses himself to the back of the ribcage cabin with a grimace, looking cornered.

Lester slumps back without a care in the world, rocking as the beast sways and bumps. "Relax," he says. "They're just people. Like us."

Before he knows it, Nate is on him, covering his mouth. The zombies watch every move. Glassy eyes glisten in the night.

They are approaching a group of abandoned cars. Among them, the moon shines on clothes. People. Standing out on the highway, waiting for them. Their faces throw menacing looks as the giant scorpion trudges on toward them, but they don't move.

"Are we gonna crash?" asks Yoshi, closing his eyes and bracing for impact.

With a swift lift, the human centipede crawls over two cars, denting the hollow trunks and roofs, shattering windows under its weight. It continues on its journey down the highway, flattening abandoned cars one after another. Still the ghouls stand by and stare in silence.

Suddenly, a stampede of headless soldiers comes running from behind the crushing monster, entering every crevice between cars and pouncing on the frozen ghouls, tearing them apart, paving the road with dead limbs in their wake. Like restless world-class athletes, they continue their massacre without the slightest abatement until not a single ghoul is left standing as far as the eye can see, then disappear into the night.

"See?" says Lester. "No need to be afraid."

"Shagadelic, Austin," says Yoshi, mocking him with a bad British accent. He chuckles and elbows Nate to get him to laugh.

"Leave Lestat alone," Nathan says, and Yoshi's grin disappears.

Behind him, over his shoulder, up ahead, Lester sees a sign with sharp, slithering old letters: LEATELRANCH: NEXT EXIT.

51

A FAINT HISS FILLS THE CHAMBER. NATHAN KNOWS IT'S COMING from the dim yellow gas lamps, but looking at the lumpy, earthy walls, his imagination plays games on him, and he can't help to think it's coming from the faces, from the open mouths, from the snakes that seem to slither around him with the flickering of the light.

"*Everyone's a philosopher at funerals*, I heard a man say once." Nathan's father looks up from the box and into the boy's eyes. His face flickers with yellow light. He looks glad. Serene. He lifts the side of his mouth in what seems to be a slight smile. "That," he says, "was a very observant man."

Nathan gets closer to him, wary of the walls surrounding him.

The man's mouth goes flat again as he draws his attention back to the box. The rag he's holding is old and gray. Dirty. Worn. It's the only thing that seems to belong to his father. That suit, so clean and formal, that blood-red hexagonal wooden box that shines under the scrubbing cloth, look like they're from another world.

"The cemetery is a puzzle, Nate. A puzzle waiting for the pieces ..."

"To fall into place," Nate completes the sentence.

"Exactly. And when you see death," he continues, "when you're around death ... When you feel the passion ... The wonders, the mysteries, they become yours." His father's voice echoes in the chamber, escaping past the broad dark arches, getting lost in the dark passageways that surround Nate.

He looks at them again and steps two inches forward, making sure this time that he's in the absolute center of the chamber, as far from the walls as he can be. He focuses on the cloth, on the dancing tail of the gray fabric, on the red shine of the marbled wood.

"The veil is lifted," Nate's father says. "Everything makes sense again. Everything becomes significant, the connections between everything. The causes. The consequences."

"Is that why you stay here, with Mom?" Nathan mutters.

His father's hands freeze. The man takes a deep breath, and Nathan takes a step back. He realizes fearing his father is a lot easier than worrying about this place. "I know this makes you angry," the man says. "But someday, you'll understand."

"I doubt it," the boy replies.

"Truth is, everything matters when you're in that state. Things make sense." His father looks closely at the box. "When you're around death, you see it."

"But I don't want to know," Nathan says. "I don't like this place."

"You want to be like the people out there," his father says. "Oblivious to all of this."

"Yes," the boy says. "Please."

His father keeps polishing the box. "Did you know that when people are about to die, in their deathbed, they dream about the dead?"

"So?"

"And when they're approaching their own death, they dream more and more of the dead, because they're closer to them than they are to the living. And it's always peaceful. And it's always reassuring. People are happy and calm afterward."

The man sets the box on the little white marble table. He looks up at Nate and smiles. "Death is a good thing," he says. "You're just too far away to see it." He pats the boy on the head and looks him deep in the eye. "Someday, you'll understand."

52

Tanks purr along the main street of the cemetery, surrounded by crypts and mausoleums. Statues smile and angels welcome them, all glistening in the rain. Thunder rumbles.

Inside the truck's tarp, under the humming of the rain, Lilith and the soldiers sit in silence. She can tell that behind the men's straight faces, behind their cold gestures, they're as scared as she is. They sit facing each other, locking their jaws nervously. A bead of sweat falls from a forehead. A hand, made into a fist, is turning its knuckles white. Behind them, a stocky tank rotates its turret to the left, and behind it, the formation continues to roll into the cemetery with more tanks and water pressure trucks and military trucks pregnant with dozens of soldiers. Engines hum. Wheels turn. Wet tires stick to the pavement like glue.

The storm blackens the sky. Cemetery lamps are off. Only the rain makes the edges of tombstones and effigies noticeable, a pale cloak thrown over confusing shapes, turning the cemetery into a series of faint angles, of ghoulish white curves, a glistening silver cobweb in the inky night.

Lilith shivers inside the cold damp anti-riot suit. The hollow rattle of the rain ricochets off it. Thunder strikes, jolting her. Lightning illuminates the entire cemetery like a photograph. A sea of headstones with crosses and stars and fishes reaching for the sky, suffering each thunder clap with a solemn eternal stance. Nothing moves. Nothing.

The procession slows down. It reaches a roundabout and sluggishly turns around a monument, a black egg with webbed wings. They come to a stop with the faint screech of old worn breaks.

Lilith's pulse quickens as the soldiers clear out of the truck. The last one to jump off turns to her. "Come on."

Her mouth trembles.

"Come on!"

"No way."

His friendly smile turns to a menacing request.

"Come down. You can't see them inside this truck, but they sure can see you."

Trembling, she puts her helmet on and forces herself up. She makes her best effort to step lightly with her heavy armored suit, to avoid any noise, to firmly climb down every rung of the ladder, to land softly on the wet pavement.

Outside, a line of tanks surrounds the rim of the roundabout. Soldiers unloading from the trucks immediately fall in line, forming a ring around the monument inside the circle of tanks. They raise their guns, pointing them in all directions.

Lilith takes a moment to gaze at the monument in the center of the formation, then at the park bench surrounding it. It looks a little older than she remembers, but it's still standing.

Nate, she mouths, and smiles.

The shriek of a rusty door opening shocks her out of the memory.

Chief Girardot jumps down from a truck. Behind him, Wolfram and Wednesday prepare to step down as well. He makes some signs with his hands, and the soldiers nod silently.

They fan out. Lines of black-armored soldiers enter the alleys and pathways around them. Patient stone welcomes them through. Laser beams slice the night, dancing among the heavy raindrops, and red laser dots flutter on the tombstones and crypts.

The clouds clear a spot for the faint moon, then close like a curtain on it, swallowing it whole, cloaking the night in darkness once again.

Lilith feels a hand on her shoulder and bolts up. It's Chief Girardot. He locks eyes with her and signals her to follow him.

Lilith has a hard time seeing with her helmet on. She takes one last peek over her shoulder. The crypts around her twist and blur in the scratched visor in front of her face, to the point that she can barely make out Wednesday as she approaches.

"*Chief, wait*," Lilith whispers.

But he doesn't hear her. He paces away from her and enters an alley.

Lilith turns back to Wednesday. Behind her, Lilith can see nothing but the curtain of rain. "Where's Wolfram?" she asks.

"What?" Wednesday asks, her voice faint in the heavy rain.

Lilith's eyes struggle to scan the alleys nearby, to discern the jagged edges of the crypts. Rain falls on dark paths, melting into the darkness. Thunder rumbles.

"Wolfram!" Lilith repeats, louder this time. "Where is he?"

"What happened?" asks Wolfram.

Lilith turns around. Lightning reveals a human shape behind Wednesday. It's Wolfram. She lets out a sigh of relief.

"Shit, Wolfie, I couldn't see you."

"He's been behind me all along," Wednesday says.

"I'm sorry," Lilith says, her voice trembling inside her helmet. "This place ..."

Her breath condensates on the glass in front of her and blinds her. Her armor makes it tough to walk. The weight on her shoulders is almost unbearable.

"I know," says Wolfram.

Lilith has a hard time catching up to the chief. She looks around, not knowing what to do with her hands, hoping she also had a gun. The crypts are smaller than she remembered them.

They are like little houses, yes, but now she couldn't imagine herself, or anyone, living inside. Windows are broken, and chains hang from doors and knobs. Everything is decayed and rotten. Or is it just her memory deceiving her? Maybe it was always like this. She peeks behind the broken windows, and lightning reveals coffins, still closed, resting on the shelves inside. She looks in front of her, and the narrow alley continues forever. Chief Girardot is gone. She hurries to the next corner and looks both ways. Nothing but shadows and darkness. Thunder cracks again, and a flash of light from the sky reveals the chief kneeling on the ground, under cover of the night. He's waiting for her. His eyes seem to say, *Catch up*.

Lilith checks again on Wednesday. She doesn't seem upset, or angry at Lilith. But being here, now, with her and her father ... Lilith feels she should say something about what happened all those years ago.

And that's when she hears it. Lilith stops dead in her tracks.

Wednesday turns to her. "What?"

"I thought I heard something."

"Like what?"

"Like ... giggling ... or something."

"It's just the rain."

Chief Girardot presses on. Lilith struggles not to lose sight of him through the limited vision of her mask. She can only see what's right in front of her. She turns her head, scanning the crypts around her, miniature houses made of stone and marble, a parade of locked doors and stained-glass windows. And paths. And corridors. And alleys. And diagonals.

She hears it again. It's a chuckle. She turns around, places her hand on Wednesday's shoulder, and pulls hard. "Are you laughing?"

Wednesday looks at her in shock.

"I'm ... sorry," Lilith says. "I thought you were ..."

Her head jolts to the sides, looking at every window, every crevice. Just when her eyes seem to be adjusting to the dark, lightning strikes, blinding her again. Her helmet heaves as she starts to pant.

"Something's wrong."

Wednesday stops, too. "It feels like a trap, doesn't it?"

Lilith senses an irony in her voice. An artificial effort, like lying, or acting. But it must be the nerves. If Lilith is scared, Wednesday must be scared shitless.

Wolfram keeps walking past them. "Just keep going."

"But it's gotta be," says Wednesday. "It's gotta be a trap."

"Well, the soldiers and tanks are here," says Wolfram, also sounding like he's reading a script. "You wanna go back to the station?"

"But it's a trap!" Wednesday whispers as loud as she can, again reading from a script that Lilith doesn't recognize, her exceedingly artificial tone confusing her.

Chief Girardot turns around. "Of course, it's a trap."

The sound of the storm suddenly goes away.

"You know this is a trap?" Wednesday asks. "So, what are we doing here?"

"Our job," he says. "We spring the trap."

Lightning flashes, shining a pale light on the wide street, and reveals a crypt that's bigger than the others. It's an inverted pyramid that covers almost the whole block, its four corners supported by pillars. Black soot of a long-gone fire covers the stone. A sign atop its charred, rotten doors reads:

COMPLETORIVM.

LILITH REMEMBERS SEEING this on the antique map back at the station. It was the biggest marking in the entire cemetery.

There's a sound coming out of it. Not quite music. Just a vibration, a ghostly tone, like the faint, sustained note of a wheezing pipe organ.

"What the hell happened here?" she asks herself inside her helmet.

"They're probably all dead," Wednesday says. "It's been years. Maybe they ate each other or rotted to shit. Maybe the ones in the park are the only ones left."

"We still don't know if they *can* die," says the chief. "And I've got a feeling that there are more zombies out there now than there were when we barricaded ourselves inside the station. And also," he says, pointing his flashlight inside the crypts, "the coffins are still closed."

As the rain thuds against her helmet, Lilith's eyes follow the flashlight beam to where it is settled on a neatly closed casket.

A gunshot echoes in the night.

"Who fired?" Chief Girardot asks to his walkie-talkie. "Goddammit, who fired!"

"Team Alpha reporting OK," a voice says.

"Team Beta reporting OK."

"Team Gamma reporting OK."

The rain is now a curtain turning the night silver. Each drop is a finger poking on her shoulder.

The chief looks up at Lilith with a grim look. The mouth under his bushy mustache is flat as a line. "I can't tell who's lying."

"I told you," Lilith says. "I told you this would happen."

"Papa," Wednesday says, "should we get out of here?"

The chief looks at Lilith, stunned. *"A walk among the dead.* It's happening just like you said it would."

"What do you mean?" Wednesday asks, waiting for either of them to answer.

Lilith smirks at the chief. "We got 'em," she says.

"Code red!" he shouts into the radio, spitting onto the microphone. "Everybody to meeting point Tango, *now!*"

53

ALL IS COLD AND SHARP IN THE MARBLE NECROPOLIS, SHINING silver in the morning light, as the black march fills the cemetery street. At the rear of the procession, Doyle Newbery looks for her face. He looks among the adults, among the black dresses and black suits. Looking up, he can see women wearing black veils, and though he knows she won't be wearing one (she would *never*), he needs to be extra careful, check for faces and veils at his own level, look through them, at the weeping eyes and wet mascara tears, until he finds her face. He touches his cheek and feels the thick scar. It still hurts, and for a moment he wishes he could also hide behind a veil. *Now's not the time*, he says to himself, *now's not the time to think about me*.

The march thickens almost to a stop in front of a tall inverted white stone pyramid held up by four pillars, with a small door in its base. Above the wide doorway a sign with gothic lettering reads:

COMPLETORIVM.

. . .

THE BASE LOOKS TOO small to accommodate all the people in the procession, and yet the line continues to march inside, and disappear.

The flow of people carries him, and before he can extract himself from the procession, he arrives at the entrance, where a carpeted staircase leads underground like a deep red throat. As the crowd forces him onto the carpeted steps, he struggles to make his way to the side of the steep staircase. He weaves among the legs and arms politely running over him, unstoppable, like death, relentless, like death. Finally, he exits the stream, finding a perch on the steps from which he can look at the procession, scan the faces, spot her as she passes.

As they funnel into the staircase, the search for her face becomes easier. He stands on his tiptoes and searches among all the legs and hands in the crowd. He bites his lip. *Maybe she entered already? Maybe things have sorted themselves out?*

He finally finds a familiar face at his own level, or maybe just a little bit above it.

"Pst! Wolfram!"

The other boy turns his bowed head until he locates the origin of the call. He swims against the crowd's current and manages to maneuver himself next to Doyle. Once closer to his friend, he stares at the fresh scar, horrified.

"This is all ... so fucked up."

"Yes," Doyle mutters, and instinctively rubs his scar. It must be getting red. *Stop it.*

They stand scanning the faces in the crowd together in silence until the last ones enter the crypt.

"She's not coming," Wolfram says, fixating on the scar again.

"She has to."

"She won't," Wolfram insists. "I've gotta go." He follows the end of the procession down the narrow staircase.

Alone, Doyle exhales, and a busy cloud of breath dissipates into the air. The cold is tightening his face, and the scar burns. He touches it again, feeling the puffy, hardened worm across his cheek.

Doyle takes a deep breath and follows after Wolfram, who is already out of sight. His foot lands on the next step. It feels cold and immovable. He pushes his other leg forward. It's getting harder with each step.

He trudges toward the door. As soon as he steps foot inside the room at the bottom of the stairs, he hears the door close behind him. He turns around to find a tall bearded man with tanned skin meeting his gaze. The man's mouth remains flat, but he seems to smile with his eyes, or make a friendly gesture with the rest of his face. He is wearing a black suit.

The walls around them are tall and painted deep red, and candlesticks hang from them. The boy walks up to a corner, hiding from the crowd, and checks for other angles, or crevices, or hideouts near him. There are many of these similar walls, set in a disturbing pattern; the room is not a square, yet not circular. He walks to the next corner, and then to the next. In the center, the people that were just pushing him around now whisper as they mingle.

I dreamt he woke up, he overhears. *He told me not to worry. Oh, to have five more minutes with him.* A part of him expects that his dead friend will come and get him, that he will open his eyes and get up and come get him, so they can both escape, go away, as far away as possible from all of this strange nonsense. Doyle has heard the word obscene before, but never understood it until now. Death is obscene. All of this, this information overload, this look into nature's naked ugliness, is obscene. Two days ago the dead were an abstract concept; now he is knees deep into that hypothetical, mythical club he thought was reserved for others, for the adults.

On the opposite side of the room, above a single closed door, there's another sign. He quickly looks away, as if traversing those letters with his own eyes will drive him mad. He keeps his gaze at his level. The room makes the whispers of the people bounce everywhere, and he can't help but hear them. He understands the words *great honor. Opportunity. One more chance with the departed.* He doesn't get it. His parents explained some of this today, but it still doesn't make sense. Who'd want to be a Delegate? Who needs the responsibility? What to say? What to ask? What to respond? Why not leave the dead alone? Whoever does this has to be crazy. Whoever *wants* it, even worse. Some things in the adult world will never make sense. He finds himself rubbing his scar and scanning the room for the third time. She isn't there.

He hears something. The door is unlatching. Everyone turns to it and slowly starts funneling inside. One by one they walk through it, leaving the room emptier and emptier. *What's the hurry?* he wonders. *Everything is going so fast. Everyone is going so fast. Why can't we stay here a little longer?*

Soon he finds himself alone. He takes a deep breath and takes one last look at the room, exploring the ceilings, the golden curves and twists decorating the edges. He looks behind the door. It leads to a second narrow staircase, another throat to the depths of the ground, and below, at the end of it, the tan stranger looks up at him. Doyle avoids his gaze and walks around the room, alone, touching the walls, feeling the textures. The big door to the outside is ajar. He peeks outside and looks up the staircase. He misses the morning sky.

He looks over his shoulder at the other door again; at the elegant bronze plaque above it, with those poisonous letters:

COMPLETORIVM.

BEHIND IT, at the foot of the narrow staircase, the man is still looking at him. He trudges toward it, shuffling his feet on the marble floor, and takes the stairs.

The air thickens. A strange music comes from below. A faint, atonal pipe organ music wheezes and stumbles, getting deeper and deeper as he descends, and starts to boom in his chest, swaying his heart rhythm, making it harder to breathe with each step. And as he reaches the foot of the stairs, as he walks past the open burgundy velvet curtain and enters the room, he hears something that curdles his blood. *Did someone say my name?*

In the center of the room, the strange tan man stands next to a little table with a wooden box and looks straight at him.

"Please close the curtains, Doyle," the haunting tan man says.

54

DOYLE SCANS THE ROOM. IT'S DARK, AND SMALL, AND COZY, with concentric circles of burgundy velvet chairs, like a circular theater. He can't tell where the strange, wheezing music is coming from. He can see the whole room, and the circular black wall surrounding it, without turning his head, and there are no speakers or organs in sight. In the center of the room, surrounded by the concentric circles of chairs, a thin ray of sunlight enters from the ceiling *(How is that possible if we're two floors underground?)* and shines on a small table. On the table rests a small brushed wooden box. The mysterious tan man with the unkept beard seems to guard it. In the far end of the room, in the dark beyond the circles of chairs, stands a pale, scrawny boy. He looks to be Doyle's own age, but he's never seen him at school.

The wheezing music fades away. Doyle looks around for an empty seat, walks silently to it, and sits down. His scar itches. He tries to ignore it.

The strange tan man starts talking, like this is a spectacle, a theater, and not somebody's funeral, not a friend's funeral, not a last chance to say goodbye. As the man talks, Doyle tries to find a comfortable position in his itchy velvet chair. Meanwhile, the man goes on and on about *completion*. About *parts that explain each other only when pieced together, like a puzzle*.

Sure, we're all pieces, Doyle thinks, clenching his teeth. *That's all we are. Who is this guy? What is he doing here? Why am I listening to a stranger talk gibberish, today of all days? What is it with all these stupid theatrics? And why isn't she here?*

And his scar. His itchy, itchy scar.

While the bearded man talks, people stare silently at the wooden box, waiting, expecting. When he finishes, it's time for the people to speak. The speeches begin with the family, sitting in the innermost row. The mother, beyond pain. The father, with his hardened face and his trembling mustache, just about to break down and cry. The devastated sister. Wolfram, sitting like a stone next to her. Then, more people say their piece, until the speakers seem to be distant family. They talk about his childhood, family gatherings, first times holding him, things like that. Some of this is new to Doyle. Some is clearly bullshit, just strangers or distant family friends trying to justify their presence in this moment that should belong to the friends, the real friends, and the family. And some ... some of the stories are so in character for his dead friend that it's hard not to chuckle at how his friend was always *him*, even as a small child, when Doyle still didn't know him. He tries to focus on his scar, to focus away from the stories, but the tone of these voices is so similar to what he feels, so familiar, that he can't help tuning in. His face shrivels, he tries to stop himself, but he breaks down and starts to cry with them.

Can they see his engorged scar? Will it bother them? He doesn't care. He shows it proud, here of all places, because it's a last living souvenir of his dead friend. He wipes the tears from his eyes and looks at the tan caretaker standing in his suit, holding the box with his rough hands. The pale boy standing next to him seems almost more frightened than Doyle. He meets his gaze, and they look each other in the eye, scared to death.

The talking stops. *They are missing one crucial part.* There is a pregnant silence in the room, an expectation. *Where is she?* Doyle asks himself. And his scar. His scar itches like crazy.

Sitting in his velvet chair, the boy hears muffled footsteps coming toward him. He turns to find that they belong to his friend's mother. She puts her hand on his shoulder, her face black with tears and makeup. Under the paint, her cheeks are blushing red. She clenches her teeth, trying to contain herself. While the father pats her shoulder, she's asking him. It's what Doyle has been fearing all along.

She grabs both his shoulders and shakes them. It's really happening. She's *asking* him.

He locks his jaw, nervous, refusing to talk. He can feel the woman's eyes probing him. Pleading. Her hands are warm, feverish. His heart is broken. His breath comes firing out of his nose, and his eyes roam the room again, roam the world, looking for the face, *her* face, but she is nowhere to be found. Finally, he looks into the eyes of his friend's mother and gently rubs his scar.

Like a dream. His mouth and breath have a life of their own, and he's just sitting there, numb, as his body starts to succumb to its role in the silent movie unfolding around him. The woman smiles and looks deep into his eyes, softly, as he responds to her request. Tears come to her eyes, and to his, as the memory develops, and the moment is fresh again for all to hear, as any new story about an old dead friend. He can hear people crying and gasping in disbelief, and he can feel their stares and their outrage and their acceptance. But the mother's bright look is one of total love, total forgiveness, and all the joy possible in a day like this. He starts to smile. All stories are dark about the dead, but this one especially. And yet, it's what the room needed, because a thick silence takes over as every gaze is on him.

Then, the faint tinkle of a small bell, coming from inside the box.

In the center of the room, the caretaker looks gravely at him. His hand still lays on the box, resting peacefully, and it wakes up, standing on its fingers, and goes into the caretaker's pocket. It comes out with a key. The man inserts it into the box, unlatching something with a rich, nutty sound.

Inside, a little bell rings, pulled by a thin black thread coming from under the box, from under the table, from under the floor.

The mother and the father cry. The sister, poor thing, looks as confused as he is. But all the people in the chairs sob silently with an uncanny sense of joy. He hears them as if through a wall. The world is a muffled, numb image at the end of a tunnel.

The mysterious caretaker looks him in the eye and mentions his name. His voice sounds calm, like a dead man's. He signals him to stand up.

The boy stands up, still spasming from the crying. He looks around at all the strangers, looking for the only face he cannot see, and frowns. "It-should-be-*her*," he mutters between spasms.

The caretaker turns to the pale boy standing next to him and signals him with his head. The pale boy looks surprised. He walks a few steps to where there's now a small door, one that was not there before, a small door under a small marble sign with embossed letters that reads:

DELEGATVM.

THE PALE BOY opens a small wooden cabinet next to the door. He takes out a gray folded cloth and starts to unfold it, nervously, in a ceremonial way.

So young, people whisper around Doyle as they shake their heads. *So young*. Only this time they're not talking about the deceased. They're talking about him.

He can't take his eyes off the cloth as the scared pale boy unfolds it. His hands are clumsy, and Doyle is thankful. He'd like to stall this moment for as long as possible. It's all so ceremonial, and yet, now, he wishes it would be even slower. He looks at the door labeled Delegatvm and wishes it were farther away.

But the pale boy is suddenly next to him, and he has unfolded the gray cloth into a robe with a hood, and he's presenting it to him.

55

EVERYONE IS USHERED OUT OF THE CIRCULAR ROOM, AND AS they climb the narrow stairs, and as the sobbing starts to fade away, Doyle scratches nervously at the scar on his cheek and wishes he could join them. He looks at his fingernails. Blood.

Stop it. Stop it.

The pale boy, in a silence that may be part of the job but he seems naturally inclined to deliver, presents a gray sleeve for him to put his arm in. Doyle's arm feels stiff. It won't move. He looks again at the exit. His dead friend's family members are the last out. They stand at the foot of the stairs and look over their shoulder, eyes bloodshot red, in a grimace resulting from an overload of sensations: grief, goodbye, and a glimpse of hope. He recognizes that glimpse and wishes he could also have it, on the safe comfortable outside of this terrible building.

The caretaker closes a burgundy velvet curtain that hides the stairs, and the room is now a perfect empty circle. The boy feels the ceiling closer to his head. *Is the room shrinking?*

He tries to put his arm inside the gray sleeve presented to him by the pale boy. It gets stuck, and he fights it. The caretaker paces toward him, and without saying a word, he corrects the pale boy,

329

moving the sleeve. Doyle puts his arm in and follows behind the caretaker as he walks toward the dreaded wooden box.

The luxurious box doesn't creak when the caretaker opens it, but he can hear the clean *tock* noise of the lid separating itself from the bottom, a hollow, dark, nutty sound that makes him shiver. The caretaker's arm raises toward the box, and though the boy cannot see what it's holding, he can see that the man is holding *something*.

The caretaker looks up at him, and the scarred boy freezes. He looks again at the curtain, thinking how easy it would be to escape now, join the others, or run past them, maybe undercover of the maze that is this damn cemetery. Maybe he could hide in one of the crypts until this all blows over. A cemetery to escape from death. He sees the caretaker's hand coming closer, handing him, *him*, the thing, the dreaded thing that is usually someone else's problem, someone else's responsibility, someone like *her, her* responsibility, not his, not here, not now, not in front of him, in the hands of a man that has the job of making sure he, *he*, will fulfill the duties of the Delegate.

The pale boy gives him a strange look. He seemed afraid before, but he's *terrified* now, seeing it, seeing *him*, knowing what will have to happen soon. Doyle remembers how hours ago, just hours ago, he first heard what a Delegate is, and was comfortably horrified that *someone* would be tasked with it. But he never imagined it would be him. That story, that legend that he heard, that horror story to scare the uninitiated kids, will forever be told about *him*.

The caretaker's eyes look at him gravely, patiently. They know that there is no escape from this, and take it without desperation, without hope.

As if he's watching a movie, the boy sees his hand extending toward the caretaker's, his shaking fingers embracing it like a trembling spider, closing on it, picking it up, and as soon as he feels the cold in his fingers, he realizes it's real, it's real and he's touching it, and it's too late to escape now.

The caretaker takes it back and places it back in the box, looking almost nostalgic, like he's saying goodbye, too. He closes the box silently, and hands it to Doyle. He takes one step aside, unblocking the boy's path toward the small door with the plaque, extends his arm politely, and points inside. He looks at Doyle with a hint of a smile, like he's thankful, or relieved. *About what?* His finger is calm, like a dead man's, as if what's on the other side is perfectly reasonable.

DELEGATVM.

THE BOY'S legs are heavy. He feels numb. His feet shuffle and doubt and tremble as he takes the first step. The pale boy, standing next to the door, looks at him with pity, looking just as scared as he, The Delegate, feels. The vision of his pale face goes blurry with each tear.

The small pale hand unlocks the door, revealing a candle-lit, cavelike chamber. Doyle is afraid to look back. If he gets another peek at the exit, at the escape route, he might think of fleeing. *It's too late now*, he thinks, taking a step forward. *Better to think it's too late now and be done with it.*

The door closes behind him. He's alone at the top of a spiral staircase. The dark wall surrounding it has paintings and candelabra lighting the way down as deep as he can see.

A muffled voice comes from behind the door. It's the caretaker.

"Now, a warning," he says.

The boy turns around, and his eyes widen. *"Now, a warning???"*

"Don't lose sight of that box. I will need it back after you finish."

Doyle nods.

"And whatever you do, don't drop it. Leave it outside when

you're done. I have some duties to attend, and I'll be back in an hour."

The scarred boy looks down at the box in his hands and blames it for all this. He doesn't reply. He takes his first step down. Old people, golden by the candlelight, stare at him as he walks down the steps. There are names under each portrait engraved on brass plaques that read DELEGATVM and some Roman numerals. He doesn't care enough to stop and look at them, except for the last one, who looks familiar. It's the tan stranger, the caretaker from upstairs.

The staircase gets narrower, leaving the luxury of the room above and slowly turning musty, ancient, earthy, like a cave that could have been dug out days or centuries ago. The boy trembles. The box in his hands rattles.

He reaches the last step, still carpeted in that crimson eternal red, and his trembling feet trudge toward an ancient marble altar, where the coffin is placed. A thin red thread goes up from it to the level above, and it still moves, and it still dings the bell upstairs, faintly, persistently.

Doyle tries not to think about it, he really tries, *Just be done with it*. And he opens the box in his hands, and he feels the moist, mushy, mysterious thing, and suddenly it's all so clear—how to use it, why, what we are all made of—and it suddenly makes sense, and it suddenly becomes easier, but it's still not enough preparation for what follows: the coffin, opening; the familiar hand, raising; the jaw, opening; and he suddenly feels a lightness in his hands and sees himself running, running away before the box even hits the ground.

56

CARETAKER MARCUS CLIMBS THE RUNGS OF THE LAMP POST AND lights the oil lamp. He squeezes the spark lighter and, with a click, he feels the warmth on his face as the flame starts. He climbs down and looks at the corridor. It's alive with warm orange light. The crypts around him dance with the golden firelight. The heat makes the light dance on the cold white stone, shiny black onyx, and veiny marble. He walks the corridor toward the next lamp. It may be the low light, but shadows seem to play tricks on him. Thick heavy doors seem ajar. Locks seem open. And a window, a stained-glass image of St. George slaying the dragon, is definitely broken, a dark hole taking the place of the dragon's head. He steps toward it. He peeks inside: In the dark, the lid of the coffin seems off. Wood tends to go bad after some years, he knows. It gets dry. It splinters. Or, it gets moist. It gets mossy. It rots. But this ...

He narrows his eyes to dismiss any effect of the dancing light. There is a wide black gap between the lid and the box. It's not ajar. It's open.

He lets out a warm breath through his nose that burns his upper lip.

He looks around him. He gazes at the far end of the cemetery, licking the horizon with his gaze. There. A few doors down. Where the light starts to die off. A human figure, a shadow, sticks to a white marble wall, then bolts, running into an alley.

He darts after it, putting the spark lighter in his pocket, and fumbles around his tool belt for the flashlight. He turns it on only to get blinded by the tiny thing. He points it forward, slowing down, shedding light on nothing but an empty wall.

He tries not to say it. If he says it, it becomes true.

"Mother of god," he hears himself mumbling.

He closes his eyes and points his face toward the dark floor beneath him. He opens them again. He can see the shape of his feet on the lighter tiles, and bolts his head up, his hand directing the beam of light toward a dark corridor. He looks behind him: The lit lamps are already distant orange dots in the midst of darkness.

He points the flashlight around. The bright yellow ring hovers on plaques, marble angels, and small windows. It hovers over a crypt door and its iron handle. There's a wide dark gap between the door and the frame.

The door's ajar.

The sound escapes his mouth. *"No."*

He hears a noise, and his neck sprints to the right. Nothing but darkness. His jolted nervous hand points the light toward the corridor just in time to see a shadow turn the corner and disappear.

He runs after it. The floor cracks under him as he steps on shards of broken glass, and the jiggly yellow circle of light reveals more broken locks and cracked windows. Inside them, lids of coffins are askew.

He dodges lamps and fountains, breathing heavily, stepping on more glass. He turns a corner, checking the crypt name for reference, and keeps going. When he reaches the weeping children, he turns right and reaches the wide corridor, the main street. He coughs, almost out of breath, and keeps going.

His zig-zag beam of light lands on a door as it opens. It's in a narrow crypt that looks like a bullet with colored windows. He takes out a zip tie from his back pocket and wraps it around the holes where the broken lock still hangs. He pulls with all his strength, zipping and tightening it just in time: The door starts to rattle back and forth, violently, held by the clamp.

On the other side of the street, inside a tall crypt, two coffins start to rattle. Hands come out, along with horrible screams. He pushes them back inside, without time to look at their faces, and after putting his flashlight between his teeth, he puts another makeshift lock on the decorative iron bars around the door. They kick and scream inside the crypt, and he hears planks of wood, or coffin lids, being dropped to the floor and kicked with anger. The sound grows louder and comes from every direction. He looks over his shoulder. The doors in all the crypts bang. The nervous beam of light hanging from the flashlight in his mouth reveals bony hands peeking out of doors, doors opening.

His lungs hurt, but he keeps running through the street, ignoring the doors opening around him. As he runs past side alleys, he sees naked bodies standing up. Shrouded figures rising. A group dressed elegantly, mingling in the street. He's not alone anymore.

When he reaches the inverted pyramid, his hand fumbles in his pocket. He hears a mumble. He tries with everything inside him not to turn, not to wonder, not to guess, but something tells him the figure he just saw out of the corner of his eye, walking down the last alley, is a woman with coins in her eyes—and she's not strolling around, not escaping like the others, but walking toward *him*.

His clumsy fingers finally find the heavy key. The dimensions of his own body seem alien to him as he tries to pull it out of his pocket, his shoulder and elbow stiff and unresponsive.

"I'm sorry," he says, and he's alarmed by the volume of his own voice. It's the first time he hears it echoing on the crypts in the empty cemetery. He pushes the black metal key into the lock and turns it.

In the dark, he enters the Completorivm passage and runs down the staircase. As he paces quickly through the empty velvet seats, the rattling noises from outside start to mute. He unlocks the Delegatvm door and hurries down the steps. He reaches the red-carpeted hall. Now, the sounds above are but a faint hum. He looks down and freezes. He mumbles something to himself, he steps on the gray robe and picks up the box lying open on the floor. He exhales, relieved. Grabbing the box with all his strength, he begins.

The humming outside stops.

He climbs back up the stairs and out the small door. As he walks through the circles of velvet chairs, he listens carefully. Once again, the cemetery is silent as a grave.

He steps outside, slices through the night with his beam of light, and clears his sweaty forehead with his forearm. Bodies and limbs lay scattered on the ground as far as he can see.

No hesitation. Hesitation is dangerous. He starts with the closest ones. Limbs get picked up. Bodies get stored. Arms get tucked inside. Stone lids get straightened out. Doors are closed. Chains and locks are collected, fixed, thrown away, replaced. Locks click.

The sun will come up soon. He picks up the woman facing down on the broken tiles, and with watery eyes, he paces to his chopper bike, his feet starting to tremble. He opens the leather saddlebags, containing nothing but a crumpled black suit, and loads the dirty shovels, pickaxes, hammer, and chisel. He kick-starts the bike, and the engine growls in the pink dawn.

He heads for the hills, where the sun is starting to rise.

As he reaches his wife's tombstone, the morning twilight mocks him with a ghostlike vision: A mound of dirt sits beside the stone, freshly dug out. He lets go of the throttle, afraid of going forward. He steps on the ground as the bike slows down. The engine purrs. It's waiting for him. Taunting him. Pitying him. Laughing at him, as he sees the open grave, the empty, open casket. He places her inside with great care.

Looking back at the necropolis, his face burns.

Nevermore.

He mounts his bike and guns the throttle, zooming toward the giant Completorivm, flying past the bodies and broken doors, screeching and braking, then purring as he paces toward the entrance, his face red and wet, his dirty hands cracking the spark lighter.

Nevermore, he mumbles as he exits. His bike roars away just as the first plumes of smoke start to escape the small door, curling in the air like black angel wings.

57

Lilith follows Wolfram, Wednesday, and Chief Girardot to the open field, splattering in the muddy ground, heavy raindrops hammering on her helmet. Behind the silvery curtain of rain, soldiers march in and join them, forming a circle, spreading as more troops gather, until they're at arms' length of each other. Lightning flashes and lights up the helmet visors as they look at each other.

Thunder cracks.

Lilith enters the circle, slipping on something. She looks down, and a small black-and-white face smiles at her. She's standing on a tombstone. She takes a careful step back onto the grass.

"*A walk among the dead*, indeed," the chief says to Lilith.

She smiles in her helmet.

"Papa," Wednesday asks her father with a thin voice. "Is this all of them?"

He looks around at the huge circle, and Lilith follows his gaze. Behind her thick scratched visor, she can barely see the silhouettes on the other side.

"Helmets off!" the chief orders.

The soldiers comply. Heads pop out in the dark and the rain.

"Flares!" he yells.

They fire up half a dozen flares, and a fluorescent red hue reveals their faces. They throw them on the ground inside the circle, blinding Lilith through her helmet visor, revealing more tombstones under their feet.

"Everybody get a look at everybody," he yells, spitting rainwater. "Someone next to you is one of them."

The men and women look at each other.

Chief Girardot calls their names. One by one, from different parts of the circle, they answer.

"All right," he says. "This is everybody."

Thunder rumbles.

"Now what?" asks Wednesday.

"Everybody strip," he says. "We're looking for bites, exposed bone, blood, any sign of violence."

Rain falls as they look at each other, trying not to look terrified. They strip. The wet uniforms stick to their skin, and they struggle to take them off, balancing themselves in the mud.

"Anybody see anything?" asks the chief.

"No," the first ones say. "No. Nothing here."

"This is stupid," says Lilith. "We should split. Now."

Wednesday looks at her and clenches her whole body.

"Papa, should we get out of here?"

"Not before we smoke out the rat," he replies.

"Do we need to strip?"

"No," he says. "Just them."

In the buzzing rain, Lilith hears something. Something in the distance, behind the heavy rain, back in the crypts area. She looks around. Yes, she didn't imagine it. Iron doors opening. Locks breaking. And closer to her, the sloshing of mud.

She looks around at the ground. It's moving. The grass seems perfectly quiet under her, but she steps back onto the plaque.

A gun cocks.

One of the soldiers is pointing her pistol at the soldier to her right. "Got him," she says. Meanwhile, behind her, on the ground, lit dimly by the red flares, mounds in the earth open, and fingers in the mud reach for the sky. She snatches his gun and points at his neck. Thunder strikes, and Lilith thinks she can see the flash photo of a bite mark.

The other soldiers ready their guns and point them at him. The metal barrels glimmer in the heavy rain.

"Wait!" someone else yells. "Got another one!"

All soldiers turn to him.

He's pointing his gun at the back of the neck of his right-side partner.

"Left-right," says Chief Girardot. The guns in the circle turn and dance a choreography. Half the circle turns their guns at the first one, and the other half at the second one.

"Mr. Girardot," Lilith says, looking at the ground around them.

"Yes, Kane."

"We need to get out of here."

"It's too late," he says, turning back to the soldiers.

Lilith looks at Wednesday. Behind the rainy helmet visor, there's a twinkle in the eyes, and the hint of a grin. She turns to Wolfram. Behind his visor is the same ugly smirk.

No.

"Got one!" says another of the soldiers.

"Another one here!"

"Zombie!"

The soldiers all point at each other, changing targets, and chuckle.

"Oh, shit," Lilith mutters.

"All right," Chief Girardot says. "I think we're done here."

The soldiers stand down. Suddenly, they look relaxed. They all look at the chief, waiting, as he turns to Lilith, his eyes releasing a rage she has never seen in him.

"I think she's good and cornered."

A bolt of adrenaline shoots up Lilith's entire body. She looks around. She looks at the soldiers, all looking at her. She looks at

Wolfram, who's taken his helmet off and stands grinning under his drenched hoodie. She looks back at the chief. She looks at Wednesday. They are smiling, dead and hungry. Thunder strikes, and their eyes glow.

Lilith's mouth trembles. She clenches her teeth. She looks into their eyes. Mr. Girardot explores her face, his eyes savoring something that she doesn't want to identify.

"Wait," she says, as her mind races.

She looks at the corpses surrounding her. At Wolfram, Wednesday, the dozens of soldiers. Behind them, among the crypts, she can already see ghouls walking toward her. She feels a tap on her foot and looks down. A hand is unearthing and reaching for her, rotten flesh peeling off its bony fingers.

"Wait," she repeats, remembering. It almost sounds too dumb to be true.

"*A walk among the dead,*" she says, facing the chief defiantly.

She takes a slow step back. The chief and the entire team ... stand still.

She turns around, waiting to hear all hell breaking loose. But all she hears is the rain. She takes another step. And another. Her feet sink deep in the mud with each step, splashing black water over the hands and arms growing from the ground like sick human flowers. Up ahead, tanks open their hatches and heads pop out, looking at her, grinning. She's too afraid to turn around, but she listens. And she hears nothing.

Finally, she stops and looks back.

The ghouls are standing, frozen like statues. Grinning.

"Why?" she asks, unsure if she should mutter the words.

She takes a step toward them. Her body trembles, and she takes a deep breath. She hopes it will calm her down, that it will allow her to think. But as the air fills her lungs, it only fuels her scream:

"Why *aren't* you trying to kill me?!"

THE WET SCENT OF THE GROUND FILLS HER NOSTRILS. SHARP blades of grass poke at her eyes, blocking her view. Heavy raindrops plunge into her open ear, filling it with water, blasting like a drum, drowning the rusty sound of nearby swings dancing in the storm. She moves her jaw, her cheeks, trying to get up. But the head, severed from its body, cannot move.

Lightning flashes behind the blurry blades of grass, and a rotten hand plunges down from above. The head tries to look up, to see the rest of the body standing in front of her. She opens her mouth and springs it shut, like a trap, trying to bite what's about to happen. To hurt it. To get even.

Thunder cracks.

The ground shakes. The blades of grass tremble and rise in front of her, swelling into a small mound. The ground is giving birth to something. Earth and mud come out of the mound like a volcano, and the head can see five bony fingers shoot up from its bowels. The sky lights up as the rotten hand coming from above grips it. As it pulls up, the mound spits out a bony forearm, and swells again, erupting black mud and giving birth to a full arm, a human torso, a body, a mess of bones and rotten meat braided with ragged hundred-year-old clothes.

The mound rises as the body stands under the rain, and it reaches the head lying on the ground, tilting it upwards. Water sloshes out of its ear, and the full force of the storm reaches her eardrums again. Thunder rumbles. Raindrops hiss. Resting on its side, inches above the grass, the head can see. Up ahead, three red wooden swings fly madly in the air, dancing in the wind, glimmering under a flash of lightning. And towering up into the sky, the standing, rotten figure pulling from above is a man in a suit. Next to him stands a dead woman in a dress. Both wear mirrored sunglasses. And behind them, all along the park, more mounds break open from the earth, as hands, elbows, arms, and skeletons come out and look up at the black sky, soaking in the rain.

The woman bends down and reaches for another bony hand sprouting from the earth. She pulls out an arm, attached to a torso connected to a skull. Standing on its own, the skeleton seems to take a moment to get accustomed to holding its newly regained weight and turns away. His feet plunge in the soft mud toward a group of ghouls climbing on each other to form a giant bony anthill. It climbs it, reaches the top, and reaches to the sky. It plucks a head that hangs from an electric wire, glistening in the rain.

The couple turns around. Behind them, behind the other skeletons, in the distance, someone runs toward them. A living woman. As she gets closer and closer, they turn to each other, and their hands meet, splotching with water, and interlock their muddy fingers. They hold identical rings.

Standing in front of the dancing red swings, the tall skeleton in colonial clothes turns its head slowly. Its hollow sockets seem to sparkle with the rainwater. It takes clumsy steps on the mud, like a toddler, closing in on the head on the ground, and if its hollow sockets still had eyes, they'd look angry, hungry, savoring a satisfaction hundreds of years old.

It towers like a giant in front of the head. It raises its knee in the rain and stomps down. The sound of its bony foot against the patches of dead hair makes a padded *thump*. The head rolls, one eye beneath a puddle of dark water, the other one barely seeing at ground level. A torso creeps its way toward it, crawling in the mud with both arms, sinking its bony fingers into the ground to pull itself forward.

An old memory of fear, a dormant instinct, kicks in. The head tries to escape. It tries to kick and wriggle and defend itself. In the distance, she can see her body, one of the hundreds of headless bodies being attacked by headed skeletons, mimicking the intended movements in a frantic, spastic spectacle as a group surrounds it, overpowers it, and rips it apart.

The crawling torso, now a shark wriggling and towering over the head, a mass of pure strength, raises itself on one arm. It pulls the other arm up into the air and closes its fingers into a bony fist. As it brings its head closer, the lonely, helpless eye above water catches a glimpse of its face. Gray, mummified flesh covers the skull, looking raw as it soaks in the rain. The hollow sockets make it look perpetually wide-eyed, surprised. It snorts with hate. The cold damp breath of a hundred years comes out of its nostrils. Its mouth twists into a grimace.

"Traitor," it snarls.

The fist comes down, and its knuckles hit the head in the nose, pushing her deeper into the mud. Both eyes are now below water, seeing only dancing shadows of the world. The head wants to blink, but it has lost its eyelids. Cold mud enters its ears and nose and throat. The sounds from outside become muffled.

With another thump it goes deeper underground. The sound of raindrops becomes a distant rumor. Now it's not she who looks or hears; it's the world who looks at her, and as she goes deeper underground, forgets her.

Another thud—and she hears nothing.

A thin root scratches her face. Soon it will grow thick, stretch and bloat like a giant squirmy worm, and its relentless tip will pierce her tender rotten cheek; it will pry her jaw open and push on until the skull and the jaw are two separate, lost pieces. It will dry up, and die, and fade off, and disintegrate. More roots and rocks and seasons will follow, the ground will shake and give and bury her further into the dark and forgotten depths. And her eyes will witness the darkness. And her ears will hear the silence. For thousands, and thousands, and thousands of years.

59

Lilith's throat burns as she gasps for air inside her helmet. Each stride in the armored suit is a struggle. The shaky drops of rain falling on her visor suddenly feel cold on her face. She's crying. *Fuck it*, she thinks, trying to keep her running pace, and she tears off her helmet and throws it away.

Cold rain pours and lashes her eyes. She runs down the cemetery's main road toward the main gate, looking around as corpses emerge from the ground everywhere, and as she enters the miniature crypt city, metal doors shriek open and glass windows break. Yet the main road is clear. Reaching the iron gate seems almost too easy.

She runs out the cemetery entrance, past the abandoned flower kiosks, and onto the puddled pavement. The wide street leading to the cemetery is well lit, and though it's clearly empty, following it would surely expose her. She tries to make out the shape of the park, but the wall of rain is too thick. Among the million drops of rain hammering her head, she hears the whiny shriek of swinging chains. The playground, she remembers, is in the center of the park. Using it as a compass, she draws a mental map of how to get across the park without being seen and steps onto the mud.

The distant shriek is closer and closer, nursed back and forth by the howling wind. The rain creates a thick curtain, and Lilith wonders where everybody went, why they aren't coming for her. She tries to make out anything around her, anything at all, and it's like she's in limbo, like there *isn't* anything around her anymore. Only her, the cold rain, and the sound of chains.

Her foot lands on something firmer than mud. She looks down. She's stepping on wet sand. She's reached the playground. She can barely make out a long twisting slide next to her. To her left there's a red seesaw, silvery under the fury of the fat raindrops. Only a few more steps to the swings. The sand is firm, but the sandbox is already flooded, and her feet stomp on soft water before stepping back onto the firm sand.

Suddenly, Lilith is startled by movement behind the wall of rain. She freezes, then releases a deep exhale. It's just the swings. They're slicing through the thick drops, chains dancing after the flying red wooden planks.

Her fingers find the cold iron pole, and she leans on it. She looks around, not knowing where to go from here. Her body trembles, and she wraps her arms around herself, clenching her jaw to keep her teeth from chattering.

She grabs the slippery wet chains. The swing wriggles like a mad dog before coming to a stop.

And she hears it again. The squeaking. It's still there, somewhere, behind the wall of rain. *How is this possible? These are the only swings in the park.*

The squeaking turns into something else. Something with a timing. With a rhythm. A familiar tune. It's a whistle, and it sounds oddly fitting for this place, like it belongs here, in her childhood. It's approaching her. Yes, it's definitely a song. Someone is whistling.

And it dawns on her. "Que sera, sera."

Thunder crackles. As it fades off, it's replaced by the squishy sound of steps in the mud. The air lights up, revealing a line of gray figures approaching in the rain. An unhinged jaw. A saggy, baggy eye.

As she looks for a way out, a hand lands on her shoulder.

"N—no n—need t—to r—rush, d—dear," a motherly voice says behind her ear.

Lilith freezes. Hollow shapes walk toward her, skeletons and corpses so rotten that the rain pours in and out of them. Bodies made of mud. Living bones and skulls. And among them, coming out of the silvery curtain of the rain, a familiar shape. The wet leathery face grins. It raises a rotting hand to remove a pair of driving glasses but cuts the motion off in mid-air, apparently remembering that they're lodged in his face.

"Pa," Lilith mumbles.

His face is a messy version of what she remembers, but melted. Displaced. Askew. Across his forehead is a purple indentation the exact shape of their car's steering wheel. His glasses, bashed in by the crash, are now part of his face. His chest doesn't beat, but his belly bloats and contracts like a bubble ready to burst. Even under the pouring rain, she can smell him, and the horrible breath coming out of his dead mouth. It's like food gone bad. And behind the mirrored glass, his eyes tremble. Is it water floating inside the sockets? Is he actually *feeling* the rage that seems to seep through those eyes?

"Hi, L—Lilybug," he says, brushing Lilith's chin with rotten gelatinous fingers.

"H—hi, d—d—arling," says a face that used to belong to her mother. Purple lips barely cover a string of black teeth. Her right eye is now an empty socket, and her left one keeps wandering from side to side, restless, trying to focus on Lilith. Her cheeks are turning a hue of green, swollen and beating with pockets of gas that exit her face in bursts. Her black gown, soaking wet, seems to hang off a skeleton.

Lilith opens her mouth, but nothing comes out. As the rain thins, she can begin to make out shapes in the night: Behind her mother's rotting face, dozens of hands and arms crawl out of the mud. There are corpses walking toward her from every direction.

Her mother's thin fingers land on her shoulder and waist. She tries to break free. She wriggles her shoulders, and the hands let her. She turns around and tries to bolt, and the hands land once again right where they were, almost like they had waited for Lilith, like they've practiced this turn before. They tighten their grip.

"You're hurting me!" Lilith yells.

She tries to run, and once again, her father's hand stops her right in front of her, slowly, methodically.

"Argh!" Lilith yells, shaking. "Help. Ma."

She looks around for a way out, but she's clearly surrounded.

"I told you this would happen!" Lilith screams. "I told you we'd end up killing each other!"

Thunder crackles again. Her mother's mummified face, deformed by the crash, has a lopsided grin that goes all the way up on one side and only slightly on the other.

"So? What are you waiting for?" Lilith explodes in tears. "Kill me!"

She stops squirming. She sobs, waiting for the blow. She looks at them defiantly. "Kill me," she repeats.

"You wanna live?" her dead father asks her.

"Of course!"

"Say it louder!"

"YES, OF COURSE!"

"Why?" he asks.

"What do you mean?"

"*Why* do you want to live?" he asks again, spitting water out of his dead mummified mouth.

"I ... I ... *What*?"

"You are so proud of how you always follow your heart. Yet you keep trying to *understand* this. You spent so much time trying to figure out how to kill us, but you never stopped to think if you should. You never stopped to ask."

Lilith doesn't understand. "Ask what?"

He comes closer. His breath smells like the tunnels below the cemetery. "What if we're right?"

He lifts his idle hand and stretches his arm behind him, pointing up. As the rain clears, Lilith sees a little white brick house. Her childhood home.

"See that house?" he says. "It has been watching you rot for forty years ... Now *you* will see *it* rot."

"I am not rotting!" says Lilith. "I am not rotting! I am not rotting!"

He leans toward her face and caresses it. His hand feels like cold leather. His eyes, two round spheres resting on hollow sockets, move like slugs, examining her.

"Look at you," he says. "I changed your diapers. Now you're wrinkly. You're *racing* toward deathf—"

His jaw dislodges and falls from one side. Ophelia's hand catches it mid-air and helps him readjust it. His eyeballs look at her with the same trembling rage.

Her mind races. Looking at the mummified corpse in front of her, it dawns on her. Suddenly the noise of the plummeting rain stops torturing her, and though she's being restrained beyond movement, she feels lighter, free. She relaxes her body, and suddenly her mother's grip is looser. She looks around at the ghouls infesting the park, waiting, not coming at her.

"You aren't gonna kill me, either," she says.

Her father pierces her with his gaze.

"You won't kill me!" she repeats as the rain hammers her face. "You don't want to kill me!"

"Oh," he says, slowly, and a hunger, an eagerness, seeps through his jagged mummy breath. The leathered mouth stretches into an uncanny smile. "Oh, we do."

"No," she continues. "Mr. Girardot didn't kill me. All those corpses in the cemetery wouldn't kill me. I thought it had to be you. But you're stalling, too. This isn't hunger. It's something else."

"You!" her mother screeches behind her. "You, you, you. It's always about you, isn't it?"

"Then who?"

"Tommy," her mother says. "W—We want Tommy. And all the Tommys in the world."

"Who—What are you talking about?"

"You lied to everyone," her father says. "Again."

"What?"

"B—Back at the police station. They asked you about Grann's visions."

"I told them everything."

"They asked you a—about w—what c—c—came after the crash."

Lilith's mouth trembles. "Well, I don't know what that means, so ..."

"It was smart, changing things," he says. "Jumping out of the car. You were supposed to crash. And, after that, nevertheless, it's something, right? Or have you forgotten about that part? About *'All the Tommys in the world?'* "

Lilith's face burns under the cold rain. "What is that? What does it mean?"

"*Oh, you don't know,*" her mother whispers behind her. "*Of course. Poor you.*"

"Don't play dumb with us," her father says. "We know why you lied."

Lilith's mind races. Should she know this?

Her father smiles a grim smile. "It's killing you, isn't it? You don't know how it works. You think if you understand us, you can beat us. Well, not yet."

Behind her, she hears her mother's voice of rustling dry leaves. "W—we c—can wait, d—dear."

Lilith jerks her arms and tries to free herself. Her mother's arms follow her movements, giving her room to move, waiting for her jerks to end, and grabbing her once again.

"You think you're so lucky, don't you?" her father asks her.

Lilith looks around at the madness, at the ghouls coming out of the ground like slugs closing in around her. "What?"

"You think you're *immune to fate* because you can see the future, don't you? You think you were so clever, jumping out of that car. The question is, was that you being unpredictable? Or was it the plan all along? And, are you slipping away from us this time?"

She shuts up. He seems to grin.

"You think you know everything!" he says. "But you only heard the ramblings of a dying woman. You didn't even get a glimpse!"

"Grann," Lilith exhales.

"You think your movies and your books made you an expert. And yet, you knew all along. And you decided to forget. You knew that night."

"What night?" she asks. "Grann died in the morning."

Her mother chuckles. "No. Not Grann. You really buried it deep, didn't you? You don't even remember why we left Leatel-ranch, you scaredy cat?"

"You took me away," Lilith says, "to the city."

"We did?" Her mother laughs. "Ah, yes, to p—protect your fragile little heart, right? Then how come you never c—came back? Not—t even visited? How come you kicked and screamed when we brought you back? We sh—shielded you from the t— truth your whole life. But death is the great teacher. We b—b— brought you here for your sake. There's something y—you need to do."

"I don't understand!" she yells. "What?"

"Oh, Lil," her mother says. "Always the rebel. You know you won't d—do it if we tell you."

"You think you've b—been making your own luck," he says, and chuckles, or whatever the dead do when they cough. "All your life, *we* made your luck for y—you!"

He looks into her eyes. Lil looks right back at him, trembling.

"You've lived a sheltered life. We made sure you knew nothing. Saw nothing. Heard nothing. But now, it's time to change that."

"You don't know me," Lilith snarls. "I went into the cemetery when I was *fifteen*," she says.

"Ah, yes. N—Nathan. Now *he* knows things."

"He taught me all about it."

Her father smiles and looks over her shoulder. Lilith turns around. Behind her, her mother is smiling as well.

"Did he?" he says. "You know he's hiding things from you. He always has."

Lilith feels an icy dagger to her chest. She tries to process what she just heard. "Nate's ALIVE?"

"You've never been to his house, have you?"

"How do you know all this?"

"And why do you think that is?" he continues.

"He was just scared."

"We're not the only ones who've been sheltering you from the truth. He knew. He always knew. Ask him."

Lilith lifts her head and locks eyes with her father. She tries to ignore his rotten grin.

"I don't know why you're doing this," she says, grinding her teeth. "I don't know what has changed. I don't know why you grin, but I can see that you're secretly hurting. You're afraid of something. And I will find out. And I will get rid of all of you. You want me to just take this. You think I'll stay in the back seat and take it. But that's not me anymore."

His grin slowly fades away.

"Kill me," she defies them, spitting rainwater with each word, turning her head to look at both of them. "Kill me, and I will show you. I will never be one of you. Even dead, I will never be one of you. I swear, all I will do, for all eternity, is destroy you."

60

A HUNDRED LEGS AND ARMS CARRY THE HUMAN CENTIPEDE across the streets of Leatelranch, splashing water with each clumsy uneven step. Old shoes, worn sneakers, and rotten bare feet march on the puddled asphalt, breaking away soles and loose flesh, stomping on the remains and leaving them behind as it marches.

Curled up in a ball, rocking with the movement, Nathan squints and looks up. The white light of the streetlights displays the rotten limbs around him in all their gore. Fat heavy raindrops seep between the elbows, knees, and hands holding the weave together and fall on his face.

He spits. "Don't let the water get in your mouth."

Lester spits and covers his mouth. Yoshi nods, silent.

Lightning strikes and Nate looks outside. He sees the first buildings: Spiked houses. Gothic restaurants. Three-story buildings with gargoyles on their roofs. A huge gargoyle holding a pizza. He clenches his teeth. He remembers this all too well.

Lester spits again. "Leatelranch. Is. The coolest," he says, spitting after each word, his pupils dilated as he looks around.

"Nathan, Lilith," says Yoshi, covering his mouth, "Now those names make sense. It's like a vampire town. You're from Gotham City."

"Yeah," Lester says. "Why did you ever leave this place?"

"You'd be relieved to leave, too," Nathan says.

"Nuh-uh," Lester replies. "You'd have to *force* me out of here. You were *scared?* You're a grown man!"

"I was younger then," Nathan whispers. "I was your age."

He sees something standing in the sidewalk. It's people. They stand idly all over the sidewalk and the street ahead, as still as the gargoyle above.

"You scaredy idiot!" Yoshi says.

Nathan jumps and covers Yoshi's mouth, looking around like a madman. "Shhh!"

The shadows outside seem to ignore the scorpion monster. He and the boys share a moment of stillness as they come through.

"I think we're OK," Lester says, as a faint rumor of growls builds around them. Ghouls on every street seem to wake from their idle slumber and turn to the formation of headless ghouls that flank and escort the monster.

"Is this bad?" Lester asks in whispers.

"They're ignoring our monster cab," Nathan says. "They just want the corpses. As long as we're in here, we're fine."

"And how long will we be in here? Where is this thing headed?"

"I guess we'll find out," Nathan says, looking around.

As they turn a corner, far ahead, he sees the columns supporting the familiar triangular structure. The iron gates. The WESTERN CEMETERY sign.

"You'd have left, too," Nathan says. "I lived in there. My father was the caretaker."

The boys gaze at the ominous entrance that's getting closer and closer. "Fuck," they say in unison.

There's a rumble up ahead. It sounds like a fight.

"And what about that *Lilith?*" asks Yoshi. "How'd you get *her* to leave this place?"

The murmur of a fight grows to the roar of a battle, of grunting, of flesh hitting flesh, of pulling and pushing, of cracking bones.

"Actually, she convinced me."

The kids look at each other, confused. Yoshi is the one to say it. "What's her problem?"

Nathan smiles. "Her only problem right now is how bad I'm going to scare her when I see her."

Their scorpion coach turns a corner, and Nathan immediately recognizes where it's heading.

"Where are we going?" asks Yoshi.

"We're going to my ..." Nate frowns, confused. Frozen. "We're going to the ..." His tone almost sounds like a question. "We're going to the ... *cemetery*?"

As the monster steps on the pavement, the rumble gets louder. Closer. They crawl to the front of the ribcage and peek through the moving mesh of limbs.

The street leads to a large park well-lit with white lamps, where the horror of a zombie battle is being played out in full glory. Hundreds of rotten skeleton zombies are taking on headless ghouls by storm. They corner them, they grab them from behind, they attack in a group.

"Come on!" yells Yoshi. "Wake up, headless zombies!"

"Are you *rooting* for that dog-whispering fuck?" asks Nate. "The one who took your friend?"

"I root for *me*," he says, pointing to the mesh of limbs. "While we're in here, we don't have much of a choice."

The headless soldiers run like rabid dogs; the skeletons, brownish with a thin layer of mummified flesh and ragged clothes still stuck to their bodies, look calm, and wait, and witness, and dodge, and corner, and endure. Each awaits its own custom demise; some get torn apart, some seem to take pleasure in burying the poor dogs of war in mass graves, already dug. Many more spill out onto the streets, a virulent anthill spitting out warrior ants.

"OK," says Lester, pointing forward. *"Now* we can worry."

A group of mud-colored skeletons lunges at them, striding forward with jarred steps. Nate shudders and braces the boys.

The limb-scorpion steers left and tries to avoid them. It climbs the curb, and the first line of legs steps on the soft, puddled grass.

Lester screams, and Nate turns around. Two skeletons, dressed in what look like rotten colonial clothes, are almost within arm's reach, stretching their arms and pulling limbs out of the human scorpion with surreal dexterity.

The scorpion's tail whips forward and reaches for them. They dodge it without even looking up and keep picking away parts. They're opening a hole in the skin of the beast, hurting it as it walks, and as the gap grows, Nate can see them more clearly. They crouch to pull out the beast's legs, making it falter. Nate cranes his neck. Among the fights and movement, in the center of the park, he sees something. He grabs two dead arms like prison bars and tries to sneak his head between them to get a better look. A name slips from his mouth as he exhales. He tries to repeat it out loud, and when it finally comes out, it's in the form of a scream that seems to emanate from the bottom of his soul.

"Lilith!"

Held by two ghouls, Lilith turns to the monstrous beast, confused. She looks for the source of the scream.

"Nate?"

The monster climbs the curb onto the soft mud of the park. Its weight compresses the earth, and it sinks.

"No!" yells Lester.

Nathan turns to him. "What happened?"

Lester is reaching down, through the mesh of limbs, trying to grab something down on the ground.

"What happened?" Nathan repeats.

Lester pulls up his arm. He's holding Frankie's arm. He smiles, relieved. "I almost lost you," he says to it.

The giant scorpion whips its tail, destroying skeletons all

around it.

"Not bad for a bag of bones," says Nate, patting the limbs next to him.

Nearby, headless ghouls cornered by skeletons sway their arms in a frenzy, not letting the skeletons touch them, and move toward the wounded monster. They group into packs and provoke the skeletons like rabid dogs, forcing them to recede. Then, they walk to the mounds of dirt growing out of the earth and pull and destroy the bones below with mad rage. The ghouls look desperate, fighting tooth and nail against the headless corpses. Nathan has never seen them like this. They seem powerless. Afraid. He looks back at Lilith and sees her looking at him as they get closer and closer.

"I think she's our target! Nate, the monster's after *her*!" Yoshi yells.

Nathan climbs up the back part of the cabin and squeezes between the limbs forming the ribs of the beast. He crawls toward the stem of the long scorpion-like tail, feeling it pull back in preparation to whip forward. The ice-cold forearms and legs below him are tense, hard at work like pistons in an engine.

He turns around for a full view of the park, now mere yards from the plodding centipede feet of the beast. Right in front of him he sees the imminent target of the swinging tail: Lilith.

"No!" he yells, and his voice seems to throw the tail off. It hits a ghoul standing right in front of her, sending him flying away.

Nathan crawls up the tail. It's composed of human legs and arms, some still covered in ragged clothing. He grabs a leg still inside its wet jeans and tries to pull it out. It's fatter and stronger than he thought, and it wrestles like a live shark, but it finally comes off, and he throws it to the ground looking for the next weak link in the mesh.

The tail wriggles again and takes out the other ghoul. A woman. As she goes flying off, Nate can't help but think that she looks familiar. Now it's Lilith, alone, in the tail's crosshairs.

Nate's eyes scan the tail, searching desperately for the weak link that will send the whole thing crumbling to the wet ground below. Then he spots it: two strong muscled arms gripping a column of tangled limbs, embracing them like a flower bouquet.

Nate grabs one of the burly arms in both of his hands and twists his body until it loses its grip, and the sting of the beast's tail falls like a massive dead weight on his shoulders.

The boys yell below him, "Get in!" reaching for Lilith, who notices them among the chaos.

The scorpion whirls its damaged tail toward Lilith, but its movements are sluggish. Lilith dodges it and instinctively hits it with her arm, knocking the tail off. She looks for an opening between the limbs and jumps in, screaming.

Nathan holds on to the end of the severed tail and smiles. "Yes!" he yells. He looks up. The monster's heads have turned around and are following Lilith as she crawls inside.

Nathan hurries back inside, swimming frantically among the limbs. Sitting next to the boys, she's as beautiful as ever, and her face lights up when she sees him.

"Nate!"

Nathan hurries to her, and they hug until their bones hurt.

The scorpion tank coils onto itself and bends its damaged tail to point at its own ribcage. Nathan looks up at the droves of arms and fingers crawling across the cabin like spiders, racing to the back of the beast, climbing the damaged tail, healing it like scar tissue, rebuilding it.

"What do we do now?" Yoshi asks, looking around. "What do we do now?"

A head enters the cabin, hovering, hanging by the hair from a closed hand, craning down from an arm, held by another arm. It looks at them in the eye with a flat dead mouth. Its eyes are milky and rubbery, but something inside them ignites at the sight of them.

"Now we hope that eternity is nice," Lester says.

At the rear of the monster, the tail inches downward, stalking them, and a thousand arms and fingers reach for them.

61

Lilith breaks her kiss with Nate and looks at him. Her cheeks burn. She's smiling so much that it hurts. Nate smiles, too, and behind him, over his shoulder, the mesh made of legs and arms opens like a giant wound and gives way to a hovering head, a dead boy that pierces them with his gaze, held by a tentacle of braided arms.

Nate notices the expression on her face and turns around. His body is electric. He pokes the head in both eyes with his fingers, stinging it with a confidence Lilith has never seen.

"Whoa," someone says behind her, and she turns around. The teenagers seem impressed as well.

"Austin Powers?" she blurts out.

The head pulls back with gooey hollow eye sockets, clumsy, blind, and as Lilith stares at Nate's fingers dripping with black goo, the tentacle arm retreats. Lilith jumps and grabs the head by the ears, pulling, prying it away from the hand at the end of the tentacle. She throws the head through the open hole just as another head starts to descend on them. Hands and fingers reach for her. The entire cabin is alive, closing in on them.

The boys jump at the second head, pulling it from the tentacle like ripe fruit. The head starts to bite in the air, its teeth chattering violently.

"I can't do it," says the bald teenager, staring at the face. "You do it!"

The Austin Powers boy, holding the head, looks even more scared. "I can't do it either!" he says. He points the head toward Nate, who prepares to poke it with his blackened fingers. Just then, the self-healing beast makes a sudden jerk and starts to move again, and he falls to his knees.

"They're getting close!" yells the boy in the black leather suit and pins in his head.

Lilith tries to keep her balance as she looks outside. More ghouls taunt the machine, closing in, and its hundred legs move to evade them. But there's no escape. When she looks to the other side, she sees a sea of ghouls. They're surrounded.

Lilith studies the ghouls' faces, or skulls, all with different degrees of dirt and flesh and blood, as they reach for her and take swings at the monster that is both protecting and attacking her, Nate, and two random kids she might never meet. They pick off limbs, trying to disassemble the beast right out from underneath her. Meanwhile, she searches among the faces. As the ghouls parade around her, as the monster tank speeds up and starts to lope, her parents are nowhere to be seen.

Hands reach inside the ribcage, groping for her. She can smell their fetid breath on her face. They grab her. They pull.

"Nate!" she yells.

Suddenly, and inexplicably, the hands let go. When Lilith looks up, the sea appears to be receding. The ghouls are moving away from the creature, walking back to gaze at them from a distance.

"What's going on?" Nate asks her.

"Shit," yells the teenager in the Austin Powers suit, and Lilith turns to him. "I dropped it again. I dropped Frankie's arm." He's looking down at an opening in the human limb mesh, where the grass is moving away rapidly.

"What are you doing, kid?" Lilith asks.

"Help! Help me!" he says, reaching down. "I can't ..."

Lilith grabs him by the shoulders and starts to pull. "Are you insane ...?!"

Nate jumps and reaches down. Lilith watches, confused, as Nate fishes up the arm and hands it to the boy.

The monster's lope becomes a drunk stride, swaying to the sides, blind, hurt. It rams against the ghouls around it, stepping right where they were a moment ago, barely missing them. Peeking outside through two severed arms, Lilith sees a dry reddish skull, the color of rotten meat, getting nearer and nearer, coming at her. Though the skull has no lips or cheeks, she can tell it's grinning. She leans back on Nate, and as the face comes closer and closer, she grips the cold dead limbs and tenses her arms, preparing to thrust her legs out from the beast and kick him. The face gets closer, close enough to reach, and the taunt in its eyes and the grin in its jaw does not move.

It knows what's coming.

Fuck it, she thinks. She grabs the limbs and pulls them apart, welcoming the horrible sight.

"What are you doing?!" two annoying teen voices ask in unison.

The beast sways forward, hurt, and the sudden lurch brings Lilith closer to the ghoul, surprising both of them. Seeing surprise in its beef jerky forehead muscles, she head-butts him.

With a slight bump, the rotten skull cracks and detaches from its body, falling off.

Voices cheer behind her.

Cheering, she thinks. *It's been so long*.

As the beast sways like a pendulum back in the opposite direction, Lilith sees the ghouls moving farther away, alternating their looks between the decapitated skeleton and the drunken wounded beast.

Out the front of the cabin, Lilith can see that they're almost at the end of the park and are heading toward the Tower, the tallest and newest building in Leatelranch. They've left the sea of ghouls behind, and their monster tank is now crawling clumsily alone in the street. It turns left and right, blind, dancing. The limbs start to sizzle.

"It's healing again!" yells the bald boy. "It's turning back! Let's go!"

The regenerating beast starts heading back into the park, where the army of ghouls is looking hungry again.

Lilith breaks open the mesh of limbs and makes the hole big enough for them to exit. "Out. Now."

She helps them climb out first, then jumps, enjoying the firmness of the pavement as soon as she lands.

Nate is already running toward the Tower, and the boys follow him. She runs after them, looking over her shoulder at the centipede. It charges against the sea of ghouls, fighting its way clumsily. Lilith almost feels sorry for it. Nate breaks the glass door, and they crawl inside, running through the lobby toward the nearest set of stairs. They climb silently, breathing heavily, mechanically, numb. The silence in the clean white stairwell is surreal. They keep going until an iron door blocks their way, and they open it.

A large roof terrace gives them a panoramic view of all of Leatelranch.

Nate shuts the iron door behind them, and they walk to the ledge overlooking the park.

"What now?" says the bald boy as his breathing calms down.

"Now, nothing," says Nate, falling to the floor. "Now, we rest."

"I don't think we have much of a choice," says the bald boy, looking down. He looks worried. Hopeless.

Lilith looks around. They're above all of the sentinel heads hanging from the streetlights and cables. "We'll be safe here," she says.

The boy in the Austin Powers suit looks down. "How the hell are we going to get out of here?"

The park is completely covered with ghouls. In the center,

near the statue of Salomone Francis, the monster defends itself clumsily from the attacks of the ghouls, who carefully extend their arms and pick away parts of its body.

As it suffers the blows from the army of ghouls, the scorpion coils its tail toward the ground and pokes softly on different spots. It cranes back up, this time with something on its end. It's a head. It places it on its front, and the tail suddenly whips around it, taking out a dozen ghouls. The tail rips apart limbs from the fallen ghouls, then places them in its own body, completing itself. Then, a new wave of ghouls closes in on it and starts picking apart its pieces.

"I wonder how long *that's* gonna last," Lilith says, sitting on the floor to watch the show more comfortably. On the street below them, a huge pack of dogs and headless ghouls are heading to the park. From this far up, the park, and the streets surrounding it, and the streets surrounding the building, all sizzle like a burning anthill, like a tireless battle between immortals.

62

MARTHA'S KNUCKLES GO WHITE AS SHE GRIPS THE RAILING OF her balcony. Down there, on the street, everyone is hiding. Even the sun is hiding, leaving an orange, pinkish sky, drawing shadows everywhere. But she's not hiding. Not Martha, no siree. She was born in this part of New Southport before it even became such a big city, back when it was all low houses and kids played out in the street, and she's not hiding.

The neighborhood is quiet. No cars. No people. No music coming from their noisy apartments. She can see them, though. She can see faces peeking out of windows, curtains folding just enough for eyes to see. So, they should come out, like her. Chin up high.

Maybe it's an age thing. Mr. Roberts, also from her generation, walks the sidewalk and signals people to stay inside their homes, guarding the street. People slide their windows open and ask him questions, and he shushes them and talks, keeping the neighborhood informed. She can hear some of the exchanges.

What happened?

The news cut off so suddenly ...

Stay inside, Phil.

Who knew? Heroes come from the weirdest places. He's even

in short sleeves, in such cold. As the sun sets and shade takes over the sidewalk, he rubs his hands and arms.

He approaches three police officers and stops to talk to them. They're standing next to a white garage door. He steps toward the door, and he seems to sigh, or worry.

That's when she hears it. A low knocking sound. She notices the glint of the metal garage door. It trembles. Someone is hitting it from the inside.

Mr. Roberts kneels and checks on something shiny. A huge lock. It's keeping the garage door shut. He stands up and joins the officers again.

The knocks get more desperate, and he looks up. The garage door is being hit harder. With each blow, it bends outward like a balloon.

And suddenly, with one of the knocks, a big crack opens in the center of the door. Mr. Roberts and the cops don't seem to notice.

Martha's hands lift from the balcony railing, preparing to signal them, to wave, to catch their attention, when the garage door rips open. Arms flail from inside and open the rip.

Martha's mouth finally opens. *Watch out,* she mumbles, and she covers her mouth in horror.

But they look like ordinary people to her. *Why would they lock them in there like that?* Two of them come out, surely in a hurry. *But who wouldn't be?* But instead of escaping down the street, they go directly for the officers. They jump them and grab them and seem to ... *Oh. But ... OH!* Martha covers her mouth and lets out a scream.

Mr. Roberts escapes. He runs across the street, and another one of the prisoners gets out and runs after him.

"Mr. Roberts!" she screams. The man looks up, searching for her voice, and meets her gaze. She points behind him, and as he turns around the prisoner jumps him and—this time she's sure— bites him on the neck and tears it apart. Mr. Roberts is gushing blood.

"Oh my god!" Martha shrieks as Mr. Roberts collapses on the street just like the policemen.

The prisoners spread out toward nearby doors.

Martha crouches and sits on the floor, hanging on to her balcony railing.

"What's going on?" she cries silently.

The floor starts to rumble. She brings her hands to it, to make sure she's not imagining it. Her balcony is indeed rumbling. And now she can hear it, too.

She stands up again and looks at the street. House doors are open. There's screaming, and people run in the street. They're chasing each other.

The rumble grows louder. She looks up. In the pinkish horizon, something moves. An insect-like rumble, like an army of cockroaches, is filling the street as far as she can see. And slowly, but steadily, they are approaching.

She looks at the mayhem down in the street. It's getting more crowded. She looks for Mr. Roberts, but he's not there anymore. *The crazies took him*.

She looks for the policemen. Only the big pool of blood remains and gets carried by the runners throughout the street. Blood is everywhere.

The rumbling grows louder. And the faces. The faces. It's like they're in a frenzy. *No, not a frenzy. They seem very much in control of themselves. They just seem to be ... in a hurry.* She spots Mr. Roberts in one of the faces. He's looking straight at her.

She gasps as Mr. Roberts starts to grin.

She takes a hand to her mouth and clenches her teeth as Mr. Roberts takes a step toward her building. He walks patiently among the running crowd, his eyes locked on hers.

His head tilts back in a sudden jerk. Somebody's attacking him from behind. The street has been taken over by an army-like crowd coming from downtown, which are ... *headless people?* A knot forms in her throat, and she can't even scream. *Headless people are attacking Mr. Roberts. Smiling, dead Mr. Roberts.* They grab his neck and ...

Oh! Oh! They are pulling off his head!

Martha grabs her own head as other headless groups spread out and attack everyone else on the street, ripping off heads and arms and legs, filling the street with blood. It all happens so fast. The sound of bones breaking, of screaming. The smell. The horrible smell. Headless people close in from every direction, cornering the already bloody people and attacking them. They enter every crevice, every hole, every alley, every building. They enter the houses, and there are more screams, and people come out, bloody, without their heads. They spread around the streets like a river of blood. The whole town is screaming.

She looks around at other balconies, other windows. Nothing. No one. Everyone in town seems to be screaming in pain except for her. She sees people trying to escape and run through the streets, but they all get chased by the headless people and get caught, maimed, killed. The headless people keep attacking the bodies even as they rise, like feral animals, and they take their heads off as they try to escape.

The screams finally die off. Everyone's standing, headless, silent, like a formation. The putrid smell makes her eyes watery.

Dogs start to bark.

A giant ... *animal?* Like a cockroach, or a spider, comes down the street, each stride stepping on the sidewalks at either side, stepping on bodies and heads, destroying everything in its path. It's surrounded by hundreds of dogs, who advance under it, dodging its strides.

A single man, with his head still on, rides on its back. Behind his dark sunglasses, he seems as lifeless as the dead bodies. He's short, and young, but there's a serious look about him. He looks angry. Victorious.

The headless people filling the street make way for it. They move to the sidewalk as the giant bug gets closer, and when it's close enough, she can see it's made of human limbs. Legs. Arms. Torsos.

The machine stops.

The man looks around. A horrible pink scar cuts across his cheek. He stands up and starts to crawl down to the street.

Martha hears a whining shriek of a door. A person—*Is that Mrs. Simpson?*—is running out to meet him, arms forward.

A pack of dogs jumps on her like a tidal wave, and a whine echoes along the street. The man jumps down from his machine.

"No!" he screams.

The pack of dogs takes the woman to the ground and tears her apart. They spread apart as the man gets closer to them. All the dogs except one, who lies on the ground next to the torn pieces of Mrs. Simpson.

"No!" the man screams again, and his scream fills the street.

The dying dog whimpers as the man kneels next to it. He pets its head and lifts it. The dog seems to look at him, and he seems to say something to the dog. Martha leans in, curious. She can't hear the words, but they actually sound ... tender. He seems to share the dog's pain. The scar across his cheek lights up, vivid.

Other dogs circle around him and whimper as well. The man hugs the dying dog. His face is shining. He's crying. He inflates his chest, then lets the air out, and inhales again, imitating the dog's agitated, last breaths, until man and dog seem to be breathing in unison. Then, they lose sync. The man slows down his breathing. The dog slows its breaths down to match. He's calming down. The man lowers his head, and the dog follows. The man turns his head to the side, opens his mouth, and exhales a heavy yawn. The dog follows.

Martha sobs. Tears are coming down her eyes.

The man looks up at the source of the sound, his face red with anger. He lets down the dog, the dead dog, and places its head carefully on the pavement. He whistles something, like a tune.

The dogs along the street start barking. The headless people, as if awakening from a dream, walk up to the houses and buildings and start tearing everything down.

Martha sees the horde walking up to her building. She hears glass shattering, metal and steel clashing (*Are they jumping on cars?*), and the metallic, high-pitched sound of brick being picked. She loses her balance. Her building is collapsing.

She grabs the balcony railing as her apartment leans forward and to the left, falling onto the street. Pieces of brick and rubble fall from above, and she feels the whole building collapsing on top of her. A cloud of dust covers everything. She's pinned.

As the dust around her settles, all she can see is the sky. The man is close, very close. She can smell him now. His face enters her sight. It's scary and cold. She also smells something else. And she hears a growl. A German Shepherd comes into view. The man is petting it. He's keeping it from lunging at her.

She can't move. She can barely talk.

"P—Please—Don't—"

The man shakes his head. He's been crying. "You're one of them."

"No, I'm not—H—Help."

The dog opens its mouth. Its yellow teeth tremble with anticipation.

"Go," the man says, and the dog's open mouth comes at her. His sharp teeth break her bones, her cheeks, her collarbone, and she feels the warm blood in her throat. She feels pulling on her feet, and as she's lifted, she can see her body dragged away by the other headless people.

The world spins. Vertigo takes over as she drops inside a pungent dark bag.

PART IV

63

Nathan squeezes Lilith's hand. It feels good to interlock fingers again, feel the warmth of her body. He takes another sip of the bottle, and the night sky is endless. There are no stars. The moon is a scythe; it could cut you just for looking at it, and if there's an opposite to glowing, that's what it's doing. Looking down, his face warm and so close to the flames, he looks at Lilith, Yoshi, and Lester sitting around the fire they built on the highest rooftop in Leatelranch. Yoshi and Lester are drunk, their eyes blood-shot red. Lester stretches toward Frankie's flapping arms and pulls them away from the fire, dragging his half-full bottle of whiskey. And Lilith, sitting next to him, is looking back at him, exploring his own features and wrinkles and gray hairs as he's exploring hers. That face. That beautiful face. Seeing her relaxed, smiling, after all this chaos, after all this time, just makes him want to scare her to death. A good jump scare. Nothing fancy. Fancy can wait. But to hear her shriek, a good shriek after all these bad ones, will be like music. But no rush. The night is young. The opportunity will come.

"You look good," Nate whispers in her ear.

She brushes against him, and he caresses her leg.

"I lost sssome weight in that station bunker," she says, slurring. "I haven't been eating."

"Yeah, I know. That's not what I meant."

"All that food we had at the station," she continues, looking into the distance, "enough to last us years ... It wasn't long until we figured none of us was really hungry—"

"Just wait until you see your green blood," Yoshi says.

"We noticed that, too, yeah," Lilith says.

"We're *zombies* now," Lester sighs matter-of-factly.

Lilith turns to him and pierces him with her eyes. "No, we're not. We're *not*, trust me. We'll know when we are."

She stares at the crackling fire.

"At first, there was some panic," she continues. "People thought we were all dead ... but then we just realized ... life itself, must have kind of ... shut down. Whatever that means."

"Yeah," Nathan says. "Not a pretty sight."

Lilith sighs. "All that training we got from movies, for gathering food and medical supplies, and fucking bullets ... All useless."

"You look good," Nathan starts again.

"You look good, too," she says.

She's lying, of course. He can see the worry in her rugged, hardened eyes.

"Those were your parents, right?" he asks her. "Back there, cornering you?"

She lets go of his hand. Her smile fades, and she scans his eyes.

"Y—yeah," she says.

"Sorry about what happened with them. It looked like ... like you were talking to them."

"Nah," she scoffs. "What? That's crazy." Her round eyes look at him nervously. Something doesn't sound right.

"We talked to a few," Lester says. "They do talk, you know?"

"They do?" she asks, looking away. "Well, they didn't talk to me. They just came for the kill. You got me out of there just in time."

Nathan doesn't understand. She doesn't trust him. Why doesn't she trust him?

Down on the street, barks, growls, and sounds of punching and dismemberment rise up in the air.

"We should check again," he says, turning around. "It was looking like the ghouls are afraid of the dogs. And they couldn't handle the scorpion machine. It definitely looked like the headless ghouls were winning this."

Lilith takes another swig from the bottle. "Yeah," she says with a mocking tone. "Sure *looked* that way, didn't it?"

Nathan sobers up all of a sudden. "What do you mean?"

She gulps, then points her whiskey bottle all around her. "That's what they want us to believe!" she says. "It's all part of the *plan*."

"They have a plan?" Yoshi asks.

He notices Frankie's arms flapping close to the flames, and he rounds them up and places them between Lester and him.

"That's what I've been sssaying!" Lilith says. "Of course they have a plan! What you told me about the bonfire? Don't you see it was their idea? That they were *expecting* it?"

Lester seems to think about it. "Oh shit!" he realizes. "The subway station! The giant zombie monster led us there!"

"They've been playing us like puppets," Lilith says. "They wanted us to be *here*. We've been predictable all along."

Yoshi takes Lester's half-full bottle and takes a long chug.

"And my parents," she says, sobering up, staring into the fire. "There's a reason they're letting me live. How do you think we escaped? They're up to something. Whatever's happening, it's what they want to happen. This is all *their* plan, not ours. They're letting *all of us* live. Until they don't."

Below them, the hum of battle fills the air.

"So, we're fucked," Yoshi says. "There's no escape."

"It's good," Lester says, trying to catch his breath. "It's a good thing. It's gotta be. These are the people who've *seen* the tunnel, and the white light, and whatever's beyond. We should trust them. Whatever their reason, they're probably right."

"You sound like sheep," Lilith says, "just taking it."

"And you sound like sheep just rejecting it," Lester replies.

Lilith's face lights up. She always enjoyed a defiant tone. And Nathan can see, somewhere inside her, wheels start to turn.

"Touché, kid," Lilith slurs. "Well, maybe if we knew what their plan was ... I ... I dunno."

Sparks fly out of the fire. Lester stretches forward and grabs Frankie's arms as they slug their way to the fire again.

"What is that?" Lilith asks.

"Our friend," Lester says.

"That's gross. You're gross."

"No, no," Nathan says. "We escaped because the ghouls were busy fighting each other. And half of them, the headless ones, don't have a plan for sure."

"It's *all* a plan," Lilith says, staring into the fire.

Yoshi gets up and walks to the ledge, looking down.

"Fuck you!" he yells at the chaos below.

Nathan bolts up and runs to him, shushing him.

"But you're right," Yoshi says from the ledge, drunk. "They're too busy fighting each other. And we're too high up, anyway. Look."

Nathan reaches the ledge and looks down. The carnage is in full swing. It's hard to tell the bodies from one another. Limbs fly off, grunts echo. Ghouls keep pouring out of the cemetery in hordes and joining the fight. From the other side, marching in from out of town, an endless parade of headless zombies also join the anthill that covers the streets of the whole town.

"Who's winning?" Lester asks, joining them on the ledge, accompanied by Lilith.

"It's hard to tell," Nathan says. "Dogs seem to win, but zombie numbers keep going up."

"As long as they're fighting each other," Yoshi says, "at least we can escape again."

Nathan points at the horizon. It's boiling with movement. "Think again."

"You know what they say about Leatelranch," Lilith singsongs, following his gaze. "Everybody's dying to visit!"

Nathan can feel the buzz leaving his body. "We're in the eye of the storm."

"Are we the only ones left?" Lester asks.

"Sure looks like it," Nathan says.

"Aren't we lucky?" Yoshi asks. "What are we going to do now?"

"You're right," Lilith says, looking down. "Look. Look at how they act around those dogs and those headless ghouls."

"What?" the boys ask.

"There's no surprising them," Lilith says, staring down below. "Everything we say, or do, they're expecting it. They've seen it already. Fuck, I thought I was so cool, twisting and jerking in my decisions, surprising them, but they were just playing me all along. But look at how they act around those dogs. And those headless corpses. Them, they *really* don't seem to expect."

Nate's mind races. "What are you saying?"

"The dogs," she says. "And the headless corpses—"

"They're slaves," Nathan says. "They're all part of the same army. That fucking zombie-whisperer fuck. We saw him *training* them. First, he cuts off their heads, I guess he doesn't want to get bitten, and then he trains them, like dogs, and bosses them around."

"No," Lilith says, looking down. "On the contrary. I think somehow they are really, truly instinctive. Look at those ghouls reacting to them. They are *new* to them. If anybody's gonna stop the ghouls, it's them."

"What about the *Delllegate*?" Lester asks, slurring.

Nate shakes his head, dismissing him, and turns back to Lilith. "That's good, right? Maybe *they* can rid us of this shit."

"No," Lilith says, staring at the battle. "That's really, really bad."

"What?" Lester asks, trembling. "Why?"

"Think about it," Lilith says, her voice deep and harsh. "There's no escape. Even if we avoid the fight below and miraculously get out of here alive, one day, we'll be dead. If zombies win, we'll become zombies. But if that zombie-whisperer fuck wins, as you so beautifully put it, we eventually become his servants. Headless, servile dogs. And guess what. One day, he'll die, too. And then we'll be headless dogs serving a corpse. Forever, and ever, and ever."

"Well," Yoshi exhales, "that's depressing."

Nathan can't stand to see her like this. He notices the dark side of the rooftop away from the fire. It would be a good place to scare her. Maybe he can lure her there somehow, and if they stood right about where those shadows seem to be lurking ...

His blood freezes.

"So, we should root for the zombies?" Yoshi asks.

"We root for *us*," Lilith says, red-faced. Her eyes are glassy beads, and the first tears fall down her cheeks.

The shadows on the opposite ledge of the roof move. Something inside Nathan—denial, fright—forces him to pretend he's just imagining it. *But they* are *there, aren't they?*

"Then, we root for the zombies," she continues. "At least as normal zombies, we have a chance."

"She's right," Yoshi says, showing his cuts, still gushing green blood. "We're all doomed already. But at least we're whole."

"Shouldn't—Shouldn't we do the opposite, then?" Nathan asks softly, noticing the shadows approaching from behind and hoping they won't notice him staring at them. "Throw them off? Do the unexpected?"

"No," Lilith says, actually smiling, and the shadows standing up with thin arms like long-legged insects come closer. "The kid is right. I'm done trying to throw them off. New plan is, we just do whatever the fuck we feel like."

She looks at Nate for approval, but he's scared stiff, frozen, mouth agape.

"So it's settled, then," Lilith says. "Tomorrow we plan the downfall of this motherfucking zombie-whisperer fuck."

As she says this, the shadows behind her silently crawl away. The night reveals their stalking faces, and Nathan recognizes Lilith's childhood friends, Wolfram and Wednesday, and their glimmering eyes. He lets out a whimper.

Lilith turns to him. She seems drunk enough to maybe have missed it, but she frowns with suspicion.

"Were you ... about to scare me?"

He scoffs, looking at the empty dark corner of the rooftop. "We got other things to worry about."

She smiles, and puts her head on his shoulder.

64

LILITH DREAMS. LILITH DREAMS ABOUT A PAIR OF EYES STARING at her underwater, or in a thick, greasy liquid, with the cavernous sound of movement around her. A giant underground maze, or palace. A strange architecture, centuries in the making. The horrifying results of time over the human mind. A climb to the Earth's surface. The humming dunes of a desert, and a giant swollen sun nearing the earth. Remains of vast cemetery cities and their wars. Endless, endless sand, and a search. The ruins of an old human city. The tall skeleton of a building. Eroded shapeless holes where windows once shone, like eyes in pain. A sandy room with Nathan, and her parents, and Grann, and a mysterious boy. The wind, the only other inhabitant on the surface. Earth, millennia, destroyed and reborn. Young Lilith sitting at the breakfast table with her parents, laughing, on a sunny morning. Behind the kitchen window, dead, rotten, zombie Lilith lurks, and meets her innocent gaze. A room, all black. Black-dressed nurses surrounding and looking down on Lilith, and on her sweaty, wide-open legs. Lilith pushing. A piercing cry.

65

Nathan wakes up shivering in the cool morning air. He tries to move under the shabby blanket and notices Lilith is awake, looking at the clear blue sky. He yawns and lifts his arm and mumbles "Morning" in her ear.

"It's killing me," she says.

"What?" he asks, trying to wake up. "What is?"

"Really," she says. "What started this? Were they waiting inside their caskets all this time, for years, for centuries? Or since when? I can't shake it off. There's gotta be an explanation, a starting point for all this, and fuck it, I can't crack it. And I'm supposed to know everything about these fuckers."

Nathan's stomach turns. He should have expected this talk. "Don't beat yourself up over it," he says. "You think it's dying off? The battle down there?"

She wraps her arms around him, and they get comfortable, staying very still. The rumble of the battle below still brews in the air.

"Doesn't sound like it," she says.

Nathan stands up and walks to the ledge. Below, the fight continues. The whole town is under siege. Feral headless ghouls still fight the calculating cold-blooded colonial inhabitants of

Leatelranch. In the distance, covering the streets all the way up to the horizon, thousands of ant-like smudges sizzle. The army of headless ghouls pouring into Leatelranch seems to go on forever.

She stands next to him and sniffles. She's crying. "We're fucked, aren't we?"

"We should wake the boys," he says.

She leans on him. "No way. Let's enjoy this moment of peace."

Nate sighs. "They're not so bad, you know?"

"Ugh," she says, shuddering. She wipes a tear from her eye and puts her head on his shoulder. "Besides, wake them up for what? This is perfect," she says, and sniffles. "Right now is fine."

He caresses her back. "Yes," he says, "yes, it is."

She gazes down below, puzzled. "Really," she says, "all this time, waiting below ground. Why?"

A knot tightens in Nathan's stomach. "Who knows," he says.

"*I* should," she says. "The goddamn zombie expert should."

He caresses her back again.

"You know," she says, "I thought I'd never see you again."

"I know," he says. "Me, too."

"And now here you are, and ..."

"Yes," he says, "this is so fucked up."

"No," Lilith says, "I mean, you, with kids."

He chuckles softly.

"How did you do it?" she asks. "Playing the parent, I mean. All the time, walking on fucking eggshells, protecting them from the world, keeping the illusion of a nice happy place, keeping the truth from them, just to delay ... I could never do that."

Nathan forces a chuckle and looks behind her at Lester and Yoshi, already waking up on the other side of the roof, squinting. "And here I was gonna suggest we have triplets," he says.

"Can you imagine?" she asks, laughing so hard she snorts. "Being pregnant in the zombie apocalypse? Talk about kids being a drag."

Nathan forces a chuckle. The boys stir.

"I mean, fuck," she says, "the last time I saw you, we were dropping one of them to the ghouls, for chrissakes."

Nate's throat closes. He waves his hands at her, trying to shush her.

"I know we had to do it," she says, and the boys' eyes are wide open. "I still keep thinking of him, though, that poor kid. That teal robe. He was *in the hospital*, the poor thing."

"Lil—"

"Frank," she says. "What kind of name is that for a little boy?"

Nathan's eyes wander behind her and widen, and the boys' screams curdle his blood.

Shocked and confused, Lilith doesn't know who to look at for an explanation.

"*You* left Frankie to die?!" Yoshi says, getting up.

"Who?" Lilith asks. She turns back to Nate. "What's happening?"

Nate grabs his face as Lilith tries to understand. "What? What's going on?" He can hear the boys mumbling something and standing up furiously.

"What are you doing?" Lilith asks them.

They mumble something as they pick up their stuff, ignoring her.

"Where are you going?" she asks.

Lester turns around and looks Nathan in the eye. His face is red. "All along, it was you who left him there to die?"

Yoshi grabs some of the stuff he gathered from the apartments and puts them into a backpack. He grabs the arms flapping on the floor. "We'll fix you, Frankie," he whispers to them as they try to break free. Nathan can't help thinking the tiny hands are reaching for him and Lilith.

Lilith stares at the arms. "*That's* Frankie?" she asks, teary-eyed.

"Wait!" Nathan says to the boys. "We need to stay together!"

Lester freezes. He looks up at him. "Oh?" he shouts. "Like you stayed together with Frankie?"

Nate grabs his face again, trying to wake up. "Guys, there's nowhere to go—"

But they're already packed, and they start walking to the iron door. "Don't follow us," Yoshi says as Lester opens the lock. "Good luck finding your *Delegate*."

The iron door rumbles. They close it with a rusty bang.

Lilith turns to him. "Wait," she says. "What's a *Delegate*?"

"Nothing," Nate says, still staring at the door.

"Delegate," she says with a blank stare. "I read that somewhere."

"Never mind, Lil."

And it hits her. "The cemetery!"

Nathan exhales.

"It's in the cemetery, isn't it?" she asks. "The big one. The inverted pyramid that looks burnt."

Nate turns slowly to her. "How do you know?"

"I saw it. Last night," she says, her eyes dashing left and right as she pieces it together. "And that same crypt was marked on Chief Girardot's map of the cemetery with that weird word, Delegatvm. The kids mumbled something about it yesterday, too, didn't they? And you changed the subject and tried to play dumb and hide it from me."

She looks up, scared, and meets his gaze. "What's going on, Nate?"

Nathan takes a deep breath. It was going to come out eventually.

"They weren't just waiting in their caskets," he says under his breath.

Her mouth trembles. "What?"

"They were dead, all right," he says. "And something woke them up."

She narrows her eyes, looking at him with suspicion. "Nate..?"

"I'm guessing, of course."

"No," she says. "You *know*. How do you know?" She goes mute, looking away. A tear runs down her cheek. "Hell, I'll just ask it. Are you dead?"

"What?"

"I don't know how this could work. You're warm to the touch. But I know you're hiding things from me." She sniffs. "Are you gonna kill me? Because if you're dead, then I don't care anymore, just go, just go for it, go."

"What? I'm not dead, Lil!"

"Then what is it?" she asks. "Why are you lying to me?"

"Wait," he says. "Is this why you've been acting so strange? You think I'm *dead*?"

"Well, why else would you be hiding things from me?"

He sighs. He sits down, leaning back on his elbows, and looks at the open sky.

"It's my father," he says. "I don't think he's alive anymore, Lil."

"How ... How do you know? What happened to him?"

Nathan sighs. "You hear any bells? Yeah. Me neither. It was his job. Stopping *this* was his job."

"You really think he ...?"

He sighs. "Well, whatever this *Delegate* thing is ... It probably means whatever he was keeping in ... is out. He must have been the last *Delegate*. And he died. That's what started this whole thing."

"Spit it out!" She says. "What's a *Delegate*?"

"Oh, god, Lil," he says. "He's dead. My father's dead."

He sobs, breaking down, and starts to cry.

She sits down next to him and hugs him. "So you *do* know what's going on. You knew about this from the beginning?"

"I suspected."

"Then why didn't you tell me? Why haven't you mentioned this thing ... like, in ... ever?"

"I was hoping I'd never have to."

"Why?"

"The less you know, the better."

Her eyes pierce through his skull. "I'm not a child, you know," she mutters. "I'm sorry about your father."

"If he died, someone else must have taken the *Delegate* mantle," he says. "They're the only ones who can stop this, and maybe they don't even know it. And that's what must have gotten us into this mess. We don't even know his fucking name, Lil. Even worse, I think it's that zombie-whisperer fuck, which would mean we'd need to reach the hardest person to reach on the planet. I swear, that's all I know. It's not like we can do anything about it."

"So, we just have to find this *Delegate*? What is that? Spell it out it already. Maybe we can stop all of this! Maybe there's hope after all?"

"Look," he says. "All I know is, it's related to this. But my father never told me the whole story. And I left before he ever trained me to host it, or whatever it is you do with it."

She looks past the park, toward the tall walls. "And it can stop this? All of this?" she asks. Her face lights up. "You're telling me you know how to stop this?!"

"Maybe. But Lil, I don't know. And more importantly, I'm not going back there. I spent my whole life trying to get out of there. I'm not going back in."

"But you came all this way, Nate!" she says, grabbing his hand. "We have to."

"Since when do you do what you have to? What happened to *I-don't-need-to-do-anything* Lil?"

"Well, this is different," she says. "If there's a chance we can stop all this ..."

"I'm sorry. I'm sorry, Lil. I thought I was past this, I really did. I thought I'd be able to handle it. But seeing that wall again, peeking inside through the gates ... And my father. He's still in there, Lil. I know it. No, no way. No way."

She opens her eyes wide. "Why? So, you're afraid of dead people, I get it." She points at the bodies battling down on the street. "Dead people like *them*, like those, covering the streets *everywhere*? And you're scared of the cemetery?"

"YES!" he explodes. "I'm scared, all right? And it's not just the dead people, Lil. Ever since I decided to come here, I've been having these ... dreams, Lil. These visions ..."

She grabs his hand. "That's just your fear talking, Nate. Remember door three-twelve? It didn't work, didn't it? It wasn't true. I didn't die in the car crash, either. So cheer up! We beat our fate already. We're free! That's why we're still here."

He sighs. "Lil," he says, "going to that cemetery ... That's what your parents want. Why do you think they brought you here?"

"I don't give a fuck anymore."

"What? But—"

"This can save us, right? I'm not thinking about what they want any more. This is what *I* want."

"Even if it could save us," he says, looking at the ghouls covering the street and the park like ants, "how do we get there?"

She gasps, startling him, and grabs his arm. "Tunnels!"

66

LESTER AND YOSHI LOOK AROUND AS THEY EXIT THE BUILDING. Salomone street looks clear under the morning sun. Trash is blown down the middle of the empty street by a gust of wind. Combat noises come from the direction of the park.

"So, which way?" Lester asks.

"Away from those killers up on that rooftop," Yoshi says, starting to run.

Lester follows him. The rustling of the trees above them covers the faint noise of their steps on the asphalt. The cool air is easy to breathe. They have the whole street for themselves.

"Why does this feel so freeing?" asks Lester, smiling.

"I know, right?" says Yoshi, striding, changing pace, playing with different strides. "The city is ours!"

"Yeah," adds Lester, "so this is how it feels to run without anybody chasing after us."

Yoshi sees a crushed can lying on the street, and he kicks it as hard as he can. It takes off, spinning in the air like a flying saucer. He looks at Lester, expecting a lecture, but Lester smiles at it.

The crushed can flies off and disappears around a corner behind a black marble church, landing somewhere with a clacking sound, followed by a hollow, echoing bark.

Yoshi and Lester look at each other. They slow down to a stop.

"*Go back*," whispers Yoshi. "*Go back*."

They turn around.

Behind the corner, the wind carries the distinct sound of shuffling steps.

They turn around again. The street is no longer empty. Up ahead, in the distance, two bodies emerge, closing in, walking toward them.

"There," says Yoshi, pointing at a narrow street that looks empty.

They stride, stepping lightly with the tip of their toes, fast and quiet. They enter the narrow street that seems to lead to a wide train crossing with lots of green and sunlight. It looks wide open.

Lester looks back, panting. Figures already crowd the intersection they stood in a moment ago. A dog, fast and furious, is hurtling toward them at an astonishing speed.

"We're not gonna make it," he says.

Yoshi wrinkles his face as he runs, straining. "Yes, we are," he says.

As they approach the next corner, from either side of the street comes a combat yell. Two groups of figures, dead, skinny, skeletal, decapitated, maimed, clothed, naked, shrouded, fight and tear each other apart, clashing in the middle of the street in a mesh of violence and growls.

They block the street.

Lester and Yoshi skid to a halt and look back. The dog is racing toward them. Its bloody teeth rattle as it prepares to lunge at them.

Lester looks around. The door to a nearby house is ajar. He turns to Yoshi, but Yoshi is already charging at the dog.

"What are you doing?"

"It's our only chance," says Yoshi.

"There's an open door right here!"

"It's more of the same. They'll get to us. I'm done running away."

"Are you nuts?" asks Lester. "You'll get killed! And maimed! Or worse! Forever!"

Yoshi looks the dog in the eye as it paces toward him.

"It's all a joke, right?" he says, looking more serious than ever, trying to brave it, as the dog charges toward him. "It's all a joke anyway!"

The dog pounces. Yoshi waits for it with open arms. As the sharp paws land on his body, as the jaw opens near his face, ready to snap, he hugs and strongholds the ball of muscle. He leans his head forward, next to the dog's, and feels the teeth and breath on his ear. A spike of pain and ringing and numbness washes over him as the dog pulls away with his ear and part of his face. He lets out an *ugh* as his back hits the pavement. The paws dig into his chest, sharp nails scratching soft skin. He clenches his arms with all his might, bringing the dog toward him until the struggling legs finally have no more room to move. He lifts his own legs around the dog, the huge dog that won't stop wiggling, and clenches his whole body, his muscles burning, his breath scorching hot.

"Stop," he says close to the dog's ear. "Stop."

The dog relaxes. He can feel it heaving under his arms and legs, but it's no longer struggling.

Yoshi relaxes his legs. The dog doesn't move. He tries to look around, but one of his eyes is closed shut. The battle is coming closer, and on the other side, Lester is standing next to him, watching in horror.

He relaxes his arms. The dog slowly steps back.

Yoshi stands up. The ringing in his ears is getting worse. He looks at the dog, and the dog looks up at him. He smiles, and it stings, something must be wrong with his face.

He turns to Lester. His face is white. His jaw is open in awe and horror.

"Dude ..."

"It's alright," says Yoshi, and his face hurts, and a cold pain runs through his whole body. He feels light-headed. Dizzy. "I did it. I faced it."

As the ghouls approach them, the dog turns to them and growls. The ghouls look down at it and freeze.

Yoshi pats the dog on the head and caresses him. It feels wet. He looks down and sees the shiny, crimson thickness sticking to his hand.

"Good boy."

Yoshi turns around. Behind them, the combat still fills the street.

"I guess it's that way," he says to Lester, trying to smile. Lester tries to smile back at him.

They walk toward the ghouls, escorted by the dog, who growls at each one of them. They make way for them as they approach.

Yoshi looks around at the ghouls as they walk among them, and he smiles triumphantly. Behind them, behind the broken and disfigured ghoul faces, behind the empty hollow eye sockets and rotten jaws, a glass window throws a ghoulish reflection at him. The face, just like his, only mangled, disfigured, bloody, smiles right back at him.

67

"WHAT DID I SAY?" SHE ASKS NATHAN AS SHE PEEKS AROUND the corner. Straight ahead, on the next block, there's the VIGILES sign with its gothic letters, and the tin POLICE sign under it. Before that, closer to her and hanging from a cable, a head faces to the side, the wind turning it slowly in her direction. She hides behind the corner.

"He was his friend," Nate says behind her. "They were all in the hospital together."

Her mind races. "What?" she says. "But he was half their age."

"He died," Nate says, dusting himself off, looking around Lilith's living room. "Years ago. They didn't."

Lilith takes a moment to process it. "Well, what do you know? Do we really have to make this stop in the Tokens shop? It would be so much easier if we could just go straight to the tunnels. We get into the police station, tunnels lead right to my place, and we cross the street to the cemetery. This way, who knows what surprises we'll find. The chances of making it ..."

"Trust me," Nathan says. "This is important."

Lilith peeks again. The head is facing away, and signaling Nathan with a pat on the shoulder, she bolts. She runs past a flower shop, its window filled with dead plants turned to mush, and a monumental masonry shop, its window full of marble grave-stones of all colors, sizes, and engravings. And a few doors before the police station, there it is: the *Tokens* shop and its window filled with all kinds of religious symbols.

Fixing her eyes on the turning head, she tries the door. It's open. Bells jingle as she enters, and she stops them. Nathan closes the door behind him, and the rumble of the battle outside fades away, muffled by the thick curtains and objects scattered around the shop. Dolls. Bells. Strands of hair. In here, only silence remains, and dust settling in the air.

"Wait," Nathan says, covering his mouth. "Don't breathe that."

She takes her shirt up to her nose and walks inside. "So, for this *Delegate* thing, we need a name?" she says, looking around. "Maybe your father kept a list?"

"It's no use, Lil," he says, exploring the dusty old shelves. "The ledger was burnt. And even if we had the list, it could be anyone in it."

"Well, most of them should be dead. All dead but one, probably."

"Exactly," he says. "It's pointless. Believe me, this is a much better plan."

"And what is the plan, exactly? What are we looking for?"

"It's ... complicated," he says, his eyes darting along the shelves, examining small wooden statues of different deities. He freezes in front of a pair of specially decorated gold coins like he's seeing a ghost. "So, this is where all this stuff comes from."

"Yeah," she says, looking around, entering a narrow corridor surrounded by bookshelves and cases with strange objects. She hasn't been here in years. She points at the different shelves. "That's eastern European, Egyptian, Catholic, Jesuit, Haitian, Rosi ... crucian? And if you think this is crazy, go check what's in the back."

She picks up something from a shelf.

"Look," she says. "What was the name of that cult?"

"Which one?" Nathan asks, browsing behind her.

"The one who renamed the dead. They said corpses were new people, so they deserved new names—"

"Oh," Nate says, looking around. "Wittican."

"Yeah," Lilith says, placing the statue back on the shelf.

"I'm looking for something else," he says. "Have you—Have you been here before?"

She searches the wall in front of her, and sure enough, there it is. A picture of Wolfram, aged ten, and his parents, Elvira and Ulfred, standing on the porch of their house.

"I used to come here all the time when I was little. We used to come with the gang. Me, Wolfram ... Doyle ..."

"You came here to *play*?"

"Wolfram's parents ran it. The Lacroixes."

"The Lacroixes," he says, nodding. "I knew them. They went in all the time. They brought this kind of stuff to my father."

She watches him as he looks around. Flowers. Runes. Crystals. Pyramids. Stones. Dolls. Braids of different color combinations.

"What are you looking for?" she asks again. "Maybe I can help."

"Who's Doyle?" he asks. "The name rings a bell."

She looks at a miniature sarcophagus next to a crucifix and stutters. "He was a friend of mine. Before I met you—"

"Look," he says, staring into the dark. "Do you see that?"

Lilith looks for something behind the dust flying in the air. There's an area of the room with shelves. There's nothing special about it.

"What?"

"The spores," Nathan says. "Somehow there are none of those spores over there."

It's true. The air in that corner seems somehow clearer than in the rest of the shop, as if the dust flying in the air is avoiding it.

"One of these amulets must work," she jokes. "It's like death doesn't dare to go near."

As he walks past her, his hand brushes against hers.

"Have you noticed something?" she asks playfully.

"What?" he asks, looking around. He takes his hand off his face and breathes in. "The air is clean here, by the way," he adds.

"We're alone," she says. "For the first time since ..."

He glances back at her and smiles. "I know," he says. He goes back to examining the shelves, browsing a large shelf in the corner filled with small shiny objects. "Are you trying to distract me? I told you, you don't need to do that. I'm fine. We will fix this. And then we can rest easy—Yes! Found it!"

She walks over and uncovers her mouth, breathing in the clean air. Nate is holding a small black key.

"What the hell is that?"

"It looks just like I remember it," he says, eyes fixed on the small key.

"What does it open?"

"The box," he says, putting the key in his pocket. "The Delegate box."

"That's great," she says, looking at it. "Come. Tell me all about it while I check something out back here."

She walks behind a bookcase and hides behind it. She crouches slowly under an old wooden desk, making sure her face is at an uncanny level, in an unusual spot, and twists her mouth into a gruesome shape, waiting for him.

"I'd— rather just show you when we're there, you know?" he says, coming closer. "Maybe, if things go well, you don't even have to be there for the actual— Lil?"

He walks past the bookcase, looking around for her in the dark corners of the shop, so scared that his eyes are almost coming out of their sockets. He's about to turn to where she's hiding—

So she jumps.

Nathan lets out a whimper and freezes, and Lilith bursts out laughing.

"Hey!" he says, coming to. "It was my turn to scare you!"

She hugs him. "I missed you so much, Nate."

Smiling, he grabs her head firmly and presses his forehead against hers, looking deep into her eyes, already breathing heavily, speaking harshly and softly at the same time, his lips close to hers.

"Me, too."

As they kiss, her hands search for the old wooden desk behind her, and she leans on it. She sweeps some stuff from the table and sits down, waiting for his embrace. Eyeless dolls fall to the floor. Dried frogs. Carved runes, colored strings knit into human shapes, a black onyx egg.

68

LILITH EMERGES OUT OF THE TUNNEL INTO HER OLD LIVING room. She enjoys the change of stale air for a different kind of stale air.

Nate vaults the rubble and dusts himself off.

"A tunnel leading to your own living room," he says. "How convenient."

"Perks of living in the old caretaker's house," she says. "What? The new caretaker's house doesn't have any tunnels?"

"They must have wised up. Tunnels in a graveyard, whose idea was that? But your house is just like I remember it."

Lilith looks around. "Furniture's different. Whoever lived here after us had shitty taste."

He's smiling at her.

"What?" she asks.

"Lilith H. Kane," Nate says. "Are you *nostalgic* about Leatelranch?"

"Fuck you."

Nate walks toward the door and looks through the keyhole. "The park is infested," he says, "but the sidewalk is clear. As long as we're quiet ..."

"It's too far, Nate," she says. "We're not gonna make it."

"Trust me."

"I trust you," she says, "but I can also hear *that*." She stares at him as they listen to the battle cries of a thousand ghouls and dogs battling across the street, in the park.

"Exactly my point. They're busy. Busy's good."

She bites her lip. "I'm finally going to see your house."

He opens the door quietly and peers through the opening. "Good," he says. "It's gonna be dark soon."

"Wait," Lilith says, placing her hand on his shoulder. "Are you sure you're OK with this? Going back there?"

"Sure," says Nate, clearly lying. "Just look out there. The world is looking more and more like the cemetery, anyway. What's the difference?"

Lilith bites her lips. "I don't know, Nate."

A pack of dogs runs past, chasing after the moaning and grumbling of ghouls.

"Now!" yells Nate. He grabs her hand and runs toward the walls of the cemetery.

Lilith catches up and runs with all her might. They pass the Requiem bar on Rodney street and its red awning, the tall trees, the seemingly empty houses. She cannot think of a safe place, but surely running out in the open is not the best of ideas.

"They—" she says, between breaths, pointing at the cemetery wall. "they're also in there."

"I know," he says. "Don't worry."

They reach the small green metal door, and Nate lets go of her hand to put both hands inside the opening, moving them nervously.

"Is it still there?" asks Lilith.

"Feels like the same," says Nate, struggling, his chin pressed against the cold rusty gaps in the green paint. "The ... question ... is ..."

Click. The lock unlatches.

Nate hurries his arms and hands, removing the lock, and finally opens the door.

He turns around. "After you," he says with a smile, and suddenly Lilith feels like things aren't so bad after all. She walks in.

Nate looks over her shoulder, back toward the street.

"Do you hear that?"

"Hear what?"

She freezes and listens. Dogs are barking. The sound is getting closer.

"Move," Nate says urgently, and Lilith quickly complies. The second she's clear of the heavy door, he closes it, chains it, and clicks the lock shut.

"Stay behind me," he says, and he speeds off down the narrow corridor of grass between the crypts and the wall.

Lilith tries to catch her breath and chases after him.

"Stay close to the wall," says Nate, looking around, finding his bearings.

Lilith looks at the plants around her, wary of any movements, and bumps against his sweaty back. Nate is standing still and looking to the right.

"What's this?" he says, his gaze locked among the crypts. "What's it doing there?"

Lilith looks at it and turns to Nate. He's smiling.

"It's not gonna work," she says.

But Nate is already sprinting toward it, entering a narrow corridor surrounded by crypts.

"Shit!" Lilith blurts out, chasing after him. She catches him by the shoulder. "All right," she says, looking around. Her chest beats like a hammer. "But let's not run a straight line like idiots."

She looks at the next corridor to the right. It looks just as empty. Just as suspicious.

She turns around and finds an iron lamp hanging from the wall. She jumps, hanging from it, and she swings, and she pulls, until it comes off with a rusty screech. She lands back on the grass with a heavy iron weapon.

"Follow me," she says to an impressed Nate.

She enters the corridor slowly, looking at the many open doors and broken windows, and as soon as she steps on the tiles, she starts flaying her arms like an idiotic dance, swinging her waist, jumping and crawling randomly, hoping to hit or break any hits coming from the openings.

Nate follows her close, evading the many swings she takes toward his side.

"When there's no more room in hell," he says with an ominous voice, "the spastics will walk the earth."

"That's—sweet," says Lilith, red-faced and sweaty, "I was going for yoga teacher with Parkinson's."

Nate dodges another swing that would have surely bashed his head in. "I can't wait until they put these moves in the next *Zombie Survival* book."

She chuckles, losing balance. "I wouldn't want to be whoever has to draw these *manouvers*."

Her arms are burning. She sees the gleaming motorbike at the end of the corridor and prepares to make one last effort.

"Is it ironic, or obvious?" asks Nate. "Now that the apocalypse actually came, there's no one to even read such a book."

"Ooh, deep," she says, exhaling hot breath, unable to keep the playful tone anymore. "Are you making conversation to keep me from hearing those dogs getting closer?"

"Ouch," says Nate.

"What happened?" asks Lilith, afraid to turn. "Are you OK?"

"Yes," he says behind her, and he clears his throat. "Fine. I'm just shitting my pants at these fucking crypts."

"Are you even trying to peek inside?" she asks, swinging the heavy lamp.

"No fucking way."

"So, for all we know," she says, turning around three-hundred and sixty degrees, ducking, and swinging the lamp like an Olympic hammer thrower, which Nate barely manages to jump over. "There could have been ghouls in each one, looking at us."

"Shit!" he yells, jolting, pushing her forward. "Don't say that!"

Lilith is glad the chopper bike is close now. She can see it leaning over a bench, in the main street at the end of this corridor. "I'm just stating the facts. I know you're scared, but ..."

Nate grabs her by the waist.

"Are you even looking," she asks, "or just following my voice and graceful moves?"

Nate doesn't answer.

They finally make it out of the corridor. Out here, the barking is more noticeable, already echoing its way toward them. Lilith drops her arms and exhales, dead tired. She lets the lamp fall on the ground with a metallic *clank* and turns around. Throughout the corridor, behind the small glass windows, pale faces lit by the moon are turned toward them.

"What ...?"

Nate hurries past Lilith and checks the bike. Lilith grabs the lamp again, and with burning arms, she lifts it.

Rusty iron hinges squeak along the corridor that Lilith and Nate just walked. Ghouls come out of their crypts.

"*Now* they come out?" says Nate, looking over his shoulder as he checks a gauge on the dashboard.

"They're picky bastards," says Lilith.

"Don't let them fool you with that trudge," says Nate. "Those fuckers can *run*."

Lilith opens her mouth to talk, but she's interrupted.

"If we have to," mumbles a dry voice from beyond the grave. Lilith looks at the faces of the things trudging toward them. An old lady, or thing, almost doesn't open her mouth to talk, but her defiant eyes pierce Lilith's soul as she gets closer.

Lilith sways the iron lamp at her, and at the whole pack. "You wanna lose an arm?" she asks. "Forever?" The fresh ones back off. Other ones, more rotten and old, keep coming at her like madmen.

Lilith turns to Nate. "Is it working?"

He's frozen, looking at the closed-mouth lady. Lilith shakes his arm. "Focus!" she says, and her voice gets swallowed by a wave of barks and growls that's getting closer and closer.

Nate shakes himself and kicks the starter again. Behind him, Lilith can see a huge pack of dogs push open the main gate of the cemetery and run inside, coming directly toward them.

"Fuck it," says Lilith, looking around. "It's not working. Let's go!"

Nate kicks the starter, and the engine growls. "Yes!"

He gets on. Lilith gets on behind him, and they speed off through the main road.

"See?" says Nate. "No different from driving in the city."

As they pass one of the glowing lamps, she sees, in passing, that its long iron pole doubles as a street sign, with names and everything. Below the street names, she even notices numbers. 300 - 400.

"No difference at all," she says.

69

LESTER CARRIES YOSHI TO THE ENTRANCE OF A BUILDING AND lets him down slowly on the marble steps. He looks at the open wounds and the green blood as the dog pants behind him.

"Are you OK?" he asks Yoshi, finding new wounds wherever he looks.

Yoshi slumps back on a step and smiles. His chest heaves and bleeds. "Ye—Yes," he replies.

"You'd tell me if you were a zombie, right?"

Yoshi laughs, and spasms, and spits blood.

"Sorry," Lester says. "I had to ask."

Yoshi's hand fumbles and looks for his backpack, lying next to him. "Let's do this."

"Give it a rest," says Lester. "We should fix you up first."

"No—No need." Yoshi finds the backpack and reaches for the zipper. The blue fabric heaves and moves; the arm inside is restless.

"He won't like it," says Lester.

Yoshi finds the zipper and tries to open it with great effort. "He doesn't *know* what to like!"

"And who are you to decide?" Lester asks.

"Ugh," Yoshi says, trying to open the zipper. "Who is *he*?"

"All right. Fuck it."

"Fuck it."

Lester leans over the backpack. He pushes Yoshi's hand away, unzips the bag, and takes out the arm with Frankie's name tag. The arm flaps and flexes and wiggles as he gives it to the dog, who's standing alert, looking around, keeping guard. His snout and teeth still shine with Yoshi's blood. It sniffs Frankie's arm.

"Go, boy," Lester says.

"She's—she's a girl," Yoshi mumbles.

The dog sniffs along the arm, shying away as it wiggles.

"A girl, huh?" Lester says. "What should we call her?"

The dog turns her head toward the park and bolts.

"Whoa," says Yoshi, chuckling, coughing blood. "That was fast. What about *Countess*?"

Lester smiles.

Countess runs alone through the empty street and aims for the ghoul-infested park. The ghouls stop fighting and make way for her as she gets near. Chunks of ground and grass fly away behind her as she trots. She's aiming for the scorpion monster in the center of the park, next to Salomone's statue.

"What's going on?" Yoshi asks.

"She's doing it," Lester says. "She went straight for that scorpion thing."

Yoshi looks up and exhales. "Good girl."

She pounces on it, climbing clumsily through the mesh of arms and legs, and seems to stop, or hang.

Lester pats him on the leg. "She took something. She took something!"

Yoshi smiles. "Almost there, Frankie."

The ghouls in the park close their formation again and resume their fight.

"I can't see her," Lester says. "I can't see her. Move, you idiots."

Lester hears the shuffling of feet on the pavement behind him. He turns around. Headless ghouls are coming to get them.

"Shit."

The crowd in the park is too dense. Lester can't see Countess anywhere. Behind him, the headless ghouls trot toward him and Yoshi.

"Countess," he says, "please hurry."

Out of the crowd and the clash, Countess emerges. She runs past shambling ghouls, making them look like spastic idiots as they try to catch her, and speeds back toward Lester.

"Yes!" he says, patting Yoshi on the leg, "she's coming back!"

The dog exits the park. She's carrying a head by the hair. She reaches the intersection and turns to the right, disappearing.

"Hey," Lester says. His smile disappears. "Hey!"

"What happened?" Yoshi asks.

Lester looks over his shoulder. The pack of headless ghouls is getting closer to them.

"Come on," he says, helping Yoshi up. "We gotta go."

"Why?" Yoshi asks, in pain. "Where did she go?"

70

The chopper bike speeds through the muddy grass and climbs up a hill, dodging the open graves and the pale crooked tombstones like rotten teeth smiling in the moonlight. Nate guns the throttle, and they roll down the hill at maximum speed. The roar of the engine and the air on their faces is exhilarating. No more graves are in the way. Nothing but soft grass.

Lilith looks back. The dogs are nowhere to be seen.

"I think we lost them."

Nate is silent.

She leans forward. "I think we lost—"

Nate's in shock. He looks forward with wide open eyes. "That's my house," he says.

"Where?"

He clears his throat. He's visibly moved. "Behind those trees," he says.

Lilith sees a small woodsy area with a sign that says Arboretvm. It's shrouded in fog, and long, needle-thin branches reach out from inside. They enter, speeding past the sign.

Lilith feels a pinch on her shoulder. Then another one. She looks up. The dark leaves block the night sky. The branches surrounding them look gray and ghoulish and seem to sway and dance above them.

"Nate," she says.

"What?"

"The trees."

"The trees what?"

She tries to shrug it off. It's impossible. It's just the speed, probably. She looks at the base of the trees. There are plaques, with names and old black-and-white pictures.

"I think the trees are moving."

She focuses on a branch far above her. It's moving down toward her, willfully, she's sure of it. As they pass under it, she feels its long thin fingers scratch her shoulder.

Nate guns the throttle. "Father never believed me when I said these trees were alive."

Behind them, through the thick trees, barks echo.

"They're back," says Lilith. She looks over her shoulder and sees the pack of dogs gaining on them.

"Where the fuck does he get so many dogs?"

"I know," says Lilith. "I've never seen so many together."

They reach the house. Nate stops the bike and stares at his childhood home. It's completely boarded up. The front door is covered in huge planks of wood. Both windows are boarded up with a very luxurious, bright wood.

"There's something ... *off* about those planks," says Lilith.

"They come from coffins," Nate says. "The windows are boarded up with coffins."

Between the planks, bushes and roots poke out, like fingers trying to escape from inside.

The dogs are getting closer.

"Ok," says Lilith behind him. "Move! Wake up!"

The bike balances as she gets down. She grabs the shovel sticking up from the bike's saddle and hands it to Nate, then pulls on the handle of a second tool that turns out to be a rusty pickax. She walks to the closest boarded-up window and strikes it.

"What are you doing?" Nate asks.

She brings the pickax behind her and swings it toward the wood with all her strength. "What does it look like?"

The wood chips and breaks. Behind it, behind the branches coming from inside the house, she can see the house's white paint.

The barking sounds grow louder and louder as the dogs get closer to the house.

"Come on!" she yells. "Help me!"

She picks apart a piece of wood and freezes as a darkened hand comes from inside. Behind it, in the dark, a human head lurks.

"Get out," it growls.

Lilith jolts and turns to Nate. He grasps his shovel tightly and swings it hard at the wooden planks. He opens a hole in the rotten wood and swings the shovel behind his head, ready to attack again, when through the hole, a head pops out and looks at them. It's a rotten, disfigured zombie.

"Get out!" it says. "You'll bring *him*."

Lilith swings her pickax at it, and the head dodges it swiftly, going back into the darkness as the pickax hits the hole.

Nate looks back. The thundering barks are getting closer. He swings his shovel at the wood. The darkened hand squeezes through the hole and grabs the shovel. It tries to pull it inside.

Lilith straightens out her pickax, dislodging it from the hole, and drives it through the hand. A howl escapes the inside of the house. She pulls to the side and back, pulling the hand away, sending it flying through the air. The severed arm moves back inside. As they ready their weapons again, planks of wood are replaced from the inside, boarding up the window again.

"Shit," says Nate. "Come here."

He walks to the front of the house and shovels the wooden planks covering the front door. Dogs are getting close.

Lilith joins him with her pickax, picking between the planks and pulling. Her arms burn.

"I see it!" says Lilith. "I see the inside!"

They keep hitting. The barks are deafening.

Nate plunges the shovel through the hole and into the wood, cracking it. He pulls the shovel to the sides, cracking the wood further. He can see the darkness inside. He pulls away the shovel, and Lilith sticks the pickax into the door again, creating a tear down the center.

"Noooo!" a voice echoes from inside the house.

Lilith glances over her shoulder. The dogs look like amped-up soldiers rounding the top of the hill, ready for battle. Behind them, atop them, something cranes its horrible unnatural shadow. It's long and thorny, and it waves to the sides as it gets closer. She recognizes it. It's the tail of the human scorpion.

She hears the wood cracking again.

"Let's go!" Nate says.

She steps into the hole and struggles her way inside. As the dogs come down from the hill and enter the wooded area, Nate pushes her further into the darkness and follows her through the hole.

71

A flash. A black-and-white photograph. That's the glimpse that Lilith gets of the surreal jungle of a living room. Gray branches growing amok, covering ground to ceiling, wall to wall. A dark empty background, as if the room had no end. Old dusty furniture against the wall. A greasy trike rolling back and forth on its own and getting stuck between two branches, but then again, maybe not. Then, the white beam of light coming from outside is sliced and swallowed by darkness as Nate covers it again.

Nathan drags what sounds like a large, heavy table, drowning the sound of barking from outside. Lilith sees the leg of the table approaching her face and grabs it. She stands up. They secure the table against the door.

Lilith turns her head and scans the dark. An inky blackness floats and swims around her eyes. She tries to focus, to make out shapes, but it's impossible. There's nothing around her but dark.

"That was my room," Nathan's voice says.

"What was?"

"The window we were trying to open. The room that's ... *occupied*."

She looks around. "Who said *this* room isn't occupied?"

Nathan stutters. "Are—are you saying..?"

417

"Not me, idiot," Lilith says. "I'm fine. But there could be someone here, watching us, listening to us. I'm fucking sure there is."

"I didn't see anyone coming in," says Nate, relieved. "And they would have killed us already."

"No, they wouldn't," she says, breathing heavily. "Let's go meet that fucker," she says. "You ready?"

There is no movement. There is no sound.

"Come on," she says, fumbling in the dark. She finds his arm. She slides down and grabs his hand. "Don't you want to get this over with?"

"That's ..." he says.

She lets him finish. He doesn't want to say it.

"That's my father in there."

She caresses his hand. It's cold and sweaty. "I know."

"Careful with the branches," he says, pulling her hand softly but firmly.

She closes her eyes, tilting her head down, feeling the first branch brush against her forehead. She uses her other hand to feel her way around, placing it in front of her face.

She stubs her foot on something hard. A root. She steps over it as branches scratch her face, and she crouches. Nathan's hand is pulling from below now. She gets on her hands and knees, following him.

The silence makes her ears ring. After the dogs, and the dragging of the table, being deaf and blind is somewhat soothing. As if death is giving them a warm welcome.

She crawls carefully, looking down, as branches brush against her scalp, caressing her hair as she moves forward. The ringing in her ears starts to fade away. Strange whispers and voices hover around, subtly, but it's hard to know if they're real, or to pinpoint where they come from.

Nathan's hand moves up and pulls her from above. She crawls a few more steps and feels the branches around her disappearing. The dark, the empty dark, welcomes her. She gets up.

"It's smooth," Nathan says. "Branches have been trimmed here."

She extends her other hand to get a hold of Nate, but she touches wood instead. She recognizes the grainy, rough texture. Her hand travels up to her eye level, and she finds it. She's touching paper.

"What's that noise?" asks Nathan.

She feels around its border, and explores the everlasting scotch tape, and touches the oily texture of crayons, and bumps into Nathan's fingers. He exhales, emotional, like he's about to start crying.

"This is my room," he says.

She holds Nathan's hand as it hovers down and it finds the cold doorknob. She can feel him hesitating.

He plunges down.

72

Countess scuttles up the station's marble steps, Frankie's head swinging by his hair like a pendulum from her mouth as she makes her way up to the wide portico.

Lester follows her as fast as he can, carrying Yoshi over one shoulder, passing just a few feet away from a group of corpses too caught in their own fight to notice. Frankie's arms wriggle inside his backpack, poking at his back, and he fights the urge to turn around, constantly feeling that someone is reaching for him. He manages to get Yoshi to climb the steps and, just as they're making it to the top, Yoshi loses his strength and slips, weighing on Lester like a sack of potatoes. Lester pushes up, lifts his friend, and reaches the top.

Countess is gone, and all the doors seem to be boarded up—except for one. One door looks to be cracked open just enough for a dog to fit through. He rushes to it, pulls it open, and steps inside, the weight of Yoshi heavy on his hip.

They've entered a giant hollow lobby. The door slams shut behind them, jolting Lester. Inside the deep dark hall, the shuffling of their steps echo. A shiny trail of blood glimmers on the dark floor, barely lit by the moonlight entering through a hole in the roof. The walls are covered with black-and-white pictures of people dressed in turn-of-the-century clothes roaming the halls of this very train station, and of large processions marching into the cemetery.

"Arghh," Yoshi cries, piercing Lester's ears. "Ouch. Ssss."

Lester examines his friend's mangled body. "You're OK," he lies.

"Leave me," Yoshi says, green blood creeping out the corners of his mouth. "It's dangerous for you."

"Dangerous?" Lester jokes. "You can't even walk."

Yoshi's breathing makes a whistling noise. His chest heaves. His face is red and wet from crying. "I guess I won't get to be pretty forever, like you, Austin," he says, trying to chuckle.

Lester smiles. "Well," he says, "at least that dog-whispering fuck won't be wanting *your* maimed body! Come on. Let's find Countess and Frankie."

Far away, on the other side of the hall, something rattles and falls with a hammering noise. It's followed by a four-legged patting on the floor. Lester turns just in time to see Countess' shadow running toward an entrance with a huge sign that reads, in gothic lettering, Mvsevm. The entrance is wide open.

"Let's go."

The museum is as dark as the main train station hall. Countess walks among dusty glass cases displaying old jewelry, rusty shovels, and worn pickaxes. She runs past a long wall covered in black-and-white pictures, ghoulish under the dim light. Some show crowds of old-fashioned-looking people disembarking a train carrying large trunks and suitcases. Others show coffins and lumps wrapped in shrouds being unloaded from a compartmented train coach that looks like a wooden closet with drawers. Solemn faces pose for the camera in front of a strange gigantic locomotive.

Countess leaves Frankie's head on the ground and goes sniffing for something else.

Lester can't make out where she's going in the dark.

"What's she doing?"

He pulls Yoshi with him as he paces toward her, stepping carefully in the dark hall, and picks up Frankie's head.

He's bruised, but recognizable.

"Frankie!" he says to it. "We got you! We got you!"

Frankie's face doesn't move. Its open eyes are dead.

Lester turns to Yoshi. "You talked to dogs," he says. "Maybe try to talk to him like a dog?"

Yoshi takes a clumsy step forward and looks Frankie in the eye, trying to get a response. They remain lifeless. He tries whispering something in his ear.

Nothing.

"Frankie!" he yells as loud as he can, making a grimace of pain. "Frankie!"

His eyes burn with fury. "We need to find that bastard and kill him."

Lester takes off his backpack and opens it. "I'm not giving up on you, Frankie," he says.

"That sounds great," Yoshi says. "But it won't bring Frankie back."

"Maybe we just need the other parts. Or do you have any other pressing matters to attend?"

Countess sneaks into a hole in a large wooden door. Above it, a sign says MAIN EXHIBIT.

"*Countess!*" Yoshi whispers. "*Where are you going?!*"

Lester puts on his backpack and carries Yoshi to the door. It's locked. He gets down on his knees and tries to sneak through the hole. Only his head fits. "What is *that*?" he asks, amazed.

"Let me see."

Yoshi gets down and looks. "What *is* that?"

Countess sneaks back from the hole. She barks at something behind them.

"Boys," says a deep voice that echoes throughout the station. "You're not supposed to be here."

Around them, the darkness gives birth to shadows, subtle

black silhouettes on black. As if coming out of the walls themselves, they crawl out the corners.

Fuck, Lester mutters.

Countess growls at them, and they stop where they are.

Lester helps Yoshi lean against a wall and looks around. "I guess you're not so brave now, huh?" he yells at the shadows, triumphantly, echoing throughout the hall like a deep resounding bell.

Lester opens his backpack and looks inside at Frankie's dead eyes. "Frankie!" Can you hear me? Can you tell them to back off?"

Yoshi rests against the wall, looking too tired to move.

Lester shakes the backpack in a frenzy. "Frankie! Please!"

"Oh, he don't speak to us anyways," one of the ghouls says, coming closer. A ray of moonlight comes from a hole in the ceiling and paints half his face with white, slicing his wide grin in half as he passes through it. Countess barks again.

Lester grabs Yoshi by the arm. "We gotta get out of here."

Yoshi grabs his chest. "Get out of here *where?*"

Lester doesn't reply. He puts on the backpack. It's rumbling more fiercely now. "We don't have much of a choice," he says, looking at the hole in the door. Let's see what Countess found."

He tries to lift Yoshi, but Yoshi resists. He doesn't want to get up.

"Countess won't hold them much longer!" Lester yells. "We have to go!"

Yoshi doesn't move. "You go."

Countess barks again. Lester looks at the ghouls closing in on them. In the dark, it's hard to tell how close they are.

"I'm sorry, Lester," Yoshi says. "But I gotta do this."

Lester turns to him slowly, trying to understand. "What?"

Yoshi pats Countess on the back. "Attack, girl!"

Countess runs toward the zombies and pounces on one of them. The ghoul dodges it and punches the dog on its side, sending it flying down with a cracking of bones as it hits the ground. Countess whines with pain.

"Countess!" Lester yells, looking for Countess in the dark. Nothing moves other than the crawling ghouls coming close. Her cries die off.

Lester pushes Yoshi in the chest. "You don't care about anyone!" he yells.

Yoshi tries to reply, stuttering. Nothing comes out.

"You're no better than Nate and the girl!" Lester says. "They give up Frankie, you give up Countess, and soon we'll all be dead, and you're just happy making enemies!"

Yoshi laughs, coughing. "You're still sore about that? It doesn't matter. Nothing matters anymore. Frankie was going to get caught anyway. Countess was going to get caught anyway. *We* are going to get caught anyway. So why—"

Lester punches him in the cheek. Yoshi's head whips back, and he takes a second to recover. When he straightens his head, his mouth is bleeding even more. He's smiling, and a new cut on his cheek continues the line of his smile, gushing out blood. "You finally did it," he says. "You found your spine."

He turns to the side and opens his mouth, letting the blood drip.

"We need to take care of each other," Lester says, looking around at the approaching ghouls. "Focus on the living."

Yoshi has a hard time breathing. He looks worse than ever. "There ARE no *living*, you moron! Don't you get it? All of us are dead! This beating heart thing is just ... temporary!"

"No!" Lester tries to explain. "Don't *you* get it? They were right all along. Maybe we should forget about Frankie, and just ..."

Lester hears Yoshi slumping to the floor.

"Yoshi?"

In the dark, Yoshi is just a mound on the floor next to him. "Yoshi?"

Yoshi's shadow stands up from the ground. After having to be carried for blocks, of not being able to put any kind of pressure on his feet, Yoshi stands straight. He looks Lester in the eye and grins.

A growl, Countess' growl, awakes.

Before Lester can react, Yoshi pushes him with unnatural force against the door to the main exhibit. The lock cracks behind his back and the door swings open, and he falls on his ass. He jumps up and closes the door, slumping his back against it, but Yoshi's fingers are holding the side of the door, keeping it from closing. He pries the fingers off, but before he can secure the door, Yoshi's foot is keeping it from closing. Lester can hear his own breathing. Through the opening, on the other side of the door, human and dog growls echo closer and closer.

Something heavy rams against the other side of the door and sends Lester flying forward. He lands on his face, burning his cheek against the smooth linoleum floor.

He stands up. A dark, steel behemoth towers over him, shining in the dark even under a heavy coat of dust.

He looks back. Yoshi's dark silhouette enters the room and slams the heavy door behind him.

Lester walks back, cornered against the cold steel of the tank in the room, squeezing his backpack. Yoshi shuffles his feet and walks up to him, and as Lester extends his hands to defend himself, Yoshi lunges toward him and bites his hand, hard, sending bolts of pain through his body.

"Yoshi," Lester says, ignoring the sharp pain radiating all along his arm. "Don't leave me ..."

Yoshi slumps on the floor, smiling. His face is green with Lester's blood.

"Gotcha," he says with a tired voice. "Welcome—welcome to the mangled-up club, Les. Your body isn't perfect anymore. Come, help me up, before I die for real."

Lester smiles, relieved.

73

LILITH'S NERVOUS FINGERS PUSH THE DOOR FORWARD AND FEEL around in the darkness for branches.

"Nate?"

"Over here." Nate's hand holds hers, still cold from being outside.

As her eyes adjust to the dark, she can start to fathom the size of the room. There are no branches. The darkness seems more breathable now, and the walls and the ceiling are finally farther away from her head. So this is Nate's home. Years have passed, but she can still imagine how it looked years ago. It smells humid. Putrid. Nate's bed is neatly made. An eerie, old chair. And in one of the corners, against one of the walls, she sees something. Chairs, and piles of clothes, or something on them. It takes an eternity inside her head to realize the new rules of this new universe. Why would that be a pile of clothes? She *knows* what shapes they really are. Even if she's never been here, she can tell that they don't belong. She follows the silhouettes as they become clearer and clearer in the dark, and she tries not to say it out loud, to shake her fear away. *That's not a person. That's not a person. That's not a person.* She tries to take comfort in what her mother told her so many times to calm her down. *If they were people, they'd be moving. Nobody can be that still.* But this comfort is from the old world.

The figures sit still, looking at them. They fill one of the room's walls. One of them stands out in the center. Outside, dogs are barking.

"You brought them in," says one of the voices.

"Of course, he did," says another voice.

A third voice, shrieky and playful, mocks them.

"Hello, kiddies."

"Father," says Nate.

The figure steps forward. It's a tall, thin figure, a skeleton the color of moldy wood. The face is mummified, cheeks sunken, two holes for a nose, a larger-than-life smile with rotten yellow teeth.

"Stay back!" says Nate. "I'm—I'm the Delegate."

A dry laugh. The face comes closer. It's uncanny to watch that jaw move.

"You're not the Delegate."

"How do you know?"

"We must be," says Lilith. "One of us. Why else would the ghouls leave us alone?"

"Yes," says a voice in the dark. "Why else?"

Nate's voice is flat. Shocked. "Mother?"

"At last," the shrieky voice says. "The whole family's together again."

The barking outside is maddening. There must be dozens of dogs out there.

"I can't take this anymore!" Lilith screams. "Why aren't you attacking us?"

"Why?" Nate's father's playful mockery of a voice replies, coyly. He lets out a chuckle. "Why ... should I?"

"Are *you* the Delegate?" Lilith asks.

Nate's father laughs with a piercing shriek. "I was. Once. Does it make any difference?"

"Lils," he continues. "Little Lilith. *You* don't know who the Delegate is?" He bursts out in laughter. "Oh, that's *rich!*"

"What?" she asks. She looks at Nate. "What's he talking about?"

Nate looks at her with a blank stare.

The others chuckle, making Lilith grind her teeth. "What's so fucking funny?"

"You think it matters," says a voice.

"You think this can be stopped," says another one.

"Wrong," says Lilith. "You're wrong *again*."

A chuckle comes from the ghouls at the back of the room.

"Why do you fear the Delegate, then?" Lilith asks.

The dogs start to scratch the walls.

Out of the shadows, one of the figures stands up. "You'll know soon enough."

Lilith steps forward. "Grann?"

"We just wanted to say goodbye. We're getting closer."

"Closer," says Lilith, clenching her teeth. "Closer to what? God, all this mystery, you sound just like—"

Out of the shadows, one of the figures stands up. He cranes his neck forward and grins.

Lilith looks him in the eye and closes her mouth.

"Hel-lo, L-Lilybug."

74

THE FIGURES STEP FORWARD IN THE DARK, APPROACHING LILITH and Nathan. The dogs outside scratch and claw through the house's boarded-up windows, tearing away the wood, and a ray of moonlight breaks in, shining on a group of old, rotten mummies, walking but not breathing.

A familiar voice sends a cold shiver through Lilith's spine.

"We c-come to s-say hello, d-dear," the dried mummy of her mother says in a mocking tone. She's shrouded in black, and the black sleeves covering her thin bony arms make the sight phantasmagorical. Her lopsided grin seems drawn on her face. Her jaw moves up and down like a string puppet, and the eerie voice seems to come from somewhere else. As the dogs tear up a piece of wood from the window, light shines on her face, and Lilith's blood curdles.

"We remember this f-fondly," her mother says. "The look on your f-face." And, turning to Nate, she says, "s-so good to see you two together again."

A ray of moonlight shines on her dry grin. Behind her, more shadows stand out in the dark. Short. Tall. Standing still. Jittering madly, like a cockroach sprayed with bug spray. The room is full of them.

Lilith kicks her, but something grabs her leg in mid-air. She hears the familiar voice in her ear.

"You th-think you're so clever," says a fatherly voice, "with your crazy *unexpected* m-moves."

"Honey," says her mother, coming closer, "it's what we've b-been expecting from you all along."

Lilith looks around for a blunt object, but her fingers grab on empty air.

"You s-soldier," her father says, coming closer, the driving glasses all the more menacing in a receding, mummified face. "We gave you so many ch-chances to figure it out."

Lilith tries to get an image of the room. Exits. Openings. But the room is crowded. The door where they came from is already blocked, and the only opening is the window behind her, being clawed by mad dogs.

"Still," her father wheezes, "we'll give you one m-more."

"Lil—!" Nathan shouts, pulled into the darkness, and his voice gets muffled, like someone is covering his mouth.

"Nate?" Lilith asks, looking around. "Nate!?"

The dogs tear up a plank of wood, and light shines on her father holding Nate in a chokehold. Nate's eyes plead with her. He looks scared. Like a child. He's panicking. His chest heaves.

"One last ch-chance," her father says. "What if I would ask you to ch-choose?"

Lilith keeps feeling around behind her, looking for something to hit them with.

"Kill him," her father says. "Go against what you f-feel is right. Or we'll k-kill you."

She freezes. Her fingers linger in the air like dead worms. "What?"

The barking outside gets louder. The scratches are sharper. Another plank of wood falls off, and she gets a glimpse of her father's grin.

"Kill Nathan," he says. "And we'll let you go."

Her mouth trembles. She looks around for a way out, only to find a wall of mummies grinning at her.

"Go against your f-feelings. Your chemical imbalances. Your whims. Show us you're t-truly *edgy*."

Lilith shakes her head. She tries to find Nathan in the dark, but the mummies keep moving away from the light.

"No!" she mumbles, feeling her body spasm as denying what's happening becomes less and less manageable. "Stop it!"

"It's only chemistry. Your body. Not you. Your fl-flesh. It was bound to happen. And now, before it changes again ..."

"No," Lilith sobs with a broken voice.

"You still don't see it? I knew you'd be in that corner b-because you're fl-flesh, and you're p-p-predictable," he says. "You just had to do what it told you. Your whims, your *freshness*, your *quirkiness*. You think you make your ch-choices, but choices are m-made for you."

"Stop it!" she yells, looking for Nathan in the dark.

"You still think *we* took you out of Leatelranch?" he asks. "You still refuse to r-remember?"

"Remember what?"

"That we've been p-protecting you all along. You know you never had a heart condition. And even now, in death, we're swerving you into salvation, because you can't do it yourself."

"What are you saying?" Lilith asks. "You're *helping* me?"

"Life was so good!" Ophelia snarls. "Life was p-perfect."

"You wasted your life fearing deatfh," Ophelia says, stumbling on the last word.

" ... and now it's not here to p-protect you." Renwick finishes the sentence as his wife manually rearranges her jaw.

Lilith takes a step back toward the window. She can feel the fury of the dogs trying to break in. The window booms with each claw.

"Have you noticed how all those s-songs you like are about *I wanna this, I wanna that, I don't wanna that* ... They're n-not about rebellion. They're about f-following orders. From f-flesh. You think you're cool for following your impulses? You're just a common dog. And N-Nathan," he says, grabbing his face, "*this*, is just another s-side effect. Rebel against your flesh!"

Lilith's hands feel behind her. She's still not reaching the window. "Wha-What?"

Another plank of wood comes off, and a gleam of moonlight enters from outside, bathing Renwick Kane's face in a ghostly white. His face is destroyed, but somehow smiling. Behind him, among the bodies, a rotten chair. A perfectly made bed. She remembers Nate's stories. His night terrors. Kaleidoscope eyes. Her, joking to Nate: *What? The new caretaker's house doesn't have any tunnels?*

"It was those songs, and those zombie mo-movies, that *kept* you from rebelling," says Renwick. "They kept you singing and dancing and watching, passively, instead of r-revolting. They kept you under control."

Lilith is speechless. She thinks she can see Nate, in the dark, trying to tell her something.

"*We* fed you that. That music. Those zombie movies. You like them because it's what you've been l-listening to and w-watching since you were a kid, the distraction we chose to keep you from learning the trutfh about what happened inside the cemetery walls. You're a p-product. Those songs and stories written by other people that you use to define your individuality. You've been following a d-design set by your mommy ..."

"No ..."

"... And your daddy."

Lilith's eyes fill with tears. Her lips taste salty.

"Well?" asks Renwick, and he shoves Nate toward her, offering him. "What does your s-servile, doggie heart *wanna do* now?"

Dogs bring down more planks in the window, and rays of moonlight shoot inside. A glimmer approaches her in the dark. Her mother is handing her a knife.

"Oh, you're seeing it now, aren't you?" Renwick continues,

smiling. His eyes are dead milky white, but his eyebrows are arched like she hasn't seen in years. He's *proud*.

"Fuck you!" Lilith yells. "I'll never do it! I won't kill Nate!"

They take a step back. "You coward," he says. "You h-hypocrite."

Lilith falls to her knees. "We can stop this! We can find this *Delegate* thing and fix it, Nate and I—"

They all laugh. Nate's father's giggles sound maniacal.

"What?"

"We were like you once. We also w-wanted to stop this. But why would you? We're all together now."

"It makes it all clear," a voice adds from the dark.

"It's invigorating," another voice says.

"You'll l-like it," a new voice adds. The timbre of the voice sounds familiar, one that Lilith hasn't heard in a long time, and it somehow brings warm memories.

"I won't," she blurts out.

A plank of wood falls down, and the full moonlight shines on both her parents' faces.

"Oh," they say with a grin. "You'll come around."

Her mother takes a step forward. "You're only afraid of death b-because your body tells you to be. It's your body that's scared. But *you* need to be more open. Welcome it. Be a true rebel."

"Never."

Ophelia points at the dogs scratching at the wood. "Do you want to end up like them? There's something worse than death. There's always b-been. And now it's here."

Dogs claw, making scratch noises in the soft brittle wood.

"So we work together," Lilith blurts out, her eyes darting between her mother's and her father's. "We have a common enemy now. Nate and I can—"

"You," they say.

"What?"

Renwick moves Nate aside and takes a step closer to her. He

kneels down and brings his rotten smelly face closer to her. He's grinning.

"We only n-need one of you alive."

Behind him, a hollow chuckle starts.

Her father's face is all she can see, but she knows which of the ghouls is laughing. She knows the voice. She's lived with it most of her adult life. She's loved it for as long as she can remember.

He could never hold himself before a good scare.

FIVE BONY FINGERS MAKE THEIR WAY OUT OF THE CRYPT'S window, shining in the moonlight like razors. Nathan notices the number on the crypt door, but it's too late; the fingers hover toward his neck, too close to avoid them. The bony tips penetrate like needles, and the hand closes, rupturing his arteries and cutting them like string. Behind them, in the dark of the crypt, two eyes shine, changing.

The whole world starts to spin—to fall. The night spills around him like an inky ocean. He manages to gargle, stretch his hand toward Lilith, who still moves and dances in front of him. The ink, cold and thick, drowns him and carries him with a strong tide, filling his veins as he loses his breath.

Lilith lands her foot after a roundhouse kick and turns back. "Are you OK?"

Death has a taste. It's smoke, and it's acid, and it's everything that makes the body catch fire with alarms of something going wrong. Because it is. Going wrong. This is what pain is meant to warn you about.

"Yes," he says, and he clears his throat. "Fine."

A fever washes over him. And it hits him. A bombardment of *all* the future, unborn moments. In death, he sees everything. He sees Tommy, his son. Months from now. His first steps. His first kiss. His graduation. His death. And that of all the Tommys in the world. He's not making calculations, because he no longer has to; he can *feel* the degrees of the unborn. It's a part of his body, a sense, just like he used to feel touch and sights and smells. Just as he used to know the location of his house even if he couldn't see it. Everything is just there now, around him, clear as daylight. A showdown in a cemetery world. A sarcophagus never meant to be reopened. A birth in a bright transparent room. And he sees his own face and his own bowels; he sees your face, and he feels vertigo and weeps. Images of everything yet to be born fill his mind. Everything yet to come. Its wretchedness.

He sees his house. He sees it bright with sunshine when it was new. He sees it being cleaned up by his father and him, fixing it, delaying the inevitable. He sees it run-down, rotten, gone. He sees it covered in creepers, blackened by oily spots created by accumulated spores, rotten, sunken sideways into the rotting ground, pregnant with a thousand wooden arms reaching for the outside, escaping in all directions like petrified black flames, wooden elbows twisting and pushing on elbows, curling and cracking his bedroom window, open palms with needle-thin fingers scratching the air. He's seen it replaced, like the rest of the world, with stone and marble crypts. He can feel the ground beneath him shaking already, breaking, giving in, as it will one day. Everything around him is about to disappear. It will happen soon. The brittleness of it all is overwhelming.

The cemetery around him rots and crumbles down like a quick passing storm. The ground gives. The continent shifts. The air burns as the sun approaches Earth. Memories become taste-less. A hug from Lilith is as bland as washing his hands. Did it last thirty minutes, or a second? Only the fact remains. No taste. No recollection.

His legs struggle to keep the same pace as before. His foot stumbles into something, and he corrects himself. His muscles are never going to heal again. Wounds are forever now.

"Let's go!" says Lilith, waiting by the chopper bike.

He starts the bike and makes sure his leg follows the familiar arc as he climbs it, matching his memory of making this very movement.

Lilith hasn't noticed a thing.

76

This is where Lilith dies.

Nathan cannot wait. The barks outside are deafening, but they are nothing compared to his hunger, the pain he's about to get rid of, the noise that needs to be stopped.

"He's coming!" Lilith yells in the dark.

Nathan looks down on the weary old wooden tiles on the floor, and the weary fragile bricks making up the walls around him. He remembers this house. He looks around and remembers all these unborn moments about to be born. Walking closer to Lilith. The firm grasp of Lilith's tense shoulders. Her parents, Ophelia and Renwick, walking toward her as she tries to set herself loose. Her pulse quickening. The hardness of teeth breaking her face and skin and sinking into her bone. The noise stopping. The hunger being quelled. In a second, she'll move toward the corner of the room. His hand shoots toward it. He waits for her, ready to touch a memory. But his fingers grasp on empty air.

How did she do that?

Oh.

Right.

441

The ringing in his ears grows louder. The buzzing of life. It teases him.

The dogs claw and scratch and bring down the last planks covering the window. The room is bathed in moonlight.

It's all so clear, and yet *this* is new. *This* hasn't happened. The vision through his rotting eyes is blurry, but he can see something moving in the dark, can still follow it. Yes. He sees her arms.

And he feels the hunger.

Such hunger.

A sharp corner. An out-of-place chair she's moved in her attempt to escape. Nathan grunts and looks down. His hand is lying on the ground. Fury joins the hunger. He looks at the stump where his hand used to be, and he explodes in a stunning scream.

"I—I didn't remember that being there!" he grunts as the group looks at him in silence. "I didn't remember!"

And the dogs. She brought the dogs. The deafening dogs. They are not what he remembers. This place was silent. This moment was quick. He wasn't supposed to lose a hand. And eternity was not bondage.

He sees the shadows in the room change formation, and he understands. It's their only chance. This is not the future yet. But it's a chance.

They are grabbing her. She's sobbing. They are moving the bed. Shadows grab the wooden legs and the headrest and move it. And under it, there it is. What he failed to see as a kid, what his father kept from him, what he now remembers forever, as much as he'd like to forget, like a recurring nightmare.

A door. A hatch.

The sight of it brings a jolt of surprise to his old body. A new wave of memories fills his mind. New angles and perspectives on his childish visions. The lady with kaleidoscope eyes crawling up the hatch and into his bedroom, watching him sleep.

He approaches the sobbing meat, hungry to stop the noise. But the dogs are tearing the house apart, and he knows exactly how much time is left.

He pulls open his pocket with his good hand and reaches slowly inside. One small scratch and he will wear it for eternity. He fumbles for it. Lilith will need it.

The world spins in his mind again. A memory that spans eons, and yet, this is new. With so many memories, it's hard to see that which hasn't happened. Which shouldn't happen. Because inside his pocket, there is nothing.

She has it already. She took it.

She scuttles down the hatch.

Behind him, the boarded window gives in. Planks of wood fly in the air, and dogs pounce inside the room. Behind the window are the pale blue hills of the graveyard, and what moves, climbing down, coming here, is a monstrous creature made of victims, bigger than the one he rode to Leatelranch. This distant memory drowns his rotting mind. The dogs, entering the house. The headless ghouls, under the spell of that human, heralding the giant new machine. The hideous human monster with its thousand arms and legs blocking the moonlight, crawling up the house, spreading over the roof, coiling around it, prying it open like a toy chest. His father, mad, scared, laughing maniacally next to him as the bricks fall, the only one laughing in a roomful of sulking corpses, looking eternity in the eye as they wait patiently to get caught.

77

Lilith's lips tremble as she crawls her way through the narrow corridor. Panting, crying, tasting her salty tears, she finds a hatch.

She steps through rotted rust-colored curtains onto the damp floor. The circular room is burnt, blackened with soot, and smells musty. Nobody's been here in years. Moonshine floods in through the caved-in roof. Around her, burnt chairs arranged in circles surround a small mossy table that looks like it might have been an altar once, now burnt, rotten. Thick cobwebs cover the antique lamps on the walls.

Across the room is a burnt rotten door, standing slightly askew. Sobbing, Lilith paces toward it, going for the luxurious knob, and freezes as a cold drop taps her shoulder.

She looks up. Water drips from the opening in the roof, falling on the floor with tiny dripping sounds that echo all through the room. It carries the soot in the room and creates a small pool of black muddy water, a stream that somehow runs through the floor and toward a specific point in one of the walls.

She looks closer. She paces through the room, splashing water with each step, following it. The water is definitely disappearing into the wall.

There's nothing special about this part of the wall. It's just as round as the rest of the room. It's blackened by fire and covered in soot, which feels sticky to the touch. She knocks. It's hollow.

She explores it, clumsily moving her hand along the wall, and coughs as the cloud of soot dissipates. She knocks again. Hollow. Her hands hurry. She bangs on it, hearing the sound on the other side, and explores it, looking for an opening, a sign, something. Above her, she finds something cold and hard. She looks up and sees a square shape. She rubs it. A sign. A word, embossed in marble.

Delegatvm.

She tries to ram the wall with her shoulder. It's hollow. It budges. A frame is suddenly visible. Her fingers trace around the wall, looking for something. And there it is. A small hinge. She fumbles with it and finally finds something to pull hidden in the wall. She twists it and pulls. Nothing. She pushes. It's heavy, but it moves. With a deep rumble, the wall opens before her.

A dark passage. A tunnel to the bowels of the earth, getting darker and darker as it goes further into the ground. Stairs lead below, carpeted, a dark red that looks worn and faded, bloated with muddy water. Under it, there is nothing but mud. These stairs are carved out of the very soil of the cemetery.

Lilith closes one eye and steps down. Below, in the darkness, something shines. The basement looks flooded. Black water licks the base of the stairs. She steps on the wet rug covering each uneven step, her feet sinking on the thick mushy carpet. She keeps her one eye closed. The passage is dark, and the only light comes from the room upstairs. She sticks to the wall to let the light in, and treads down, jumping over the wet steps, two at a time, three at a time, not caring about anything anymore. She finds herself at the bottom of the stairs, sees the mirror of water below her, and jumps.

The murky water reaches her waist. She wades through the thick liquid, going further into the cave, leaving the faint moonlight from above behind, putting her hands ahead of her but hurrying her steps madly as if she could still see, or as if there was nothing to fight for anymore.

She closes her eye and opens the other one. There are hues of dark now. Shapes. Towering over the waving water, an altar stands high. A shiny box rests on it.

She waves her arms to push harder through the thick water, raising her knees like she's kicking death in the face. The waves lick the top of the altar and splash away. She gets her hands on the box.

Her trembling fingers find a lock.

Her eyes spring open. "Oh!" she says as she fumbles in her pocket. "Oh!"

She takes the key out and tries it in the lock. She turns it, and the lock unlatches.

She opens the lid.

Her face turns into a twisted grimace.

She closes her eyes, disgusted, and forces herself to touch it. A white chicken membrane sticks to her fingers as she dares to grab the thing inside. It's cold. Moist. Tender. It's no bigger than a thumb. And as she takes it out, there is something on the box's lid. She takes out as much of the membrane as she can, and narrows her eyes. She mouths the words as she reads in the dark.

Her cheeks burn. This is impossible.

Suddenly the room makes sense. The roundness of the hall upstairs. The chairs. Even the strange candelabra. This all has one obvious, simple meaning. And her parents. Everything they said. Everything they did. Everything they pushed her to do. A procession of faces, their heavy burden, all the previous holders of this horrible miracle.

"I can ... He can ..." she says, and as her heart starts to race, her voice ramps up into a yell. "We can stop it!"

Her voice bounces and echoes up the stairs.

She closes the box and wraps her arm around it, pushing it against her chest as she fights the water and hurries up the stairs, struggling with her heavy wet clothes. Across the circular room is the exit door. She turns the knob, and it comes off. The heavy door is askew. It's only resting on the door frame. Behind it, more planks of wood and marble block the exit.

"No!" she screams, panting and hitting her fists on the door. "No!"

The echo of her voice bounces on the walls and escapes upward. She's locked in.

She sits against the wall on the cold, damp floor, and looks around. She looks up at the broken roof and the full moon.

"He can stop it!" she yells to the sky, hearing her own voice echoing in the chamber.

Outside, out of the oppressing silence, the faint sound of barking appears.

Great.

She paces the room, hitting the walls to check for more hollow sounds, finding none. She looks at the burnt rusty chairs.

She places one on top of another and pushes down. It holds.

She piles another one. And another one. And another one, until she forms a burnt totem of angles and chair legs. She climbs the openings between the twisted metal. The tower trembles but holds. She goes down and brings another chair to the top, testing it again. It holds.

As the barks get closer, she continues piling them on, seeing how with each new chair, the pile towers higher and higher toward the hole in the ceiling.

She goes down to fetch the last chair. She climbs back, carrying it, and tries to fit it on the top.

The metal beneath her feet gives in. She jumps backward and

lands in a crouch as the tower falls. She covers her head as broken metal showers over her.

When the last of the pile has tumbled, she sits on the ground and covers her face with her hands.

"I'm sorry," she says. "I'm sorry." And she mouths the names she fought so hard to forget all these years, and they taste salty with her tears.

78

THE NIGHT IS FULL OF INVISIBLE CRICKETS. THE COLD AIR carries the smell of fresh grass. But it's more than just cold, the girl thinks, unable to stop shaking, rubbing her arms with her numb fingers. There's something chilling about it. She looks at the tall stone wall that looms over her and the boys, lit by the pale streetlights. It spans for as long as she can see, and it's as tall as the huge trees on the other side of the wide empty sidewalk. Along the wall, up high and covered in cobwebs, hang eerie old artifacts that look like oil lanterns. Next to each of them are cheap yellowish light bulbs that already look as dry and old as the lanterns. They are spread far apart along the endless wall. Lilith tries to imagine this street lit by firelight, how much warmer it might have seemed.

"We should go back," the tall boy says, shivering.

Next to him, Doyle seems to ignore him. He looks around, worried, and exhales. He's shorter than the rest, but his puff of breath turns to a cloud big enough to hover over all of them. "Just a little more, guys," he says.

The girl looks through the big cloud as it dissolves in the air. "Of course," she says. "Our parents won't mind," she lies.

451

"I don't know," the boy with the impossibly blue eyes says, looking back. "We should probably go back soon."

"I know," Doyle says. "Just a little more."

The girl can see the worry on his sweet face. She throws a look at the boys. "No problem," she says, making it clear that she's speaking for everybody. "Hey, do you smell that?"

The boys sniff the night air. "Yeah," the tall boy says, "so what? It's grass."

"It's freshly cut grass," she says. "That smell means death, you know?"

"What?" asks the tall boy, shivering.

"Nate told me," she says. "The grass sends a distress signal when it's cut. That's what we find so enjoyable. The grass, dying, yelling for help."

"That guy is dark," the tall boy says.

"Yeah," Lilith boasts. "Where's Wednesday?"

"Home," the boy with the blue eyes says. "Doing homework."

"Homework?" the girl says. "What a nerd."

"It's freezing," the boy with the impossibly blue eyes says. His teeth rattle. He's holding his chest with both arms. "We should go back."

"You know," the girl says, pointing her chin at the wall nonchalantly, "I've been inside."

The worried small boy doesn't seem to care. He just cranes his neck and looks around. The tall boy looks at her, scared to even ask. The boy with the impossibly blue eyes, on the other hand, *is* interested, or maybe he just wants to keep his mind from the cold, just like her.

"I have," she says. "Twice. Nate took me. And years ago I took my Ma and Pa inside."

"What's in there?" the boy with the impossibly blue eyes asks.

"The cemetery," the tall boy says.

"Duh. But what's it like?"

"Guys, really," the small, worried boy says. "Are you even looking?"

"We're looking," the girl says, seeing nothing but darkness on the empty street around them, and on the ghoulishly white sidewalk. The boys nod. "Uhuh."

"So?" the worried boy says, looking around, impatient. "Tell us. What *did* you see?"

"Oh, so you *are* paying attention," she says. "Anyway—nothing. Nothing you should worry about. *Yet*."

The tall boy looks at Lilith, scared. He's shivering more from fear than from the cold. "Tell us."

The sound of their steps becomes a creepy menacing echo in the night. She looks ahead. They are alone. "Nothing, really. I saw crypts, like little stone houses, where they put the dead. A fogbow, which is like a rainbow but made of fog."

The tall boy is hooked. "*Whoa*."

"Really," the boy with the impossibly blue eyes says. "Let's go back. Our parents—"

"I also saw an *entombing*," Lilith blurts out.

The tall boy is interested. "What's that?"

"Oh, you don't wanna know."

"Yes, I do," the tall boy says.

She laughs. "Wolfram, you're *shaking* with fear!"

"It's not fear!" the tall boy says. "I'm cold!"

"Come on!" says the boy with the impossibly blue eyes. "Doyle, I'm sure that if we go back—"

"Hey!" Lilith says, pointing at him. "Stop being such a wuss."

The boy looks down, ashamed.

"What's *that*?" Wolfram says, looking up.

They all stop. Doyle, already ahead by a couple of steps, turns around.

Above them, a large marble fixture protrudes from the wall. An oblong box topped with a plaque, facing downward like a giant dagger, looms over them.

"Shit, that thing is big," he says. "How the hell didn't we see that before?"

"And look," Doyle says, pointing far ahead, "there's more of them."

Spaced out, between the old lamps, the boxes multiply in the distance, all the way until the night's breath swallows the wall.

"Let's go see—" he continues.

"I've seen them before," Lilith says, nonchalantly.

"No, you haven't," Wolfram says, looking down at her. "You'd have told us."

"Yes, I did—"

"No, you didn't—"

"Guys," says the small worried boy, "you can check out the next one. Or come back tomorrow. Let's just—"

"I bet I can climb that high," says the tall boy.

"Wolfram, shut up," Lilith scoffs. "Look at how these things are placed. Look how they point down like daggers. Like thorns coming out of the wall. I really think these things are a kind of warning. Nature's way of telling you to stay away. We should go on."

She looks at Doyle. He smiles.

"Where do you see a thorn?" the tall boy asks.

"It's a *metaphor*, stupid. The thing *does* look like a dagger ready to fall on us, right?"

The tall boy moves closer to the wall, staring at the box from below. It looks heavy. It's gigantic. It's big enough to fit two people high and two people wide. "What's that thing poking out?" he asks.

Doyle, worried, walks a few steps forward. "Guys? Please?"

"He's right," says Lilith, "Let's go."

"It looks like a coffin," says the boy with the impossibly blue eyes.

"Guys, I'll tell the story if we keep going," says Lilith, looking at Doyle's worried face, trying to cheer him up. "C'mon."

"More like a giant ... marble ... toilet," Wolfram says.

Lilith looks up. "What? That's obviously a giant coffin. With a tombstone."

"Oh, right," says the boy with the impossibly blue eyes. "Yes. Yes, I see it."

"No, look," Wolfram explains. "The gravestone is the water tank, because the markings on the top right almost look like a flush lever."

Lilith narrows her eyes and chuckles. "Oh, yeah."

"Hold on," says the boy with the blue eyes, stepping forward, fixating on the slab. "I think there's something written on the tombstone."

"You mean on the tank."

"Go," says Lilith, pushing them from behind. "Move. We gotta go."

The worried boy stops walking and looks up at the thing. He narrows his eyes. "You mean that pointy thing?" he says. "It *does* look like a lever."

"No, all over. Next to the lever. It's engraved, I think, that's why it's hard to read."

They all narrow their eyes. "Oh."

Lilith looks up and examines the sculpture. There's something about these figures. All this time living next to the cemetery, and she never paid attention to them, yet they are unmistakably huge.

Wolfram jumps against the wall and tries to propel upward as he bounces off, flaying his arms toward the box. He's still far from reaching the bottom.

"Nice try," says Lilith as he lands on his hands and feet next to them. "You done? Let's go."

He stands up and looks at the box again. "Hey, I know," he says. He walks up to the wall and leans his back against it. "Here," he says to the boy with the impossibly blue eyes, "I'll give you a boost."

"Wolfram, stop," Lilith says.

Wolfram just smiles and looks at the boy with the impossibly blue eyes.

"No way," says the boy.

"C'mon," Wolfram insists.

The boy with the impossibly blue eyes throws a scared melancholic look at him. "I don't know," he says, looking up. He's trembling, and it's not clear anymore if it's because of the cold.

"OK," Wolfram says. "Wuss. Come here. You give *me* a boost."

The boy sighs, relieved, and walks toward the wall. He stands upright with his back to the stone and cups his hands for Wolfram, just as the tall boy lifts his leg and steps on his shoulder. He jumps up and gets his other leg up, stepping on his other shoulder. He reaches up toward the box. His hands still can't quite reach. He stretches, standing on his tiptoes.

"Watch out!" Lilith says, taking a step toward him. Doyle, still with a worried look on his face, looks at the scene from afar.

Lilith tries to peek inside the stone coffin perched against the wall. There's a sliver of darkness between the lid and the box, and she narrows her eyes to see inside. Somehow, whatever secrets death is holding from her are inside it. Whatever her Grann saw. Everything the grownups are keeping from her. Everything that's true, and dark, and tough, but true. It's the beating heart of the cemetery, exposed, available, at reach. The thin sliver of darkness seems to sizzle like an anthill, waiting for her.

"You're almost there," she says. "Help him up."

"I—can't," The boy with the impossibly blue eyes says, also trying to stand on his tiptoes. He manages to lift Wolfram just a little bit.

"That's it!" says Lilith, stepping closer. "You almost got it!"

Wolfram's feet tremble on the boy's shoulders. He leans on the wall, inhales, and tries to stay as still as possible. His hands stick to the wall as he stretches his neck, trying to read the slab.

"Can you read anything?" she asks.

"I—can see the bottom," he says. "This thing is old. The marble is rusty around the edges. There's—a black line separating the lid, like it's a real coffin—a—real lid."

"Sure, it is," Doyle says.

"This—angle," Wolfram says, struggling, "doesn't—help."

The boy's hands fumble nervously on the bottom of the box,

feeling the rusty, dirty marble, and finds a base on which to cling. He puts his fingers inside.

"Oh, wait," he says, "this is hollow. It *is* a real lid!"

"Wolfram, get out of there," Lilith says. She looks at Doyle. He looks even more worried than before.

Wolfram stretches his arms as much as he can. "I—can't —reach."

The boy with the impossibly blue eyes just stands there, silent, miserable, supporting Wolfram's weight on his shoulders.

"Well," Doyle says, "OK, come down and let's keep walking. I'm freezing over here."

"No, wait!" Wolfram yells. "I know."

"Can you read anything?" Lilith asks.

Wolfram reaches up. He's almost touching the box. "Not ... yet ..."

"Guys," Doyle protests. "Let's go ..."

Wolfram jumps up and grabs the wide dagger-shaped box by the sides. He's hanging from the bottom now.

"Look out!" yells Lilith.

"Shit, he's gonna fall!" Doyle yells.

"He's not gonna fall," Lilith says, smiling.

Wolfram's arms are stretched around the big coffin. He swings his legs to the sides like a pendulum, managing to slowly climb a hand upward with each swing.

They hear the heavy sound of stone brushing against stone.

"Shit!" Wolfram yells.

Doyle is holding his head. "Careful!"

The coffin's lid is ajar. Dirty water starts to seep out.

"I'm OK," says Wolfram, hanging on the askew lid. He climbs and hugs the top half of the giant marble coffin. He clamps his feet on the bottom and stretches toward the inscription.

"Shit, guys, we should get going," says Doyle.

Lilith can't hear him. She's deeply involved in watching Wolfram as he cranes his neck, moving his head from side to side as he tries to read the words carved above the coffin.

"Hey," Doyle says, "are you listening?"

Wolfram finally stays still. He moves his lips, reading.

Lilith strains to hear him from her position on the sidewalk. "What? What does it say?"

"I got it!" Wolfram says. "It's ..." He opens his eyes wide. "Oh, shit," he says, in shock, and his feet start to slip out from under him.

"Careful!" Doyle yells.

The wall crumbles under Wolfram's left foot, and a spray of rubble rains down on his friends below. His leg hangs in the air as he clings to the sides of the coffin with both hands. Hugging it harder, he lifts himself with his other leg, and with his last bit of strength, he jumps up toward the protruding tombstone above. His hands grab the big stone lever as his feet hang loosely in the air.

Lilith stares at him in silence. She tries to call him down, but she's paralyzed. He's too high up. If he falls ...

"I'm reading it!" he yells. "I can read it!"

His weight brings the lever down. A guttural sound comes from inside the box. The deep sound of stone grinding against hollow stone.

The lid is opening.

"Come down!" Doyle yells. "Come down now!"

"No!" she says. "The lid is opening! Keep doing whatever you're doing!"

"What?" Doyle asks, mystified.

"I need to see," Lilith says, burning with anticipation.

She notices a pair of impossibly blue eyes staring at her, scared, mute.

"I really don't," Doyle says. "I just wanna get out of here and do what we came here to do."

Wolfram mouths something as he reads. His own breath exits his mouth and forms a white cloud that hovers in front of him, preventing him from reading. As the cloud slowly vanishes, his body spasms in shock, and his grip on the stone lever weakens.

Down below, his friends gasp.

"Tom!" Wolfram calls down to the sidewalk, still holding on to the tombstone. "Give me a hand!"

The boy with the blue eyes looks worried.

"Don't do it, Tommy," Doyle says. "Wolfram, just come down!"

"I'm OK!" Wolfram yells from above. "Tommy, just look inside the box! I'll keep hanging from the lever!"

The boy looks at Lilith, scared.

She smiles. "Do it," she says.

Lilith stands against the wall and boosts Tommy up toward the coffin. He stretches upward until he grabs the bottom of the box and leans his face toward the open darkness. Drops of water fall from inside and zip by his face.

"No, wait!" Wolfram yells from above, trying to regain his grip on the handle, to pull himself up and continue reading, his fingers slipping on the cold stone. "Tommy, wait! Don't!"

"There's something inside," Tommy says, his impossibly blue eyes peeking through the crack. He presses hard on Lilith's shoulders, then puts one foot against the wall to boost himself further up. Loose rubble falls on Lilith's face and hair. His hand grabs the heavy lid and, pushing against the wall, he pulls it open.

"No!" yells Wolfram. "Tommy, don't!"

A strange mud falls from the opening, covering his face and mouth.

"Tommy!" Doyle screams, running to help lower Tommy back down onto Lilith's shoulders, holding his legs as Tommy kicks and wriggles. There's a harsh sound as Tommy's fingers slip from the bottom of the box, and his legs swing, kicking Doyle in the face. Doyle's head whips back, but he again manages to grab hold of Tommy's legs, and Lilith reaches up in time to help him slow Tommy's fall. Tommy lands and kneels on the sidewalk, and Lilith and Doyle bend down to check on him.

Wolfram closes his eyes and steadies his breathing. He swings his legs, aims for the open coffin, and jumps down, stepping on it before dropping down to the sidewalk. He lands on his hands and feet and rolls on the ground.

"Whoa," he says, getting up, "did you guys see that?"

But Lilith's looking at Tommy. He's still in shock, wiping his mud-covered face.

"Are you OK?" she asks him.

"Yes," he says, catatonic.

She helps him clean up. Doyle and Wolfram move closer, but Tommy stands up and resumes his walk like nothing happened.

"What the hell was that?" Doyle asks, holding his cheek.

"Nothing," says Tommy, shrugging it off, spitting out more of the dark water. "Just mud, I guess." Lilith looks at his eyes. The bright blue seems to glow a different shade.

"No, not you," Doyle says, and turns to Lilith, piercing her eyes with his gaze. "You. What was that?" His cheek is bleeding from the kick.

"Me?" she asks.

"Yah. We should have just kept going." He feels the deep cut along his face and finds a shard of brick lodged in his cheek. He pulls it out and looks at it, furious.

"And you!" He turns to yell at Tommy, punching him hard in the shoulder. "What were you thinking?"

Lilith punches Tommy in the shoulder, too. "Yeah, you idiot! We were worried."

Tommy just keeps walking and laughs it off. "Don't you worry about me," he says. "It's just some mud. Promise me, if I die, you'll name your first kid after me."

Lilith laughs, relieved. She turns to Doyle and looks at the cut across his cheek. "Are you OK?"

A faint hollow sound comes from the dark distance, and Doyle's worried face lights up.

"Bandit!"

The barking sound booms closer to them. Joyful anticipation beams from Doyle's face despite the blood pouring out one side of it. Out of the shadows and into the white glow of the streetlights, a German shepherd comes running toward them, alone on the vast sidewalk, and it pounces on Doyle.

"Bandit!" he says, hugging his pet. "I was worried sick!"

The others share smiles and scratch the dog's head.

"I guess we can go back now," says Lilith, petting Bandit. "Thank god. I can't feel my fingers anymore."

Wolfram chuckles. "What do you say, Tommy?" he asks, turning around. "Maybe we should give that wall one more try before we go?"

Lilith and Doyle chuckle, but Tommy doesn't respond.

"Tommy?"

Without a word, the boy with the once-impossibly blue eyes falls backward, landing with a dull *thump* on the sidewalk.

"Tommy!"

79

LILITH STARES AT DOYLE'S EYES AS HE SPEAKS, TRYING TO AVOID looking at the wall behind him or its terrible coffin-shaped fixtures. He's doing the same, only breaking eye contact with her to look down at his dog and to wipe the tears from his eyes. The cut on his face has turned to a fat pink worm scuttling across his cheek.

"Why didn't you come?" he asks.

Lilith's stomach turns. She looks up at the night stars, and at the deserted street around her. "I couldn't. I had to get ready," she says. "I'm sorry. I had to."

"There was a wake," he says. His mouth trembles. The scar on his cheek wiggles. "They ... chose me."

"I couldn't go," she says. "I'm sorry. It's ... too hard."

His lips twitch in a way that makes Lilith take a step back. "Too hard?"

She looks over Doyle's shoulder. At the end of the unusually long, unusually wide sidewalk that surrounds the cemetery and goes on forever, under clouds that slither over the black sky and cover the stars, the red sedan purrs, idle, waiting. She can't wait to get in.

"I wanted to see you before I left."

"What?" he asks. His frown may contain some confusion but is surely chock-full of hate. "You're *leaving*?"

"My parents," she says, "they're making me."

His eyes are red. He looks tired. His silvery scar seems to beat. "Why?"

"Who knows," she says. "Protective, I guess. You know, my heart condition."

Bandit licks his hand. He signals the dog to sit and wait.

"Look," Lilith says. "First my Grann, now Tommy ... It's like everyone around me is dying in front of my eyes. I just couldn't cope. I couldn't deal with another."

He sniffles. "Wait. So you know about the Delegate already?"

A cold heavy drop falls on her shoulder. Then another, directly on the top of her head. It's starting to rain.

"The *what*?" she asks.

Drops start falling on his face. "Did you go to her wake?"

"No," she says, confused. "My parents wouldn't let me then, either. And I know, I know, I'm older now, I should be brave, but I guess I'm not. I can't."

"So which is it?" he asks. He seems to pant, with the spasms that come just before crying. "Today. They didn't let you, or you didn't want to?"

Rain pounds on her head. She doesn't answer.

"So are they really forcing you to leave?" he asks. "Or are you running away?"

"What do you think, *I* asked to leave? To move away? From you guys? From my home? From Nate?"

He stares at her. Bandit's breathing intensifies. "So they just up and packed? Today?"

"Yep."

"All that talk about going inside the cemetery," he says, "about how easy it was, how beautiful it all was. Why would you skip it today, of all days?"

"It's not that simple," she says as the rain gets worse. "They wouldn't let me."

He burns her with his gaze.

"You always hated how adults kept things from us."

"Adults suck," she responds, and tries to smile. "We should make a pact—"

"They're right, aren't they?" Doyle says. His mouth trembles. "Some things are better … kept."

Lilith looks at him gravely.

"We used to be best friends," he says.

"We are!"

"Ever since you met that *weirdo*," he says, "things haven't been the same."

The freezing cold rain seeps inside her clothes.

"What changed?" he asks.

Lilith sighs and looks him in the eye. "I guess I did."

The rain pours on the sidewalk and the immense wall. Even from here, she can hear it hammering on the car's roof.

"I'm glad we found Bandit," she says, reaching down to pet him. The dog growls.

"Don't you say his name," the boy mutters among millions of drops falling to their death. "You're not worthy of saying his name. He's loyal. He'd never do what you did. He loves me. And you … you …" He scowls at her. "You're dead to me."

She looks into his eyes, and all she can hear is the rain and Bandit's panting.

"I'm sorry," she says, breaking their stare. She walks past him, then quickens her pace as she gets closer to the car. Among the raindrops, Bandit's heavy breathing fades away. Over her shoulder, she calls to Doyle one more time. "I'm sorry!"

The car purrs in the rain. The trunk is still slightly open. She opens it, and rain falls on Nathan, lying on top of suitcases and bags. She pretends to rummage through her hastily made bags.

"Everything OK back there?" her mother asks from the front seat.

"Yes," she says, "just making sure I didn't forget anything."

"Who was that?" Nathan whispers.

"A friend," she says. "Are you sure about this?"

"I don't want to talk about it," he says. "Ever. I just know that I don't want to be involved in anything like that ever again. Trust me. Take me with you."

"But—"

"Promise me," he says. "Promise me you'll never ask me about today."

She smiles and nods. "Only if you promise the same," she says, and warm tears blend with the rain on her face.

She closes the trunk, making sure there's an opening for him to breathe. She enters the car and sits in the red upholstered seat.

"Everything OK?" her mother asks.

"Yes," she says.

"Are you sure you want to do this?" her father asks.

"Yes, please," she says. "I'm afraid. For my heart."

Lilith's parents share a worried look. Her mother turns around to face her.

"Your heart?" she asks, confused. "But your heart's fine, honey. We told you. We ... may have exaggerated, told a white lie, years ago, to keep you from going into the cemetery when you were little—"

"Please," Lilith says, grabbing her chest, and she turns around and looks back over the seat. Doyle is kneeling down and hugging his dog in the rain. "Let's go. Please."

80

LILITH HEARS A RUMBLE BEHIND HER. THE FLOOR WHERE SHE sits trembles. The metal pile next to her starts to shake.

She springs up. "Fine!" she yells at the walls around her. "Come and get me!"

The walls start to quake. The cracks around the hole in the ceiling spread like dry arteries. Finally, the seams give way, and the ceiling crumbles, sending chunks of granite down around her. She presses herself against the circular wall to avoid the falling debris.

She struggles to see through the rising cloud of dust, trying to find where the rumble is coming from. It's everywhere. She can feel the tremor in the wall behind her intensifying. She moves away from it, stepping on the chair parts and leaping over broken hunks of ceiling to reach the center of the room.

The wall explodes with a deafening bang as a massive steel locomotive breaks through it, its wheels rolling on the ground, cracking open the granite, sending metal flying through the air.

As the dust settles, she can see it. The steel machine is monstrous. Like a brutal, bulletproof Model-T, or a sturdy gothic tank. Its sharp corners and lines gleam in the moonlight. Though its name is printed along its side in old gothic lettering, Lilith recognizes it from a long-forgotten memory: The Citizen.

As Lilith runs away from it, a thick sheet of glass opens from one of its sides with a shriek, and Lester's head pokes out.

"Get in! He's coming!"

Lilith is out in the open now, in the middle of the cemetery, and she can see the trail of destroyed crypts behind the wake of the steel behemoth. Far back, at the end of the path of destruction, the massive train station and museum has an enormous hole in its wall. And the barking is closer now. Raw.

She shakes her head. "N—No. You're dead. Everyone's dead."

"What?" Lester asks. "Shit. Something happen to Nate?"

"He's dead. They're all dead. They're all slaves for that fucking zombie whisperer."

Yoshi pokes his mangled face out of the cabin window and looks at Lester. "See? I told you that scream was her."

Lilith takes a step back.

"No, no," Lester says. "He's fine. Just look out for his funny side. It's acting up. He just played zombie just to teach me a lesson. The fucker's not afraid of anything."

Yoshi tries to smile, and a cut in his loose sagging cheek starts to bleed green. "I had to do it," he says.

"That's not funny," Lilith says, horrified. "You know what?" she asks, defiant, and walks up to the machine. "Yes. We have to do this."

Holding fast to the polished wooden box, she climbs a ladder on the side of the locomotive.

She enters the cabin and addresses the unlikely engineers. "Let's do this."

"Do what?" they ask.

"I know who's the fucking Delegate!"

"The what? Who?"

"I'll explain on our way to the city. First, get us the fuck out of here!"

The steel beast breaks through the tall cemetery wall, its furious chimney setting the night sky on fire. The sharp, V-shaped pilot shovels its way through the park's soil, cracking the ground below in two.

Lester steers the beast, looking forward. "What happened to Nate?"

Lilith stares at the metal plates on the floor, sulking. She feels dirty. The soot and ash from the old locomotive mixes with her sweat. "Just go."

"Which way?!" Lester asks, grabbing two sturdy levers, balancing against the shaking and rocking of the beast.

Lilith kneels on the old riveted metal plates of the cabin's floor next to Yoshi, who's leaning on a control panel on the cabin wall. Between them is the blood-red *Delegatvm* box. She can't believe what she hears. "You can *steer* this thing?"

Lester pulls the left lever with the weight of his whole body. With a hydraulic howl, the locomotive snakes and zigzags to the sides, bumping into a tree and sending it flying off onto the front of a house. Lilith loses her balance and holds on to a leather strap hanging from the ceiling near her head. The locomotive merges into an empty street.

Lester grins. "You can steer this thing."

Lilith remembers. *"An advanced machine, even by today's standards. It has its own track-changing system."*

She peeks out the window. "There," she points. "That way."

He leans back, pulling the monstrous smoke-colored lever, and the gothic monster turns. The cabin rumbles. They go through the corner of a brick house.

"Oops," says Lester. "Still getting used to it."

"Better get us outta here, Les," Yoshi says. "That guy's gonna want to kill us when he sees what you did to his house." They laugh and high-five.

Lilith turns back from the window to shoot the boys an approving glance. "You guys are OK," she says.

The locomotive turns left on the main street, toward the city exit.

Lilith looks at Yoshi's disfigured face and bloody clothes. His face is pale. Dark bags hang under his sunken weary eyes. "He really *is* going to die if he doesn't get help," she tells Lester.

"We're all gonna die," says Lester, keeping his eyes on the road.

"Nate told me he found you in a hospital. Did you pick up anything about wounds?"

"It wasn't that kind of hospital."

"Whatever," says Lilith as she stands up. "Take care of your friend. I'm driving."

She balances her way to the machinist seat, holding on to the leather straps on the roof, and switches place with Lester. She sits down and grabs the cold levers, pulling on them slightly to see what they do. The cabin rocks and sways as the locomotive crashes the shells of abandoned cars in the street, blowing them away like toys.

They take the ramp out of Leatelranch. The highway is plagued by the dead, roaming out in the light of dawn. It's a procession. An exodus. The entire population of Leatelranch, anyone with a head still attached to their necks, seems to be fleeing, leaving town and taking the highway.

"We're not the only ones going to the city," says Lester.

"They're fleeing," says Lilith. "Everyone's finally dead. We're the last ones."

"That zombie-whisperer *fuck* has won."

"Not yet," says Lilith. "Look."

The locomotive is running a corridor between two lines of fresh stone crypts. The highway has become an endless, sprawling necropolis. Headed bodies, hard and mummified, strain under the weight of large pieces of junk and steel and concrete, working together to build, build, build around themselves. Rabid corpses fight for parts and destroy one another in efforts to seize victims' crypts. Skeletons pull bones from other skeletons. Groups close in on the smallest skeletons, as helpless now as when they died, and break them apart, sharing the loot.

"Does this mean we'll beat him?" asks Lester. "They're planning long term, it seems."

"Maybe," Lilith says. "Let's not celebrate just yet."

As they speed through the gruesome construction zone, the corpses seem to tense, like they're sensing the group's arrival, and they scatter to the sides of the road. The sea of corpses opens up for them. The behemoth zooms by, and soon they're the only ones on the highway.

"Well, that was easy," says Lilith.

Lester looks around. He balances as the cabin rumbles and sways, and he stretches toward a lid and opens it. Empty. He opens another lid. There's a white box, a first aid kit, old and dusty. He opens it.

Empty.

"Pass me the backpack," he says, turning to Lilith, "I left it below the seat."

She checks the backpack and pulls back in horror.

"There's a head in here."

"Yeah. Frankie."

Lilith raises her gaze and stares at Lester. "What."

"We found him. Countess—Long story."

She looks at him with pity. "You can't just grab any head and pretend—"

"It's him, lady! Don't you recognize him? You left him to die."

Lilith looks down again.

The bag starts to growl.

Lester and Yoshi look at each other. They turn to Lilith.

"He recognized you!"

Lilith stares at the head in terror.

"Take him out, see if you can make him talk. And see if you can find a piece of cloth or something to stop the bleeding!"

Lilith grabs the head by its thin corpse hair and pulls it out. She extends her arm to keep it as far away from her as possible and looks inside the backpack again.

She tosses Lester a roll of toilet paper. "See what you can do with this."

Lester catches the roll and looks up, moving his head closer to the window. A low hum, almost imperceptible, can be heard in the distance.

"What's that?"

"What?" Lilith asks.

"That sound."

"I don't hear anything."

"Nah. It can't be."

The cabin falls silent as Lester works to stops Yoshi's bleeding, and Lilith concentrates on steering the Citizen down the dark highway.

Suddenly, over the sound of the Citizen's giant engine, they hear a thundering rumble. A helicopter hovers above them.

Lester looks through the narrow windows on the side of the cabin to find them under siege. Tanks are flanking them. Fighter pilots zoom above them, dropping bombs, but the trusty steel locomotive pushes through. An unsteady helicopter shoots a missile and misses. Tanks try to ram them from both sides, but they also move erratically and miss. One of them wanders into the path of a missile from a helicopter that whooshes past, intercepting it before it can damage the iron giant.

Lester looks up at the ash-colored roof. Not a scratch. He knocks his fist against the wall of the cabin, and it feels like hitting a submarine. Solid. Eternal.

"This thing is amazing," he says.

Lilith looks around, checking for damage, and seems as amazed as he is.

Yoshi leans against a wall with his eyes closed. He smiles.

They take another blow. It rocks the locomotive harder this time.

Lilith shakes it off. She grabs the head by the hair and talks to it. "Doyle!" she pleads.

"Who's Doyle?" Yoshi asks.

"Doyle," she says to the head, "we're still alive, you're not alone here. We need your help."

"You *know* that fucker?"

Frankie's head stares at Lilith.

"You don't want us dead," she says. "Not yet. There's something I need to tell you. Something about that night."

The head is mute.

Lilith cries. "I'm sorry!"

The steel giant takes another hit, and the cabin rumbles.

The head moves. Its jaw opens slowly.

The boys look at each other wide-eyed.

"Fuck—you—Lilith," the head says.

"Well. He *clearly* doesn't want to talk to *you*," says Lester, looking at the head. "Let's turn here and go live somewhere else, what do you say?"

"There's still time to abandon *us*, too, if you want," says Yoshi.

"Don't be a dick," Lester mumbles.

"I'm sorry about your friend," Lilith says to them both. "I'm sorry, Frankie," she says to the head. "I had to do it."

The boys look at each other. "We know."

"And I'm sorry about you, too, Doyle," she says. "I'm sorry I left you guys behind. I've been selfish and shitty, and maybe I deserved to be the one left behind."

The tanks and helicopters suddenly turn away. They move off in the direction of the city.

"He called them off?" Lester asks, suspicious.

"He's probably raising some hell, wherever he is," Yoshi says, and it's not entirely clear if it's a response to Lester or if he's begun hallucinating.

The tanks speed off to the side of the road, leaving the locomotive alone on the highway once again. For a while, the only sound they hear is the grumble of the machine cutting through the pavement. Until it is joined by that now-familiar low growl, starting from a distance and growing louder as they speed forward.

"Oh-oh," says Lester.

Soon, Lilith can see them in the distance, getting closer and closer.

"Shit," says Lilith, narrowing her eyes. "These ones still have their heads on."

Lester turns to her. He's worried. "They're the real ones."

Lilith nods in agreement. "You guys have worked some shit out," she concedes, ready to welcome a little help trying to figure out the next move. "Should we ... run over them?"

"Get off the highway," says Lester. "You saw what they did to that scorpion thing. I doubt this machine can heal itself."

Lilith looks around for an exit. Her hands tremble. They are barreling toward the ghouls at a maddening speed.

"Yes," she says, gripping the levers, "I guess the smart thing *would* be to turn away."

She looks up. She reaches for the horn pull cord and hangs from it with the weight of her whole body.

Toot! Toot!

The locomotive's whistle screams at the top of its mechanical lungs, piercing the sky.

Yoshi and Lester turn around. "Come on, fuckers!"

The ghouls move over to the sides, parting to let the beast pass between them.

"Yeah!" Lilith cheers.

But the ghouls turn back and jump onto the iron beast, clinging to it and piling onto each other like cockroaches, and begin crawling up toward the cabin.

Lilith strides toward Lester. She pulls back her hand as far back as she can and slaps him.

"Fuck!" he says. "What's that for?"

"Dunno," says Lilith. "Just trying things that don't make any sense."

The boy loses balance and falls backward, hitting some buttons on the panel. The back of the locomotive drops, and they hear the iron wheels rolling away from them, released from the chassis. A mechanism activates at the front. The locomotive sways from side to side, fending off dead bodies like a dog drying its coat. A second, bigger front steel pilot comes out from the inside of the machine, mowing down ghouls and carpeting the highway with a dry greenish paste.

As it sways, it barely misses hitting a sign that says NEW SOUTHPORT: NEXT EXIT.

81

THE IRON WHEELS OF THE CITIZEN SAW INTO THE TENDER highway, leaving a wake of broken asphalt. Up ahead, the dawn sky glows fiery orange above the New Southport skyline.

Lester finishes bandaging Yoshi's neck and turns to Lilith. "Are you sure you can get this guy Doyle to stop all this?"

Lilith looks straight ahead, pushing and pulling levers, trying to keep the beast steady. Her eyes burn with the reflection of the orange cloud getting closer and closer. She opens her trembling mouth, about to speak, and closes it shut.

"That's reassuring," Lester says. "And how do we find this fucker?"

Lilith's voice comes to him heavy and blunt. "He'll come to us."

She hears a faint sigh, a feverish *ugh*, and turns around to see Yoshi standing up. He looks weak and pale. He grabs hold of two of the leather straps hanging from the cabin's roof and looks ahead.

"Yoshi!" Lester yells. "Don't get up!"

Yoshi raises his arm and points forward. "I ... have an idea where he might be ..."

Straight ahead, over the city, a swarm of helicopters and jets are firing everything they've got down to a single spot behind the buildings, raising a cloud of smoke.

Lilith lets go of the right lever and unzips the backpack. She grabs Frankie's head by the hair and looks him in the eye.

"Doyle," she says, "I don't know if you're listening. But we know it's you. We know what you did." She looks at the boys. They're staring at her, confused. "And we're coming for you."

Yoshi looks at the helicopters swarming toward the city, at the jet fighters zipping by, all flying together toward the epicenter of the chaos. "Uh ... Is it really important that we go *there*? Right to the middle of it?"

Lilith stares at Frankie's face, gazing deep into its milky dead eyes, looking for a sign that the message went through. His pupils just stare at her, lifeless. "Yes," she says. "I have to be sure."

Lester looks at the orange cloud of smoke. "But we're gonna die if we go there!"

"Yes," Lilith says. "Yes, we are. And that's why it's important we do this first."

Lester's face hardens.

"If we don't stop him," Yoshi mutters, "he'll get to us, even after we're dead. If he's the last one to die, we all become dogs."

Lester turns around. Yoshi stares at her, too. The sound of gunfire in the distance is getting closer.

"Take the exit!" Lester yells, looking ahead.

Still holding on to Frankie's head, Lilith pulls one of the levers, and the mammoth locomotive steers to the right, taking the exit to New Southport.

They zoom through a dark street. The tall buildings muffle the sounds of the battle. Above them, around them, dead faces gaze at them from behind every dark window.

Entire blocks populated by their previous inhabitants, still haunting the city with their decrepit corpses. Ghouls rot in their suits with the uncanny, string puppet movements that only a dead body in motion can make. Mummified bodies walk in pairs pushing strollers silent as little graves. Naked skeletons wander aimlessly, rotten, insane. They all turn like spectators to watch the locomotive as it tears through the streets, zigzagging through empty shells of burnt cars. The locomotive is the single float in a parade of hair-raising speed, heading for the epicenter of an epic battle.

As they get closer, the scenery changes. Headed corpses are nowhere to be seen. Packs of headless ghouls break apart cars and bodies, collecting their bounty, kings of the streets. They come out from building doors and form like carefully orchestrated platoons.

Every torso turns to the locomotive.

"Oh oh," Lester says. "These ones are not ignoring us."

The headless ghouls bolt after them. They can run at unnatural speed. The pack in the front seems to outrun the locomotive, then slow down and chase it on both sides, like dogs to an oncoming car.

"Shit!" Lilith yells. "Shit!"

They flank the locomotive, closing in on them.

"OK," says Lilith, looking around for weapons. "Grab something."

The ghouls keep running forward. Ignoring the locomotive, they outrun it and head downtown.

"It's like the others are not even trying," says Lester. "Most of them were like, *watching TV*, just waiting to be called in."

"Maybe they're trying to minimize casualties," Yoshi jokes.

"I think that's exactly right," Lilith says. "That's what they're doing."

Lilith's face burns with anger. At the turn of a corner, the locomotive barely hits the glass window of a store too run-down to be recognizable. Lilith straightens it and makes it back to the center of the street, and gasps. The street in front of them is taken by men, all dead, among army tanks, police cars, national guard jeeps, all looking straight at them. Three tanks barricade the street in front of them. Their cannons seem to concentrate on the locomotive as it approaches them.

"Stop!" Lester yells, jumping on Lilith and pulling both levers to his chest.

"No!" yells Lilith at his side, fighting for the controls. "We're ramming them!"

Lester struggles. "Don't you think they expect that?"

"I don't give a shit what they expect."

"You're both insane," Lester says, letting go.

Blam. Three cannons blast their ammo at them, shaking the steel mammoth. Lilith's ears ring. She lets go of the levers and covers her ears, losing balance when the locomotive shimmies to the sides. She grabs the levers again and pulls them back and forth, randomly, clenching her teeth. The projectiles fly by them with a piercing whistle.

The Citizen's V-shaped pilot wedges between two huge tanks and stops cold, sending Lilith flying forward against the painful levers. Yoshi goes flying and falls on Lester, next to her.

"You OK?" She asks them, trying to stand up.

Lester nods. Yoshi grabs his head in pain. Only a handful of pins remain loosely attached to it. "Hmpfh."

Lilith stands on her feet, still disoriented. She checks her chest and belly. She looks down and sighs, relieved. "I'm OK."

The shuffling of running bodies outside makes Lester take a peek through the small window. "They're coming!" He says. "Go! Go!"

Lilith moves the levers around, and the beast responds. *It's still alive!* With a roar of twisted metal, the locomotive charges on, pushing the tanks apart, making way until they're out of the way, and, as it gains speed again, it hits the cars and jeeps like they're made of paper.

"Yes!"

"Are we dead?" Yoshi asks.

"No, we're not," says Lilith, looking at Lester, like it's an order. "None of us."

"Don't look at me," he says. "I'm fine."

She looks straight ahead and pushes the rusty levers until they can't go any further.

Lester grabs his head, still dizzy from the bump. "They missed? How did they miss?"

Yoshi doesn't open his eyes to talk. He seems to be in a tremendous amount of pain. "You mean *why* did they miss."

Up ahead, the street is blocked again. A formation of soldiers faces away from them, all shooting their weapons at something ahead. Lilith squints, trying to make out what it is. Behind the soldiers, the street seems to go up, like a ramp, or like a mountain. It stands tall between two buildings. It seems to move, to buzz, like a wave of dead limbs that's about to crash against them.

"What *is* that?"

The soldiers take up the whole street, and they shoot their machine guns and bazookas and grenades at the mountain, which moves and sizzles like an anthill. Above it, the swarm of helicopters circles erratically like a flock of drunk crows. They shoot a fiery rain of bullets on it. The mountain explodes with limbs and regroups, repairing itself, expanding, transforming in the air, dodging and stretching toward the attacks.

"Are they missing on purpose?" asks Lester.

"Yeah, why do they fly like that?" asks Lilith. "It's like they're on drugs."

"Look!" Yoshi says. "There! The guy flying that helicopter! Look at that face! It's like he's in a frenzy! Have you ever seen them like this?"

"They're getting worse," says Lilith. "They're decomposing."

"They're losing their minds," Yoshi says, rubbing his head, still in pain. "Now we're really alone. Is it depressing that I'm gonna miss them?"

Lester burns him with his gaze. "Yeah. We're sure gonna be alone *now*." He opens his eyes wide and grabs Lilith by the shoulder. "Turn! We're gonna hit them!"

Lilith pulls the left lever with all her strength, and the locomotive's steel wheels skid, turning the behemoth to the left.

"It's falling!" Lester yells. "It's falling!"

To the right, the giant anthill seems to melt, revealing a building beneath it. An avalanche of human limbs tumbles down to the street in a massive exodus, climbing down and taking the street like a giant ocean wave. As it crashes down, its tide turns, and it crosses the street, and crawls up the building opposite the first one until the new building disappears.

"That must be him," Lilith says. "Those are his *bodyguards*. He's moving from one building to the other."

"So luxurious," Yoshi says. "What a life."

Lester frowns. "OK, so let me get this straight. All the zombies in the world cannot get to him, but *we* will?"

The gunfire continues, and behind the ocean of dead bodies, Lilith sees the glimmer of the dead army's firearms. Limbs fly away, and the helicopters fire off more missiles, blowing bigger chunks away, but the moving parts reassemble after every shot, moving into position to absorb every loss. A helicopter stops firing and flies away, then is immediately replaced by another one that continues the attack.

As they get away from the action, Lilith focuses on the road. Up ahead, a swarm of headless ghouls runs toward them. She holds the levers steady, preparing to ram them. But the crowd gives way to the locomotive and runs around it, tearing each other's arms off as they run. As the locomotive clears the crowd, the ghouls take a hit from a helicopter missile, but its dwindling population keeps running until it dives into the ocean of limbs, making it bloat and grow.

"Anybody have a plan B?" Lester asks.

Lilith turns to the head again. "You can stop this, Doyle. I know you can."

The head just stares at her.

"Nice try," Yoshi snarls.

"Look, sonny," Lilith yells without even turning to him. "I know you think you're the shit, but believe me, you're just a bratty bitch."

She tries again.

"Listen to me!" she yells at Frankie's head, trying to ignore the horrible feeling of its dry hair around the ears, and the weight of a real human head in her hands. "You are the Delegate! The cemetery caretaker took the mantle from you, and he was the last Delegate, and now he's dead, and that's what started this whole thing. And I think somehow you became the Delegate again. So it's up to you to stop it!"

The head's mouth opens, and like air from a deep cavern, a voice emerges.

"Why did you leave?" Doyle asks. "Why did you disappear that day?"

Horrified, she forces herself to react. "I—don't know," she says. "I wasn't thinking. It wasn't a decision. I just had to."

"You ... always ... do ... whatever your ... body tells you?" the head speaks.

She doesn't respond.

"Have you ... been keeping ... him alive?" The guttural voice sounds like an echo coming from a long hollow tube.

"What?"

" ... Tommy," the head says. "Have you ... been ... a good Delegate for him? Remember him often, do you? You are his Delegate, too, you know. We all are."

Lilith's mind races. "No. What?"

The head just stares blankly at nothing.

"You can stop all this!" she pleads. "Please, for the love of god, stop!"

The head's eyes turn and focus on her.

"Come close," it says, "and I'll kill you."

Lilith's eyes swell. Horrified, she pulls the head away from her, just as its mouth starts to open again.

"Lilith," a familiar voice says, and she quickly thinks of Nathan. The echo multiplies and becomes a plural cry. "We are waiting for you."

She looks up at the boys, and the three of them stare at each other in horror.

"Well, thank god we tried *that*," says Lester.

Lilith's body shakes with anger. Her cheeks burn. She's suddenly very much aware that she's holding a talking putrified head, and that she's trapped in an iron cage, in a dead world, and that she has nowhere to run. Her arms tremble, Frankie's head wobbles, and a scream bubbles up her throat.

"Aargh!" she explodes.

She throws the head on the floor and enjoys watching it bounce and roll away.

"Hey!" Lester yells, struggling to stand up among the chaos. He balances his way through the cabin to fetch his friend's head. "Leave Frankie out of this!"

Lilith clenches her teeth. She grabs the polished blood-red wooden DELEGATVM box, stomps her way to the front of the cabin, and pulls open the heavy iron furnace door. She tosses the box inside, closes the door, and turns the handle to a satisfying stop.

"NO!" Lester yells, throwing the head into the backpack.

"What's the point?" she roars.

"Why?" Lester insists. "Wasn't that the key to this whole thing?"

Lilith is fuming.

"Answer me!" Lester insists. "What's the plan now?"

"I dunno," she says, strangely relieved. "Que sera, sera, kid."

Lester stares at her, furious.

"Do you hear that?" Yoshi whimpers, fixated on the war zone around them.

Lilith waits for her heartbeat to stop drumming in her ears. Yes, she can notice something. Yes, especially now, growing louder.

Screaming.

"I thought we were the last ones?" Lester asks, glowing with hope, and he hurries to one of the narrow windows.

The ground shakes. Something is moving toward them along the side street. Something huge. Lilith and the boys freeze, staring at each other, and the quaking stops.

"What the—"

The ground shakes again. And again. And again. It shakes in deep intervals as if something massive were steadily plodding along, towering over the fires, crushing cars in its wake.

The tremors get stronger. Deeper. Closer.

Whatever it is, it's coming from just around the corner. The screaming doesn't stop. A constant shriek pierces Lilith's ears.

As the locomotive zips through the intersection, Lester's jaw drops, and his gaze travels slowly upward.

"Fuuuuuuuuuck," he says, his voice now muffled by all the screaming. "Not again."

Lilith turns around. A giant, a monster, a mesh of faces and bodies packed like sardines, a high-as-a-building leg comes out from behind a building, whistling a thousand screams as it soars.

"Oh," she says. "They have toys, too."

"Yes," Lester says. "We've met before."

Yoshi tries to look up, but he's too weak.

The monster approaches the ocean of corpses climbing the building. Its mushy, darkened extremity breaks off into a giant open hand. Its fingers sink into the hive and close into a fist. It pulls back, tearing away the mesh covering the building, its skin whistling with a thousand open-mouthed faces.

Lilith turns the locomotive toward it.

"What are you doing?" Lester asks, covering his ears.

"You'll see."

"Are you crazy?!"

As they approach the giant, it turns its head toward them. It raises one leg, preparing to crush them. The shrieking is deafening.

"Go back!" Yoshi yells.

The monster's foot looms over them, about to fall like a hammer.

"Oh shit!" Lester yells. "Jump! Get out!"

Lilith grabs him by the shoulder, without taking her eyes away from the incoming rotten faces grinning at her from the sole of the monster's foot. "No," she says.

"No what?" Lester tries to break loose.

"They won't kill us."

The monster's foot hovers right over them.

The locomotive speeds off, and the monster steps on the street behind them, missing them. The stomp makes the ground shake, and the locomotive rocks wildly from side to side.

Lester jumps to grab the levers. "What happened? Why didn't it kill us?"

While the locomotive continues to twist out of control, the giant resumes its heavy steps toward the war zone, away from them.

"They want us alive."

Yoshi seems to wake up. "*Us?*"

The heavy tank of a locomotive moves erratically through the street, zigzagging and shimmying.

With a boom, a missile hits them, throwing them against the hot metal floor. Smoke spills out of every crevice into the cabin, making it nearly impossible to breathe.

The locomotive starts to go down an incline. They're entering some sort of tunnel.

Lilith coughs and looks ahead. Her eyes widen in panic.

"Hang on to something!"

82

___

The black blotch on the wall bloats and contracts like a sick dying heart. Around it, a cluster of blotches scatters around the endless granite wall.

Standing still in his hazmat suit, Holt stares at it, frozen.

"Hey, Ellen," he says, his voice muffled by the mask, "come take a look at this."

Ellen's boots squeak on the floor. Her steps echo in the hollow chamber. She takes off her helmet and looks at the blotches, breathing heavily under her mask. She can see the panic in his eyes.

"Relax," she says. "It's safe."

Reluctantly, he turns back to the wall. "That's Sammy, ain't it?" he asks.

"And Lenny," she says. "And Mrs. Leuwen."

"It's eating away the wall."

"We'll be fine," she says, "for now."

He doesn't take his eyes off the wall. "You sure?"

"Michael's been playing around with that black stuff in his lab—"

"Michael?" he asks.

"He used to be a veterinarian," Ellen says. "He says—"

"A veterinarian?"

She throws a stone-cold look at him. "Yes. A veterinarian. Mrs. Leuwen was our last biologist. Getting picky now, Holt?"

He doesn't look convinced.

"Don't worry about it yet," she says. She tries to put her arm around his shoulders, but he's squeamish. She stops in mid-air and looks him in the eyes. He reluctantly accepts the hug.

"C'mon," she says. "They're having a toast for her."

They walk along the giant warehouse toward a superstore-like maze of shelves that reach high into the ceiling. They walk among canned food, bottled water, tools.

More people in yellow hazmat suits walk past them, carrying parts and tools, escorted by armed yellow people.

When they get to the medicine aisle, she stops to browse through the boxes. He waits for her as she climbs the aluminum shelf and reaches for a plastic bottle.

"Somebody sick?"

"Nothing serious," Ellen says, coming down.

They continue along the hall until they reach a double bullet-proof glass wall. Behind it, people are talking, laughing, toasting with food in their hands.

She takes off one thick rubber glove and presses her thumb against a reader. The glass door opens, she steps in, alone, and the door closes and seals behind her. The cabin buzzes with mechanical tests, and a light turns green. Another door opens, and she steps into the room to join the celebration in progress.

Holt repeats the same procedure behind her.

"Come sit!" a welcoming voice calls out to Ellen, offering her a mug.

She smiles politely. "In a second, guys."

She walks toward a hall lined with glass chambers on both sides, like a glass prison. People press their buttons and say hi to her through speakers.

"Come to the mess hall," she says, "there's some sort of party going on."

"Nah, thanks," says the woman in one chamber.

Ellen brings the pills to a one-person, transparent cell. She presses a button and talks to a mic. "Michael said to take these, just in case. I'm sorry, but I need to see you taking them."

She puts them in a glass drawer and closes it. The man inside presses a button, and the drawer opens. He looks up at her and smiles. He presses another button, and his electric voice runs through the corridor. "Thanks."

"You need some water?"

"Nah, I'm fine," he says, taking the pills. "Thanks, El."

She walks back to the mess hall. The small crowd makes room for her at the table.

"To Sammy."

"To Sammy!"

"She was one of the good ones."

Ellen raises her mug. "To humanity!" she says. "We'll carry on!"

"We'll carry on!" say all, hundreds of them, from each of their speakers in their cells along the corridor.

They drink. A pregnant silence takes over the room.

Holt looks at the faces around him.

"Michael," he says, "I'm worried about those blotches."

Michael looks nervous. He looks at Ellen. He stammers.

Other voices come from the hall cells, speaking electronically through their speakers.

"Are they getting worse?"

"Oh, god, there's no hiding anymore," one of the electric voices says.

"Oh, god," says another voice.

Ellen throws a look at Michael. He clears his throat.

"They're OK," he says, looking at her. "Spores aren't so bad yet. Maybe in a few years we should start worrying about them, but trust me, we can stay safe in here for a very long time."

"Michael," a crackling voice comes through the intercom, "for all we know we're the last remains of humanity, the last couple thousand humans on Earth, and you're saying there's a small chance we're in danger, and we *shouldn't worry?*"

Ellen looks around, gauging people's reactions. "We're fine," she adds. "Nothing can penetrate these walls. Nobody can come in unless we try to leave. We have food and supplies to last us forever. We have everything we need to go on for generations."

People around the table look more serious than before.

She hardens her expression to mimic them. "If you have a better idea on how to handle our own dead, I'm happy to hear it. But seeing as we need to burn our dead in here, this is the best possible scenario. Blotches will keep appearing. They will contain the dead remains. And we'll stay away from them."

An electric *click* announces one of the cell speakers. "You mean they'll *increase.*"

A moment of silence.

"But can't we throw them out somehow?" Another voice asks.

Michael clears his throat again. "No," he says. "There is no way to get rid of them. Unless you want to risk going outside to throw them out, which could draw them toward us."

"If that is the case," Ellen says defiantly, "you let me know." She looks around. "So I can shoot you."

Holt waits for someone to laugh. He fakes a loud chuckle. "You wouldn't dare shoot anybody. You're too afraid to make a noise."

Electronic laughs echo around the hall.

Ellen smiles and looks around. "Oh, yeah?"

"Yeah!" someone shouts.

She walks to the door and presses her thumb on the reader.

"Oh! She's gonna do it!" Holt shouts.

She steps outside of the secured glass structure and out into the warehouse. She can see them cheering and laughing behind the glass.

She pulls her gun to the thick gray wall. She turns to them.

Holt is smiling at her through the thick glass. She can see his mouth move. "She won't do it!"

She narrows her eyes. She grins.

"You won't do it," he mouths, defying her.

Ellen turns to the gray wall and prepares to gently squeeze the trigger.

Bang.

The shot echoes through the huge chamber.

Bang.

She looks over her shoulder. The guys aren't laughing anymore. They seem impressed. She turns to the wall and prepares to fire again.

Bang.

The wall explodes, and a massive black locomotive crashes inside, filling the air with dust. The wall caves in and closes behind it.

PART V

83

LESTER FOLLOWS YOSHI AND MICHAEL TOWARD THE CITIZEN. The white floodlights bounce on the glossy cement floor and make the tall vast hall look as bright as day. The body bag on his shoulder is heavy and kicks hard, almost throwing him off with every swing. In front of him, Yoshi is also struggling with his bag. Even though his bag is smaller, lighter, and only has single limbs, it's rubbing against the scars on his neck and shoulders, and Yoshi can't hide signs of discomfort.

Michael reaches the locomotive and opens a big hatch on its side. He unzips his bag and dumps the wriggling parts into it.

He steps aside. Yoshi painfully unzips the top part of his bag, and he tries to dump it on the iron shelf. As he tries to roll it down his shoulder, his face turns into a grimace.

Lester drops his bag to the floor and sprints toward him.

"Let me, you moron," he says, picking up his bag.

He leans into the container, dropping the parts with a thump that echoes all through the warehouse.

"Thanks," Yoshi mutters.

Michael locks the hatch. "All done!"

They turn around and start to walk back to the cells.

"A locomotive whose furnace doubles as a built-in crematorium," Michael says, rubbing his hands. "You can't make this shit up."

"If you think that's weird, you should visit Leatelranch someday."

"Maybe," says Michael with his bulletproof smile. "Someday."

Lester looks again at Yoshi's scars. They're healed, but noticeable. A scar runs from his mouth up through his cheek up to his scarred ear, like a smile.

"Still hurts, huh?"

Yoshi turns to him. "What?"

"Still hurts?"

"Nah," Yoshi lies, looking away.

Michael hugs the boys and jams his head between them. "So," he says, "are you in on the pool? Think today's the big day?"

"We're not in the pool," says Lester.

Michael smiles. "Well, I am. And I'm betting it's today."

"Maybe," says Yoshi. He looks at Lester and signals him to wait.

They slow down and wait until Michael walks past them.

"This is it," Yoshi says to Lester. "We should have enough fuel to get back out there."

"Cut it out!"

"Pussy."

"You're gonna get us all killed!"

Yoshi grabs Lester by his shoulder and looks him in the eye. "Don't you want to put Frankie together?"

"Not anymore."

"That fucker's got his body."

Lester tries to break free. "It's useless. He's gone. You know he won't even talk to us."

"He will if we put him together!"

"Why would he?"

"I don't know! But isn't it worth trying?"

"And what about Lilith?" Lester asks.

"Let's ask her to join," says Yoshi.

"Very funny, moron. I'm serious. Can we at least discuss this when she's able to come?"

He speeds off and catches Michael.

"Michael."

"Yes?"

Lester points back to the locomotive. "You ... heard that back there, right?"

"Heard what?"

"Those scratching noises."

Michael's bulletproof smile remains.

"Behind the wall," Lester says.

Michael doesn't even blink. "Yeah."

"They're breaking through," Lester says.

"Probably," Michael says, his teeth whiter than they have any right to be after living so many years underground.

"You don't seem worried," Lester says. "We need to move."

"Nah," Michael says. "Impossible. They won't get to us here."

"We should probably at least scout—"

"And in any case," Michael says, stopping him, "this is the safest place on Earth. If they indeed find a way," he says, without blinking, "then that's it."

He turns to the door and places his finger on the reader. He looks at the woman on the other side of the triple glass.

"Hi, Marion," he says.

The woman smiles at him and presses her finger. "Morning, Lester."

The door opens with a *whoosh*.

"So, we agree!" Lester says. "We need a new place. With no biological stuff at all. Maybe underground caves. With the spores everywhere, we need a place where nothing is alive. I've thought about it. Just inert matter. Think granite, cement, maybe a factory?"

"Like a cemetery," Michael jokes.

They reach another door.

"I'm serious," Lester says. "Same goes for electricity, and all the luxuries we have. Lights, security, water pumps, heating, music. Soon it might go away. If the zombie whisperer dies, even of old age, who knows if whatever's powering this part of the city doesn't die with him—"

Michael turns to him and lowers his head, looming over Lester.

"You mean to say you're sorry that you put them on alert when you crashed in here with your locomotive, and now you've doomed us all?" he says.

A shout comes bouncing off the hall. "Michael! Michael!"

McKenzie comes running, breathless, and leans on Michael, trying to catch his breath.

"What happened?" Michael asks.

McKenzie is white as a ghost. "It's Lilith."

Michael keeps his smile. "Don't panic. Let's go."

He strolls calmly toward the sleeping quarters. McKenzie leans over and puts his hands on his knees, still trying to slow his breathing.

"What's the matter?" Yoshi asks him.

McKenzie looks up at him. "You know, at her age ..."

Lester follows Michael into the halls. They run through the white-lit corridor surrounded by the glass cells on both sides. People watch them with worried faces as they go.

One of the intercoms buzzes, "Is everything OK?"

"It's Lilith," Michael says with all the calm in the world, keeping his pace.

They turn the corner, reaching an identical corridor with identical multiple glass cells.

They knock on the thick glass door of Lilith's cell, and Lester looks at the floor. There's blood. She's in pain. She stretches up, presses the button, and the door opens.

Michael enters and kneels in front of her.

"I see you started without me!" he jokes. Lilith responds with a shriek of pain.

A loud rumble comes from behind them, where they left Yoshi. A massive wall crumbles and falls down.

"Shit!" says Lester, looking back. He bolts, running back through the halls as fast as he can.

A piercing cry fills the room. Michael smiles, relieved, and holds the baby up for Lilith to see.

"Have you thought of a name yet?"

84

Lester finds the Citizen lying dead on its side on an empty street, a stranded iron whale at the end of a trail of cracked pavement. Around it, nothing but rubble and the faint whisper of the wind blowing in his ears. The street is a war zone. Buildings are torn apart. Rubble makes the streets as bleak as the sky above. Around him, sick gray vegetation has taken over the empty carcasses of buildings, twisting around their holes and crevices.

Up ahead, ghoulish white figures march away. Their bare backs are white as chalk. They seem to walk and crawl and run as hard as their mangled bodies allow, following a high-pitched whistle coming from afar. Behind them, a lone figure hides and follows them from a distance.

Yoshi!

Lester follows him. As he gets closer, the piercing whistle grows louder and louder. He looks up. Large speakers located atop the buildings on both sides of the street are emitting the shriek.

The Slayers' old comm system.

He runs to Yoshi, kneeling behind a large piece of debris, and taps his shoulder. Yoshi turns in silent panic, and suddenly his deformed face looks glad.

"You came," he whispers.

"Of course, man."

They sprint toward another big block of debris closer to the marching ghouls and crouch behind it, leaning on a half-demolished wall covered in baby-blue wallpaper with dancing clowns, and part of a window frame.

The shriek from the speakers gets louder. Yoshi covers his scarred ear, trying to avoid the deafening pitch, and grabs Lester's arm. In pain, he silently points to a mountain of rubble leading up to a high-rise building's roof.

Lester nods and follows Yoshi as he takes off. They climb through the rubble carefully to avoid drawing any attention. Big chunks of concrete, brick, and steel bars roll down as they step on them, but the high-pitch noise covers it all.

The top of the building is not a rooftop—below the dust and the rubble, there's carpet. This used to be an apartment.

He follows Yoshi toward a low edge leading to the turmoil. It has the same dancing-clowns wallpaper as before. A massive explosion takes him out of his thoughts.

What was that?

Lester looks down below. On the street, war is raging between hundreds or thousands of ghouls. Destroyed, maimed, the headless dog-ghouls fight to their last bone against careful organized dead. Others, decrepit but still sporting a cool head, also seem enraged beyond reason. They throw themselves at fights, teeth first, like rabid dogs hell-bent on destroying everything, following not instinct but insanity.

Yoshi pats his shoulder and points just below them. A group of headless ghouls are separated from the fight by an L-shaped wall, hidden, waiting, a reserve army.

"What?" Lester whispers.

"Look!" Yoshi says.

The dust paints the whole street a dry white. He narrows his eyes, struggling to give the scene definition. Among the dusty bodies in the dusty war zone, something finally stands out. A hint of turquoise. It's Frankie's hospital gown.

Yoshi unzips the backpack, and as it opens, a moan comes from inside. He takes out Frankie's head, his face a grimace, a roar, his mouth wide open for the first time in years, his fetid breath exiting as it tries to scream in a frantic reaction to the pitch.

In a rush, Lester uses the empty backpack to wrap his hand and covers Frankie's mouth. He makes the head face the riot on the street. It tries to bite him. He can feel the teeth springing shut through the backpack's thick fabric.

"Don't bite," he says to its ear. "Look! We found your body!"

The head continues to moan, muffled by his hand.

Yoshi checks for any change in the expression on Frankie's face.

"Nothing," he says to Lester.

"Am I pointing correctly?" Lester asks. "Is he *seeing* his body?"

Yoshi looks. "I think so."

Lester can still hear the vibrations of Frankie's airless breath on his hand.

"Shit."

He sets the head back on the floor and starts to unwrap the soft backpack from around his hand. "Now what?"

Yoshi looks down. "I guess we put him together." He looks again at the battle raging below in the street. Only blocks away, the human anthill that surrounds the zombie whisperer awaits, surrounded by fighting ghouls of every size and state of decay. The street is pure carnage.

"Really?" asks Lester. "We just get up there in the middle of all the ghouls, and assemble his body, and everything will be OK?"

Yoshi looks him in the eye. "Do you have a better idea? If we're gonna die, and we're gonna, then I'd rather spend eternity with our friend."

Lester nods. "But how do we get to him? He's surrounded by ghouls."

Lester looks around. The way to Frankie is impossible. But

just above him, a fallen building looks clear of zombies. Another fallen building leans on it. He knows they can make it.

"We need to get up there," Yoshi says, looking in the same direction.

"It's too close," says Lester.

"Again. Better plan?"

Lester starts walking toward the building. There's an opening in the base, like the mouth of a cave. The wind howls through it and blows on his face.

"Do you hear that?"

"Hear what?" asks Yoshi, turning his head, trying to hear with his mangled ear.

"Voices," Lester says.

Yoshi takes a step back. "I don't hear nothing."

Lester jumps on a big piece of concrete and examines the opening. It's a crooked apartment. Dusty furniture seems ready to fall on him.

He jumps to the apartment floor and lands on something soft. Carpet. A cloud of dust puffs around him as he tries to stand up.

He turns around. Yoshi looks scared. He stands at street level, examining the apartment.

"Are you coming?"

"You said you heard voices?"

"I don't know what I heard." He turns around and looks at the gray furniture. It's just an empty apartment. "There's no one here."

Yoshi shoots him a weary look of distrust. "Of course I'm coming."

85

LESTER CLIMBS ANOTHER STEP ON THE TILTED CARPETED FLOOR. He tries to keep his balance as he looks around the crooked apartment. It's dark, but the light coming from the demolished wall behind him shows black spots and greasy pools everywhere. On the walls. On the furniture. On a couch. On a cupboard. On a long TV table, and on the broken TV facing down on the floor in front of it. The whole place looks like the greasy ceiling of the hospital's kitchen. Up ahead, at the far end of the apartment, a thread of light comes through a door's keyhole. And next to it, a large painting still somehow hangs from the wall. In it, an old woman watches over the room. She seems to stare at him. Her face, cut out from a black background, shines with an unusual glow in the otherwise pale dusty room. There's something about that face that bugs him. And it hits him. It's the first new human face he's seen in years.

"So?" he yells down at Yoshi, and he can hear his own voice muffled by the apartment.

He can still see Yoshi below him on the rubble, the pale morning light shining on him, looking for something to climb on to boost himself into the angled apartment. He stands on a large chunk of debris and finally jumps in, but immediately slips and starts to fall back down.

Lester climbs down with firm careful steps. He holds on to a door frame.

"Grab my leg."

Yoshi's hand tightens around Lester's ankle, and he climbs his friend's body until he manages to get up next to him.

"Thanks," he says, catching his breath and trying to regain his balance. Lester can see the worry in his eyes as he scans the apartment.

"Careful with the sticky black stuff," Lester says. "Actually, careful with everything. It looks really loose."

"Yeah, yeah. Look at this. An actual apartment. A couch!"

Lester smiles. "Yes. And that over there on the floor is a huge TV."

"People really lived like kings," Yoshi says.

"At least our glass cells were on a level."

Yoshi takes a step upward. "Is there even a way out of here?"

Lester looks up. "We should check that door."

"Great," says Yoshi, struggling to climb another step up.

"Stay here," Lester says, about to rest his hand on Yoshi's shoulder and remembering that it's a sore spot for him. "I'll check it out."

"Why?" Yoshi says. "We can both go."

Lester takes a couple of long strides and quickly passes Yoshi on his way to the door. "Sure," he says.

Behind him, he can hear Yoshi struggling. "I'm just ... gonna ..."

A strange crisp sound stuns him. It's coming from above. A small cymbal-banging monkey toy walks and bangs his cymbals across the floor.

"Shit!" yells Yoshi, falling and tumbling down.

Lester's heart beats fast. He looks down. Yoshi is leaning on the couch's thick armrest.

"You OK?" he asks him.

"Fuck," says Yoshi. "How does that thing still have batteries?"

Lester looks at the oily blackened toy. The toy turns its head and looks at him. "I don't think it's running on batteries."

The couch slides down, taking Yoshi by surprise. It drags him down and zigzags toward the hole where they came in.

"Yoshi!" Lester yells.

Yoshi jumps to the side just in time, and the couch slides down and falls out of the hole.

"See?" Yoshi asks, getting back up. "You worry too much."

"Oh!" Lester yells. "You think!?"

The crashing cymbals are making Lester crazy.

Yoshi tries to gain his balance again. "Fuck, Les, calm down."

"No!" yells Lester. "Stop thinking this is a joke!"

"But it *is* a—"

The curtain reaches for him and wraps around his ankle, pulling him down to the floor.

"Oh, good," Yoshi says, laughing, "remember these?"

Lester climbs down to him and grabs his hand. He tries to pull him up. "Stop—laughing!"

Yoshi chuckles. "But it's all just too much—"

The curtain springs toward Lester, too, a ghost with a hundred sleeves. It wraps around him and whispers little screams in his ear. They're saying, *We've got you now*.

Lester pulls harder. The curtain retreats and clings to Yoshi, tightening around his body.

Lester tries to pull it to the side. "Don't breathe!" he says to Yoshi. "Don't get any of that shit in your mouth!"

Yoshi's voice, coming from beneath the thick cloth shaped like his face, is a drowned chuckle.

Lester manages to pull the cloth to the side, revealing Yoshi's face once again. He inhales. He's smiling.

"Help me, you moron!"

Yoshi laughs. "Now?" he asks. "Later? Until when?"

Lester manages to unwrap Yoshi and sends the drape kicking and screaming down the hole and out to the street.

Yoshi drops to the floor, laughing. Lester tries to get ahold of himself, but he can't help to throw a weak kick at his friend.

"Look at your face!" he yells. "This is not a joke! Haven't you learned anything?"

Yoshi just laughs. "Lighten up. *Things* are attacking us. Don't you get it? We're fucked. We're fucked anyhow."

Lester looks around. The apartment waits for them, still, silent. He looks at the door. The way toward it seems safe. Nothing is in the way. His gaze meets the old woman's in the painting again. With the wind, the woman appears to breathe.

"We're not fucked. We're gonna get Frankie back. And he'll get that zombie-whisperer fuck out, somehow."

Yoshi explodes in laughter.

"You know," says Lester, climbing up to the door, "I'm really getting tired of your bull—"

He feels a draft in the back of his neck. The curtain has flown back up, and it's dancing in the air next to him, raising the dust from the furniture as it flies by, uncovering the greasy black stuff that makes the furniture shine with a lively, greasy look.

The dust starts to settle, but the floating spots don't fall downward; instead, they seem attracted to each other. They form a shape. The spores stick to the black oily surface covering a chair, and the chair drops to the floor. It cracks, its legs swinging up in the air. The cloud of dust reaches the painting on the wall and sticks to it and pulls the face off the frame, and it joins the small tornado forming in the center of the living room.

A tingling. Light fixtures hanging askew from the hunched ceiling fall into the tornado as well. Lester can see Yoshi struggling to climb just below the moving cloud.

"Come on! Hurry!"

Yoshi crawls on all fours toward Lester.

"Hurry up! Come on!"

Out of the small tornado, a lively hateful face comes out and spins around, shining its electric lightbulb eyes at Lester. A sleeved arm reaches down for Yoshi and pokes him in the back, sinking in the flesh, pulling out green blood. Yoshi lets out a scream.

"You're almost here!" yells Lester. "Give me your hand!"

Yoshi looks up as the ghost's arm pulls up and gets ready to strike again. He stretches toward Lester. Lester reaches for him, and the image of Yoshi struggling to climb is suddenly blocked by a face, that horrible oily grinning-old-woman face, hovering in front of him.

The painting bends. It smiles.

Lester finds the maddening cymbals. He grabs the monkey and throws it at the ghost's arm, knocking it off. The chair leg flies down to the street down below.

Yoshi crawls toward him. They lock hands, and Lester pulls him up.

They're close to the door now. Lester stretches his arm toward it and finds the handle. Pulling it down is enough for the heavy door to open. Sunlight floods the room as the door hangs from the crooked wall.

His arm burns as he swings Yoshi toward the opening. Yoshi tries to grab the doorframe, but he misses. Lester makes a final thrust and swings him up again. He knows he won't be able to do it a third time. When Yoshi gets ahold of the doorframe and climbs up, lending him a hand, he sighs, relieved.

86

From the first floor of the destroyed building, Lester leans over the jagged ledge and looks below.

"Careful," Yoshi says behind him. "This looks like it's gonna crumble any minute."

Next to the sidewalk where ghouls roam are the remains of a building with no roof and partially destroyed walls. Inside, the floor seems to move. Frankie's little armless body, a lump of pale skin covered in a faint turquoise gown, wriggles below him. His name tag is still attached, old and faded. It's chained to other headless bodies, some even without their legs, squiggling and flapping, reminding Lester of the hospital's nursery, where all the babies were put on display.

Yoshi takes the moaning head out of the backpack and hands it to him. Lester takes it with both hands and reaches down, trying to connect the head to the frantic aimless body.

Yoshi tightens his grip on his ankles, and he stretches further, hanging down past the destroyed roof. The room stinks of sweat and decay, like food left out to rot. Down below, he can see the dry flesh in the severed neck.

"Can you reach?" Yoshi whispers from above.

"Just—almost—no."

Yoshi's hands spring open, letting go of his ankles, and Lester falls to the ground below, landing on a scraping pile of concrete rubble. As he feels his burning back starting to bleed, the backpack starts to moan, louder and louder.

"Ha," whispers Yoshi from above. The scar running along on his face makes it look like he's smiling wide. Or is he actually grinning, the bastard?

Lester clenches his jaw.

"Uh-oh," says Yoshi from above, looking out on the street.

Lester freezes. "What?"

"They heard you. Quick, try to free him before his moaning gets any louder."

Lester stands up and checks Frankie's rusty old chains. He pulls, trying to break them, but they won't budge. The body starts to move like it's waking up from a deep slumber. The moaning in the backpack gets louder.

"Oh, fuck," says Yoshi. Lester looks up at him. He's looking around. He seems impressed. Amused.

Lester opens the backpack and pulls out the head. He looks around the rubble on the ground and finds a piece of cement with a steel construction bar coming out of it. He smashes it against another piece, freeing the iron bar, and impales the head with it. He feels the iron penetrating the dry, hardened flesh around the neck, and hitting bone. He lifts his arms and sinks it into the body's truncated neck. As he lowers Frankie's small head to his body, its humming gets quieter. Its green eyes, still wide open, seem to focus on him. And, when it finally sits on top of his little torso, it becomes almost silent.

"They're still coming," Yoshi's voice comes from above.

Lester looks at Frankie in the eyes. "Frankie?"

The face remains stiff. It locks his eyes on Lester, idly, defiantly, still a stranger.

"I told you," Yoshi whispers. "We're fucked. Fucked and out in the open. I told you."

Lester looks around him. There's another steel bar protruding from one of the pieces of rubble. He smashes the piece, freeing the iron bar, and takes out Frankie's arm from the backpack. He nails it to the torso from the side.

The hum lowers even more. The one-armed ghoul looks at Yoshi. Something in his pupils changed. He's calming down.

"It's working!" he whispers to Yoshi.

Yoshi crawls down. He lands on his hands and feet on the loose pieces of rubble with an *ouch*, and trudges toward Lester and Frankie.

"Frankie," he whispers, "are you still in there?"

The eyes scan him, moving vividly for the first time.

"We're still missing one arm," Yoshi whispers, examining Frankie's eyes.

"Fuck it," Lester whispers. He looks at the ghouls chained together to Frankie. Half a dozen headless adults rock back and forth idly. They've all had their limbs removed. Lester looks at the last one in the chain. A thin dry mummy-like arm hangs from her shoulders, still holding to a small rusty useless ax.

"Don't make a sound," whispers Yoshi, looking through a small hole in the nearly destroyed wall.

"Are they coming?"

"Not anymore. But they're still around."

Lester clenches his face in disgust. He grabs the girl's hand, grabs her forearm, and places his foot on her chest. With a firm yank, he tries to pull the arm off. The ghoul wriggles and protests. The other ghouls seem to wake up, shuffling their feet loudly on the rubble. Yoshi can only think of the rubbery feeling of the girl's hand.

"Shit."

He pulls again, harder. He hears the sound of a dry tree branch cracking in two. The arm comes off with a puff of dust.

He walks by the wriggling torsos and hands the arm to Yoshi. He looks for another piece of iron bar.

"There," Yoshi whispers, pointing at another lump of rubble.

Lester grabs it, sinks it in Frankie's shoulder, and attaches the arm.

A loud groan stuns him. Frankie pushes him away with his own arm, and flaps and flails with an open hand at them. His ankles and arm rattle the chains tying him to the other ghouls, and the metallic clanking noise fills the room. On the other side of the wall, ghouls start growling and groaning.

Lester and Yoshi look at each other with wide eyes as the shuffling steps from outside move closer. They peek through the hole. Out on the street, the headless ghouls seem to be alert, aware of them.

"Frankie," says Lester. "You have to help us."

Frankie's pupils seem lost, scanning Lester's eyes and the surrounding roofless room.

"It's not working," says Yoshi, looking out on the street. "We should get out of here."

More growls come from above. Ghouls are marauding the floor above them, looking for them, trudging on the ledge they just came down from.

One of them steps on the ledge and slips. The cement crumbles under it, cracking, dissolving the whole floor, and, like an avalanche, half a dozen headless bodies fall down to the room in a cloud of dust.

"Ha-ha," Lester chuckles nervously, and now even he cannot help but smile. "No escape now. Frankie, I guess you're not gonna help us after all, right?" He chuckles again. His eyes are wet with tears. Lester sees the fallen ghouls starting to get up and assemble around Yoshi, who turns to him.

"How do we get out of this one?" he asks.

And it moves. The parts Lester and Yoshi have gathered and carried and cared for finally spasm and shiver. Their friend. Their last hope. Their chance to end this. Frankie, alive, stretches his arm toward Lester.

"Frankie!" Lester yells, ecstatic, relieved, and Yoshi joins him with a loud cheer behind him.

But Frankie's tiny fingers tighten around Lester's throat.

Lester smiles, nervous. "Hah," he manages to let out.

Among the growls, he can hear Yoshi's voice. "No! No!"

The ghouls surround Lester, ready to claw their way into his chest. He kicks the first of them away and looks again at Yoshi, who is also surrounded. The ghouls poke their arms and hands into him. Yoshi seems to be trying to defend himself, deflecting the many arms coming at him, but more arms find their way inside.

Lester feels hands poking at him, fingers reaching for his skin. It tickles.

"Stop—haha—stop."

He kicks another torso away, but two hands grab him by the forearms from each side. With a jerking motion, he sets himself loose. He avoids the ghouls' thousand fingers and tries to move toward Yoshi, who is buried under a huddle of corpses. Looking down on his own chest, Lester finds mangled, bloody clothes. Stripes of flesh come out of him.

"Ha-ha," he chuckles.

Yoshi's arm shoots up from inside the huddle. "Help!"

Lester holds his fleshy wounds and makes his way toward Yoshi. A cough, or laughter, bubbles up his throat.

His bloody teeth open in a hungry smile as he pounces on Yoshi. His hands turn into fists and bury inside the ghouls surrounding his friend, reaching Yoshi once, twice, many times in a repetition of suffocating punches to the stomach, chest, neck, and face.

"You maniac!" shouts Yoshi between heavy breaths. "What are you doing?"

"It's so fucked up!" Lester shouts, frantic, his heart pounding a thousand times a minute. "Isn't it?"

Like a whirlwind, his arms keep punching his friend, his nails shredding through Yoshi's flesh.

Yoshi's eye, buried in the mountain of ghouls, widens. Its pupil retreats in confusion.

Lester's hand sinks deep into Yoshi's mangled chest and keep tearing flesh apart. Shreds and pieces hang down as he reaches the bone, and he picks apart the innards of Yoshi's chest through his ribs.

Yoshi, dead, looks at him in terror.

Lester, panting, blood coming up his throat, shoulders heaving, scans Yoshi's eyes and savors them, rejoices in them, in looking at Death in the eye.

He turns around. A roomful of ghouls close in on him, and he bursts out in laughter. He bends down and grabs an iron bar. He stabs himself in the stomach. He feels the thrust, yet there is no pain. He pulls the bar out and stabs himself again in the chest, maniacally, pushing and circling until his hands freeze and his laughter fades away, turning into something completely different. His body stops heaving.

He turns to Frankie, who looks at him with a frightened gaze. Lester tilts his head to one side, and as if he were under a spell, Frankie's head falls to the side as well. Lester moves toward his hastily assembled old friend with calm unbreathing steps. He brings his face close to Frankie's crusty stinking head and whispers in his ear.

Frankie's eyes open wide.

* * *

SOMEWHERE NEARBY, Frankie's missing hand lifts its rotten index finger. A dog barks.

87

THE GERMAN SHEPHERD BARKS AT THE SEVERED HAND HANGING from a nail on the wall. It stretches its fingers like a star. Each bark booms around the vast luxurious room, making the thick golden drapes shrug in fear and the hundreds of severed fists bump against the wall they hang from.

The man steps on the thick carpet. His sick shaky arm stretches toward the severed hand and lifts a tired finger toward it, then stops in mid-air, frozen.

"They're ... g—gone?" he mumbles, confused, scared.

Around him, more hands start to move. Fists bloom into open hands. His tired eyes spring open. His pale face hardens. His thin silver hair rises on the back of his neck.

"Impossible," he babbles. "They're all gone?"

He shakes his head. His gaze dashes frantically around the room. The yellow light fixtures fly around like neon lines as his mind races. Paintings, glass chairs, blackened, buzzing windows, and hands, hands everywhere, open like spring flowers.

His trembling hand hovers toward the drapes, and clenching his teeth, he pulls them open. A swarm of black dead limbs swims on the other side, pasted together like a car crash, crawling like worms, swarming like a beehive, thick enough to block any light from outside.

He turns to a man's head hanging on the wall like a safari prize. It gazes at him with open eyes.

He sighs. He waves his hands in a secret sign and looks down, already regretting it.

The somber white of daylight starts to shine on his face. The buzzing hive opens up, like a tunnel clearing out. Far away, he can see a white dot. The sky. Limbs crawl away and open up until the bleak light of day blinds him. He covers his eyes with a shaky arm, and, getting accustomed to the light, he tries to focus on the world outside. He moves and peeks from different angles, trying to get a view of the street below, but from this window, the sky is all he can see.

He strides into the penthouse living room, past decorations and stolen treasures, and continues toward a heavy door. He plunges the knob with the weight of his whole body, pushing forward, but something squishy blocks the door from the other side. He paces between his dogs toward another head hanging on the gold-wallpapered wall and signals it.

He swings the door open as the horde behind is still scattering away like scared spiders. Next to the window, a ghoul sits on a chair, naked, and the horrible leathery skin of its back almost makes Doyle sick. It's leaning on a simple wooden table, its dry mouth open next to an old microphone, eyes vacant, staring out the blocked window. Its dry mouth is open, and from it comes an immortal whine, a breath without lungs, a death rattle.

The man signals the head atop the room wall, and as the living room window clears away like a flock of sparrows, light shines on the hollow-eyed ghoul's face sitting on the chair, the electric version of its whine coming back through the open window multiplied ten times by the speakers placed out on the street. The sound fills the room, and as Doyle struggles to scan the streets below for any signs of victory among the chaos, a figure emerges from the sky.

Before Doyle even sees it coming, the figure crashes through the window, squashing the singing corpse and dropping the microphone to the floor.

The speakers outside shriek and die off.

Doyle steps back in horror as the odd-looking figure stands up. Its blue jacket glitters as he fights the dead singer and tears him apart. Its two heads turn, looking up at Doyle, and smile. The one perched on the body's right shoulder looks beat-up, with a scar running along his cheek. The other one looks fresh. Plump. Recently departed.

With a whistle, a wave of limbs crashes on the two-headed teenager and pushes it out of the hole it created in the wall when it came crashing in. Doyle watches in horror as it disappears.

They haven't been this close in years.

An electric silence falls over the room. Doyle looks down at the street from the gaping hole in the penthouse window. A subtle idle hum comes from the speakers placed around the street, and the horde of headless ghouls seem to search, lost, for the master's voice.

A hand grabs the ledge in front of him, just inches from the front of his boot. Another one joins it. And then the faces. Those harrowing faces rise from the side of the building and enter the apartment.

Doyle steps back, speechless. His lips tremble, and his eyes swell and stare. He exhales a warm deep breath through his nose, his chest heaving. He can hear his heart beating.

Hearing an unusual grunt, he turns around. His headless security detail tilts to the side, curious, picking up on his nervousness. With a wave of his hand, a pack of dogs surround him.

The beehive around what's left of his window thins out, as if he released his tight grip on it.

"No," he says, losing control. "No."

Steps approach him from behind, and he turns around. He raises his hand to the headless group that he has relied on for his safety all these years. "Stay back."

The group stops. They look at his hand, trembling, shaking. They look back at him.

They take another step forward.

Doyle's entire body starts to tremble in fear. Cold sweat runs over his face. The heads hanging from every intersection of the city wake up and roar free, and a loud communal scream rises through the city like a wave.

He gazes in horror at the group trudging toward him. "Tch!" he says, pointing two fingers at them. He snaps his fingers. "Stop! Stop!" he says, trying to regain a dominant tone, but his voice falters.

And before he can send his dogs to the two-headed ghoul coming in through the broken window, before he can send his dogs to attack, his own headless bodyguards have their dead hands on him.

"What the?" he says, wriggling as his feet leave the floor.

The dogs, still loyal, forever loyal, attack and bite the ghouls as they carry their master toward the fresh gap in the living room wall. A scream rises in Doyle's throat as the two-headed ghoul moves out of the way to let his former allies pass by.

He closes his eyes while the wind rushes past his ears.

Doyle lands on a pile of limbs that, only moments ago, covered the building he's been calling home. As he slides down into the war zone below, as he tries to stop himself by clinging to the bones and undead muscles, he hears the approaching stampede. Down below, an out-of-control mob of headed ghouls enters the street and sprints among frozen headless ghouls, tearing apart the suddenly meek and docile bodies. With a roar, an epic war catches fire throughout the street, and the order in his ranks is taken over by chaos. Limbs are torn apart just below him, creating a widening hole in the pile he sits atop, waiting for him like a fiery hungry mouth.

"No," he repeats as he tumbles and slides down. He snaps his fingers. He hears an acknowledgment, a growl, and dogs begin jumping out the penthouse window and rushing to his rescue. They run down the hill of limbs and surround him, clenching their teeth on his clothes, pulling him up just before he hits the pavement.

The deafening sound of a jet flies by, and it carpet-bombs one of the streets. Hundreds of bodies blow away. More are set ablaze. The whirring of tanks closes in through a side street.

Doyle stands up and looks around him. The headless crowd is falling like dominos, and a tidal wave of rage and violence approaches him. Before he can react, strong arms and sharp fingers sink into his skin and flesh. From above, the twice-grinning two-headed ghoul in the blue jacket approaches faster than he's seen any ghoul move . It swings its bare hand right at his face, and a cold sharp pain tumbles through his body. Unable to move, unable to stop it, Doyle can only watch as it claws and punches and drives its nails into his insides, pulling out entrails and muscle and heart and blood. His head falls down with a *thud* against the floor, landing on its side, his open eyes now like an idle discarded camera filming the moment of his death. The mob kneels and keeps punishing him, squishing his heart with open fingers, munching on his lungs with cold sharp teeth.

He opens his mouth, whining and pleading for help. A dead black light washes over him, and he dies, and he sees, and he is, and he understands, and he remembers.

The uproar stops.

They stand up. His own family, his dogs, his friends, circle around him. They bow their torsos, and they whine, and they mourn him, and they welcome him.

They spread around. They start to walk away. Even headless, he recognizes all of them now, but one group is particularly familiar. He had met them in life. They are led by a male, and now Doyle knows everything about him, everything that happened and everything that is about to happen, and he recognizes in him the boy that he once knew in a dark and cold ceremony, and he sees him walking away, his black T-shirt with the white waves walking away, waking up from his spell and walking away, free, free to find Lilith.

88

LILITH'S EYES THROB. THE BLURRY BLACK-AND-WHITE MONITOR in her cell shows a gray shape, a person shape, lugging away pieces of rubble.

"Is it them?" a metallic voice asks through the intercom.

"I told you this would happen!" another metallic, altered voice shouts as Lilith squints her eyes. "I told you they'd come back for us! Now they know all our secrets!"

"Shut up!" Michael yells through the intercom. "We're OK. You all know how safe this is."

"We shouldn't have let them out," another voice says.

"We didn't *let them out*," Michael snarls. "They *escaped*."

Lilith looks again at the monitor. Between the inky blotches crawling the corners of the buzzy monitor feed, the figure's being methodic, patient. His arms swing and throw away each piece of granite from the mound left by the Citizen when it busted out of the compound. It's impossible to see behind the black that seems to radiate from the corners, but it's not hard to guess that he's close to making it inside.

"Mommy, mommy."

Lilith turns to the cell next door. Tommy looks at her with his puppy eyes.

"Joy Division," the boy says, pointing at the monitor, drawing waves in the air with his finger.

Lilith turns back to the monitor. The figure is wearing what looks like a faded black shirt. The lighter figure in its center is a set of lines. Waves. The ones she taught Tommy how to draw on his cell wall. That gray shape, that person shape, that corpse, lugging away the rubble in her small black-and-white monitor, that head that keeps bobbling like a floating balloon above his shoulders, is Nate.

Someone thumps on her thick cell glass. She steps back and gasps in horror.

"You think he'll make it?" a playful old woman asks, sitting calmly, looking at her own monitor, amused.

The gray figure on the screen turns its loose balloon head up to the camera. His face turns into a grin and pierces Lilith's eyes.

He seems to be saying something.

"Do we have audio for this thing?" Lilith asks, and someone turns it on.

The figure says, " ... We have all the time in the world."

Lilith's hand hovers toward her red door lock button.

"Oh, God," the old woman says. "Do you know him?"

Lilith turns to Tommy. He's silent. Scared. "Open up, please," she says, facing front.

Silence fills her cell. She can feel the people in the nearby cells staring at her.

"Are—are you sure?" the old woman says.

"Open up, please," Lilith repeats. She presses the button. Nothing happens.

She turns to the woman. "Open."

The woman looks at her with a motherly look. "Lil. Don't go," she says. "Just let it be."

"He'll never get through," says another voice through the intercom. "You're not worried, are you?"

Lilith can see the guy uttering the words a few cells ahead of her. "Even after clearing all that rubble, they'll never get inside the secure rooms."

"And even if it does," says an older voice, "we have plenty of traps in here. Tried and tested."

"I almost wish he tries," says a third voice.

Lilith looks up at the monitor. Nate looks up at the camera, finishes clearing up the rubble, and gets inside the cave. Her thumb is still pressed against the button.

"Please," she says. "Open."

Lilith hears the *whoosh* of a door opening nearby. Michael walks over and looks at her through the glass.

"Lilith, listen to me."

She turns to the monitor.

"Lilith. You don't need to talk to him. Forget about him. He poses no threat to us in here. We can live forever in here."

"Please," Lilith says, "Let. Me. Out."

"Oh, it's harmless," says the old woman. "Let her go to him."

The woman presses a button on her console. Lilith sees other arms raising in nearby cells.

Her glass door slides open, welcoming her to the main hall.

She gets out to the blinding white lights of the main hall, the all-revealing, no-secrets, surgery-room white floodlights. People look at her with pity and fear.

Her feet are heavy as she paces the white floor toward the next section hatch. She presses her code on the keypad, inserts her key, and turns it.

"Lil—," a younger man says to her from a cell nearby, "don't go."

"I have to," she says. "Please turn the key."

The man inputs a code in his cell's console and turns his key. The red light above the hatch turns off, and a green one turns on. She unlatches it and crosses over, hearing the heavy automatic lock close the hatch behind her.

Section after section, hall after hall, she's too numb to think it over. She can see the looks on people's faces, pitying her, but her feet seem to have a life of their own as she treads down the hall. She lets the lights test her, the scanners scan her, and the X-rays blast at her. Before she knows it, there she is: facing the final hatch. And the big, glass window leading to the cave, where Nate stands, waiting for her among mountains of rubble.

It's uncanny. She can't look away. She knows Nate is dead, and he's nowhere to be found in this life. But that body looking at her behind the thick glass wall, that decapitated torso with a head loosely resting on its neck, is the mocking proof, the vessel of the void. It's the exact place where he's not.

Her heart races. Her palms sweat. She pants.

He doesn't.

She presses a button next to the window.

"You're paler than usual," she says to the intercom, trying to smile. She sniffs.

His hollow eye sockets scan her without really looking. His blue lips are still as a photograph.

She presses a button on the intercom. "So," she says. "You're one of them now."

He gazes and lingers for a little while. He looks disgusted.

"No," comes his voice, electric and strange. "*You're* one of *them*."

Lilith sniffs again at the sound of his voice. It's like somebody's puffing air out of a dead man's throat, imitating the voice she hasn't heard in a while.

She presses the button again.

"How's life as a zombie?" she asks, trying to sound cute, to spark a conversation. To contact good old Nate.

"Are you here to do the zombie thing, and kill me? Or are you still a true rebel?"

He smiles as if an invisible puppeteer is pulling strings at both ends of his mouth.

She sniffs again. Her eyes are faucets. "I'll never let you in. You know that. I let you in, you kill everybody."

He just smiles. "You're the last ones."

"You know there's no way to enter unless I let you, don't you? You're wasting your time here."

His smile remains. He looks like he knows something.

Behind him, among the rubble, more figures come forward. A thick cut along their necks shows that sticking their heads back on was not a flawless operation. How could it be? They are thin dried-up mummies. A disfigured skeleton shrouded in black seems to grin. A taller one with driving glasses melted into his face. The old woman who once told her about the afterlife. The childhood friend she saw climbing the cemetery wall. A woman whose eye sockets hold something shiny. Lester, grinning in his vampire clothes, with a beaten up, angry-looking Yoshi head attached to his shoulder. Other putrefied corpses she cannot recognize.

"You knew!" she screams. Her own voice echoes around the empty hall, stunning her. "You all knew. Why didn't you tell me?"

They wheeze like deflated balloons, "To protect you. Let us in, and you'll see it."

Lilith's mind races. The pieces start to come together. Could it be this simple?

"You want to kill Tommy," she says, "and *all the Tommys in the world*. We've been racking our brains trying to figure what it meant. Why. But even *you* don't know why, do you?"

Nate's smile slowly fades, and she chuckles. It's so simple, after all.

"All your plans and schemes," she continues, "your fucking prescience, your gloomy inevitable fate bullshit. And after all, you're no better than anyone. It's the same reason anyone does what they do."

Nate's hollow eye sockets can do nothing to hide his dead mind racing, like a dog chasing his tail.

"Instinct," she says, "that's all. Just your dead bodies, wanting *for* you. There's no *why* other than that. You're just following orders."

Nathan just stares at her.

"So *you* rebel," she says. "Remember who you are, Nate, and rebel."

Behind the glass, his hollow eye sockets seem to widen. "You're afraid. Your body's telling you to protect Tommy. Nothing but flesh and chemicals. Give in. Betray that body that betrayed you your whole life. Betray all bodies." He opens his arms again and smiles, waiting for the hug. "Open up. Come to us."

Lilith sobs. "He's our son! Our son!"

No body has ever been so still. "Yes."

"So help me protect him. Go away. Stop trying to get me to do whatever you're trying to do."

Nathan's hollow eye sockets swallow the light around him, calling for her. "Protect him from what? Do you even know?"

She struggles with the thought.

"What if what we're offering is *release*?" His smile fades away, and Lilith's eyes swell as he continues.

"It's over," he says. "Doyle is dead. You don't have to fear an eternity of bondage. Sooner or later, you'll be one of us. We're offering you a younger body to spend eternity in. Open up."

The news hits Lilith like a punch to the gut, flooring her. *Is he lying? Is it true? Would she even want it to be true?* Her mind races, and the answer comes quick. *Would they be here otherwise?* Suddenly she's very aware of how deep in the ground they all are, how boxed-in they all are, how the only way out is behind those corpses, and how it's not much of a way out after all. The world is a box, shrinking in around her. The walls, the ceiling, the blinding lights, it's all conspiring against her. It's hard to breathe.

Lilith tries to pull away from her thoughts, to be present again, alert, to get a grip on what's happening. Her eyes focus again on the corpses in front of her. She looks around. They must be up to something. They must have found a way in already. She goes through a mental checklist of the traps, the mechanisms, the medical gear, and the hidden weapons around her.

"You always wanted to be a rebel," Nathan says. "Are you ready to finally go mad? To test your weary heart? To learn what you've been so afraid to learn?"

She checks the ghouls in the back for any sudden movements, or even for slow movements. The small crowd seems frozen, waiting. But waiting for what?

"You want to see it, don't you?" Nathan asks. "You always have. Stop lying to yourself, stop stopping yourself, stop being such a coward. If you want to really understand, if you're going to feel it, there's only one way."

"If you're here," Lilith thinks out loud, "it's because you know I'll accept."

He smiles.

"So I just won't," she sings, faking a smile, and she wipes the first tears from her eyes.

"We're here," he argues calmly.

"I let you in, you kill everyone. Isn't that boring. I know there's more to you, Nate. Ma. Pa. You know you're better than this. You used to be cool."

"We're cool now," they say. "We can start over," they say. "It's a new world now."

"That's disappointing," Lilith says. "We always said, Nate, that even death wouldn't turn us into one of them."

"Death is the greatest teacher," Nate says. "I was wrong. You'll see. Zap zap."

"Oh, I'll be the coolest zombie ever," Lilith insists, trying to hold back her tears. "Even a zombie, I'll be on team humans," she says, and tries to chuckle.

"Really," they ask, stiff mouths not moving.

"Yes, really!" She yells.

"How much would you bet?" Nathan asks. "All that remains of humanity?"

Lilith doesn't understand. "Yes, and more."

"Prove it," they say. "Prove us wrong."

Lilith looks around through watery eyes. Of course, she has thought about this. Of course. How is she different from them until she proves it? And yet, now, suddenly *(But what does suddenly mean anymore?)*, surrounded by warning measures and defensive objects and blinking defibrillators and weapons *(Face it, Lil, you already picked the one, for God's sakes.)*, it's clear that there is no point letting this go on any longer. If she's gonna know, then why not now? Why? Why not, really? Isn't this, really, the way to protect Tommy, to have it happen in a controlled, secure environment? And if Nate doesn't really think she'll do it, if there's any chance he's bluffing, isn't this her chance to surprise him, and have the final scare?

89

AT THE FAR END OF THE HALL, THE MECHANISM UNLATCHES. AN echo travels the glass walls, and Tommy shudders.

A door swooshes open. A human-shaped smudge comes out of it.

Ma.

The door slams shut, and the stain starts to get bigger. Footsteps echo closer and closer to him, louder and louder.

A faint voice from a cell next to her asks, "Lil?"

She seems to turn her head and walk up to it. A cell door opens with a distant *swish* sound, and she disappears.

Two people walk out. They walk the hall, stand next to other cells, maybe they're talking to them. Another *swish*, another talk, another *swish*. Both figures disappear.

Four people walk out.

Tommy looks at the man in the cell next to him. He looks as worried as he is. He tries to smile. "She's OK," he says, and he can't avoid turning again to look at the hall. "Don't worry."

The figures seem to split up. Two of them walk and disappear to the left. Two of them disappear to the right.

One of them comes closer. It stands behind a transparent

hatch. After a short muffled exchange that Tommy can't hear, the hatch opens.

A man comes through. He's followed by a woman. It's Lilith.

A voice, clearer now, closer, breaks the silence.

"You're one of them!"

The man turns to the right. He speaks softly, but Tommy can hear his voice on the intercom. "No, we're not, honey," he's saying. "Open up. Look at this."

And another door swishes open.

Voices come through the intercom.

"They're dead!"

"Don't open your doors!"

"Oh god, oh, god!"

"Scan them!"

A storm of electric shouting and yelling follows.

Tommy turns to his cellmate. The man in the other cell looks at him, worried. In the reflection, Tommy sees a worried pale face.

Out in the hall, a man presses some buttons on a panel next to the hatch.

Lilith and the other man enter the scanner. A green light shines above the door.

"They're OK!" somebody yells.

The door opens. The man comes through, pats the guard on the shoulder, and they both walk out to another hall.

Behind them, Lilith walks in. She looks fine. Same as she did minutes ago when she went out. *Would she look any different?*

Her gaze locks on his, and she paces toward Tommy.

His fingers hurry toward the intercom.

"Ma, are you all right?" he asks through the cell window. "Who was that?"

Lilith brings her face close to the glass and smiles. "We got rid of him. It's over. It's all over."

"Really?"

"Really," she says, crying. "We can get out now. It's over. The war outside is over."

He looks at the cell next to him. The man is already opening the door and going out to the hall, his face radiant with relief.

He looks at her. She looks fine. She looks relieved.

Tommy brings a finger to the unlock button, but he freezes.

He explores her smile again. Her still smile. He watches her chest, inflating and deflating. Normally. Regularly. Forcibly. He looks around at the glass doors around her, looking for his mother's back in a reflection, looking for wounds. There are none. But why is he checking? Why is he feeling so bad about all this? He focuses on her face again. She's grinning.

"Yes, honey," she says. "We're all dead."

He looks behind her. They all stand still. Their chests don't move. Tommy's heartbeat starts to pound in his ears.

"You want to know what it's like," she says with her motherly voice. "Come and see. Really. There's nothing to worry about."

His pulse quickens. He looks at his glass cell. The reflection of his pale, scared face is all around him.

He clenches his teeth, and his finger lands on the button. The door mechanism starts its whirring sound, and she smiles as the door swishes open.

He sobs. "No, Mommy. No."

Her smile widens. She can't wait for the door to open.

"Will it hurt?" he whimpers.

"Oh, honey," she says, savoring him already. "I will make a mess out of you."

He sobs. "Please, mommy. I don't want to die."

"Honey," she says, entering the cell. "You'll come around."

90

LILITH HAS ESCAPED THE THOUGHT OF HER OWN DEATH FOR her whole life; she's put it off until it later, always later, a hypothetical later when it would finally be necessary, like old age, or after some kind of warning, an illness, an accident. Up until now, this sudden, confusing now, she thought of death as for the dying. But it's happening. It's happening to her.

And she remembers the mathematics of death. Loss, over and over. A procession of dates. She can feel them, just like her body used to feel touch and sights and smells. All the roads not taken. Everything she missed. Everything she didn't finish. Everything she didn't know would happen to her if she chose differently. If she had been brave enough to choose what she actually wanted. And it's so clear: Her parents were right all along. They were protecting her, and she didn't let them. Why, oh, why didn't she let them? They did everything for her. And now it's too late.

Her body rattles with rage. Today is the day. Now is the time. Now, without warning, death happens to her. Everything that she knows has already started to end, and she never got a warning. Lights off. Darkness. Nothingness.

All desire leaves her. No more purpose. No more questions or cares. No need to escape. Nowhere to escape to. Just witness. All those things she's seen already, she'll see them rot once again. Forever. Corpses, relieved. Resting. Tommy, asking what happened. Corpses ignoring him. Worried. Discussing what to do next. With visions gone, they talk and remember what they saw. They try to complete an image, long forgotten, about the one threat they will have to defend against. Underground cities. Centuries of construction. Cities turned to deserts and jungles. Some don't remember seeing them. A shrinking universe. An incoming sun. They mention *those things*. What comes next, nobody seems to remember. Some are becoming hopeless. Some start changing their tone. They are beginning to panic. They start behaving like animals. They start having violent fits.

The grey wall, alive, beating like a thousand black hearts. Gooey arms stretch and spread, gaining on it, painting it a shiny, oily, lively black. A procession of ghouls walks out of the compound. A line of hundreds takes refuge in the new world. Outside, the foulest stench is in the air. A blinding scorching sun takes center stage in a fiery orange sky. The wind carries clouds of skin flakes. Skin that never rots. Skin that can nest and bloom inside the body. Caves collapse. Empty shells of thousand-year-old buildings watch them with empty windows. Their hollow doorways whisper warm winds. A new threat. An epic wall to keep it out.

A wheel rolling by, covered in oily blots, wheezing, screaming. A calcified structure that looks like a giant warped skull. Her old Raggedy Ann doll, walking with deaf cotton steps, whispering something as it exhales. It's the message of a thousand years and a hundred people, destroyed, parted, pulverized, trying to scream without lungs. Remains of mixed bodies meld together. New organisms making new nightmares. Ghouls head-butt their spore-covered faces against the hard marble, destroying themselves in madness. Others, mummified by the elements, lie on the ground and stretch their arms at the sky, barely able to move. Greenish skeletons open and close their jaws, trying to scream, putrid beyond recognition. Others go crazy. Rabid. Bacteria and spores swell and beat inside of them. Walking skeletons collect spores in cartwheels and take them away.

Corpses going into a cave's deep dark throat. The sweet and musty smell of methane and hydrogen sulfur and ammonia.

And she will live through all of it.

But her teeth still work.

And her jaws still work.

Fuck all this, she thinks. *Fuck nature. Fuck flesh.* The world is rotting around her, and she just wants to bite it, destroy it, lock her jaws into pink new innocent flesh and feel it crush under her teeth, hear it break, taste its suffering.

ALL THE TOMMYS IN THE WORLD

ABOUT THE AUTHOR

Javier Gombinsky was born in Buenos Aires, Argentina, in the neighborhood of Chacarita, the real-life inspiration for the town of Leatelranch.

His love of horror started with Argentinian children's books by Elsa Bornemann. Then came The Twilight Zone, Tales from the Crypt, Freddy Krueger, and finally zombies with the greatest zombie movie ever made: Return of the Living Dead. Since then, he's been consuming all things horror and zombies, and keeping a list in the back of his mind about all the things he wanted to happen, but didn't. That list ultimately became All the Tommys in the World.

He lives in Amsterdam with his wife.

This is his first book.